"Truly GRIPPING." Malorie Blackman

"THRILLING and ROMANTIC." Ruth Warburton

"Will have you THRILLED, SCARED and HEARTBROKEN." Teri Terry

"HEART-STOPPING." Mizz

"WONDERFUL, ORIGINAL." The Sun

"Packed with SUSPENSE and DRAMA." The Daily Mail

PRAISE FOR
L.A. WEATHERLY

BROKEN SKY

L.A. WEATHERLY

TRUST NO ONE

Of all the ways to lose a person, death is the kindest.

– Ralph Waldo Emerson

PROLOGUE

THE RAIN BEAT DOWN.

I stood half-hidden in a doorway with my hands jammed in my coat pockets, staring out at the gloomy city street. The glow from the street lamps daubed at the shadows. In the downpour, the light itself looked streaked with damp. Distantly, I was aware of the emptiness in my stomach – a hollowed-out feeling, as if someone had gouged away my insides. It was two days since I'd eaten, not that it mattered. If I could just get what I needed, I'd be fine.

A light went on in the diner opposite. Five a.m. I could see a bleached-blonde waitress tying on her apron, and silver stools with red leatherette seats. My hands tightened in my pockets. It all seemed so ordinary.

I was desperate to get in there and see a newspaper, but forced myself to wait until other people had drifted in: a postman, a woman who wore sensible shoes like a nurse, a few more. Then, my heart beating hard, I flipped up my coat collar and left the safety of the doorway. My boots splashed in the puddles as I jogged across the street, shattering reflected light with each footfall.

My boots. They were regulation boots, nothing like the pretty shoes that most women wore. I prayed no one would notice and stepped into the diner.

The sudden warmth and dryness was an embrace. Conscious of how bedraggled I looked, I slipped onto the seat at the end of the counter – the one nearest the door, in case I needed to run.

The waitress came over. Her upswept hair was in stylized curls. "Help you?" she said cheerfully, swiping at the counter with a damp rag. *Betty*, read her name tag, with a symbol beside the letters that looked like a lashing tail. I tore my gaze from it.

"Just coffee, please," I said.

Six months ago I wouldn't have known what the symbol meant. Now I knew it was the glyph for Leo, the lion. People didn't have to display their birth signs yet...but plenty were.

Don't think about it. Just find out what's going on.

The coffee came in a large white mug. I stirred in a dollop of cream and cast a sideways glance down the counter. The postman sat munching bacon and eggs with a copy of *The Angeles Advent* propped in front of him. I could just see the date at the top: March 17th, 1941 AC.

March 17th. I'd been on the run for four days.

His gaze crawled back and forth across the sports section. After an eternity, he picked up the paper, slowly shook it out, and refolded it to another page.

My fingers gripped the mug.

"Is that the only paper?" I asked Betty when she came to refill my coffee.

"Yes, sorry," she said. "Morton comes in every morning to read it. Cheap so-and-so; you'd think he could buy his own once in a while."

She didn't bother to lower her voice. Without looking up, Morton waved his mug at her. "More coffee, less talk, you dizzy dame."

Betty refilled his coffee and then leaned her hip against the counter. "Any news on Wildcat?" she asked him brightly.

My knuckles turned white. I stared down at my coffee, letting my bobbed dark hair fall forward around my face. *The door's only a few feet away,* I told myself frantically. *I can escape if I need to—*

Morton squinted up at her. "Who?"

"*Wildcat.* You know. That World for Peace scandal. Come on, half the country's talking about it! You been living under a rock?"

He grunted and took a slurp of coffee. "I'm reading about last night's game."

"Well, is she still on the run?"

"Don't you have someone else you can bother?"

"Oh, but *you're* so sweet I just can't help myself." Betty shot me a dimpled smile, inviting me to laugh with her. I smiled weakly back and hoped I wouldn't throw up.

"She's still on the run," called over the nurse. She got up and started pulling on her coat. It fitted snugly at the waist, with broad shoulder pads. "Or she was last night. I heard on the telio."

Betty shook her head and scooped up the change the nurse had left on the counter. "Shocking, isn't it? Gee, we're supposed to be able to trust those pilots. If *they're* crooked, who knows what else is going on?"

"She's as low-down as they come, all right," agreed the nurse. A golden crab brooch glinted on her lapel. "They're talking about trying her for treason when she's caught."

"*Really?* I thought it was just murder!"

"Yes, but it's treason too, isn't it? Anyway, she'll be up for the death penalty. Good riddance."

The coffee tasted like bile now. I choked more of it down. After the nurse left, Betty switched on the battered wooden telio that sat on a shelf. A black-and-white daisy whined into view as dance music filled the air.

I gazed tensely at the telio's small round screen with its curlicue speakers to either side. This wasn't one of the times of day when the daisy disappeared and a programme came on. I wished it was. The music reminded me too much of Collie...of how I'd danced in his arms that night, with candles flickering around us like fireflies.

Was he still alive? My throat tightened. I ducked my head against the memory.

Finally Morton left, and Betty passed the folded paper across. My fingers itched to open it. Somehow I waited until she'd turned away.

Please, it's got *to be in here by now*. I took a sip of coffee as if I hadn't a care in the world...and then flipped to the front page.

My own face stared back at me.

Ice slammed through my veins. WILDCAT STILL AT LARGE! screamed the headline.

They'd released my photo. They'd actually *released my photo*. Around me was the low buzz of conversation; the rise and fall of music; forks clinking against plates. Trying to look casual, I refolded the paper and glanced towards the door.

The way was clear. My fingers felt thick and clumsy as I tucked the paper inside my coat. *Stay calm, Amity.* I put a few coins on the counter and slid off the stool. Keeping my head down, I started for the door – but hadn't gone two steps when it swung open.

A pair of policemen came in. The taller one took off his hat and shook the rain from it.

He had a newspaper under one arm.

Without pausing, I veered for the restrooms. Behind me I could hear the policemen sitting down, calling for coffee.

The Ladies' was a haven of black and white tiles. I locked the door behind me and slumped shakily against it.

The window. I leaped across the small room the moment I saw it, but it was painted shut. I yanked at it in frustration; it didn't budge. The only way out would be to break the panes – but they'd hear that in the diner, surely?

My heart felt like it was trying to escape from my chest. I unlocked the bathroom door and opened it a fraction. I pressed one eye to the crack. The policemen were sitting at the counter; Betty was pouring coffee for them.

"Just a quick cup," I heard the tall one say. "Take the edge off that damp, right, Vince?"

His newspaper lay on the counter. My gaze flew to the black-and-white image of my face. Would the waitress notice it? But no, she'd already turned away.

"Keep your shirt on, I'm coming," she called to another customer.

I swallowed and eased the door shut; bolted it again. I'd have to wait them out – slip away once they'd gone. I hesitated...and then pulled the crumpled paper out from under my coat.

> Amity Vancour, an 18-year-old Western Seaboard pilot, has been known as "Wildcat" by the press since her daring escape four days ago, following the murder of a Central States pilot during a regulation Peacefight. Her case has caused international furore, leading to the unprecedented step of the World for Peace waiving its

anonymity policy for Peacefighter pilots and releasing her name and photograph.

"I'm delighted that the WfP has seen reason," stated John Gunnison, leader of the Central States. "Vancour must be captured – and will be. I have seen it in the stars."

I'd devoured stories about Gunnison for months now; it was very strange to read one where he mentioned me. An astrology chart accompanied the article, supposedly predicting my downfall. How could people *believe* that stuff? Especially here in the Western Seaboard, where we weren't even under Gunnison's rule.

At least the story didn't mention Ma and Hal. The last thing my family needed was the press sniffing around; they were in enough danger already. *Stay safe,* I begged them silently. *I'm sorry if any of this is my fault.* But going over and over it in my head…I still didn't see what else I could have done.

The photo was the official one from after my induction ceremony. It showed a girl with sleek dark hair falling to her jawbone; light brown eyes under stark eyebrows; a strong-boned, oval face. I wore a serious expression even though I'd been wildly happy.

Just a few months ago, Collie had studied that photo in my bedroom back on the base. "Wish I'd been there," he'd said as he gently touched the frame.

"You're here now," I'd answered, and he'd grinned and wrapped his arms around me.

"Yeah, and guess what? You're never getting rid of me, Amity Louise."

I pushed aside my longing, my fear for him and rifled through the paper. There *had* to be something in here by Milt. He'd promised to write it all down exactly like I'd told him.

When I found the small story on page nine, it knocked the breath from me.

"No," I whispered, clutching the paper. I read the words again, willing them to be a mistake. "*No.*"

I started as the doorknob rattled.

"Hello?" called a woman. A knock rapped. "Is anybody in there?"

My gaze flew to the thin silver bolt locking the door. Faintly, I heard the waitress's voice: "Is there a problem, ma'am?"

The woman sounded peevish. "Well, I don't know. I didn't see anyone come in here, but the door's locked."

"No, that girl went in," called out someone else. "The one sitting at the counter drinking coffee, about ten minutes ago."

A high-heeled stride and then a different knock, rat-a-tat-tatting at the wood. "Hon? You all right?"

My throat was sand. "I'm fine," I managed, lifting my voice. "I'm sorry, I...I don't feel very well."

"Well, you can't stay in there all morning," grumbled the woman.

"I'll just be a moment." I'd folded the paper again; I pinched my fingers up and down its crease. I could still hear them standing outside, only a few feet away, murmuring together.

I dropped to my knees and pressed my cheek against the tiles. Through the thin slit under the door, I saw two pairs of women's shoes...and two pairs of scuffed black men's ones, heading this way.

I scrambled up just as an authoritative knock pounded. "Miss? You all right?"

I felt electric with fear. I took a step back and glanced at the window. "I'll be fine," I called. My voice sounded reedy. "Please, just...leave me in peace for a minute."

"Hon, if there's something wrong, you can—" The waitress broke off. "Oh!" she gasped. "Officer, your paper! That girl on the front page!"

I shoved my own newspaper down my denims and yanked off my coat. In an excited babble outside I heard: "That's her, that's the girl in the bathroom! All she ordered was coffee, but I could tell she was hungry—"

"Open up!" shouted one of the policemen, beating on the door. It rattled on its hinges. "You're under arrest, Vancour!"

With my coat wrapped around my fist, I punched the window. It didn't give. I punched again and again, frantic now, and then jumped up onto the radiator to kick at the glass with my boot.

It shattered, falling to the alleyway in discordant tinkles.

"She's getting away!" screamed the waitress.

"Stand back!" Gunshots echoed through the tiny room; one of the tiles on the wall exploded.

The wooden window frame was still in place. I beat at it wildly with my foot, my hands. Just as the door swung open, the frame gave way with a splintering crack and I propelled myself out the window, taking the rest of the glass with me.

"Stop!"

I landed on a scattered mess of wood, glass, trash from the alleyway. Pain – my hand was bleeding – I lunged to my feet and ran, pausing only to push over a trio of garbage cans and send them rolling in my wake. Panting, I veered out onto the sidewalk, my boots thudding against the concrete.

The clatter of trash cans from behind me. "Stop that girl! Stop her!"

Rain muffled the words. It was coming down in solid sheets now, the sidewalk busy with early-morning commuters hunched into their trench coats, jostling past each other with streaming umbrellas. There was a grey knit cap in my coat pocket. As I wove through the river of people I pulled my coat back on and yanked the cap onto my head.

I slowed to a brisk walk, keeping my hands in my pockets, face down. My pulse beat against my skull; with each step I expected a hand on my shoulder. When I came to an intersection my instincts shrieked at me to turn.

Instead I crossed the street and kept going straight. Finally I risked a glance back. The policemen were standing on the corner, staring up and down the cross street. One spoke urgently into a talky; I could see its long antenna.

I let out a trembling breath and kept walking, fists clenched in my pockets. My right hand throbbed. It was slick with blood.

By the time I heard distant sirens, I was over ten blocks away. I kept going until I couldn't hear them any more, until the only noises were the mundane ones of the city. The elevated train was up ahead. No one paid attention when I paused under its bridge. People passed by as the trains rumbled above, shaking the ground at our feet.

A shard of glass glinted from the fleshy part of my thumb. I gritted my teeth and pulled it free, then found a handkerchief in my pocket and wrapped it tightly around the wound.

The whole time, my thoughts were tumbling, screaming.

I knew that I had not misread the story on page nine. But I pulled out the paper and read it again anyway:

> JOURNALIST KILLED IN AUTO CRASH
>
> Milton Fraser, 28, was found dead yesterday evening after he apparently lost control of his auto and broke through a safety rail, crashing over fifty feet into a canyon...

I swallowed hard as another train rattled overhead and

the trash whispered against my ankles in the breeze. They'd killed Milt, an ordinary journalist who they shouldn't even have *known* about. How deep, how broad, did this whole thing go?

Collie.

My sore hand clenched its bandage. Suddenly I felt short of breath. He had to still be alive; he *had* to be. And I had to get back to him, somehow – we both had to escape if we could—

With the rain still drizzling down, I started to run.

From *My Vision* by John Gunnison, required reading for every Central States schoolchild:

> ...it is my duty – no, my destiny – to make your life happy and harmonious. How? By using the ancient tool of astrology. The power of the stars allows me to find Harmony's true way and make good decisions for you and your family.
>
> HARMONY is the key. Everything I do, I do for the sake of Harmony and for you...

Chapter One

THE PREFLIGHT ROUTINE WAS AUTOMATIC. My hands moved across the plane's control panel, flicking levers as I studied the dials. Undercarriage down, flaps up, throttle half-inch open. I checked the temperature gauge and then primed the engine, working the handle quickly in and out.

I switched on the ignition and the small plane roared into life, trembling with power: a MK9 Merlin Firedove, one of the finest machines ever built. It was just like the Dove I'd learned to fight in. We understood each other, this plane and I.

I gave the primer pump another stroke. Anyone watching would've said I was scowling: I could feel deep furrows ridging my forehead, like always when I'm fully absorbed. Underneath my concentration was a rock-hard resolve.

Today, of all days, I had to win.

I signalled to the fitter and he ran to pull the chocks from my wheels. "You're good to go, Miss Vancour!" he shouted.

With a distracted wave I eased open the throttle and started taxiing, facing into the wind. The plane was trembling, eager, picking up speed by the second. The undercarriage bumped against the ground as fields rushed past in a blur...and then I was airborne.

Usually I loved the moment when I lifted into the sky, so light and free. This time my jaw felt tight. I headed south-west at four thousand feet. Once I'd left the complex of airbases behind, I could see faint, ancient lines sketching the earth where streets had once been, and fragments of ruins up in the hills.

No cloud cover. Good. Some Peacefighters hate that, but I know how to use the sun.

The European Alliance pilot was already over New Bay when I reached it. His MK9 had stripes instead of camo swirls; that was the only difference. Our battle would be skill against skill.

The ocean glinted silver. On its beach stood a commentator with a bulky field phone, describing the scene for millions clustered around their telios. Few Peacefights were broadcast live. That this one was, just cemented my resolve.

My opponent and I faced off, circling each other as we waited. The vibrating drone of my engine filled my senses. Far below, seagulls wheeled over the water.

The instant the clock showed 15.00, I banked and headed for the sun.

I used it mercilessly, hiding in it, darting out at him from its glare. My thumb worked the firing button. A muffled staccato sound shuddered from my wings. Tracer shot through the sky, raining damage down on him.

He whipped away and came at me from above. Gunfire rattled across my windscreen's bulletproof glass. I swore and rolled; sky and ocean spun. I got him back in my sights, shot again. The way my opponent flew was familiar – I'd fought him before. Today he didn't stand a chance.

"You will *not* stay up," I told him softly as I jammed down on the firing button.

The other pilot twisted away unscathed and went into a screaming turn that held his plane a knife-edge from stalling. Tricky, but two could play. I stayed right on his tail, making the turn tight – tighter – feeling the G's as my plane juddered, rattling my bones.

Hold it. *There.*

I fired, spraying his fuselage. Smoke started streaming from his tail. He broke the turn, tried to climb, but I was right there ahead of him. *Fire.* Bullet holes peppered his hood. The horizon tipped on its side as I peeled away.

Suddenly the only engine I could hear was my own.

The other Dove had gone silent, flames leaping up from its hood. The pilot bailed. I watched as his plane twirled down to the bay, black smoke spiralling, while the white circle of a parachute floated languidly, the pilot a dangling stick-figure clutching its cords.

Base already knew, just like the rest of the world – but I reached for my mic and completed my job: "Victorious. Opposing pilot bailed and needs assistance."

When I released the button, I could breathe again.

The airfield looked tiny as I brought the Dove back in. And now, despite what day this was, I was so light inside that I couldn't help humming – some stupid song that was playing a lot on the telio, from one of those band leaders, Van Wheeler or someone, whose smile is more of a smirk but no one seems to mind; everyone flocks to the clubs where his band plays and dances the night away.

Love me in May,

Oh, please say you'll stay…

I could see the crew below. On impulse I did a victory roll right past them, laughing out loud as the world spun. Grinning, I soared high and came in again from an angle. When I got below a thousand feet, I shoved open the hood for the landing.

Wind whistled through the cockpit. I throttled back and lowered the undercarriage and flaps. The Dove slowed obediently, nose lifting; forward visibility vanished.

Love me in June,

Oh, darling I'll swoon...

I peered out the port side, wind snapping at me. Right on track for the runway. I gave it a touch more throttle, still humming. A bump, then a pause – another jolt, and I was down, taxiing.

I was singing aloud by then. I eased on the brakes and finished the song just as the plane stopped. I killed the engine. From the propeller's blur, four flashing blades emerged and slowly stilled.

In the sudden silence I peeled off my leather helmet and gloves, then gently touched the ID tags that hung around my neck.

"I did it," I whispered. A smile burst across my face. "I did it!"

The fitters came running up as I climbed from the cockpit. "Good job, Miss Vancour!" Edwards stretched up a hand to help me. I'd given up telling them to call me "Amity". The Western Seaboard base was full of traditions and that was one of them.

"Thanks." My smile threatened to split my face. I jumped down from the wing. I always felt more *alive* after a fight. Colours were brighter, the air cleaner.

"Heard it on the telio," Edwards said, his eyes shining. "Man, what a great day for a rumble!"

My Dove sat behind us on the runway: a small grey and tan plane that looked sleek, muscular. Its nose jutted upwards as if eager to leap back into the sky. The other fitter had just put the chocks under my wheels; he bobbed up with a grin.

"The other guy didn't have a chance, the way you held that turn! I bet he's *still* wondering what went wrong."

"He'll get me next time, probably," I said. The pilot I'd forced to bail was excellent. I didn't know his name, but knew the way he flew. He beat me as often as I beat him.

An open-top truck with the Western Seaboard sunburst emblem on its side came hurtling across the airstrip. The driver was half-standing, whooping, leaning on the horn.

Russ, my team leader. He screeched to a stop and jogged over, a big black guy with a face like a boxer. "How's my favourite wildcat?" he boomed, scooping me into a hug that lifted me off my feet. "Vancour, that was perfect! Just what I like to see: insane flying with no regard for personal safety."

"What was the dispute?" I gasped eagerly. We weren't allowed to know before a fight.

With slow ceremony, Russ drew two cigars from his breast pocket and held one out to me. My eyebrows shot up. This was a first.

"That good?" I asked.

"Oh, yes." He waggled the cigar seductively back and forth, its cellophane wrapping gleaming in the sun. "*And* it was a clean win. Go on, kiddo, you deserve it."

I started to say no, then laughed and took the cigar. Why not? Russ was right; the clean win made it even better. The other pilot hadn't been able to get his plane down – if he had, then whatever dispute I'd just won could be challenged sooner. Now the European Alliance would have to wait the whole five years to appeal.

Five years of a clean win felt mighty sweet.

Copying Russ, I bit off the cigar's tip, then let him light it for me with a quick scratch of flame from his metal lighter. I took a deep, considering draw and managed not to cough.

The fitters were grinning. "Wish I had a camera," said Edwards.

"Nothing to see here, gentlemen," said Russ. "Just a pilot enjoying a well-earned stogie after a fight, that's all."

With a wink at me, he looped an arm around my shoulders and we headed to his truck. The airstrip stretched out around us, shimmering into heatwaves and lined with palm trees. It was warm here in Angeles County, even now in November. In my home town further north, a chill would be huddling up against the bases of the mountains.

Home. Even now, I kept forgetting that Ma and Hal didn't live there any more. I pushed the thought away, refusing to let it dampen this moment, and opened the truck door.

"You still haven't told me," I said as Russ started the engine. His own cigar was clamped between his teeth. He twisted around to glance behind him, squinting against the sun.

"What do you think of your celebratory cigar?"

"It's foul."

"Ah, but it's the principle of the thing, isn't it?"

"*Russ.* Tell me."

He faced forward and gunned the accelerator; we careered across the airstrip, the warm breeze stroking our faces. Russ drove the way he flew – the way he pushed all of us to fly. *Harder, faster, trust the plane,* he was constantly shouting. *Have I got pilots or a bunch of pantywaists?*

"You know I'm not really supposed to tell you," he said, lifting his voice over the engine.

"And you know I'll just comb through the paper until I figure it out."

He raised a scarred eyebrow. "What is this, insubordination?"

"Just telling it like it is. Sir." I took the cigar out of my mouth and licked my lips, trying to get the taste of it off them. "This is terrible. How can you stand the way the tip goes so soggy? It looks like something you'd scrape off the bottom of your shoe."

Russ chuckled. "Give it back if you don't appreciate it." He wasn't much older than me, maybe twenty-one. Most Peacefighters were still pretty young.

I stubbed out the cigar in the overflowing ashtray. "Are you going to tell me, or not?"

"All right, here it is, Vancour." Russ intoned the words like a quiz-show host on the telio. "In your fight today… against a representative pilot of the European Alliance… you successfully rejected their claim…"

"*What?*"

"That twenty-seven per cent of our oil rights should be ceded to them."

I gaped as the magnitude of this sunk in. "That actually passed the Conflict Council?"

Russ shifted gears. "Yep. They got it through on an ancient dispute claim. It was on the table, but *you* took it off."

At first I couldn't respond. This was why we weren't allowed to know what we were fighting for beforehand. "Why...why was that a Tier Two fight and not a Tier One?" I said finally.

Tier One fights didn't happen often – they were for the gravest, most monumental disputes. Russ might have fought it instead of me in that case; he was a T1 pilot as well as my team leader.

He grinned at me. "Just missed being T1 by a hair. Heard they debated it for days. Aren't you glad?"

"*Now* I am. If I'd lost..." I swallowed, thinking of raised prices – hardship – millions affected.

We reached the office, a worn building with sky-blue paint and our sunburst emblem over the door. Russ pulled up with a lurch. "But you didn't," he said, his voice firm. "Now go make your report and then celebrate. A few hours to rest on your laurels before you're nothing again."

I smiled. I knew the drill. "'You're only as good as your next fight'," I quoted.

Russ let out an expansive stream of smoke. "'So don't cock that one up and you'll be fine'," he finished.

Chapter Two

In the locker room later I took a quick shower and then stepped out of the cubicle, wrapping a towel around me. Some of the guys were getting dressed; I had a glimpse of bare backsides and damp chests. Above, ceiling fans whirred lazily.

I swung open my locker and grabbed a pair of denims and a clean shirt. As always, my eyes flicked to the sepia photo tucked behind my mirror: a laughing man with flight goggles pushed on top of his head. A younger me stood pressed against him, smiling widely.

We had the same sleek dark hair and tilting brown eyes, the same olive skin like a perpetual tan. There was a biplane on the grass behind us; the man wore a leather jacket. The smell of it came back to me, rich and primal.

I won, Dad, I told him silently.

I studied my father's face, remembering what happened on this day five years ago. I'd been trying to shut out the details, but now they came vividly. The field of grass rustling in the breeze. The sound of my father's dying gasps, mixing with the creak of grasshoppers and my own sobs.

I won, I repeated to myself. The victory felt hard inside of me now.

"Congratulations," said a bright voice, making me jump.

I turned away from my locker and started getting dressed. "Thanks."

Vera had the next locker over. She was my age, eighteen, with cherry-blonde hair set in pin curls. Her gaze went to the photo too, but she didn't comment. Not a soul here ever would. That was why it felt safe to have it on display. No one would ask about the memories it contained.

Or about the half of it that had been ripped away.

"What was your win, do you know?" Vera asked instead. She mechanically undid the curls; wavy locks tumbled free. She wore them set under her flight helmet if she had a date later.

I glanced in my mirror and combed my own hair from my face, not looking at the photo this time. "I retained some of our oil rights."

Vera smiled. "Oil rights...hanging onto those is pretty good, I bet."

"Well, except that people will have to find other ways to get rid of their money now."

It was supposed to be a joke, but Vera gave me a quick glance and I knew I'd done it again – sounded too dry and sarcastic and made someone feel like I was poking fun at them when I wasn't. Why couldn't I ever manage the light tone that others handled with such ease?

"Sorry," I said awkwardly. "Yes, it's good. It means the price of fuel won't go up – at least, no more than usual."

Vera seemed placated. She was an open, easy-going girl, pretty much the opposite of me. She fluffed out her hair and stepped into a bright blue dress.

"I lost my fight," she said. "I tried to get down but I had to bail." She sighed and started fastening her buttons, each like a tiny pearl. "At least my fights aren't as important as yours. So maybe it wasn't anything too serious."

Though I didn't say it, sometimes the smaller fights made a big difference, their consequences spiralling out unexpectedly as the months passed. I made a mental note to figure out from the papers which Tier Three fight she'd had; I knew Vera wouldn't check. A lot of the team didn't. They didn't want to know what they'd won or lost; it made it easier for them.

For me, though, I *had* to know. I couldn't stand not knowing something so important. Even before I became a Peacefighter, I always read the paper front to back, trying to understand what was going on in the world through all the flowery prose. I'd write down my questions in a special notebook and wait impatiently for my father to come home.

Or else my best friend and I would try to figure things out for ourselves. My eyes went to the photo again – to the face that wasn't there.

No. Irritated with myself, I pushed it all away.

Vera still looked glum as she rummaged through her locker.

"Try not to worry about it," I told her. "'A peaceful loss is better than war.'" That idea was what the World for Peace had been founded on.

She smiled slightly. "I know. Thanks."

She sat on a wooden bench to pull on her stockings, rolling them expertly up each leg. I stood in my denims and brassiere and rubbed my favourite lotion on my arms. It smelled like summertime. Like home.

"Hey, Vancour!" A muscular brown-haired guy named Harlan appeared around the end of our locker row. He wore only a towel and had a scantily-clad woman tattooed on one bicep. "Rumour has it you're the hero of the hour," he drawled.

I couldn't help laughing. "The rumour where? In the funny papers?"

Harlan grinned. "Careful with those daredevil fights, girlie – if there's not enough left of you, they'll just throw you out with the trash. Not that *we* care, but it might make your mama sad not to get a funeral."

"Noted."

"How'd you do?" Vera called over to him.

Harlan punched both fists to the ceiling. "Vic-to-ry!" he chanted.

"Hey, good!" I pulled on my shirt and started doing up the buttons. "Who were you fighting?"

"The Scando-Finns. Don't know what our beef was with them, but we've won it now."

Vera laughed. "The Scando-Finns? I bet you just won us some moose rights."

My spirits fell slightly. "Too bad it wasn't against Gunnison," I said.

The one thing that would have improved my own win was if it had been a strike against the Central States' dictator – his power seemed to be growing every day. You could hardly watch a single news story without seeing John Gunnison's grainy black-and-white grin. He looked so inoffensive…yet we'd heard stories about a vicious police force called Guns, and of people he disapproved of being taken away in unmarked vans.

"Maybe we can use our new moose rights against him," said Harlan. "Stop pissing on my picnic, Vancour. I *won*."

I shrugged. "I'm just saying, that's all. It *is* too bad your win wasn't against him. Mine, too."

"That's for sure," muttered Vera. "He's got a screw loose, that guy."

It was strange to think that only twelve years ago the Western Seaboard and the Central States had been one country: Can-Amer, stretching from the west coast to the Mizsippi River. But the eastern provinces had thought the west held too much sway. I could still remember all the debates about it, with people shouting at each other on the telio.

Then Senator John Gunnison announced the stars had shown him the answer: the vast region east of the desert should secede. The idea caught fire; tensions exploded. When the civil war Peacefight came, millions huddled around their telios listening. I hadn't really understood it all back then, but my heart had still clenched when we lost.

The newly-formed Central States split off with Gunnison in charge, and then he'd slammed the borders shut. You could still get in; getting out was another matter. All that we knew about life over there now came from his official, glowing news releases…and the underground pamphlets that sometimes popped up with more chilling stories.

"You know what I heard?" Vera gazed into her mirror, stroking bright red lipstick across her mouth. "Gunnison's got something against Virgos now. They're all having to go in and answer questions."

Harlan's brow furrowed. "What's a Virgo?"

"Virgo the virgin. It's an astrology sign." Before Harlan could make some crack about virgins, I went on: "And no, I think Virgos in general are supposed to be okay, but not if their moon's in Libra or something. It's complicated."

"It's nuts." Vera peered behind her, adjusting the seams of her stockings.

"Hey, he's still better than that clown *we've* got in charge," said Harlan. "The Central States ain't exactly poor."

No, and that was why plenty here in the Western Seaboard gazed at them with such envy, despite Gunnison. No one could call us prosperous any more.

"Well, President Lopez can't magic resources out of thin air." I propped my foot on the bench and pulled on my shoe. "Anyway, Gunnison can claim whatever he wants. He doesn't let anyone out of the place, so who'd even know for sure?"

It was just turning into the kind of conversation I enjoy – something I could really sink my teeth into – but then Harlan shrugged and said, "All right, enough about the loon across the border. You playing later?" The ongoing nightly poker game had reached epic proportions.

I shook my head. "I'm going out."

"You?" said Vera. "Miss Hermit?" She glanced at my denims and wrinkled her nose. "Want to borrow a dress?"

I laughed. "I've got one, *actually*. I need to go home and change; I didn't have one with me when—"

I broke off as Clem, a T4 pilot, came in.

At first I thought the expression on his face was because of the locker room. It took a while to learn to act casual around all the naked bodies; then one day you realized you actually did feel casual about it. But Vera and I were fully dressed. And Clem's freckled face was ashen.

He sank onto one of the benches.

Silence fell. I straightened and clutched my locker door – so hard that the metal dug at my skin. *Not this,* I thought. *Not today.*

When Clem spoke, his words held a terrible sense of déjà vu. "I, um...I have some bad..." He choked to a stop.

"Who?" Vera said softly.

Clem swiped a hand over his eyes. "Stan. He was fighting against the Indasians. His plane went down over the water. He drowned."

My lips went dry. I deliberately didn't look at the locker across from mine, with the name scrawled at its top on grey masking tape: *S. Chaplin.*

Only two hours ago, Stan had stood there joking with me.

"You know what I love about you, Amity?" he'd said as he pulled on his trousers. "You look so *capable.*"

I'd been buttoning my shirt, trying not to think about what day this was, but I'd still had to laugh. This was a new one. "I look so *what*?"

"Capable." Stan had scanned me up and down, a teasing glint in his eyes. "Like, if someone dropped you in the middle of the Arctic, I bet you'd just strangle a polar bear and then build your own igloo."

My fingers had paused on my buttons as I stared at him. "Why would I strangle a polar bear?"

"I don't know. Maybe you don't like polar bears."

"So you see me as violent and erratic."

"Strong and spontaneous," he corrected. "My kind of woman." He put his hand over his heart and heaved a dramatic sigh. Stan was quick and wiry, with dark hair and a thin face, and he'd thought of a new compliment for me every day since I'd known him.

Over three hundred offbeat compliments now. He never repeated the same one twice.

"You'll have to run out of things to say at some point, won't you?" I'd mused as I pulled on my leather jacket. With Stan, banter was easy...and today I was grateful for it. "I mean, there must be a limit."

"With you as inspiration? Never."

"Man, just ask her out, Chaplin. This gets boring, day in, day out," said a guy named Levi as he brushed past from the shower, his dark skin damp.

Both Stan and I had probably looked a bit horrified; then Stan caught my eye and we laughed. Not everyone knew he was gay. "We could go out if you want," said Stan, tucking in his shirt tails. "Hey, want to go into the Heat tonight? I feel like celebrating."

I glanced at him, suddenly noticing how buoyant he seemed. "You do? Why?"

He winked. "Maybe I'll tell you someday. I did something I should have done months ago, that's all... Come on, you up for it?"

I reached for my ID tags. My father's and mine, on the

same chain. I ran my finger slowly over them, then put them on and cleared my throat. "Sounds good. But only if you don't talk about polar bears."

Stan didn't comment on my tags. No one here ever had. "I am not hampered by having to limit myself to other topics," he informed me with dignity.

I laughed. "No, I bet you aren't."

"See you later, then." He grinned. "Better brush up on your igloo-building techniques, just in case."

It was the last thing he'd ever said to me.

The silence in the locker room was stifling. Stan, trapped in his plane as it crashed into the water. Scrabbling for his straps, struggling to get out as the water rushed in… I couldn't speak.

Finally Harlan sighed and pushed his hand through his hair. "Took the big swan dive, huh?" he murmured. "Well…the man went out doing what he loved."

Vera nodded, eyes bright. "Marcus and I will lift a glass to him in the Heat tonight."

"Hell with that; we'll all go in," said Harlan firmly. He clapped Clem on the shoulder. "Pilot down. That means we give him a good send-off."

A good send-off. Usually the words felt comforting, even for people I'd liked as much as Stan. I swallowed hard, seeing green fields of gently waving grass, hearing the sound of grasshoppers.

"There's a new jazz player at one of the speaks," Vera was saying. "Stan would've loved that – let's spread the word."

"You're on," said Harlan. "We are going to paint the Heat *red*."

I clanged my locker door shut. The photo of the laughing man disappeared from view. All at once I felt hot. I stepped across to Stan's locker and slowly ripped away the name tape; it made a noise like tearing paper. I crumpled it, stickiness plucking at my skin, and kept crumpling until it was a tiny ball.

I threw it aside. It rolled across the floor and came to rest under a wooden bench.

"So we've got a free locker," I said into the silence. "I don't know why we even bother to put names on these things."

"Amity…" said Vera softly.

I kept my gaze away from the screwed-up ball on the floor, where a curve of the *S* was still visible.

Finally I let out a breath. "You're right. We'll give him a good send-off," I said.

Chapter Three

When I'd first arrived at the World for Peace complex, the vastness of it had awed me: sixty-two Peacefighting bases, one for every country in the world. Taken together, they spanned hundreds of square miles. Each base was the territory of its own country – effectively, a mini-nation.

The Heat alone was neutral territory. It was really Heatcalf City, named after one of the World for Peace founders, and was a dense, throbbing metropolis right at the heart of it all. It was where pilots went to unwind; it was a slice of the whole world. You could start out in a Western Seaboard diner eating chowder and end up in a New Moscow bar throwing back shots of vodka.

Vera's speak turned out to be a dark cellar with scuffed tables and a wailing jazz trio – too noisy for conversation, and I was glad. We sat toasting Stan with shots of some terrible liqueur that tasted like almonds. The saxophonist seemed in a trance, closing his eyes and swaying as the notes soared out.

"Do you like this music?" Harlan bellowed in my ear.

I nodded. It was wild, discordant. It suited my mood. Levi sat on the other side of me, eyes half-closed as he patted the table to the beat. Clem had some girl on his lap; they were kissing like tomorrow might never come.

Vera leaned towards us. "He's really good, this guy!" she shouted.

Harlan made a face and pushed his chair back. "More drinks," he announced.

Vera propped her cheek on her hand, gazing at the band. Marcus sat beside her, his arm around the back of her chair. He was thin, with a good-natured face and hair so pale it was almost white. He said something to her and she nodded; they got up and started moving together on the tiny dance floor. He held her close, as if different music entirely were playing.

Marcus worked at a restaurant in the Heat. Pilots didn't date pilots. There wasn't a rule; it just didn't happen much. We saw each other as teammates, poker buddies, and saved our dalliances for the Heat. If I'd wanted to date, I'd have done the same as Vera: found some guy who had nothing to do with flying. Though Marcus had to be kind of dense – what had happened to Stan could happen to any of us. Didn't he know that?

But I guess if you've never had your heart ripped out, you don't think to protect it.

I swallowed and looked down. What had Stan wanted to celebrate? Something he should have done months ago, he'd said. Maybe he'd gotten out of a bad relationship.

A matchbook with a shamrock design lay on the table. I fiddled with it blindly. I had on a blue dress sprigged with flowers; I wondered what compliment Stan would have given me. *You are like a daisy, Amity. No, wait, I've got it – like midnight with tiny pink blossoms.*

If it had to happen, why did it have to be today?

Harlan appeared and put another shot glass in front of me. "Drink," he said.

I drank.

Later, with the music reaching a shrieking climax and the pulse in the speak something palpable, I pushed my own chair back and headed to the restroom. I stopped halfway, squinting through the smoky darkness. Russ sat in a corner with two other men.

The mood at his table seemed out of place, somehow. Russ leaned forward on his arms as he spoke, his expression intense. One of the men laughed and wagged a finger at him.

An irrational anger touched me. Whatever Russ was saying that was so important, it wasn't about Stan. He didn't know – he hadn't been at the base when we'd rounded everyone up.

My thoughts were a little blurry by then, but one thing felt clear: my team leader had to be told. This instant. I started across the crowded, table-packed room, almost having to climb over people.

"Hey, pretty thing," laughed one guy, trying to pull me onto his lap.

I batted his hands away and kept on. As I drew closer a woman got up; when I could see again Russ was sitting alone and the two men were heading past me towards the door. One had curly hair. The other was bald, and wore a neck chain with a gleaming gold pendant.

A hand took my arm. "You trying to abscond?" shouted a voice in my ear. "If I have to listen to this crap, you do, too."

Harlan. I shook my head. "Russ doesn't know," I called back stubbornly.

Harlan peered drunkenly at the dimly-lit corner. His blunt, handsome jaw turned as determined as mine. "Well, we've gotta tell him then!"

Russ sat looking down. His head snapped up as we reached him; he tucked something in his jacket pocket and rose. "Vancour, Taylor. Night out on the town?"

There was something tense about his smile. I didn't dwell on it. "Stan's dead," I said, lifting my voice over the music.

All my life, I've never known how to soften news. I especially couldn't do it after drinking shots. Russ winced.

I thought I saw him say, "Oh, no," though I couldn't hear the words.

"You're giving him his send-off?" he said finally.

"Over there." Harlan nodded at our cluster of tables.

Russ didn't ask for details. I guess he didn't really need to.

"Come on," he said. "I'll buy the next round."

The residential section of our base was like any other Western Seaboard town: leafy streets lined with houses. They were all dark as I walked past them hours later. The others were still in the Heat. I'd left them to it and caught the streetcar back alone, resting my cheek against the car window and gazing at the reflections of other passengers.

The small house Vera and I shared was silent. I groped for the light switch; the front room with its worn furniture sprang into view. Magazines lay fanned across the coffee table.

After we'd all left the speak we'd wandered the heaving streets for a while and ended up in the Stardust Ballroom, built in some of the Cataclysm's ruins, drinking shots that tasted of peppermint this time. I'd danced with a guy I didn't know – stupidly good-looking, clutching me close as we swayed to the orchestra, surrounded by uneven walls and pieces of ancient concrete.

When he'd tried to kiss me I'd let him. It's been so long since I've been held that it just…felt nice for a moment.

I'd wrapped my arms around his neck and pretended he was someone I cared about.

I rubbed my head and put my handbag down on the coffee table.

An orange striped cat came mincing across the rug, meowing. I smiled, somehow wanting to pretend for him. "Hello, Peter," I murmured as I picked him up. "Did I wake you?"

I carried him with me into the kitchen and put him on one shoulder as I opened the icebox. Its shelves held a jar of mayo, some olives, a murky-looking pint of milk. I'd have to grab something at the canteen in the morning. It was open now – nothing here ever closed – but I didn't feel up to facing anyone. There were times I didn't feel like it even normally. Here at the base it wasn't like the outside world; no one would ever say, *Amity, you look so serious! Smile!* But still, people at least expected you to talk to them.

You always have to talk. To connect, even if it's only superficially. Sometimes it seemed like everyone had the knack except me.

That hadn't always been true. A memory came of sunlit fields: a day of green and gold, and an endless, aching blue that was the sky. My best friend and I had lain in the grass and pointed out clouds to each other, arguing about their shapes (*A fire engine. No, don't be stupid, that's a pony!*) and when my father had landed his plane we'd run to meet him, clamouring to be taken up. *My two pilots,* my dad had said.

Everything about the memory was engraved in crystal... but especially the sense of belonging so completely to those two people. Now one was dead, and the other might as well be.

Over four years without a word.

I realized that I was staring blindly into the icebox, letting out its cold. I closed the door with Peter still balanced on my shoulder.

I needed coffee. I made some, then sank tiredly onto the sofa and flipped through the magazines. One cover showed Gunnison, a solid-looking man with blond hair going grey at the temples. He was smiling, holding an astrology book. Behind him was his infamous Harmony symbol: the stark red-and-black swirls that were a corruption of the old yin-yang.

I knew better, but opened the magazine. The main article began: *With a warm, genuine smile, President John Gunnison shakes my hand. "Call me Johnny," he says cheerfully. "Nicknames make things friendlier, don't you think? Mind if I call you Bill?" When I ask how the Central States stays so prosperous, Gunnison winks. "The power of astrology, Bill. You folks in the Western Seaboard should tell President Lopez to try it."*

The story left out what else we'd heard Gunnison did with the so-called power of astrology. If he thought someone was a "threat to Harmony" then they were dubbed Discordant, sometimes just because of their astrology chart. The Discordant apparently didn't last long.

Gunnison's chief advisor, Sandford Cain, dealt with them, though the papers remained vague on the details. In the single photo I'd seen of Cain he'd gazed coolly out at me, with eyes so pale that I'd thought of grubs that lived under rocks.

I usually felt a sick fascination when I read about Gunnison's regime. Tonight the sight of his easy grin just made my throbbing head worse. How could people *believe* this garbage? I drained my coffee abruptly and went into my bedroom.

Peter sat on my bed and watched, tail flicking, as I got undressed and pulled on my pyjamas. His expression said, *Hurry up, stroke me, you've lollygagged long enough.*

We'd inherited Peter a few months ago, when a pilot I'd known only distantly had gone down. Before that he'd belonged to someone else. And someday, if what had happened to Stan happened to Vera and me, he might move on again.

Strange, to realize that something I loved as much as flying might kill me.

Peter waited for me to slip under the covers. Then he settled purring on my stomach as I stroked his smooth back.

It's not the goal to kill the other pilot. The World for Peace wouldn't sanction that; no one would. But deaths happen, and you couldn't have too many regrets or you'd go crazy.

"Three," I murmured, and my voice startled me in the quiet.

That was how many pilots had died after battling me in the year I'd been a Peacefighter. Three was *low* – I was just thankful it wasn't more. I was fiercely glad of the anonymity policy. I would never learn those pilots' names or view images of their faces. And if I died, the other pilot wouldn't know who I was, either.

"Not much different from here on base, is it, cat?" I said softly. We had tattoos with no stories attached, laughing banter that said nothing, photos that no one would ever ask about.

After my father died I'd shut myself away in my bedroom, seeing the crash over and over. I'd been there. I'd kneeled beside him, pleading with him to stay alive, to please be all right – but though my hands had grown wet as I frantically tried to stop his bleeding, I hadn't been able to keep him from slipping away.

I hadn't been able to do anything at all that had helped.

Afterwards, the only person who'd been able to reach me was my best friend. He'd come into my room and sat beside me on the bed. Just sat, holding my hand.

On the bed now I shut my eyes tightly, my chest suddenly shuddering.

"No," I said aloud. I was not going to do this. But everything crashed together in my head: Stan, drowning in his cockpit; my father, dying in a field. Peter scrambled away as I rolled over and clutched my pillow, muffling my tears in its softness.

People say it's a release to cry, but this wasn't like that. It felt raw, painful; I hated every sob. Peter curled up next to me, resigned that the stroking had stopped and settling for my body warmth instead.

I stiffened at the sound of Vera's light, high-heeled tread coming down the hall. She hesitated outside my door, and I knew she'd heard – could almost see her pretty, freckled face screwed up as she decided what to do.

"Amity?" she called.

I didn't move. "I thought you'd be staying over at Marcus's," I said finally, lifting my voice so it would carry. I didn't realize I'd just given her an explanation – *I wouldn't have let myself cry otherwise* – until I said it.

"Not tonight." She cleared her throat. "Do you...want to talk?"

"No. Thank you."

"Are you sure? I know that..." She trailed off uncertainly. She wouldn't mention Stan's name again. No one would. Once you'd given someone their send-off, they were gone.

Better that way. Without a doubt.

"No, I don't want to talk," I said.

"All right," Vera said, her voice faintly relieved. "Well... goodnight, then."

I heard her go into her room. The slight *thump, thump* as she took off her shoes. Her telio went on, and the music started.

Love me in May,
Oh, please say you'll stay.

I switched off my light and lay gazing into the darkness as the mindless lyrics drifted in. Moonlight turned the room soft-edged. I listened to the music and to Peter's purring as he pressed against me…and as I finally fell asleep, I imagined couples holding each other and twirling on a dance floor, around and around until they could see only each other.

Chapter Four

The Cataclysm should have put an end to war, but it didn't.

Nearly two millennia ago, four great powers simultaneously launched massive attacks. We'd learned in school about the mushroom-shaped clouds that bloomed on the horizon. Cities toppled, leaving only rubble and broken bodies.

"Cataclysm" was an understatement. The world was destroyed. Whatever technology that had built those bombs was thankfully lost.

Slowly, humanity struggled back to its feet through centuries of dark ages. Now, generations later, we were in a modern age again; shining new cities had arisen from the ashes. We had autos, moving pictures, airplanes. And we had something the ancients never dreamed of: peace.

Yet even with the ruins of the Cataclysm as a reminder… there had still been war until only ninety years ago.

My family originally came from Oceania. One of my ancestors there was named Louise, and as she was walking home from school one day, soldiers attacked. Troops swarmed through the streets; shots echoed; people were screaming, running for cover. Louise sprinted home, somehow making it there safely, but when she opened the door, everyone had been killed.

She saw her mother lying on the kitchen floor with her stomach sliced open. She saw her older brother's body sitting slumped against the wall; it ended at the bloody stump of his neck. His head lay on his lap, staring at her. Her father was simply gone. Bloody scuff marks led out the door, as if he'd been struggling when he was dragged away.

"I don't understand," I'd whispered when my father told me this story. I was nine years old, and the words felt shrivelled as they left my mouth. "Why did the soldiers kill them?"

"They'd spoken out against the opposing forces." My father was sitting on the side of my bed. His sleek dark hair, so like my own, fell across his forehead. His square, firm hands were a larger version of mine too.

I felt hot, like when I'd had a fever once. "Those soldiers were evil!"

"Were they?"

"Of course! They did terrible things!"

My father had smiled sadly. "But, Amity, that's what happens in war. Louise's side might not have acted any better, if they'd had the chance."

I'd been so happy at first to spend time with my dad, but his story had been nothing like I expected. When I didn't – couldn't – reply, he went on.

Louise had fainted. When she came to, she was still in the house and still alone. She walked out the door, not shutting it behind her, not caring any more whether the soldiers killed her too. But the streets had gone strangely quiet. No one stopped her as she started through them.

Though she had no place to go, she kept walking until she left the city far behind. And without her realizing it, some small part of her decided that she still wanted to live. When she saw troops approaching, she hid in the bushes until they passed…and then started walking again.

She was thirteen years old.

The war Louise lived through eventually led to the Final War. It was long, bloody; the whole world took part. All across the far Pacific, countries were torn up into battlefields. Terrible gases were used; the fledgling technology of flight sent bombs screaming through the air. Tens of millions died.

And suddenly humanity realized that the path it was heading down had been taken before.

Louise was middle-aged by then. Along with many others, she told her story and warned, *The ancients destroyed themselves. We must never do the same.* It was the greatest protest movement the world had ever known. Louise was at its forefront, working tirelessly for decades.

Humanity listened.

The International Peace Treaty was signed by every nation. It took years for the current system to develop – lots of false starts, my father said – but now the World for Peace was as accepted as the rising sun. For the first time in history, a neutral organization governed all conflicts between nations. Military forces were found only in textbooks; weapons of mass destruction were forbidden.

For almost a century, disputes had been resolved by Peacefights: a single pilot against a single pilot. Skill against skill.

No more war. Ever.

I'd licked my lips as my father had finished, Louise's story still haunting me. "Why do Peacefights have to be dangerous, though?" I blurted. "Why can't opposing countries just play chess or something?"

Yet even as I'd asked I'd known the answer.

"Because people are violent at heart," my father had said softly. "Without risk, it wouldn't feel as if we'd really won something." He stroked my hair.

"And you're named Amity," he added, his voice intent. "For 'peace'. The fight for peace is in your blood."

* * *

The daily pilots' meeting was held in an old hangar, a vast space that smelled faintly of machine oil. When I got there the morning after Stan's send-off, Commander Hendrix was already at the front: a tall man with a kind, careworn face. I'd felt star-struck when he'd first arrived on base to take command soon after I'd begun. He was one of the highest-rated Tier Ones in recent history, not to mention that he'd served with my dad.

"Good morning, pilots," Hendrix said as we all took a seat, over a hundred of us, metal folding chairs scraping against the cement floor. He read out the roster. I didn't have a fight that day and didn't know whether I was sorry or glad.

Finally Hendrix pulled off his reading glasses and rubbed the bridge of his nose. I stiffened, bracing myself.

"A moment of silence for Stanley Chaplin, who was killed in combat yesterday," he said quietly.

The hangar went still. I sat motionless, gazing at the neck of the pilot in front of me. I carefully studied the way his hair made little whorls against his skin and tried not to think about Stan's laughing face...or about grasshoppers singing in a summer-hot field.

"Farewell, brother," said Hendrix finally. I let out a breath.

A telio set crouched on a wooden stool at the front; Hendrix turned it on. As its small, round screen flickered into life, he said, "Pilots, stand."

We rose. This was one of the few times of day when a programme was shown instead of just music playing.

The whole world might be watching this now.

The World for Peace's flag appeared on the screen, snapping in the breeze: two clasped hands encircled by a laurel wreath. The same flag hung at the front of the room now, with the Western Seaboard's sunburst flag below. Music soared from the speakers. I stood tall as glimpses of all the bases were shown.

"Repeat after me," said Hendrix, and our voices echoed through the hangar:

I swear to fight fairly,

I swear to defend my country to the best of my ability,

I swear to honour the sanctity of life.

At this moment all of the world's Peacefighters were making the same vow from every base in this complex. Our voices faded. My spine felt straighter as I gazed at the two flags on the wall.

"Remember that you're a part of something larger than yourselves," Hendrix said. "The world thanks you for your service. Pilots dismissed."

My Dove howled over the Western Seaboard practice fields. Fly straight at the other plane, fire, *roll.*

"Ha! Got you," I muttered as field and sky swapped places. Another plane swung into view; I roared on one wing after it, the g-force a giddy weight in my stomach.

All that existed up here was adrenalin. I wanted to stay in the air for ever.

When I landed I heard Russ shouting. I glanced over as I climbed from the cockpit and saw him striding towards another pilot, bellowing, "Listen up, Ramirez! If you don't start pulling out the way that machine is capable of, I swear I'm gonna—"

Despite everything, my team leader's constant refrain made me smile. I hopped down from the wing.

Vera was in line at the canteen when I went to dinner later. She gave me a rueful look as I joined her. "Two losses already today. We could use a win."

"I know," I said, though Vera had no idea how right she was. I'd been catching up on the papers. My win against the European Alliance had been important, but Gunnison was our main opponent these days – and half his recent victories had chiselled away at our eastern land rights. He really did seem to have the stars on his side, the number of wins he managed. Some people actually *believed* that.

Vera slid her tray forward. Her voice brightened. "I saw on the board that you've got leave next week. Going home?"

I didn't look up as I spooned peas onto my plate. "Just for three days," I said.

We Western Seaboard pilots were lucky: our country bordered the huge complex of Peacefighting bases. But though visits home were easy, I didn't see my family as often as I should have. That morning I'd requested leave on impulse.

This time it will be different, I promised myself. *Please. I need it to be.*

As Vera and I turned to find a table, I slowed abruptly. A cluster of new pilots sat nearby. Something went still inside me – though we'd been short a few even before Stan died. They arrived every few months, so clean and fresh-faced.

No one was talking to them. Not avoiding them, precisely...but combat fighting for real was a steep learning curve from training school. It usually felt safer to wait awhile before including someone.

Especially if they arrived the day after a send-off.

"So I guess you and Marcus will throw a wild party at the house while I'm gone," I said to Vera as we moved through the crowded room.

My tone was too dry again; she didn't get that it was a joke. She hesitated. "Oh, I don't know...he's gotten so serious lately. It's not really fair to him, when..." She broke off, her face fleetingly vulnerable, and I knew how much the send-off had affected her, too.

"Never mind," she said, and forced a smile. "Hey, maybe I'll throw a party on my own and seduce Harlan."

I made my voice jovial. "Good idea. He can teach you to belch and play poker."

Vera giggled. "He does have his charms, it's true."

Just then, one of the new pilots rose from their table, an empty water glass in his hand. I stopped short, clutching my tray as he headed towards me. The breath left my chest.

Vera stood watching me in bewilderment. I couldn't move; the canteen seemed to fade away. The new pilot had halted too, gaping at me.

He was tall, with shoulders he hadn't quite grown into yet. His hair was dark blond, streaked with sun. Full lips, a strong chin. His nose was slightly crooked, thickened across the bridge from when he'd broken it falling off his bicycle once. I'd been with him that day; we'd gone to the pond to catch tadpoles. I couldn't think, now, why we'd wanted them.

Good thing he broke that nose, or else he'd be too pretty, Ma had said once.

My thoughts tumbled crazily past. I stood rooted, gripping my tray.

The new pilot swallowed. "Amity?" he said softly.

"Collis," I whispered in wonder. It broke the spell. "Collie!" I cried.

My tray hit the floor, scattering food and broken glass as I lunged at him. He caught me up; we hugged each other tightly. I was shaking. He even smelled the same – a warm, boyish scent that brought back sprawling on the living room rug listening to *The Claw* on the telio; the time we'd run away from home together; the way I'd come downstairs at dawn sometimes and find him already there in the kitchen, eating almond butter sandwiches and grinning at me, his tanned legs swinging from a chair.

Our first – our only – kiss.

Finally I drew back, staring at him. The canteen had gone silent, everyone watching. Collie looked dazed. "I didn't – I didn't expect to see you here," he stammered.

My rush of joy was fading into confusion. "What *happened* to you?" I burst out. "Why didn't you write?"

He winced. "I did."

"You didn't!"

"All right, I…" He glanced over his shoulder at the other new pilots and hesitated. "I didn't," he admitted. "It…just seemed best."

"Best?" I echoed. At my feet, my broken glass of milk had pooled around roast chicken slices and peas, like a white lake with islands in it. Why was I noticing this?

Collie's expression was pained. "Amity…"

"When you left, we both—" I broke off, remembering his hands gripping mine. *They won't keep us apart, Amity. I promise.* He'd only recently grown taller than me then – we'd only recently started to move from best friends to something else.

Collie seemed to become aware of the stares. He nodded at a neighbouring table. "How's it going?" he said brusquely. A few mumbles as the pilots looked away.

"Isn't there a better place we could talk?" he asked me in an undertone.

I grabbed his arm and we walked through the canteen. A low buzz of conversation started up.

I shoved through the swinging doors and we stepped outside. The day had turned overcast; a chilly wind from the bay bit at the air. I leaned against the outside wall and crossed my arms tightly over my chest.

"Talk," I said.

Collie glanced around us. "Here?"

"It'll do."

There was a bench against the wall; after a pause, Collie dropped down onto it. My mind kept trying to reconcile him with the lanky fourteen-year-old I'd last seen, whose cheek had been silk-smooth when I'd shyly touched it. Now there was a golden shadow on his jaw where he'd shaved recently. He rubbed it with one hand.

"All right," he said. "Where do you want me to start?"

"Why are you here?"

"I'm a Peacefighter now," he said. "The same as you, apparently."

Collie's eyes had always had a trick to them: sometimes blue, sometimes green. They looked very blue now, like pieces of sky. He sat taking in my face as if he were trying to reconcile me with old memories, too.

"I guess I shouldn't be surprised to see you here," he added quietly.

My throat tightened, recalling my father, landing his plane near the hay bales while Collie and I ran towards him.

"No. You shouldn't be," I said. "You know it's all I ever wanted."

As if thinking about something else, Collie frowned at

his hands. "It wasn't, but I can see how you came to do it," he said.

"What are you talking about? I've always wanted to be a Peacefighter!"

Collie straightened a little. "Amity. No, you didn't. You wanted to be a transport pilot, remember? You said that you loved flying but didn't want to use it to fight, and—"

A chill touched me. "That's not true."

"Of course it's true."

And in fact, it was coming back: Collie and me lying on our stomachs beside the river, setting scraps of pine bark off down its currents. I'd put twigs on mine, pretending that the bark pieces were planes and the sticks my cargo.

Collie was watching me. "You remember now, don't you?"

I sank slowly onto the bench beside him and stared out at the dusty road lined with palm trees, recalling the way I used to feel so guilty that I had a name like *Amity* and didn't want to fly for peace. That's how Dad always described it: flying for peace.

I sighed. "It's all I want now, though," I said. "It really is, Collie. After Dad died..." I couldn't finish.

"I know." His voice was soft. He put his arm around me and looked down, his expression troubled. The warmth of his hand on my shoulder felt so familiar – right in a way that other hands touching me had never been. I hated knowing that, yet I didn't pull away.

"Why didn't you write?" I asked.

His fingers tightened on my arm. "I started to," he said. "Please believe me, Amity. I started to so many times. But, you know, Dad had just made us move, and Goldie was worse than ever…"

Collie stopped talking, and after a beat I realized that this was all he was going to say. "I don't understand," I said blankly. "Are those supposed to be reasons?"

"No, there were other things, too."

"Like what?"

"Like…I really don't want to do this, Amity."

"Do *what*? You disappeared for four years without a word! Where did your family go? I never even knew that much!"

His face had closed. "It doesn't matter."

"Of course it matters!"

Collie took his arm from my shoulders and cleared his throat. "Look, I didn't know you were going to be here. This is all—" He broke off, his jaw tense. "I could spin you a line about why I didn't get in touch," he said finally. "Let's just say I had my reasons and leave it there, all right?"

He sat leaning forward with his head down, hands linked together between his knees. His hands were a man's hands now, not a boy's. I stared at them, my chest hurting with everything I wanted to say. *Dad died, and then you left and it was like you'd died, too. Collie, I haunted the mailbox every day for months, and there was nothing…*

I stood up. "We can leave it wherever you want," I said. "We won't be talking much anyway."

He glanced up with a surprised frown. "We won't?"

"No. It's very easy to not talk to people here."

Collie started to say something else and then stopped. He looked off down the road with that same troubled expression and rapped a fist against his palm.

"Yeah," he said at last. His voice was flat. "That's probably for the best."

Chapter Five

The doorbell rang at exactly the time Kay had expected. She glanced in the mirror, tensely patted a curl into place, then put on a bright smile and swung open her apartment door. A man in a fedora hat and pinstriped suit stood in the hallway. On his lapel was a small silver Taurus pin.

"Did you bring your dance shoes?" asked Kay in a clear voice.

For a second the man stared blankly. Kay widened her eyes at him, and he swallowed. "Yes – yes, of course." He patted the briefcase under his arm. "Right here."

She ushered him in, first glancing up and down the hallway. The other apartment doors were all closed.

Once inside, Kay quickly locked her door and put a vinyl disc on the phonoplayer. Dramatic tango music poured from the trumpet-shaped speaker. She twisted the blinds shut against the orderly brownstones that lined the Topeka street, and the slanting bars of sunlight that had fallen across the room vanished.

"You told me on the phone it was urgent," Kay said, her smile gone. "You know, Mr Hearn, I don't usually see people unless—"

"No, please! You've got to help me." Mr Hearn pulled off his hat and sank into a chair at her consultation table. "Look, I've got them right here." He opened the briefcase and took out a large brown envelope. He hesitated as he studied Kay. "You're very young."

She raised an eyebrow and sat across from him. "I'm nineteen. You're welcome to find someone older."

He winced. "I had a hard enough time finding you."

He handed over the envelope. *Hearn Family*, read the lettering on its front. The rubber-stamped date – November 22nd 1940 – was from the most recent sweep, only days previously.

Kay studied it. "You stole this from a state astrologer?"

Her client shifted uneasily. "Let's say 'borrowed'. Can you tell me if my family's in danger?"

"Yes," said Kay.

There was a pause. Mr Hearn frowned. "Well, *will* you tell me?"

"I just did," said Kay, patiently. "Look." She pointed at

a small, pencilled mark on one corner of the envelope: a circle with a jagged line through it.

"That shows that someone in the family has been found Discordant," she said. "It saves the sorters from having to check each family's charts when they come in."

Mr Hearn went rigid. He stared at the circle with its lightning-bolt slash. Kay knew what he was thinking. A few years ago, being made Discordant meant having to wear a "D" on your clothes and losing some of your civil rights. But now Sandford Cain, with his bland face and pale eyes, was handling the Discordants.

Neither Kay nor Mr Hearn said the words "correction camp".

Kay took an eraser and carefully rubbed at the mark. The circle with the jagged line faded. "This will buy us a little time."

Mr Hearn's knuckles were white. "There must be something you can do," he said tightly. "*Please.*"

Kay slid out the birth charts. Each showed a circle divided into twelve parts, or "houses", with one astrology sign per house. Kay always imagined a snapshot of the heavens taken the moment someone was born, with the astrological wheel then superimposed over this. Numbers and symbols showed which astrology signs the sun, moon and planets were in at birth and to what degree. At the charts' centres, geometric shapes showed the unique, complex ways the planets interacted for that person.

Or would interact, thought Kay, if any of this were true.

Astrology might be intricate to master, but only fools believed in it.

She examined the charts, and tapped the one labelled *Margie Hearn*. "This one's the problem."

Mr Hearn made a small, strangled sound. "My daughter," he whispered. "She's ten."

"Well, they'll have found her Discordant anyway. She's got Pluto in the seventh house, plus her ascendant is Aries. That shows a subversive attitude towards—"

Mr Hearn's voice rose to almost a shout. "*Subversive?* She's ten! Seventh house, ascendant – what *is* this crap; what's it got to do with Margie?"

Kay's glance was almost amused. "Oh, dear. Haven't we been paying attention in our astrology classes?"

Her client blanched as he realized his blunder. All citizens were required to study basic astrology, "to preserve our harmonious society".

"Don't...don't report me," he said.

Inwardly, Kay shrugged. Even with perfect stars, you could be found Discordant. But the black market was where the money was, not reporting people who were supposedly a threat to Harmony.

"My goodness, I wouldn't dream of it," she said mildly. She studied Margie's chart again. "The ascendant's the sign that was rising on the eastern horizon at birth," she added. "Your outward personality. Your daughter's sun sign is Libra, but Aries rising means she comes across more like an Aries."

Mr Hearn swallowed. "And...that's supposed to be bad?"

"Depending on a chart's other elements," said Kay. And on whatever new ideas President Gunnison had gotten into his head.

Every Central States citizen knew how Gunnison, once a poor farm boy, had "found himself" through astrology. In countless interviews he'd described his fascination on learning that astrologers had predicted the Final War – though those old predictions were so vague, thought Kay, that they could mean anything.

From the very start, Gunnison's policies had been driven by the stars. Excited that astrology had also "predicted" their new country, people had at first embraced it with enthusiasm. The thought was hard to believe now. Kay's clients all wore the same tense, desperate look.

But if you had the right contacts, there was a great deal of money to be made.

"All right, here's what we'll do," Kay said. "I'll recast your daughter's chart. By the time they do another sweep, she'll have a new birth certificate with a safe time and date."

Cautious hope crept over Mr Hearn's face. "You can do that? Put a new birth certificate in the record's office?"

Kay smiled sweetly. "If you can afford it."

He gave a terse nod. Kay took out a blank chart and her ephemeris. She noted Margie Hearn's date and time of birth, then flipped through the thick book of planetary graphs.

A knock banged at the door.

Kay froze and looked up. In the background the dance music played on.

"Are you expecting anyone?" Mr Hearn whispered urgently.

No. She was not. The knock came again – louder, harder. Kay lunged from her chair.

"Coming!" she called.

She grabbed the ephemeris and shoved it back into her bookcase; the spine read *Famous Quotations.* She swept up the charts and jammed them into the envelope. She placed it on the rug. Trying not to let her hands shake she quickly rolled the rug into a tight cylinder, exposing polished floorboards.

"I've been teaching you the tango," she hissed to Mr Hearn. Without waiting for a response she glanced in the mirror again, making sure her Scorpio brooch was visible, then smoothed out her skirt and went to the door.

When she opened it there were three Guns. They wore identical grey uniforms; their buttons gleamed. The red-and-black Harmony symbols were stark swirls over their hearts.

They shoved past before Kay could speak. "What's wrong?" she cried. "I'm just giving a dance lesson!"

They didn't reply. Mr Hearn stood in the middle of the room like a statue. One of the Guns held Kay's arm in a painful grip; she watched in cold terror as the other two tore her home apart. Someone had tipped them off –

or else her contact in the records office had been captured.

They found the ephemeris easily enough, knocking all the books from the shelf until they had it. Then one of the men flapped open the rug. The *Hearn Family* envelope fell out onto the floorboards.

The Gun's lip curled. He picked up the envelope and glanced inside. "These are yours, I take it," he said to Kay's client. "Who's the Discordant? You?"

Mr Hearn took a shaky step backwards, hands up. "I – please, I didn't do anything wrong! I was just—"

The Gun reached for his holster. Kay had a confused second to register the blunt black shape of a pistol, and then a gunshot thundered. Mr Hearn collapsed to the floor, stumbling over the skewed rug. Red bloomed on his chest. He gasped: a terrible choking sound. Panting, he touched his chest – stared blankly at the blood on his fingers.

The Gun walked over to him. Mr Hearn looked up, his eyes round and panicked. "Please…" he whispered.

The Gun shot him again, in the head this time, and then kicked his lifeless body hard. Blood spattered across the floor.

"Discordant scum," the Gun said.

Kay couldn't move. Mr Hearn's face had a hole in it. Part of his head was gone. *Gone.*

The Gun still held the envelope. Where the circle with the jagged line had been there was now a streak of blood. He put the weapon back in his holster and turned to her.

"So very sorry to trouble you, Miss Pierce," he said coldly. "Come with us."

They surrounded her in a small cluster as they strode down the hallway. Kay saw Mrs Lloyd peek out her apartment door, then quickly close it again. The vindicated look on her face was unmistakable.

Kay went taut. Had Mrs Lloyd been the one to report her?

Outside, the sky was very blue, the sidewalk spotless. One of the windowless grey "Shadowcars" waited at the kerb: tall, with rounded lines; a silver grille leered at its front. As the Guns shoved Kay into the van, passers-by avoided looking at her.

There were no seats. The cold metal space smelled of sweat and urine. When the Shadowcar began to move, Kay's tense fingers closed around a pencil stub in her sweater pocket, along with a crumpled receipt. She pulled out both items and gazed at them, mind racing. She balanced the scrap of paper on her leg and began to write.

Finally the van stopped. When the doors swung open Kay saw that she'd been taken to the centre of downtown Topeka; the city of millions pulsed around them with its gleaming el-trains and streetcars and honking taxicabs.

Just in front of her was a stretch of lawn and a marble building she recognized as part of the Zodiac: the massive twelve-domed capitol complex that housed John

Gunnison's regime. Kay was unsurprised. Dread shivered through her.

The Guns yanked her from the van. They'd parked in front of the "Libra" building. Its broad white dome towered overhead as they hustled her inside. She was even less surprised to find out that there were jail facilities deep in the building's bowels.

As she was pushed into a large cell full of people, Kay clutched one of the Gun's arms.

"I have vital information about Gunnison's Dozen," she said, and pressed the scrap of paper into his hand. "It would be very worth someone's while to listen to me."

They left her locked up for over seven hours.

Kay sat hugging herself on a bench, feeling sick. From the low, frightened buzz of conversation, her cellmates were all black market astrologers, too. A few times someone was ordered out, and the whole cell went tautly silent at the distant sound of screams.

Finally Kay was taken to a small room near the cells. It held a plain wooden table, two chairs. The Gun who'd brought her left and locked the door.

Kay sat down gingerly. She stared at the walls. They had faint reddish-brown stains, and she had a sudden terror that she should have kept her mouth shut.

She waited, her imagination running rampant. Who would walk through that door? Sandford Cain? Gunnison's chief right-hand man was known to be a violent thug. The correction camps he'd established in the far north were notorious. There were whispered rumours of prisoners forced to work in the snow until they froze to death, of secret midnight shootings in the woods, of anonymous graves piled high with bodies.

The door opened. Kay straightened with a jerk.

No, it wasn't Cain…though the man who stood before her was in the news as often. Malcolm Skinner, the Chief Astrologer of Gunnison's regime. He was thin and narrow-shouldered; his double-breasted suit was sharply creased.

Skinner dismissed a pair of underlings with a wave. As the door closed, he sat across from Kay. The look he gave her was dry as a bone. "Miss Pierce, is it?"

"Yes, sir."

"You claim you have information about the Twelve Year Plan. I'd be very interested to know how."

Kay swallowed. "Because I cast a chart showing the Plan's 'birthdate' – the exact time and date of its inauguration," she said softly.

When Gunnison first took power just under twelve years ago now, he'd announced the Twelve Year Plan: a scheme to bring boundless prosperity. How exactly he would do this was kept secret. Occasionally the press would mention that "Gunnison's Dozen" was on track; that was all.

Casting this chart was forbidden even for state astrologers. At Kay's admission Skinner's gaze narrowed.

He flipped through a stack of papers he was holding. His cufflinks showed the symbol for Capricorn.

"Talk," he said, and shoved a paper her way.

The chart for the Plan. Kay started to give a wildly positive interpretation. Something about Skinner's tense mouth made her speak from instinct instead.

"There are themes of idealism," she said. "But there's uncertainty too. Not in Mr Gunnison's vision. He knows exactly what he wants; you can see that with Mercury in Taurus."

Skinner gave a small nod that Kay doubted he'd been aware of, and she had a flash of thankfulness that she didn't actually believe in astrology – otherwise, given the chart's generally positive aspects, she wouldn't have hinted at trouble. But she'd become masterful at "cold reading". Many of her clients not only believed in astrology, they wanted insight about their lives, and people's body language always told you when you were on the right track.

Just as Skinner's was doing right now.

Gaining confidence, Kay sketched a line on the chart. "See, look at this T-square: an exact Jupiter–Pluto opposition. Nothing's been as straightforward as President Gunnison would like these last twelve years. And given Jupiter's trajectory, our country's facing great challenges if his vision is to become reality. It's make-or-break time."

Skinner held himself so carefully that Kay knew she'd struck home. "An interesting interpretation." He put the chart away. "You're a black market astrologer," he said after a pause. "You've helped Discordants escape justice."

Only for the money didn't seem a wise answer. Kay replied cautiously: "I have an unregistered ephemeris and see clients, yes. If any of them have used the information I gave them to elude justice, I'm unaware of it. I care very deeply about a harmonious society, Mr Skinner. The only reason I'm not a state astrologer is that I couldn't afford the registration fee."

If her contact in the records office had been captured too, she was dead.

Skinner sat frowning, tapping his index fingers together. Abruptly, he rose. He went and opened the door.

"Take her back," he said to the lackeys.

They left her in the cells for twenty-two hours this time.

Kay lay huddled on one of the hard concrete benches, thinking, *Have I saved myself, or made things worse?* The only thing she was sure of by now, given that she was still alive after claiming she'd never knowingly helped Discordants, was that her contact in the records office hadn't been caught.

No. Someone had reported her.

Finally a Gun appeared. "Kay Pierce," he said, and unlocked the door as she stiffly sat up. She felt hollow with hunger and fear.

The same office. This time Skinner was waiting for her.

Kay took the seat opposite and noticed for the first time that one of his eyebrows had a tiny bald patch.

Skinner flipped through a stack of papers. Without looking up, he said, "If you repeat what I'm about to say, I'll have you shot."

Kay's stomach flipped. "I…I understand."

For the next five minutes, Skinner spoke tersely. What he said shocked Kay to her bones, though she tried her best to hide it. She'd thought herself jaded, beyond surprise… but *this*? The Peacefights had always been sacrosanct.

When Skinner finished, he gazed coldly at her. "I will repeat, Miss Pierce, you are not to mention a word of this. People who cross us regret it…such as the Western Seaboard pilot who had an attack of conscience recently and tried to weasel out of his agreement. And *then* the fool thought he could just continue Peacefighting as usual."

Skinner leaned towards Kay. He spoke deliberately. "Well, he paid for it. His next fight wasn't broadcast and we had him shot down over the water. He drowned."

Kay's hands were clenched in her lap, her mind spinning with all she'd been told. "I understand," she said again, her voice faint. "I won't say a word."

"Good." Without further ado, Skinner shoved a batch of astrology charts towards her. "There's a vital rematch tomorrow between the European Alliance and the Western Seaboard. Which Western Seaboard pilot should fight it?"

From the way he said it, this pilot might not live to tell the tale, either.

Kay sifted through the charts and wondered fervently what the right answer was. How exactly were they planning to ensure the Western Seaboard's loss? Did Skinner have a particular pilot in mind?

She came to an unusual chart and paused. At its centre, a square with an "x" through it showed that four planets formed a "Grand Cross" – an uncommon aspect.

Suddenly Kay noticed how still Skinner had become, how intent his gaze.

"A Grand Cross," she commented. "Rare."

Skinner didn't respond, though she thought his nostrils flared slightly. Kay looked through the other charts. None provoked as strong a reaction. She steeled herself and slid the Grand Cross forward.

"This one," she said.

"You're certain?"

"Positive. The Grand Cross signals difficulties. With Saturn entering Aries this month, the pilot won't stand a chance."

Skinner gave a small, satisfied smile. He traced the "x" at the chart's centre.

"Very fitting," he said softly. "After our misguided Western Seaboard pilot made his fatal decision, we had to take him off a crucial fight with the European Alliance. This pilot fought it instead. She was unaware; she actually *won.* It's because of her that we have to have the rematch. Well, I hope she enjoys her next fight."

Kay's muscles sagged. She'd guessed right…for now.

Skinner gathered all the charts and tapped them together. His tone turned curt. "All right, you're free to go."

"Go?"

"Yes. Go home. Don't see any more clients. In fact, don't do anything at all until we're in touch with you again." His gaze raked over her. "You *will* be watched. If you try to leave the city you'll regret it."

Kay rose, her knees suddenly weak. "I won't," she said.

As she reached the door, Skinner said, "Oh, and you'll give us your client list, of course."

"I didn't keep one," Kay said truthfully. "But I'll tell you everyone I can remember." A thought came. In a steady tone, she added, "Mrs Lloyd, my neighbour, was one."

She left the jail. No one tried to stop her. She went up the stairs and found the main door out of the Libra building. When she stepped outside the sunlight dazzled her eyes. She lifted her face to the sky and savoured the cool breeze that stroked her skin.

She wasn't safe yet. She knew that. Skinner had been very clear how important this rematch was to the Central States, and to what lengths they'd already gone to ensure their desired result. If the European Alliance didn't win tomorrow, Kay was dead.

As she started the long, weary walk home, she tried not to think about the grisly mess that might be awaiting her. Her lie about Mrs Lloyd concerned her not at all. It'd serve the old hag right if she'd been the one to turn Kay in.

She wondered briefly, though, which Western Seaboard pilot the Grand Cross chart belonged to and to what fate she'd submitted them.

Better them than her.

Chapter Six

My boots crunched on the gravel as I walked towards the airstrip. Against the sunset the palm trees were dark, fringed outlines; I could smell oranges on the breeze. It was the day after Collie had arrived. I'd been relieved to learn I had another fight against the European Alliance – a night battle this time. I felt too edgy to sit around doing nothing.

I reached a plain white building and opened the door quietly, feeling the smoothness of its worn wood. Inside, candles cast a gentle glow. A few other pilots were present, some with heads bowed, others looking deep in thought.

I slid onto one of the benches. I came here often; it was a place where you could breathe. My father must have come here, too. Maybe he'd sat on this very bench.

On the wall was a tapestry of the World for Peace flag, with rich embroidery outlining its figures. Its laurel leaf threads gradated from palest green to rich emerald. A white-draped table sat beneath. On it was a bronze statuette of a Firedove.

I touched my ID tags, running my thumb over the raised letters of my father's name. I shut my eyes and pressed the tags against my lips.

Let me fight fairly.

Let me defend my country to the best of my ability.

Let me honour the sanctity of life.

And deep down, I added another plea: *Don't let me be distracted by the thought of Collie.*

When I took off the night was overcast. Then I emerged up through the cloud cover and found a glittering sea of stars. Below my plane, moonlight stroked across the cloud tops, transforming them into a weird, silvery landscape.

In the distance a shadowy shape appeared from a cloud, then ducked away into it again.

It was time.

From the European Alliance plane's tight control, I knew already it was the same pilot I'd shot down a few days before. Perfect – I was in the mood for a good fight. I eased my stick forward and dropped into the clouds, speeding towards him with the roar of the engine in my ears. Ghostly scraps of mist whipped past.

When I burst out into the starry night the other Dove was directly ahead; the pilot hadn't spotted me. *Yes!* I fired. Gunfire juddered as eight streams of tracer shot through the sky.

Too late, I saw my plane's moonlit shadow cross the other cockpit. He reacted instantly, banking sharply away into the clouds, unscathed. I swore and plummeted after him; he flickered in and out of view as we howled through the greyness together.

He was gone. Jaw tight, I came up through the clouds again, craning down through my goggles for the gleam of moonlight on his wings.

A wall of cloud towered to my right; suddenly he came roaring from a tunnel, firing. *Damn.* The Dove and I half-rolled and plunged into a dive; seven tracer passed harmlessly over my starboard wing. A single cartridge clawed a furrow in the metal.

Stars and clouds shrieked past as I dived; pressure plastered me against my seat. At four hundred miles per hour I eased back – a wave of darkness tugged, but I was out of the dive now and didn't pass out. As I soared from the clouds they turned gracefully upside down, meeting my plane's nose. Stick forward, left, and I'd rolled out right way up.

My rival was still right on my tail. Despite myself, I felt a bolt of admiration.

"Nice try, but not enough," I muttered to him. I circled quickly, then came straight at him from above and fired.

My wings barely trembled this time – only one tracer snaked out. What? I tried again, jamming down hard on the button. Nothing. Heart suddenly pounding, I checked the air gauge. Eighty. Way too low. He must have hit me a second time, got my air bottle without my even seeing.

Had he, though? You could usually feel a hit. Had I had a malfunction?

My attention snapped back to the fight. My opponent had swung into firing position; tracer streaked towards me. Before I could move, a hail of machine-gun fire shook right across my fuselage.

My engine sputtered once, coughed…and died.

The only sound was the hum of my enemy's aircraft. Across my plane's nose, the propeller's four blades went still. Flames flickered from the engine, bright orange against the stars. Smoke billowed past my cockpit.

I knew I should bail. I didn't move. It'd be a clean win for the EA: five years until we could challenge. *Five years.* Remembering the magnitude of the stakes last time, I went cold.

My rival's plane drew close. I glanced up sharply – if he shot again now, it would be against every rule. As his Dove flew alongside mine, I glimpsed the pilot's face through the smoke for the first time. A few dark curls had escaped from the edge of his leather helmet; from behind his goggles his eyes looked just as dark. His mouth was shouting silently at me.

Bail!

He jabbed a finger at his parachute, then pointed at my own, still shouting, his meaning clear: *What's wrong with you? Get the hell out of there!*

I decided. Ignoring the other pilot, I checked the hydraulics, flicking the lever a few times. No response. I glared at the dancing flames. *All right, don't worry, Amity. You can still get the wheels down when you land.*

With luck.

I glanced at the other pilot, shrugged – then banked into a screeching dive. The world turned misty, lit by eerie glimpses of snapping flames through the smoke. I kept one eye on the altimeter, tracking my descent. The flames kept sputtering down with the wind, then rearing up again, higher than before.

Come on, go out! Struggling against the pressure, I raised my seat to the full up position in case I had to bail; my eyes darted to the lever I'd pull to jettison the hood. *If you're on fire, don't open the hood until the last moment; it'll draw flames into the cockpit.* Useful sentence from my training.

Don't think about the fact that the gas tank is sitting right between you and the flames. Do. Not. Think about it.

Finally the fire gave a last defeated flicker and vanished from sight. Was it really dead, though? Smoke still curled around the edges of the control panel. The cockpit was an oven – sweat streamed down my face.

"Let's go with the idea that it's out; I like that one best," I muttered. Now the wheels.

Dark fields came racing towards me as I burst out of cloud cover at two thousand feet. I took the dive as low as I dared; before I could pass out I pulled up sharply, making the angle as vicious as possible. A tumbled glimpse of lights from the Heat and the underside of clouds again, and then the world righted itself as I went into a glide.

"Please," I gasped, glancing at the smoky controls. But pulling out like a lunatic hadn't worked – the landing wheels hadn't budged.

All right, I could handle this; the Western Seaboard's base was only a mile away. I kept gliding, keeping the nose level, my gaze locked on the lit runway just visible in the distance.

Still one thing left to try. I worked the rudder pedals like I was trying to stamp my feet through the floor. The plane rocked wildly, the airfield lurching in my view.

"Come *on,* come *on,*" I chanted through gritted teeth. Suddenly the green indicator light flicked on: my wheels were down. I slumped back against the seat…and saw a tongue of flame flicker up from the hood. And then another. In a second the engine was merrily on fire again.

"Oh, you just couldn't stay out, could you?" I breathed. The runway was still too far ahead – I wasn't going to make it before the plane blew.

No. I have to.

The moonlit fields were rushing towards me. Ignoring the flames, I went into the usual drill: UMP and Flaps. My undercarriage was already down. Mixture control to rich.

Propeller speed – what propeller speed? I didn't even have an engine. Flaps down.

The plane slowed – her nose dropped slightly. The fire raged, surging up over the hood.

Now the part that might get me burned to a cinder. I set the emergency exit door at half-cock position, careful not to get my arm in the airflow…and then I shoved back the cockpit hood.

Smoke hit me in a solid wall. Flames came whipping back into the cockpit; heat crackled at my leather jacket. I couldn't see the air speed indicator – couldn't see anything. I closed the throttle, bringing the stick back. The tail bounced and I was down – and I'd just made the edge of the runway after all, rumbling and jouncing over the asphalt.

Yes! Now I could get out of here. I fumbled with my straps. For a second they didn't budge and my heartbeat trebled; I gave a panicked tug and they fell away. I scrambled from the cockpit.

The port wing raced along below me, the pavement a blur underneath. I slid down onto the wing and didn't let myself think about it: with a rush of wind I dropped over its edge.

Pain – a blur of asphalt and then grass. I staggered to my feet, clutching at my ribs. With one hand I shoved back my goggles; I stared after my plane.

It trundled to a stop, lit by orange flames and the runway lights, the painted circles on its wings like bloodshot eyes. Sirens howled, growing closer. Shadowy figures ran across the landing strip towards the blaze.

I sprinted to meet them. "Get the fire out!" I shouted. "The air bottle! There may have been a malfunction; we've got to—"

The plane exploded with a rumble that shook the night. With a cry I dropped to the ground. I covered my head as scraps of metal and burning shrapnel pattered around me.

When it ended I stumbled to my feet, eyes streaming with smoke. What was left of my plane was still on fire, in a defeated kind of way. The fire engines arrived and screeched to a halt. The hose came rattling off its cylinder.

Edwards was there. I grabbed his arm and quickly explained. "I'll tell them, and see if we can salvage it," he gasped, and raced towards the fire crew.

After that there was nothing else I could do. I stood watching my plane burn. *I almost didn't make it out,* I realized blankly. Just a few more seconds…

The roar of another Firedove. Distracted, I glanced up. It was my European Alliance opponent, cruising low over the burning plane. I stared. He was breaking at least a dozen rules coming here. But remembering how he'd told me to bail, I suddenly understood. There were probably too many lockers with the names torn off them in his changing room, too.

I stepped into the circle of the plane's burning glow and waved, showing him I was down and safe. The other Dove waggled its wings. It banked gracefully, then headed off towards the EA base.

I stood very still, studying the shape of his plane as it grew smaller against the stars. Then I saw Russ jogging up. He paused, staring at my burning Firedove, then broke into a run. I forgot everything else as I pounded towards him. When I reached him he grasped my shoulders.

"Vancour, what happened?" he barked.

"I lost," I panted. My rib was kicking me now. I hardly cared. "But I got it down, Russ! We can appeal the wait-time!"

I told him what had happened, the words tumbling over each other. Across the airstrip, the black, burned-out shadow of my plane looked skeletal as the firemen withdrew. Water dripped from its charred carcass.

Russ gazed at me as if he couldn't believe his ears. For a long moment he didn't speak.

"Russ?"

On the grass nearby a small, still-burning piece of plane sputtered. Slowly, a lopsided smile spread across Russ's face. "Holy hell, kiddo – you are one amazing pilot." Still seeming stunned, he ran a hand over his head. "Okay… so we can appeal the wait-time now," he said. "Good job, Wildcat."

"What was the dispute?" I asked urgently.

He grimaced. "You don't want to know."

"I do! I have to!"

"That fight of yours the other day," Russ said at last.

"The one that retained twenty-seven per cent of our oil rights. The European Alliance managed to challenge on a technicality – you just fought the rematch."

The world dropped away. "*What?*"

"I'm sorry, kiddo."

"They can't do that!"

But I knew they could. Rematches happened. Fact of life.

I spun to face Edwards as he appeared, his face smudged with grime. "Miss Vancour, it looks like the air bottle wasn't destroyed, but we can't check it out here. We'll take the plane into one of the hangars – give it a thorough going-over."

"Yes, please!" I gasped.

"Your air bottle?" Russ said sharply.

As Edwards jogged off, I explained about the possible malfunction – how I hadn't been able to fire. I tried not to sound desperate with hope and failed. If I was right, we could get a whole new fight – we could obliterate what had just happened.

Russ frowned over at my plane. "I doubt there was any malfunction, Vancour. You know how carefully these crates are checked out. You were probably just hit and didn't realize it."

"It's a possibility, isn't it?"

He seemed to rouse himself and glanced back at me. "Sure, it's a possibility. I'll let you know what they find out."

"You won't have to. I'm going to go along while they check."

"Forget it," Russ said flatly. "The only place you're going is Medical."

I'd forgotten my rib. I still had one hand over it. "It's only a cracked rib; I'll be fine!"

A cluster of trucks was parked nearby. Russ signalled to them and a driver came hurrying up. "Get her to Medical," he said, jerking his head towards me.

"I've got to know!"

"*You'll know.* I'll come and tell you." Russ clapped my arm, his eyes intense. "Listen, that was excellent flying, kiddo. First rate – I mean it. At the very least, we'll get an appeal to challenge the wait-time. Now go get fixed up and write your report."

The driver helped me into the truck. My rib throbbed. *Please let me have been right about the air bottle,* I thought. *Please.* I'd won that fight for my father. I couldn't let it be taken away from me now.

As we drove away, I looked back. Russ's shadowy form was striding towards what was left of my plane, its shape black against the stars.

Chapter Seven

"AMITY!" CALLED MY MOTHER AS I stepped off the train in Sacrament.

At first I couldn't see her on the crowded platform; then I spotted a frenzied handkerchief waving at me above the fedoras and styled, upswept curls. I struggled over and we hugged. It hurt my rib, but I didn't say anything. I hadn't told her I'd cracked it.

"It is *so* good to see you," Ma murmured. She drew back, holding onto my upper arms and beaming. "And looking so well! What a pretty dress! Isn't she beautiful?" she demanded of my little brother Hal.

Hal hung back. He was thirteen, thin and lanky, with the same sleek dark hair and olive skin as me. He gave an awkward shrug.

"She's all right," he said. "Hi," he added to me.

"Hi, Hal." After a beat, I hugged him, too. I never knew whether he'd welcome it or not – he was at a funny age.

Not to mention that I'd left.

"Here, let me carry that for you," said my mother when I reached for the bag that I'd dropped at my feet.

"Don't bother, it's not heavy."

"No, give it to me," Ma insisted. "You must be tired."

"Why would I be tired? It's only ten in the morning."

"You work so hard, though." She tried to take the bag from me; my fingers tightened around its handle.

"Ma, please stop fussing. I'm not tired."

"Hal, *you* take it," said Ma, and I sighed and handed it over to him.

"Fine," I said. "Can we go now?"

A huge bronze timepiece hung over the station's main exit. *Time since the end...lest we forget,* its ornate lettering read. The numbers clicked steadily, up in the millions now: the minutes since the bombs causing the Cataclysm had dropped.

As we headed towards it through the station, Ma spoke in deliberately cheerful bursts. "You look so *pretty,* darling. Where did you find that dress? Blue suits you so well! Why, you could be a model if you weren't a pilot! And I know you must be exhausted, whatever you say. I don't want you to do a single thing while you're here." She patted my arm.

My smile was pasted on. *She's only trying to be nice,* I reminded myself. But I felt like a cat held on someone's lap and very determinedly stroked.

Outside autos and buses grumbled past. Everything looked slightly shabby: the cracked sidewalks, the billboards advertising toothpaste and cigarettes, the overflowing trash cans. An ancient structure that was once a capitol building still stood, its dome a smoggy grey. Other buildings tiered upwards like elongated ziggurats, but were just as grimy. Many had *For rent* signs.

No wonder people envied Gunnison's gleaming cities whenever a glimpse of them came on the telio.

The streetcar home was crowded, but we found three seats near each other. As the car clanged away from the kerb, Hal glanced at me. He had his hair slicked back, and wore grey trousers that were rolled up a turn or two, showing his socks.

"So what's it like being a Peacefighter?" he asked under the noise. "You never say much in your letters."

I heard the restrained eagerness in his voice – and saw a *Peace Power* comic sticking out of his back pocket. When pilots died in the comics, all you had to do was turn the page.

I tried to smile. "There's always too much to tell."

"You're home for three days, though. You've got time."

"Yeah, I guess I do."

My brother's full name was Halcyon. Our names both meant "peace".

Ma wasn't listening; she smiled widely at the heavyset woman behind me. "Helen, hello! Have you met my daughter Amity? Amity, say hello, this is Mrs Blackstone."

I had to turn in my seat and smile and smile as Ma chattered away, her inflections hushed and dramatic. "She's a Peacefighter, you know...only home for three days and I know she's just exhausted, poor thing...but a very skilled pilot, exactly like her father..."

Ma reached across the aisle to pat my arm again and then kept her hand there, resting her fingers on my skin as she talked. Mrs Blackstone sat gazing at me with awe. The woman next to her was listening too, eyes wide, not even pretending to be doing anything else.

When Ma paused for breath, Mrs Blackstone leaned forward. "Thank you for your service, Miss Vancour. Everyone in the Western Seaboard is proud of you."

"It's an honour," I said, trying not to sound stiff and failing. It *was*, but I could never say it and sound natural, not with people gazing at me with shining eyes.

Besides, everyone in the Western Seaboard would not be proud of me if they knew I'd lost almost thirty per cent of our main fuel source.

Russ had come to find me after I got taped up by Medical. "The team checked; there was no malfunction," he said as I signed myself out. "You've got two bullet holes right through your back panel."

My heart had dropped. I put down the pen. "Really?"

He gave a reluctant nod. "They pierced your air bottle and snapped off the nozzle – that was why you couldn't fire. You must not have felt the hit, that's all. It happens."

He was right, but the disappointment almost knocked the breath from me. "Well, thanks for telling me," I said finally.

Russ gripped my shoulder. "Hey, you got it down, kiddo," he said quietly. "That means a lot. At least we can challenge the wait-time."

On the streetcar, I reminded myself that nothing would change for the Western Seaboard until after the appeals court heard my case. If you got your plane down after a defeat, it meant the other pilot hadn't totally bested you. You could appeal for time off the standard five-year wait before your country re-fought the issue.

Three years off, maybe. Four, if I was lucky. No matter how bad things got for people as a result of my loss, at least it wouldn't last for very long.

Ma kept talking to Mrs Blackstone. I gazed out the window as she confided how difficult it was when Truce died, but Amity had been *such* a help – and now, of course, she was a hero just like him—

"Oh, honestly," I muttered. My hand twisted at my skirt. Ma's ability to rewrite history drove me crazy. It also made me nervous; I think she really believed what she was saying. Already, the vague idea I'd had when I booked this leave that I could share my feelings about Dad with her – and maybe even about Stan – was receding.

The disappointment tasted sour. Why did I ever expect anything different?

"Remember the night I got arrested?" I asked Hal, lifting my voice.

He glanced up from his comic. "Sure," he said.

"It was after we moved here from the country, remember? I hated it here, and I was still upset over Dad – I got into a lot of trouble for a long time."

Hal looked confused. "I know all of this," he said.

Mrs Blackstone hadn't. She was more agog than ever.

Ma tried to laugh. "Amity! You weren't *arrested.*"

"I was. For shoplifting."

"Darling, don't exaggerate. It was a misunderstanding," she added to Mrs Blackstone. "The store was so apologetic afterwards."

"The store wanted to press charges. I almost got sent to a juvenile detention centre."

"But how can you be a Peacefighter if—" started the stranger next to Mrs Blackstone. Her cheeks reddened as she realized she'd butted in.

"It didn't matter," I said. "I told them everything in my admissions interview. They accepted me into training school anyway."

"Madeline helped," said Hal.

"No, she didn't," I said sharply.

Madeline Bark, an old friend of the family, had been a Peacefighter with my father and was now a high-up in the World for Peace. "I didn't even tell her I was applying,"

I said to Hal. "I wanted them to let me in on my own merits, or not at all."

"Well I never," murmured the woman.

Ma managed an *Isn't that cute?* chuckle while looking daggers at me. "But tell me about *George,*" she said to Mrs Blackstone. "Didn't I hear that he's going to need surgery, poor man?"

I propped my chin on my hand with a sigh and stared out at the passing buildings, feeling like I was ten years old again. I started to say something to Hal, then stopped short. "What's that?"

We'd entered Ma's neighbourhood, with its familiar once-genteel buildings, now as run-down as the rest of the city.

Hal looked up. "What's what?"

"*That.*" I pointed, chilled. Where a florist's had once stood, there was a sign showing the swirling red-and-black Harmony symbol. The lettering read: *Birth Charts Cast, Destinies Explained.*

"Is there an *astrologer* here?" I gasped.

Hal turned a page of his comic. "Sure, there's lots now. I guess people are interested 'cause it's in the news so much."

"It's in the news so much because Gunnison's a maniac," I said curtly. "And why's his symbol on the sign?"

We were long past the astrologer's now. Hal blinked at my vehemence. "Isn't it just a good-luck symbol? Ying and yang, or something?"

"Yin-yang, and it hasn't been lucky since Gunnison took it over."

The streetcar clattered to a stop and Ma rose. "This is ours," she said to Mrs Blackstone. "So nice to see you! Say hello to George for me."

"I will, and it was certainly a privilege to meet your lovely daughter." Mrs Blackstone beamed at me as Hal and I got up – but I could see her wondering about the shoplifting.

After that red-and-black swirl, I'd almost forgotten it.

"Here, give me that," I muttered to Hal, and took my bag from him as we went down the streetcar stairs.

Our brownstone wasn't far away, right next to the fruit seller's. Apples and pears sat in open display crates; the smell of strawberries hung in the air. It was a relief how normal it all seemed. Though I scanned the street, I couldn't see any more of those stark red-and-black symbols.

It's not my concern if people believe that garbage, I told myself.

Ma climbed the steps to our building's front door and stood rummaging through her purse. "Now, where are my keys…?"

Suddenly I felt a rush of affection for her. I couldn't remember a single time when Ma had let us into the building without first losing her keys in that bag. "Try the inside pocket," I said.

"No, under your wallet," put in Hal.

Ma held up her keys with a jingling flourish. "Inside pocket," she said, dimpling. "Amity, you're so smart."

Our third-floor apartment had always felt overcrowded to me: full of all the nice things we had when Dad was alive, crammed now into a too-small space. I longed to throw half of it out so that I could breathe.

"Now, Amity, you must sit down," commanded Ma once we got inside, unpinning her hat. She rested it on a small marble-topped table. "Can I get you anything? Are you hungry?"

I stayed standing. "I'm fine, Ma. Thanks."

"A sandwich?"

"Really, I'm not hungry. I'll just have some water. I'll get it," I added before Ma could offer, and went into the kitchen.

"I bet you'd like some coffee!" Ma called in brightly, like someone who's just found the answer.

"*Please* stop fussing."

"Why, darling, I'm not fussing! I just want you to relax while you're here." She came in and watched as I filled my glass from the tap. The gurgle of water sounded overloud in the small room. "Don't you want some ice with that?" she said.

"No, thanks."

"Here, let me get you some ice." She started for the icebox.

"Ma, *no.* I'm fine." My fingers were tight around the glass.

Perversely, now that she'd said it I *did* want some ice, but I drank my water without it. I wished that she'd scold me for mentioning my arrest. A few years ago she would have. Now she just stood gazing at me, eyes shining.

Just like Mrs Blackstone, who didn't even know me.

When I'd finished my water she took the glass from me and washed it. "Well, I'm dying to hear absolutely everything!" she said. "Tell me all about life at the base. Have you been in many fights? We don't see you nearly often enough, darling!"

On the train earlier, I'd vowed that I wouldn't shut her out this time. I'd be charming, open, the daughter she'd always wanted. For once, we'd manage to really share our feelings – not just about Dad, but all kinds of things.

Yet now something in me shrank. Her avid expression didn't seem to have anything to do with *me* at all.

"There's not much I can tell you," I said awkwardly. "A lot of it's classified."

Hal had drifted in. "You can tell us about the rumbles, though, right?" he said, his voice eager. "I mean, not which fights were yours – just the flying part. Please?"

"Collie's at the base," I said.

It came out with no warning; I'd been debating whether to tell them. Ma gaped. Suddenly it was as if she were seeing me, Amity, again.

"*Our* Collie?" she said.

"Yes. Our Collie."

"But what's he doing there?" she asked blankly.

"Same as me. He's a Peacefighter pilot. He just arrived last week."

Hal's expression darkened. "Where was he all those years?"

"Who knows?"

"He hasn't told you?"

"We've hardly spoken."

"Oh, Amity!" broke in my mother. "You have given him a *chance,* haven't you?"

"Of course I have. He doesn't want to tell me."

"You should have brought him with you," she said.

"*What?*" But it wasn't really a surprise. Ma had always adored Collie. When we used to get into trouble together, he'd be the one to sweet-talk us out of it.

"We're more his family than anyone – we always have been," she went on. "Oh, isn't that *wonderful,* that he's there with you now! You two were always such pals—"

I gritted my teeth. "Ma, please stop."

"How is he getting on? What's he been doing?"

"Didn't you hear me? I have no idea."

She sighed and patted her hair into place. "Such a good-looking boy," she murmured. "He was like having a second son all that time. I used to feel so sorry for him…his own family just didn't seem to care, and he was so bright and able…"

I refilled my glass and drained half of it in a gulp. "Well, I'm sure he still is. If that's any consolation."

"Maybe over lunch you can—" Ma broke off then, looking fretful. "Lunch! Oh, I almost forgot; I need to get us some carrots to go with the roast beef. I know how much you love my glazed carrots."

I couldn't work up the energy to protest. "Do you want me to go?" I asked resignedly.

"No, no, of course not!" Ma was smiling as she went back into the other room and put on her hat again. Watching her inspect herself in the mirror, humming, I knew she could hardly wait to tell people about Collie. She could claim that she was practically the mother to *two* Peacefighter pilots now.

After she'd left, Hal poured himself some water, too. He opened the icebox and popped some ice out of the metal tray.

"So...Collie, huh?" he said over his shoulder.

Yes. Collie. I rubbed my forehead, thinking of all the times that I'd seen Collie around the base these past few days. Once or twice our eyes had met. Collie always looked as if he wanted to say something, but neither of us had.

I forced a smile.

"Hey, want to hear about my fights?" I said to Hal.

So I told Hal some stories about flying, making them as exciting as possible. Peacefighting *was* exciting. Battling other pilots with speed, power, my own skill – why was it so hard for me to share this with my little brother, when I was so proud of following in our father's footsteps?

I didn't know. It just felt as if only telling him the enjoyable parts was a lie.

We were in the living room, sprawled on the sofa; Ma hadn't gotten back yet. Hal's eyes shone as he listened. "I'm going to be a Peacefighter too, just as soon as I'm old enough," he said. "According to my chart—" He broke off with a guilty look.

I straightened. "Your chart?"

Hal chewed his lip. "Um…"

"What chart? Your *birth* chart?"

"Ma had them done," he said finally.

I stared at him.

"Don't tell her I told you. I'm not supposed to know." He twisted on the sofa and pushed aside the heavy curtain behind it. Sunlight ventured in like a stranger. "Over there," he said, pointing.

At first it was the same view as always: a dingy courtyard shared by four buildings. Then I saw the sign on one of the windows opposite – that Harmony symbol again, with lettering underneath: *Madame Josephine: Astrologer, Fortunes, Dreams Explained.*

"Oh," I said faintly.

"Ma goes there a lot," Hal said. "I've seen her when I'm playing stickball. Here, look." He went to an antique bureau that sat against the wall and tugged open one of its heavy drawers. When I followed, he passed me a large envelope labelled *Vancour Family*.

Sketched lightly on one corner was a circle with a jagged line through it.

I frowned, wondering what it meant. Then I opened

the envelope and slid out four circular graphs, each divided into twelve pieces and littered with spiky characters. There were charts for me, Ma, Hal…and Collie.

My fingers tightened as I stared down at Collie's name. Hal shifted his weight. "I, um…guess Ma was trying to find out if he was okay," he said.

"Yeah," I muttered. Despite myself, my eyes went to my own chart. It was as indecipherable as the others.

Hal pointed to my chart's centre, where there was a square with an "x" through it. "That's called a 'Grand Cross'," he said.

"A what?"

"*Grand Cross*," he repeated. "It's pretty rare. You've got four planets in opposition, which gives you lots of challenges."

"Wha-at? How do you even know this?"

"I've been reading up on it. The library has plenty of—"

"*Hal.*"

"What? It's interesting. See, Collie is Leo with Gemini rising," he added. "That means he's outgoing and good with people. And you're Aries with Sagittarius rising, and *that* means—"

I jammed the charts back in the envelope. The circle with the crooked line vanished from view as I shoved the envelope away in the dresser again. "Hal, come on," I said testily. "It doesn't mean anything at all. 'Madame Josephine' is a complete charlatan."

He hesitated. "It seems pretty scientific."

"Trust me, it's the opposite! Ma doesn't actually *believe* this stuff, does she?"

Hal started to say something, then stopped. He leaned against the polished wood of the bureau and shoved his hands deep into his trouser pockets. He'd gotten so tall, I realized. Soon he'd be taller than me.

"Well...why not?" he said finally. "Everyone has to believe in something."

CHAPTER EIGHT

JOHN GUNNISON'S VOICE BOOMED THROUGH the speakers: "Remember, the stars love Harmony, and we are harmonious. We're going to lead the whole *world* to Harmony, my friends!"

Their leader was just a dark speck on the platform, far away over the sea of people. Even at this distance, Kay thought that Gunnison somehow made you feel he was speaking to you alone.

His voice was deep, relaxed: "Bryce Hill. The Rocky Flats. Monroe. The Twelve Year Plan is coming to fruition, folks! Soon the Central States will embrace its true destiny – and the Discordant elements of the world will be done away with!"

Gunnison punched the sky. The crowd roared and Kay cheered along with them, waving a fist to show even more enthusiasm than usual. She believed what Skinner had said – that she was being watched.

The dusty desert regions Gunnison had mentioned were formerly Western Seaboard territory. All had recently come under the Central States' control through Peacefighting wins. Like everyone else, Kay pretended to be ecstatic that their western borders were expanding…but was sure she wasn't alone in wondering what they were all meant to be so thrilled about. Some of the places weren't even towns, just tiny, fly-specked pieces of desert.

She wondered how many of those wins had been fixed. Skinner had made it clear to her that a small, crucial number of Peacefights were not left up to chance and skill. Not only that, but certain members of the World for Peace *knew.*

The WfP's sanctity was so ingrained that even now Kay felt shocked. Betrayed.

Don't be a child, she chided herself.

When she arrived home after the rally she found herself entering the building at the same time as Nadine, a young mother of two. "Were you at the rally?" asked Kay brightly. She fingered her silver scorpion pin, making sure her neighbour saw it.

Nadine beamed. "Oh, yes. Wonderful, wasn't it?"

They crossed the foyer together. Kay started to say something else and then stopped, her neck prickling.

Shrieking sobs were heading towards them down the stairwell.

"No!" cried a woman's voice. "You've got the wrong person! *No!*"

Kay and Nadine glanced at each other. Nadine gathered her children close. The two boys had gone silent, eyes wide.

"Maybe we should—" started Kay weakly, but there was no time to leave. A trio of Guns burst through the stairwell door, dragging a sobbing woman. A thrill of excitement – of guilt? – raced through Kay as she recognized Mrs Lloyd.

The small group approached. One of the Guns wore a grey suit with a Harmony armband, and Kay held back a gasp. There wasn't a person in the Central States who wouldn't know that bland, pale-eyed face; she'd seen it in a hundred newsreels.

Sandford Cain.

"I'm not Discordant!" wept Mrs Lloyd. A purpling bruise stained one cheek. "I swear to you – please—"

"Stop," said Sandford Cain to the Guns.

Kay saw Cain's mouth twitch and realized he was enjoying this. He drew a heavy lead blackjack from his pocket and patted it against his opposite palm, his expression contemplative.

Mrs Lloyd shrank back. "No...no, please..."

In a quick motion Cain struck her hard across the temple. The sound was a muffled crack. Mrs Lloyd sagged in the Guns' arms, head lolling. Her crisp curls looked as if she'd just had them styled. A flower of blood appeared and trickled down her cheek.

The signet ring on Sandford Cain's finger flashed as he tucked the weapon away again. "There now," he said. "We can have some peace."

To Kay's relief, Cain paid no attention to her and Nadine. Once he and his men had left, dragging Mrs Lloyd between them, Kay let out a breath, her heart crashing against her ribs.

Nadine licked her lips. Both her sons were crying. "*Mrs Lloyd,* Discordant?" she whispered. She seemed to catch herself; she touched her Libra brooch and shot Kay a fearful glance. "Well...well, I suppose the stars are never wrong."

"Actually, I'm not surprised," said Kay after a pause. "I always thought there was something inharmonious about her."

Back in her apartment Kay slumped against the door, shaken. What did it mean for her that *Sandford Cain*, Gunnison's most valued right-hand man, had taken care of this personally? If they'd accepted Kay's word about Mrs Lloyd, that had to be good, didn't it?

Yet there was also the Peacefight for which Kay had chosen the Grand Cross pilot. She felt nauseous every time she thought about it. According to the papers, the Western Seaboard pilot had somehow gotten the burning plane down; the wait-time was being appealed. Kay doubted very much that this was the result that Skinner and his people had planned for.

She put some dance music on the phonoplayer and sat doodling in a sketch pad, trying to quell the sick tension in her stomach. She avoided looking at the new rug she'd had to purchase.

Though Mr Hearn's body had been gone when she returned home that day, the bloody evidence had remained.

Chapter Nine

The letter was waiting for me when I got back to base. Vera had left it propped on the coffee table. I stood in our living room reading it over and over, with Peter twining around my ankles.

The Official Appeal Board of the World for Peace requests your presence…

"So soon?" I whispered, gripping the thick stationery. I'd gotten these letters before, but only weeks after a fight. This said the appeal was *tomorrow.*

Tomorrow.

Was the fact that my appeal had been expedited good or bad? I didn't know, but I'd go crazy if I hung around here thinking about it all night. I shrugged back into my jacket and left again.

I ended up at Harlan's, playing poker.

"Cut," he ordered, shoving the deck at me. He wore a sleeveless undershirt and had a shot glass full of clear liquid in front of him. He kept a still out back and made his own rotgut for the fun of it.

Levi wrinkled his nose. "Man, it's even more like paint thinner than usual." He helped himself to another glass from the bottle. "Can't tempt you, Vancour?"

"No thanks, I prefer my liver unpickled." My mind was still on the letter.

"Nectar of the gods," intoned Harlan as he started to deal.

"Don't make me laugh. It hurts my sore rib."

Harlan flicked my last card to me. I tried to forget the appeal and studied my hand. Pair of threes, pair of jacks. I arranged the cards, wishing the stylized images didn't remind me of those astrology charts of Ma's.

I'd ended up mentioning them to her; I couldn't help myself. I pretended that I'd found them on my own, looking for some stationery. The conversation hadn't gone well. "It doesn't do any *harm*, does it?" Ma kept protesting.

All I knew was that anything connected with Gunnison made my skin crawl. I threw out the lonely five and got another three. When it came my turn to bet, I slid twenty credits to the centre of the table.

Harlan lit a cigarette and blew out a stream of smoke as

he gazed at my bet. "Now, what we have here," he said, "is either confidence or a bluff. Which is it, Miss Vancour?"

"A bluff, of course."

"Of course." He studied his own hand. "All right, girlie," he said. "I'll match your bluff…and raise you ten credits."

"I'm out," said Levi.

"Too rich for me," agreed Steve, tossing his cards down.

"Let me think about this," murmured Clem. He ran a hand over his head. He had a dozen IOUs in the game already. "Okay, yeah…I'll see your thirty credits, and call."

Before we could show our hands, a knock came. Harlan slapped down his cards. "I swear, some people got no respect…"

He swung open the front door, and I stiffened. A tall pilot with dark blond hair stood there. I took a gulp of lukewarm beer and managed to keep my face expressionless.

"I hear there's a nightly poker game," said Collie. "Need another player?"

"Nope," said Harlan, folding his arms over his broad chest. "Invitation only."

Collie seemed to be deliberately not looking at me. "Even if I've got a stake of a hundred credits?" He jingled a denim bag.

Harlan wavered, eyeing it.

Collie quirked an eyebrow and grinned. "You've got an empty seat," he pointed out.

In the pause that followed, I knew what was going

on in Harlan's head: Collie was still an inexperienced Peacefighter. If he didn't make it, his hundred credits would stay in the game.

"All right, you're in." Harlan opened the door wider. "Guys and girl, meet fresh meat," he said as Collie stepped inside.

"Collis," said Collie to everyone. He'd always introduced himself by his proper name, even when we were kids.

Levi, Clem and Steve gave unenthusiastic hellos. Collie was still too new for anyone to really warm to him yet, plus no one gatecrashed the poker game – ever.

The empty seat had been Stan's. It was next to me, of course.

"Amity," greeted Collie in an undertone as he sat down. He had on a blue shirt, tan trousers. "I brought some beer, too," he added to the guys, resting a paper bag on the table.

"I'll take that." Harlan whisked the bag away into the kitchen; I heard the icebox open.

Levi and the others had started talking. I could feel Collie's gaze on me. He hesitated, then nodded at my pile of coins. "Hey, I see you're still a card shark."

I studied my full house without responding. He'd made himself very clear that first day, and so had I. What was he trying to prove, coming here?

Collie crossed his forearms on the table. I knew without looking that the left side of Collie's mouth had quirked upwards, just like always when he joked about something that bothered him. "So...I guess I missed the part where you said hello to me."

"No. I haven't said it."

"Are you planning on it?"

"I have no idea what it matters to you."

"It matters," he said.

Though I'd been doing my best to ignore Collie's presence on base, I somehow knew that he was a T3 pilot – a rank higher than most new pilots – and had already completed his first two fights. I seemed powerless to resist checking the board to see when he was going up and then keeping an eye out until he returned.

A deep dread had been growing in me this last week. I kept thinking of all those long summer days we'd shared – the hundreds of memories with Collie in them. They made me feel exposed, fearful.

I was glad now that he'd refused to explain anything; almost glad for the pain of his four-year silence. Because I'd realized what forgiving him could mean. It had always suited me fine, the way people on base kept to themselves. I hadn't let anyone close since Dad had died and Collie left. I thought of Stan's empty locker and my grip on the cards tightened.

All I knew was that I wanted Collis Reed to stay far away.

Harlan returned with fresh cold ones and dealt Collie in. Collie studied his hand. After a pause he moved a card from the outside of the fanned spread to the inside. Anger touched me.

"Oh, just bet, already," I muttered.

"Patience, Amity Louise," he said without looking at me.

Everyone's eyebrows flew up. No one had known my middle name. Harlan glanced from me to Collie, and I tensed.

"Amity Louise, huh?" he said finally.

Collie straightened. "All right, I'm in. What are the stakes? Thirty each?"

When we all laid down our cards, he had a royal flush. He scooped up the credits with a shrug. "Beginner's luck," he said.

Clem eyed him cautiously. "Are you always that lucky at cards?"

Collie took a swig of beer. "About average, I guess." He looked over at me. His eyes were blue-green tonight, like a sea that edged white beaches. After a beat, he said, "What would you say, Amity?"

"How would I know?" I said stiffly. *Don't do this, Collie. Do not drag me into having a shared past with you when I don't want it.*

As the game went on, the usual banter sprang up. I was glad to have the cards to focus on. I suddenly had a deep need to obliterate Collie's pile of coins. The words swirled around me as the hoards of coins in front of Collie and me ebbed and flowed. No one else seemed aware that the game had turned into a private grudge match.

Collie knew. He gave me a wry look as I raised him again. "Sure you can afford this?"

I knew I'd think of something wittily scathing at three in the morning. "Bet or fold," I told him.

Collie started to take a swig of beer and then saw his bottle was empty. "I think I need something stronger to make this decision."

"Fine – it'll cost you five credits," said Harlan, deadpan.

Collie raised an eyebrow but flicked a coin across at him. Harlan poured him a shot of the clear, thick liquid. Collie stretched back in his seat, tipping it onto two legs, studying his cards and swirling the drink in its glass.

Since when do you drink rotgut? I almost said. I bit the words back. Since sometime within those four years of silence, obviously.

Collie knocked back the liquor. He started coughing; his chair came down with a thump. He pushed the shot glass aside, wheezing and choking. Harlan stared at him in amazement, then clouted him hard on the back.

"Thanks," Collie said croakily. He reached for my beer and gulped half of it down at once. "I, ah…I was trying to impress a girl."

Harlan laughed in surprise; for the first time he looked at Collie as if he were more than just some new pilot who might die tomorrow. "Yeah, she seems real impressed," he said. "You impressed, Vancour?"

"I don't think she's impressed," said Levi.

The rueful grin Collie shot me was one I'd seen a thousand times. "Yeah, and I bet I know what she's thinking now," he said.

"Collie—" I started.

"She's thinking about the time when she was eight and I was nine, and we built this bridge across the stream at the back of her property. They had this big place, out in the country – acres of fields and woods."

I sat frozen. Collie didn't seem to notice how still everyone had gone. His hair looked as if it had been gilded by sunshine: thick streaks of dark gold with brown underneath. He went on with a smile, pushing one of his credits around in a circle on the table.

"So we built this bridge. I mean, we spent an entire day sloshing around in the water in our underwear, stacking stones and slapping clay over them and laying planks across. And then when we finished Amity said it wasn't sturdy enough, and I said yes it was, and we got into this huge fight – and so of course, to defend my masculine whatever, I had to prove I was right and walk across it. And of course the whole damn thing buckled and I fell off and broke my arm. So after that, whenever she wanted to prove a point, all she had to do was say, 'Remember the bridge to nowhere?'"

The others had gone completely silent, staring at us with a mix of interest and wariness. My cheeks were on fire. I felt raw – split open.

Harlan snorted finally. "Bridge to nowhere," he said. "That's deep, Vancour."

"Yeah, that's me," I said.

"I, um…wouldn't have taken you for a country girl," said Levi.

"Of course she is," put in Clem, trying to joke. "Remember what Stan always said – that she looked like she could wrestle a steer to the ground with her bare hands." Then he realized who he'd mentioned and his cheeks flushed. He scowled down at his cards.

Collie glanced at me. I could see him wondering, *Who's Stan?*

"Are we going to keep playing poker?" I said. The words tasted like metal slivers. "Or do we want to hear more childhood stories?"

Collie's brow furrowed. As he studied me, his eyes slowly took on that concerned look that had once touched me so deeply that nothing else mattered.

Harlan sloshed fresh drinks into everyone's glasses. He put the bottle back on the table with a definitive noise.

"Poker," he said.

Between the appeal and Collie, I couldn't sleep that night. I just lay in bed listening to the faint sound of dance music floating in from Vera's room. At five a.m. I gave up – I got dressed and slipped out of the house. I went down to the airfield, where I signed out my new plane.

"I thought you were grounded with a broken rib for four weeks," said the purser, checking his sheet.

"From fighting," I said levelly. I didn't explain further. Finally the purser shrugged and okayed it.

I spent almost an hour pushing myself to the utmost:

performing screaming loop-the-loops; banking so tight that I left my stomach somewhere far behind; tumbling my plane sideways into vicious barrel rolls.

When I finally landed, I felt as if I could breathe again. I went to the changing room and took a long shower, then stood in front of my locker, dripping and towel-clad, drying my hair with another towel.

"Fun crowd you hang around with," said Collie.

I spun and stared. I hadn't been in the locker room since my last fight, but now I saw the new strip of masking tape where Stan's name had been. *C. Reed*, read the scrawled letters.

"*This* is your locker?" I said, aghast.

Collie shrugged and pulled off his shirt. The thin boy had turned sleekly muscular, with a dusting of golden hair on his chest. "It's the one they assigned me. I didn't argue," he said.

A faint line of hair led from his navel to his waistband. When he reached for his belt buckle I looked quickly away, realizing I was breaking the first, most basic rule of the locker room: *No staring.*

"Amity, what *was* that last night?" said Collie in a low voice.

"I don't know what you mean."

"Oh, you do."

I wasn't capable of whipping off my towel in front of Collie – it didn't seem to matter in front of anyone else. Furious, I grabbed a clean pair of underwear and struggled them on under the towel. No, this wouldn't do. I snapped the towel off and kept my back to him as I put on my brassiere, feeling his gaze warm on my skin – but when I looked, he wasn't watching; he was pulling on his flight trousers with a frown on his face.

"I was playing poker with my friends," I said. "Then *you* came in, and felt the need to tell everyone about—" I broke off.

"What? That stupid story about when we were kids? Is that so taboo here?"

"You don't understand," I said tightly. "You've barely been here a week." I stepped into the green dress I'd brought; I was leaving for my appeal straight from here. "Why did you even *come* to Harlan's, anyway? What happened to it being best for us not to spend much time together?"

Collie turned then. "It *is* best – for more reasons than you know," he said quietly. "And fine, maybe it was stupid to just show up, but I can't do this any more, Amity. I can't not talk to you."

"You managed it just dandy for over four years."

"I told you, I had my reasons!" He saw the photo in my locker then, and his face changed. Before I could bang the door shut, he stepped close and pulled the sepia image out from behind my mirror.

My father's right arm was around me. His left arm was torn off. The person he'd had that arm around had been ripped away.

Collie stood gazing down at what remained of the photo. When he finally spoke, his voice was hoarse. "You really hate me, don't you?"

He still had his shirt off. I could smell the warmth of his skin.

I took the photo and shoved it back into place, hiding the torn edge. I got out the rest of my things and closed the locker door. It gave an echoing clang.

"I don't hate you," I said. "I just...missed you a lot, after you left."

Collie didn't move; he was standing only inches from me. "I missed you, too," he said.

I turned away and sat on the bench. I started pulling on my stockings and didn't answer.

The room was quiet; for a change, there were hardly any other pilots around. "Are you going home for a visit?" Collie asked finally.

"No," I said. "I went home just a few days ago."

"You did?" He sat on the bench next to me. "How are Rose and Hal?"

"Fine." I stared down at my legs as if rolling stockings up them was the most fascinating thing in the world – even more interesting than doing a loop-the-loop.

"Did you tell them I was here?"

I started to snap at him and then saw the look in his eyes. They were pure green under these lights, and full of longing. Ma had been more of a mother to him than his own ever was.

"Yes, I told them," I said.

His throat worked; he looked down at his hands. "Maybe...maybe I could go with you sometime."

"Collie, what do you want from me?" I burst out. "*You didn't write.* For four years! What was I supposed to think? You might as well have died, just like Dad!"

"I know," he said softly. "I'm sorry." To my surprise he gripped my hand. "What if I told you where I was?" he said, his voice intense.

"I don't want to know any more. It doesn't matter." I pulled away, trying to ignore how his skin had felt against mine.

"I want to tell you."

"Collie—"

"We were in the Central States."

I stared at him, my hands frozen on the flimsy stocking. "What?"

He smiled grimly. "Want the details?"

"No," I said after a long pause, even though this explained everything. Gunnison didn't let letters out of his country, not without a lot of rigmarole. A schoolboy's letters to a girl back home wouldn't have had a chance.

Collie hesitated, then held out his hand. "Here," he said.

A small tattoo marked the base of his thumb: a circular blue swirl. "What is it?" I asked, chilled. It reminded me of those charts of Ma's at home.

"The glyph for my sun sign. Leo, the lion. I was trying to fit in. You have to pretend to be nuts about astrology."

Collie studied the tattoo with a sour look; his hand closed into a fist.

"Anyway, I managed to escape," he said. "I didn't tell you that first day because seeing you threw me so badly. Then I wasn't sure what to do. I'm still a Central States citizen. I couldn't be a pilot for the Western Seaboard if that got out."

I felt locked in place. "What did you mean about not writing being 'for the best', then?"

Collie let out a breath. "I don't know. We didn't go to the Central States right away, and…I guess at first, it did seem for the best. I was *fourteen,* Amity; who knows what I was thinking? It just seemed too hard. But then once we got there, I—" He stopped; his jaw tightened and he looked down.

"I did write you a letter at the border," he said finally. "You probably didn't get it. I had a feeling the guard wouldn't send it."

No. I hadn't gotten it.

"Are your parents all right?" I asked at last.

"I don't know. They're still there."

My desire to take his hand again shook me. I pushed it away, along with all my questions. To get answers would mean getting close to him again.

I couldn't do it. Not any more. Not here.

I went back to rolling up my stockings. "Well, I'm sorry to hear it." My voice sounded odd, stilted. "I'm glad you're all right."

Collie studied my face. I'd never felt so thoroughly *seen* before. "Amity, you asked what I want from you?" he said in a low voice. "I want to pick up where we left off. *I missed you,* don't you know that? It was like part of me was gone. I don't think a day went by when I didn't think, *Amity would like that,* or, *I've got to tell Amity.*"

I stood up and fastened my stockings to my garter belt. I smoothed my skirt down over my thighs to hide the fact that my hands were shaking. "We can't pick up where we left off. We're different people now."

"We could try!"

"What if I don't want to?"

He rose slowly. His eyes scanned mine. "Is it Stan?"

The name lashed at me. "No, it's *you.* It's *me,* it's the two of us *here* – it's impossible, and...and I can't talk about this now. I've got to go."

I yanked on my heels and snatched my handbag up from the bench; I strode from the locker room.

Collie followed, shrugging into his shirt. "Amity, wait!"

He caught up with me as I stepped out into the corridor; he took my arm. "Can't we at least talk? Please?"

"*No.* I'm not going to get close to you only to—" I broke off.

Collie's shirt hung open over his chest. His gaze stayed locked on mine. He shook his head. "Only to what?"

I took a step away, gripping my handbag. It was just a clutch, and I knew the way I was holding onto it, my fingernails would leave dents in the shiny black leather.

"Stan's dead," I said. "He died the day before you got here. You've got his locker."

"Oh," said Collie softly.

"It's not like you think! But you could die too, any day, do you realize that? You're a new pilot, you're inexperienced—"

"I just went through six months of training school!"

"New pilots die more often," I said. "Why do you think hardly anyone talks to you? People here aren't *mean;* they're not *unsociable* – it just hurts to get close to someone and then lose them."

The words hung in the air – and I knew we were both thinking of the four years of silence.

Collie's jaw took on the determined lines I knew so well. I had a sudden image of him the day we'd built the bridge to nowhere, splashing through the river, holding a rock as big as his head.

"All right," he said. "How long?"

"How long what?"

He moved aside as Levi went into the locker room, ignoring Levi's sidelong stare. "How long before you decide that I'm not going to die in my next fight, and that it's safe to let me in again?"

I started down the hallway. "You could die anytime. We all could. Stan had been here almost a year."

He darted in front of me and put his hands on my shoulders. "Are you saying *never,* then? I won't accept that."

"I've got a train to catch, Collie."

"I've been here over a week already. Two more weeks? Three? A month?"

I jerked away, wishing he'd button his shirt. "Are you *listening*? I have to leave; I've got to be someplace in an hour."

He let go of me then and I headed for the doors, wishing I knew how to walk better in heels – wishing Collis Reed had never taken it into his head to be a Peacefighter – wishing I could go back in time to when he'd first arrived so I could stare at him blankly and pretend I had no idea who he was.

"A month," Collie called after me. His voice echoed through the corridor...deeper than I recalled but still Collie.

Chapter Ten

When I was growing up we lived out in the country, in a town called Gloversdale up near the Lassen Mountains. In the summertime it was so hot that the fields caught fire sometimes; in the winter, snow covered everything, gently muffling all sound.

Our house was an old place that had belonged to Dad's great-great-grandfather. Hal and I loved it. Ma didn't. She was always buying antiques and experimenting with new wallpaper, trying to make the rambling rooms look like the sleek ones in the magazines she read – the ones that came all the way from New Manhattan in far-off Appalachia.

On rainy days, Collie, Hal and I would play hide-and-seek in the house and it could take hours to find each other.

Outside was better still: over twenty acres filled with fields, a small patch of woods, even a river. The fields were deep green in spring, and when they were full of golden hay bales in summer it was like living in a painting.

Flying was our main love, though.

Dad had retired from being a Peacefighter when I was five, but he still worked for the WfP. He trained new pilots, gave talks, made sure everyone knew the importance of fighting for peace. By the time I was ten he wasn't home very much, but I understood. Everyone needed him.

I lived for him coming home. I lived for being taken up in one of his planes. He had two: a MK3 Firedove and a biplane, a Gauntlet Jenny. The Gaunt was a two-seater, and as soon as I was big enough to see over the control panel, he'd sit beside me in the cockpit and say, "Let's see how you do."

I remember sitting up straight, so determined to do well, excitement pulsing through me like an extra heartbeat. Dad would let me do the take-off and fly it, sometimes putting his hand over mine if I needed to throttle back a little.

"Good," he'd say. "You're a natural pilot, Amity."

And I'd scowl because I was too happy to trust a smile, and I'd dream about flying for a living someday.

Collie was crazy about flying, too. He lived next door, though that was a good quarter of a mile away. We met when I was six and he was seven, when we were both walking to school and realized we lived on the same road.

It turned out that Collie had spent a lot of time hanging out at the fence that divided our two properties, peering in and wondering about who lived there – though I'd never seen him, and he'd never gotten up the nerve to climb over. He said later he was afraid we'd chase him off. I guess our house looked very grand to him, though to me it was just ordinary – I loved it, but didn't know it was anything special. Collie's house was small and cramped, nothing like ours.

It took me a long time to understand that this meant his family didn't have much money.

From the second we became friends, Collie practically lived at our house. My parents both loved him. Everyone loved him. He was like bottled sunlight: a thin, scrawny boy with a smile bigger than he was and mischievous eyes.

The first time he saw my room, he'd stared in wonder at my books and board games and model planes. "Amity, you're so *lucky*," he'd breathed, gently touching a toy Firedove.

"I am?" The thought had never occurred to me.

He gave me a look that said maybe I was the stupidest person on the planet but he liked me anyway. Then he'd swooped the plane through the air, buzzing it close to my head. "Come on. Let's take it outside!"

It also took me a long time to wonder why Collie's parents never seemed to miss him.

I only went to Collie's house a handful of times. Once was when I hadn't seen him for a few days. There'd been no Collie knocking at our kitchen door just in time for breakfast, and he hadn't been in school, either. So I went to his house. I took Hal with me, even though my little brother was only six then – I felt more apprehensive than I wanted to admit.

Collie's house was small, darkly shadowed by the yew trees that flanked it. The front porch sagged, and I stepped onto it nervously. No doorbell. I knocked on the screen door's weathered frame. There were holes in the screen, and I stared at them, thinking, *But how do they keep the flies from getting in?*

The inside door flew open. A woman smoking a cigarette stared out at me. She had Collie's golden-brown hair, though hers spilled wildly past her shoulders. She slumped a hip against the door frame and blew out a stream of smoke. "Yeah?" she said.

"Is – is Collie here?"

"Collie?"

I squeezed Hal's hand. "I mean...Collis."

"*Collie,*" she said, as if remembering who I meant. "Yeah, he's here. You his little friends?"

I nodded, terrified. There was something wrong with the woman's eyes. She kept peering at me, then drawing her head back as if she couldn't quite focus.

"Isn't that nice – Collie's got little friends," she said. "C'mon in, Collie's little friends." She held the door open.

Hal was tugging at my hand. "Amity! I don't want to go in there," he hissed.

"Shut up," I whispered fiercely. I didn't want to either, but we stepped over the threshold.

It was like no place I'd ever seen. There was hardly any furniture, but there were piles of things everywhere: magazines, empty bottles, overflowing ashtrays, those novels Ma called "trashy bodice rippers". I stared at a stack of old newspapers with dust on them. The walls were grimy with cigarette smoke.

Hal jerked at my sleeve. "Let's go," he pleaded.

"I'm Goldie," announced the woman, rummaging for something on a table. "On accounta my hair. Like mother, like son, huh?" An ashtray fell off and she swore.

I felt tight inside. Collie had hardly ever mentioned his mother, but I'd thought... I swallowed. I didn't know what I'd thought.

Goldie found a lighter and lit another cigarette; she puffed a stream of smoke towards the ceiling. She took a sip from a small brown bottle and offered it to me. "Want some? I won't tell."

"Where's Collie?" I blurted. "You said he was here."

"Oh, sure, he's here." A battered-looking telio set sat in the corner. Goldie snapped it on and started swaying as dance music drifted out. "Oh, yeah, this one's my favourite," she murmured. Humming, she spun, then peered at Hal. "Hey, wanna dance, little boy?"

Hal shook his head violently.

Goldie giggled and ruffled his hair. "Aw, too bad. Bet you'll break some hearts one day."

"*Where's Collie?*" I repeated.

But Goldie was off in her own world, dancing with an invisible partner.

I looked around wildly and spotted a door. "Come on," I hissed to Hal, and dragged him across the room.

"Amity, I want to go *home*!"

"We have to check on Collie," I snapped, fear making my voice sharp. I was trying not to notice the filthy kitchen I could see through an archway, or the smell coming from it. I knocked at the door and pressed my ear against it. "Collie?"

No answer. My heart beating hard, I edged open the door and we slipped inside. We were in a tiny, dark bedroom. A huddled figure lay in the bed.

"*Collie!*" I was beside the bed in a heartbeat. "Are you all right?"

He rolled over and stared blankly at me. "Amity?"

"You're sick!" I realized. I sat beside him. His cheeks were flushed, his eyes glassy.

Collie struggled to prop himself up on his elbows. His pyjamas were at least two sizes too small. "What are you doing here?" His fierceness took me aback.

"Hal and I came to check on you. We were worried."

"Well, I'm fine."

"You're not!"

"You've got to leave, Amity."

I started to rise. "I'll go get Ma. She'll know what to—"

"*No!*" He grabbed my wrist with hot fingers. "I'm fine.

Goldie gave me some aspirin. Please, just – just go away, all right?"

To my dismay, I realized he was close to tears. Collie never cried, not even the time he'd fallen off his bike.

"But..." I hesitated and stared around his room, knowing I was making things worse yet helpless to stop. It was cleaner than the rest of the house, but with hardly anything in it. A scarf my mother had knitted for him – blue-green, to go with his eyes – hung neatly over a chair, though it wouldn't be cold enough to wear it for at least another month.

When I looked back at Collie, his cheeks were still flushed in a feverish way I didn't like, but his mouth was hard.

"Go away," he said in a low voice. "*I don't want you here.* Can I say it any clearer? *Get out.*"

I felt dizzy. "You'll – you'll come for breakfast again as soon as you're better, right?"

Abruptly, he rolled away from me. His shoulder blades looked thin and sharp against the worn fabric of the pyjamas. He shrugged.

My chest felt tight with all the words I didn't know how to say to him. I grabbed Hal's hand – he'd been staring frozen at Collie as if he didn't know him – and we left.

Goldie was still dancing. I don't think she even noticed us.

I did tell Ma, though I thought Collie would never speak to me again. She went down to Collie's house with soup and comic books and told me later that he'd been glad to see her.

"We played cards," she said. "And I gave him some more aspirin. If he's not better soon, I'll get a doctor in."

Her mouth was tense; she stood chopping vegetables for a stew. I watched her, at a loss. Why had Collie been glad to see her and not me? At the same time I felt so grateful to her that a scowl darkened my face. Ma could be silly and fluttery sometimes, but when Hal and I were sick she bathed our hands with cold cloths and made all our favourite foods.

"Did you bathe Collie's hands?" I said finally.

Ma stopped chopping. "Come here," she said, and hugged me hard. I pressed close, though I didn't usually like being hugged – I'd decided years ago that pilots were too tough for that.

"Yes, I bathed his hands with a cool cloth," she said. "And his face, too. And if I could, I'd take him away from that mother of his and raise him right here, with you and Hal. Now go play – I'll call you when dinner's ready."

Then she'd turned quickly away and I'd known better than to hang around.

Collie appeared a few days later, knocking at our kitchen door as if nothing had happened. "Scrambled eggs, great," he said, sliding into his usual chair. His eyes were stormy blue that day, daring me to say something.

I didn't – not ever. But something ached inside me whenever I thought of Collie lying in that almost-empty room, with the scarf Ma had given him so carefully arranged.

I thought he was the bravest boy I'd ever known.

I was thirteen when I found out Collie was leaving. My father had died four months before and nothing had been right since; the sorrow was a boulder constantly weighing me down.

Yet there was also the memory of how Collie had held my hand, that day in my bedroom after Dad died. He did that sometimes now. He'd touch my hand, or my arm, and electricity would shoot through me. I didn't understand it. This was *Collie,* who I'd known since I was six, who'd seen me in my underwear as we slogged through the mud together.

We hadn't been swimming in almost a year, though. I felt too embarrassed by my new curves, and hated it fiercely that things had to change. Sometimes I'd look at Collie when the light hit his face a certain way and my stomach would go tight. *What's wrong with me*? I thought.

When he told me that he and his family were leaving, that very day, the two of us were sitting under a tree in one of my family's fields. The news was too much; it shattered me. I leaped to my feet and took off running, pounding over the grass. I heard Collie call after me but I didn't stop. When I reached the barn, I ducked inside and tugged the heavy door shut after me.

The large space plunged into shadow. I headed straight for the shape that crouched in a far corner. I was sobbing by then; I couldn't help it. I folded my arms against the side of my father's Firedove and hid my face as my shoulders heaved.

A sliver of sunlight fell into the barn, then disappeared again.

Footsteps. Collie appeared beside me; I felt his hand rest on my shoulder. He squeezed it hard.

"Please don't cry," he said hoarsely.

At last I straightened and swiped my palm over my eyes. "Why?" I got out. "Why do you have to go?"

Collie took his hand away and jammed his fists into his denims pockets. He'd grown a few inches lately: a thin, lanky boy with eyes as changeable as the sea.

"I don't know," he said. "I think my father owes people money. Well, he always does, but it's pretty bad this time." Collie's voice was bitter. From what little I'd gleaned, his father was always either off making "deals", or sitting around drinking with Goldie.

He stared at his feet and added reluctantly, "And… I could be wrong, but…I kind of have the impression that Tru's death made things worse for us."

I went cold. "*What?* Why would it?"

"I don't know! Maybe your dad was going to offer mine a job or something."

I couldn't even process the idea that my father's death might have brought this about. Finally, hesitantly, I took Collie's hand. He didn't look up; our fingers wove tightly together.

"Don't go," I whispered.

He rubbed his eyes. "Do you think I want to?"

"Then stay here with us! Collie, you know Ma would—"

"I *can't.* I can't leave Goldie; it's not like my father ever looks out for her. And besides, if I stay here, what is there for me? You know what everyone thinks of my family in this place."

His voice had turned bitter again. Collie had a couple of uncles, too, and cousins, all a few years older than him. *Those Reeds*, people called them.

"But if you live here with us, people won't—"

"It doesn't matter anyway," he broke in shortly. "My father wouldn't let me stay in a million years."

"Why should he have any say in it?" I cried, close to tears again.

Collie pulled away. "Because the law says so, that's why. He'd set the police on Rose if I tried. I wasn't even supposed to come here today, but…" Collie looked at me. His throat moved. "But, Amity…I couldn't leave without saying goodbye to you."

I felt locked in his gaze. Neither of us moved. Every moment of this past year when Collie had affected me so strangely seemed to surge together at once and my heart beat hard. I was suddenly very aware of his closeness.

The barn felt vast, silent. Collie hesitated. He put his hands on my shoulders and bent his head to mine.

Our lips touched. I kept my eyes open as we kissed,

staring in wonder at his dark gold eyelashes, the freckle near his eyebrow. There had never been anything as soft as his mouth against mine.

We drew apart. I swallowed and rested my hand on his cheek. The smooth curve of his skin filled me with awe.

He reached up and gripped my fingers. "Amity, I…I've wanted to tell you for so long…"

"Tell me what?"

The world held its breath. Finally Collie shook his head, looking miserable. "I've got to go," he whispered. "I don't want my father coming here."

Panic touched me. This could not be happening. "No, wait! You have to say goodbye to Ma!" On some level, I knew that my mother would not let this happen.

Maybe Collie knew it, too. "You tell her for me. Tell her how grateful I am to her for everything." He clutched my hands fervently. "They won't keep us apart, Amity, I promise. I'll write to you all the time. Every day. And then when I'm older, I'll—"

Collie choked to a stop. He kissed my cheek, then pulled away and ran from the barn before I could stop him, his long legs churning. Sunlight angled in as he wrenched the door open.

"Collie!" I shouted, racing after him. "*Wait!*"

He didn't stop. A moment later he was gone, running away over the fields.

* * *

I haunted the mailbox for months after that, scarcely able to believe it when nothing came, day after day. Finally Ma sold some of our land and rented out the house and we moved to Sacrament, with its noisy streets and its skies crowded with buildings, because she said she couldn't keep up the farm without Dad.

We left a forwarding address but still no letter came. I was going crazy by then, certain that something terrible had happened. Ma was worried, too, and put feelers out – and finally, in response, she got a letter from a friend of hers in Vegas, who said she'd seen Collie and his parents there a while back.

They seemed fine, told me they were just passing through. Collis looked happy. He was playing ball with another boy when I saw him, she'd reported.

That was when I stopped caring about much of anything, and decided that I might as well act in the same cold, dark way that I felt inside. I'd shoplifted, mostly. I liked the thrill – it got my adrenalin pumping the same way flying once had. I hung around with this sleazy boy in our neighbourhood named Rob, who Ma hated. That was good enough for me. He wasn't Collie, which was even better.

I lost my virginity to Rob when I was fifteen. He wanted to, and I just thought…why not? It was in the basement of his parents' house; they were making it into a rec room but hadn't finished the work yet. There was sawdust everywhere.

I didn't like it. Or hate it. I didn't let myself feel much of anything, but deep down I must have, because I broke up with him soon after that. Then I got arrested for shoplifting a few weeks later. I had to sit in a jail cell for hours, full of drunks and prostitutes – and it hit me so hard then, what Dad would think of me.

That was when I decided to become a Peacefighter.

There'd only been one other boy since – someone I met in training school. He was a nice guy and I'd liked him, but I wasn't in love with him. Or him with me. We were both lonely, I guess. We only saw each other for a few months; then he dropped out. I think I was almost relieved when he left.

That was it. My romantic career so far. And now Collie was back…and he was insane if he thought I'd ever let myself risk being so shattered again.

Chapter Eleven

When I rushed into the courtroom antechamber, Russ was already there, unfamiliar in a blue pinstriped suit. He leaped up, twisting a fedora in his hands.

"Where have you *been*, Vancour? I've already testified."

"I was delayed." I glanced at the closed courtroom doors. I'd missed my train because of Collie and had to catch a later one; I'd run all the way from the station. I thought I'd kill for a glass of water. I swallowed and smoothed my hair with one hand.

I should have worn a hat, I thought belatedly. Something small, with a veil. At least I'd brought gloves. I dug them out of my purse – silly little white things that I seldom wore – and struggled them onto my sweaty hands.

The heavy wooden doors swung open. "Miss Amity Vancour," called the bailiff.

"All right, at least you made it in time." Russ clapped my shoulder. "Go on, Wildcat, knock 'em dead." His smile looked tense. It reminded me of something – I couldn't think what, just then.

Inside the courtroom, the bailiff directed me to the witness stand and I was sworn in. Three WfP officials – two women and a man – sat behind a long, ornate table; the familiar flag with its laurel wreath and clasped hands hung above. They questioned me tirelessly about the Peacefight, referring to typewritten pages.

"You were aware that your plane was on fire at six thousand feet?"

"Could you explain, in your own words, the dangers of not bailing from a burning plane?"

"You are familiar with the phrase 'sanctity of life' and what it means to the World for Peace, is that correct?"

I gripped the podium and managed to keep my voice level as I answered. I couldn't read anything from their faces, their tones. The stenographer typed every word into record; the steady clicking played on my nerves.

While they deliberated I sat in the anteroom and plucked at the fingers of my gloves. The minutes ticked past. Russ tapped the wooden arm of his chair, looking like he wished he had a cigar.

I almost wished I did, too. I gazed blindly at a painting on the wall: the current World for Peace leaders, a committee of twelve who'd given up their respective citizenships to be truly neutral. Just then their expressions seemed grim, unsympathetic.

I jumped as the outer door opened. A woman with wavy red hair and worried eyes entered, her heels clicking against the marble floor. "Amity! I came as soon as I heard."

Madeline. I let out a breath and rose to meet her; her perfume wrapped around me as we hugged. I hadn't told her about the appeal, but in the back of my mind I'd been hoping she'd come.

"Thanks for being here," I said.

She squeezed my arm. "Don't be silly."

When Dad was alive, Madeline often spent long, lazy summer weeks at our place. She'd even gone swimming with Collie and me in the river, shrieking like a ten-year-old at the cold. She and Dad had given flying exhibitions together – and seeing her laughing and confident in her battered leather jacket had impressed it on me even more than Dad's praise: *girls can be pilots too.*

Now she worked here in the Heat where the main WfP offices were, but I didn't see her very often. I was touched that she'd come. I introduced her to Russ; they shook hands.

"How's it going so far?" Madeline perched on a seat and glanced tensely at the closed courtroom doors. Despite her businesslike skirt and broad shoulder pads, she still looked like an overgrown tomboy, with freckles misting her nose.

Russ grimaced and didn't respond.

"I'm not sure," I admitted. "From the way some of the questions were going..." I trailed off and tugged at my gloves again, then realized I was doing it and stopped.

"Well, you know what your dad would say," Madeline commented after a pause.

I glanced up quickly. She had a small smile on her face. "No, what?" I asked.

"To hell with it – full speed ahead."

I smiled a little too. I could hear Dad saying it, and Ma protesting, "Tru, that isn't helpful."

The door to the courtroom opened. "Court is reconvened," said the bailiff.

I took a deep breath. Madeline gripped my hand. "I'll wait for you here," she said in an undertone.

A few moments later Russ and I stood behind a wooden railing with the long table in front of us. One of the women rose and read from a crisp-looking sheet of paper.

"The Appeal Court in the case of Miss Amity Vancour, Peacefighter pilot 100982, in regards to conflict AT34 on November 29th 1940, the Western Seaboard versus the European Alliance. This court finds that Miss Vancour's landing of a burning plane from six thousand feet was a reckless manoeuvre, against the precepts that the World for Peace holds dear, and we therefore rule that the wait-time before said dispute can be challenged shall remain five years as standard, with no..."

Beside me, Russ closed his eyes. I stood stunned as the words droned on. *Nothing*? If you got your plane down, you almost always got at least a year, except in cases of total irresponsibility. Did they really see me as that reckless?

"...while no penalties shall be issued, Miss Vancour is officially warned not to partake in such a manoeuvre again. Case dis—"

"No!" I gripped the railing. "Wait, this *can't* be right! I was in control of that plane every moment!"

The only sound was the stenographer's steady typing. He came to the end of my outburst and the room fell silent. The WfP official raised an eyebrow as she gazed at me over the top of the paper.

"Are you questioning our judgement, Miss Vancour?" she asked.

The only honest answer I could give was *yes*. I said nothing, words churning inside me.

"Case dismissed," said the official after a pause. She rapped her gavel on the table.

As I exited the cool building the sunshine felt like a spotlight on my failure. *Twenty-seven per cent* of our main fuel source gone. The Western Seaboard wasn't prosperous; we couldn't import what we'd lost. Prices would skyrocket. There'd be hardship – poverty.

All because of me.

Russ had hardly spoken. He put on his hat and snapped the brim to an angle. As he walked beside me he shoved his hands in his pockets. "Well, you got shafted...but at least you tried."

"Fat lot of good it did," I said bitterly. After a hug and a few words of condolence, Madeline had had to return to work. I felt very alone, even with Russ there.

The Appeal Courts were in a staid part of the Heat never known as anything but Heatcalf City. In places, the planners had left pieces of ancient ruins on show. As Russ and I walked, we passed ages-old footprints set into the sidewalk, alongside names I didn't know. I stared down at them, lost in my thoughts.

"Excuse me, Miss. Are you a pilot?"

I turned. A guy in his twenties with auburn hair and ruddy cheeks had caught up to us. A press card was stuck into his hatband. He held out his hand. "I'm Milt Fraser – a reporter for the *Daily Laurel*."

Russ rolled his eyes. "Buzz off, you know better."

"Hey, I noticed there was a case today, that's all. Thought you might have a scoop for me."

"No," I said shortly. I started walking again.

"You sure?" Milt Fraser jogged to keep up; he grinned. "Aw, come on, help out a struggling hack. There hasn't been anything good since that big gambling scandal last month. Total anonymity, I promise. If there's anything you want to—"

"You heard the lady," snapped Russ. "Beat it."

Milt pressed a business card into my hand. "Okay, didn't mean to make you sore. But if you've ever got anything for me, just give me a call."

After he left I crumpled the card and pitched it savagely at a trash can. "I could have his job for that," I muttered. Reporters weren't supposed to talk to us; usually fending them off was a game. This time I felt like murdering someone…or crying.

Twenty-seven per cent.

Russ must have seen it in my face. He looped an arm around my shoulders and we started down the sidewalk again. "Come on, kiddo," he said. "I'll buy you a drink."

Though it was only eleven o'clock in the morning, I let him. We went to a small bar not far away and I drank whiskey neat. Russ grew expansive as he downed shots of rye, telling me about some of his own hair-raising Peacefights.

The bartender stood drying glasses; only a few other customers were there at this hour. One sat slumped over the bar with his head on his arms. There was a telio set on in the corner, its drone low and steady. For a change, music wasn't playing. News footage was on instead: one of Gunnison's Harmony rallies.

The small screen showed the Central States leader in grainy black-and-white. He waved a fist, shouting, then surveyed the rally with that call-me-Johnny grin that prickled at my spine. A man I thought might be Sandford

Cain stood beside him, his small smile just as chilling. Then came the thunderous crowd. So many people – so many flags snapping at the air with their stark swirls. In real life they'd be red and black against grey, like blood on grimy snow.

Russ knocked back a shot. He'd fallen silent as he watched. His expression was troubled, faintly resentful… yet suddenly the odd sense came over me that this was a celebration drink.

I stared at him.

"What?" Russ said, glancing over at me. He'd loosened his tie and taken off his jacket. His white shirtsleeves were rolled up, contrasting with his dark, muscular forearms. He looked the same as always.

I shook my head. I'd had too much to drink already. "Nothing," I said, and downed the rest of my whiskey. "Maybe we should order some food."

Though I thought I'd pushed the strange moment away, on some level it refused to leave.

Russ stayed on in the bar. Hours later, walking back to the streetcar stop, I passed the speak we'd gone to the night of Stan's send-off. I stopped and gazed at its glossy black door.

On impulse I went inside. I walked slowly down the narrow stairs. With no band playing yet, it was a different world from the dimly-lit, pulsing place I remembered.

In the corner was the table where I'd seen Russ sitting with two other men. I stood looking at it.

"Can I help you, miss?" asked a waiter.

I came back to myself with a jolt. "No," I said. "Thank you."

I'm just tired, I told myself as I rode the streetcar home. *I'm imagining things that aren't there.*

But I felt cold inside. Unwelcome thoughts had started to flower – wild, rampant vines that I couldn't control. Once I got home I tried to relax but it was impossible; I paced our small living room as Peter lay sleeping on the sofa.

Russ's smile when I'd gone into the courtroom… I knew now what it had reminded me of: he'd had that same tense expression in the speak, when Harlan and I had gone up to his table. And those men he'd been talking to – what had they given him? My memory of that night was fuzzy, but I thought I recalled Russ tucking something into his jacket pocket.

It could have been anything. A cigar, probably. The thought hammering through my brain didn't even make sense, because Russ had been thrilled when I won that first fight. He'd given me one of his terrible stogies.

Images came anyway, one after another: Russ snapping his hat brim jauntily into place this afternoon. His initial silence when I'd gotten the burning plane down. The Russ I thought I knew should have been exuberant – scooping me into a hug, shouting a hosanna to the sky.

No. I dropped onto the sofa, clutching my head. Russ was my team leader. Things like this just didn't happen in the World for Peace; it had been run on the honour system for generations. We *cared* about what we did. A memory rushed back – dozens of new Peacefighter pilots, all in our dress uniforms, our right hands raised:

I swear to serve the World for Peace and all it stands for...

Russ, with his strained smile. He'd told me that my air bottle had been hit, even though I hadn't felt it happen.

I'd believed him.

Blood beat at my temples. I jumped up from the sofa and yanked on my shoes; I grabbed our flashlight from the kitchen. As I raced from the house, I was thankful that Vera wasn't home to ask questions. I was sure I was going crazy.

But I had to see the bullet holes for myself.

There was a scrapyard where they put the wreckage of planes that were past repair. I'd never been there but knew it was on the eastern side of the Heat, which was a kind of no-man's-land. I took a streetcar as far as I could and then walked for over a mile. It was dusk now and the paved road was empty, slicing through an avenue of bedraggled-looking palm trees. Wind whispered through the long, dry grass.

I couldn't believe I was here. I couldn't believe I was thinking this.

Finally I saw the chain-link fence; it stretched off across the fields. Inside was a huge cluttered lot. In the fading light I could make out the shadowy hulks of hundreds of planes, their jutting wings creating an alien landscape.

The gate was locked. I found a spot dark with shadow and climbed over, hooking my fingers into the chain-link diamonds. The fence rattled as I dropped to the ground, and I ducked behind a nearby shed.

There was only the pounding of my pulse and the ocean's distant murmur. Finally I exhaled and stepped out into the yard. I shone my light over the nearest heap of mangled Firedoves. All right, my plane had to be here somewhere...I just had to find it.

The planes were organized by country, with rough paths between each section. I walked down one dark path and then another, shining my flashlight on the Doves' call letters. They flashed into view, ghostly and forgotten. Shards of broken glass glittered where my light fell on them.

The moon travelled slowly up through the jagged palm fronds. The night air grew cooler, prickling at my arms. Finally my flashlight started picking out call letters beginning with *WS*.

No sign of my plane. I circled the Western Seaboard section twice as the moon crept higher. Was my plane even here? Angry at the panic seeping in, I swept my flashlight wildly, searching in great arcs – and then let out a fierce, relieved breath as the blackened call letters WSO67 suddenly swung into view.

It wasn't at ground level. It had been dumped on top of two other planes: a tangle of wings and shattered cockpits.

Holding my flashlight tightly in my armpit, I began to climb, ignoring the kick of pain from my ribs.

The first plane creaked when I lifted myself onto its wing, but remained stable. I stepped onto the side of the cockpit and jumped to grasp the second plane's wing. As I clambered onto it the world tilted sideways with a groan. I froze, my fingertips icy.

This is insane, I thought.

I could see my plane above me in the moonlight, its back panel hidden by the angle of the wing. The answer was *there* – only feet away. I balanced myself carefully, and then jumped again. The second plane groaned as I left it; I got my leg over the third wing's edge and pulled myself up.

It was the same Firedove I'd flown so many times, now half-burned, unrecognizable. I was too taut to feel any sadness. I gripped the open hood, scanning the plane's port side fervently with my flashlight.

Nothing.

Steeling myself, I stepped into the charred, smoke-smelling cockpit and then out the other side. The wing here sloped upwards, pressing me hard against the plane. I leaned over and shone my flashlight onto the panel behind the cockpit.

There were two bullet holes.

I gasped out loud. But maybe I was only seeing them because I wanted them to be there. I craned far to the side and ran my hand over the holes, over and over, digging my fingers into them.

They were real: two round bullet holes whose crisp metal edges had been charred in the fire. The piece of panel was now attached only by a single bolt. Struggling to keep my balance, I swung it open. When I shone the light in, my air bottle had a bullet hole, too; its edges glinted in the light. The bottle's nozzle had been blown off, just like Russ had said.

I felt limp with relief. It had been ridiculous to come out here – risk breaking my neck on this teetering pile of scrap. I creaked the panel shut. Had I really doubted my team leader because of a drunken half-memory? Because his *smile* was too tense? He'd made the same vow as me.

I climbed down. Maybe there was still plenty to worry about in the world, but all I could do was my job. And I would, as good as before.

No.

Better.

Chapter Twelve

The same day that Kay read the results of the Western Seaboard pilot's appeal, a knock came at her door.

It was late; she'd been getting ready for bed. She went rigid, staring at the door in apprehension. There was nothing for it. She pulled her bathrobe tightly around herself and opened the door a crack.

Malcolm Skinner stood there, looking thin and hollow-cheeked. He pulled off his hat; his sparse hair clung across his skull. "Let me in," he said.

Kay did so and then stood fiddling with the tie of her bathrobe. "Would you like some coffee, sir?" she asked. "Or—"

"This isn't a social call," Skinner snapped. He sat on the

sofa and opened a briefcase. "Sit," he ordered.

Kay slowly lowered herself to the edge of her armchair. Somehow the Chief Astrologer was more frightening here, in her own territory, than he'd been in the small, stained room in the basement of the Zodiac.

"Celia Lloyd has been found Discordant and sent to a correction camp," said Skinner. "As for the Western Seaboard pilot you chose for us…" He narrowed his gaze. The odd bald patch on his eyebrow was larger now – or maybe it was a trick of the light.

Kay bit back a mewling plea and straightened her spine. "I'm confident that the Grand Cross chart was the correct choice."

And incredibly, Skinner inclined his head. "It seemed unfortunate at first, but going through the official appeal process has put an extra seal of validation on the EA's clean win. Mr Gunnison's most pleased."

Kay managed not to gasp out loud with relief. "I'm so glad," she said. Yet she still felt nervous. Skinner wouldn't have come here just to tell her that they were pleased.

"I believe I *will* have some coffee," he said.

Kay went to the kitchen, where she gripped the counter hard with both hands. "Calm," she ordered herself in a mutter. "Calm."

Ten minutes later, Skinner blew fussily at the hot coffee in his cup. "You haven't been seeing clients," he said. It wasn't a question. So she *had* been watched.

"No," said Kay. She took a sip of coffee and forced her fingers to stay relaxed around the cup's handle.

Skinner reached into his briefcase. He took out a thick file, and then two more. He stacked them neatly on the coffee table, lining up their edges.

"Your duties," he announced. "You're now an official astrologer of the Twelve Year Plan."

Kay somehow arranged her expression to one showing only surprise and pleasure. "*Really?*" she exclaimed. "But I'm not even a state astrologer!"

"Nevertheless. Mr Gunnison has been very interested in your input."

Kay's mind was whirring. This could be her salvation or her death. But if she could get it right – could play Gunnison at his own game and win—

"I'm extremely honoured, sir," she said after a pause. "I'll want to get started immediately, of course." She cleared her throat. "And if I may say so…it's always best to have the client present."

Skinner looked shocked. "You mean Mr Gunnison? Impossible."

Kay started to protest that he'd get much better results. She caught herself; astrology was supposed to be dispassionate.

"I like the personal touch," she said.

Skinner sneered. "How sweet. But no." He drained his coffee and rose. "I'll expect you at headquarters first thing tomorrow. Goodnight, Miss Pierce."

After he left, Kay sat staring at the files, almost too frightened to touch them. The apartment seemed to be pressing in on her. She sprang up and hurried into the bedroom; she blindly threw on some clothes and then grabbed her coat.

The walk she took was brisk, unseeing, her footsteps echoing against the sidewalks. Topeka was a metropolis of millions, surpassed only by New Chicago. Even this late, it was pulsing. Kay passed brightly-lit moving-picture palaces; state astrologers' signs flashing the Harmony symbol; a building with a bas-relief of Guns helping citizens.

Finally she reached the broad expanse of the Bradford Bridge and stopped near its central arch. She leaned against the railing, gazing down at the dark, churning depths of the Souri River. The bridge's cables hummed in the wind.

People jumped from here, sometimes. The papers always portrayed the suicides as deranged, crazy...but almost everyone in the Central States understood the real reasons.

Behind her, traffic rumbled. Seeing a passer-by duck his head against some sight, Kay turned and saw a Shadowcar glide past, its tall, rounded lines like a ghostly hearse.

She let out a short, fierce breath.

In the black market underworld, it was common knowledge how frequently one of the Twelve Year astrologers got arrested and sent to a correction camp.

Gunnison tended to go with the astrological interpretations he liked best...and woe betide any astrologer who got it wrong.

The Grand Cross pilot that Kay had chosen for the Peacefight had been Skinner's favoured choice. She'd seen it in his face. To last as a Twelve Year astrologer she had to see Gunnison's face...or else she might as well flag down the next Shadowcar she saw and climb inside.

No, Kay thought, fists clenched. *Never.*

The Twelve Year astrologers met in a boardroom below the Pisces dome – far from the Libra building where Kay had once been held prisoner. The soaring view showed three of the Zodiac's other domes and downtown Topeka beyond. Carved wooden panelling depicted astrological figures. A mirror glinted across an entire wall.

Kay and seven other Twelve Year astrologers sat around a long table with Malcolm Skinner at its head.

"Page four in your packets," instructed Skinner. "Now, this chart is of particular interest..."

Kay's gaze flicked to her reflection: careful waves of upswept hair; a new dress with a neat row of buttons. She looked unruffled, businesslike. She was glad of that... because the rumour was that it was a one-way mirror and John Gunnison sat on the other side.

The thought terrified her. Yet she fervently hoped it was true: if so, Gunnison might become intrigued by her, want to meet her in person. So far, she could see no other way of getting close enough to read his body language.

Kay studied the chart Skinner was discussing. The mirror story had to be only a rumour, she thought tensely. Gunnison wouldn't have time to spy on his astrologers. No, but he could have a lackey do it for him.

A lackey would have to do.

Since her appointment as a Twelve Year astrologer a week ago, Kay had mostly kept quiet, modelling her responses on the other astrologers'. In no time she'd realized how backbiting and frightened they all were.

Four empty seats gaped around the table: the only evidence left of astrologers too stupid to learn how to play the game.

Kay hadn't slept much recently; she'd been obsessively reading the files Skinner had given her. Though the contents left the ultimate goal of "Gunnison's Dozen" shrouded, the gist was clear: power.

The John Gunnison portrayed in the files was a patient man. When it came to the Peacefights, for instance, he'd at first held back from controlling them, apart from a few crucial conflicts...such as the fight that had won the civil war, allowing the Central States to split off on their own.

Kay had gaped at the words, then reread them. *The civil war Peacefight had been fixed.* Now that she knew, it seemed obvious. Of course Gunnison wouldn't have left that fight to chance.

In the decade following, though, he'd mostly left the Peacefights alone. He'd instead cultivated people sympathetic to him – manoeuvred them into key positions in other countries and then seen them rise slowly through the ranks. Numerous countries would now be horrified to learn how many of their high-ranking citizens were Gunnison loyalists: senators, councillors, CEOs of major companies.

With this support system in place, Gunnison had only recently started manipulating the Peacefights in earnest. The elaborate system of Peacefight wins, losses and kickbacks wouldn't be obvious to anyone without serious digging.

And every single manipulated fight supported the aims of the thickest file.

Its contents had been shocking, mesmerizing. That first night Kay had stayed up until four a.m., hardly able to believe what she was reading. When she'd finally gone to bed, all she could think of was one name: Rita Pulaski.

Rita had been Kay's neighbour years ago; she'd disappeared when they were both seven. Kay recalled knocking on her door, asking if Rita could come out to play. Mrs Pulaski's eyes had been red-rimmed.

"Rita doesn't live here any more, Kay," she'd said. "She's gone away."

Kay had taken a step back. "I...I'm sorry," she'd stammered, responding to Mrs Pulaski's eyes rather than the words.

Rita had preyed uneasily on Kay's mind for a long time, but as no grown-up seemed to think that action was needed, eventually she'd forgotten her. Until the file marked *Operation Mars*.

Mars, the ruler of Aries, the first sign of the zodiac… and the ancient god of war. The year Gunnison took office, six- and seven-year-olds from all over the CS had been taken from their parents. The families had been told only that it was an honour; the highest accolade that the newly-formed state could give.

The children, now adults, had been in training for twelve years.

As Skinner droned on, Kay readied herself. It was vital that she steer the conversation that she was about to spark in the way that would be most advantageous to her. She managed not to look at the mirror again…but prayed someone was watching who would tell Gunnison of her fire, her competence.

"Yes, we can take that as a given," said Skinner in response to someone's question. "Now, if we next turn our attention to—"

"Excuse me," said Kay clearly. "When are we going to attack the Western Seaboard?"

CHAPTER THIRTEEN

"WHERE'S EDWARDS?" I ASKED IN surprise. I'd just gone out to my plane; it was my first fight after being put back on the roster.

My new fitter, a tall guy named Regan, lifted his voice over the sound of an incoming Dove. "I think he's working on Tier Threes now."

Fitters got reassigned sometimes, but it made me feel as if I'd been grounded for months instead of just four weeks. I pushed away my faint wistfulness and climbed into the cockpit. All that mattered now was doing my job.

The loss of our oil rights had hit the news soon after I lost my appeal. I read all I could about it, hating every word. People had started panic-buying fuel; food prices had rocketed. It was better than war, I knew that...but oh, why had I had to lose *that* fight?

When I wasn't fighting, I was practising. I think I was determined to never lose again, though deep down I knew how crazy that was. If I saw Collie, I ignored him. He seemed to ignore me, too, though I thought I felt his gaze on me sometimes.

I never looked to see.

"What's going on with you and that new pilot?" said Vera one morning. We were in the kitchen getting ready to go to the morning meeting. She didn't look up as she spooned cat food into Peter's bowl.

I tensed. "Nothing. Why?"

"No reason." Then she glanced at me. "Did I tell you I broke up with Marcus a few weeks ago?"

I'd been pouring myself a cup of coffee. I stopped and stared, remembering the two of them slow-dancing to the wailing jazz. "You did?"

"Yes," she said flatly. She rose and rinsed off the spoon. "It wasn't fair to him to let it get so serious, not with what we do. Be careful, Amity."

I didn't need her to tell me that. Yet passing by the Tier Three practice field one day, I stopped and watched as a blue Firedove sliced through the air. Somehow I knew it was Collie. The pilot went into a shrieking turn, holding it just a hair from stalling; he rolled sideways and got his opponent in a spray of fake bullets.

As I watched I remembered a dog-eared pamphlet I'd

seen in the Heat. It had been written in short, punchy text, as if whoever wrote it didn't have much time. *John Gunnison is a madman. His lackeys are violent thugs. Don't believe what you hear about Gunnison's policies being good for the Central States. We live in uncertainty and fear. Neighbours turn against neighbours to save themselves...*

My scalp had prickled as I read about correction camps: *places of misery and murder.* Was *that* what happened to the Discordants?

And Collie had lived in the Central States. How much of all this had he seen...lived through?

Now I stood peering upwards, shading my eyes as I took in Collie's sharp control. I wasn't surprised that he was such a good pilot; he'd always flown really well when Dad had taken him up. I wished that Dad could see him now.

Far across the field, the Firedove came in at an angle, its swirling pattern glinting. It touched down with hardly a bump.

Without thinking I started to jog across the grass, suddenly wanting to tell Collie how well he'd flown. I stopped myself as he climbed down from the cockpit. Even from this distance, every move of his lean form was familiar.

The ache that went through me startled me – stiffened my spine. *No.* Shaken, I turned and left the field. The grass rustled at my feet, whispering things I couldn't catch.

I half-expected Collie to see me and come running after me, but he didn't.

* * *

The die showed the symbol for sunset.

The controller stood hunched, holding the phone's chunky black receiver between his ear and shoulder. He scribbled down what I'd rolled, and then checked the schedule for a slot.

"17.25," he said into the phone. There was a pause. "Holy Hills," he informed me.

Dusk, then. Over the hills, that meant mist. When the time came, I jogged out to my plane, my parachute bouncing over one shoulder. A few minutes later I was speeding down the airstrip, engine roaring; then my plane lifted away from the ground and pierced the sky.

I headed west, where the Holy Hills crouched darkly against the horizon. Tucked high in their folds were a pair of ancient letters: an "H" and an "L". Whenever I saw them, I mentally added an "A" for my brother's name. Once there'd been homes up here, too. You could still see the flattened foundations, and kidney-shaped holes that had been swimming pools.

Now it was just another battlefield.

I entered the airspace over the hills. Mist flying was tricky – too much of it and you had to turn tail and reschedule. Tonight it was just right: pockets of white rose up from dips in the land below like ghostly invitations, with clear sections in between.

At exactly 17.25, I spotted the Alaskan plane. Its blue and tan swirls ducked away into the mist.

"Here we go," I murmured.

The world fell sideways as I banked, my fingers gentle on the stick. I roared through patches of white, trying to guess where the other Firedove might be hiding.

All at once my opponent appeared right below me. My pulse skipped with adrenalin and surprise. I twisted into a dive and screamed towards them, firing. Eight streaks of tracer bullets turned invisible in the mist, then visible again. Holes rained across the other Dove.

"Usually a good idea to check your mirrors," I said softly.

I circled above, watching to gauge the damage. I could feel myself frowning: that sort of clumsy mistake didn't usually happen in Tier Two fights.

Black smoke billowed from the other plane's hood. The engine skipped a beat, then died. I saw my opponent shove the cockpit open – and I must have gotten their steering system too, because the Dove started to plummet towards the ground. The pilot hastily undid their straps, then stood up and bailed.

"*No*," I breathed, my fingers suddenly tight on the stick.

I could see it all unfolding in a kind of terrible slow motion. The pilot half-fell from the cockpit, exactly as we're trained – and then the Firedove went into a spin. The pilot slammed against the side of the falling plane; their belt got snagged on the cockpit hood. They lay caught flat, struggling as their parachute billowed open above.

"Get it off, *get it off!*" I shouted.

I was damp with sweat, cold all over. I dived after the other plane, wildly thinking that maybe there was something I could do. There wasn't. The trapped pilot writhed and kicked against the hood. Their parachute cords got more tangled with every spin. I glimpsed the raw panic on the Alaskan pilot's face as the ground sped closer and closer. Finally I pulled out of my dive; I had to.

The plane crashed below.

With a dull *whump*, the gas tank blew: for a long, fierce moment, flames plumed up. Then there was nothing – just the crumpled shape of the plane visible through patches of mist.

I circled once, frantically looking for a spot to land, then brought my Dove down on the grass and rocks. The world bounced violently – my straps bit at my shoulders. The ground loomed as I almost somersaulted, then the Dove righted itself with a heavy jolt.

I grabbed for my mic. "Pilot down!" I gasped. "Over the Holy Hills – send someone fast!"

I yanked off my straps and scrambled from the cockpit. Utter silence. I dropped to the ground and started to run. Faint paths showed through the mist; there was a rocky indentation that might once have been a house.

The other Dove lay ahead. It had hit nose-first, crumpling the hood like tinfoil. Its tail stuck almost straight up, and one of the wings had come off. Smoke drifted upwards, looking oddly peaceful.

I was breathing hard. I jogged to a halt and pushed my goggles up – I stared at the wreckage. No one could have survived that. Then I heard a faint moan and jerked into motion again, sprinting towards the plane.

The Alaskan pilot lay on the ground by the shattered wing. Their body looked small, huddled. One leg was bent at a weird angle.

I dropped to my knees beside them. I couldn't speak. It was a girl about my own age with dark eyebrows. That was all I could tell. Her features were wet with blood. A mangled-looking injury bloomed at the edge of her leather helmet: blood so dark it was almost black, and shards of white that I realized were bits of her skull.

The world fell sideways. I was crouching in a field of tall grass – there were grasshoppers singing, and my father lay choking on his own blood.

The girl shuddered. I somehow shook away the vision and touched her shoulder. "You're all right – you'll be just fine," I told her. My voice sounded too loud, falsely hearty.

She opened her eyes and saw me, though her goggle lenses were streaked with blood. Her mouth moved. I couldn't hear her and leaned close.

"Please can you..." The words were a stir of breath against my ear.

Her hand moved feebly. I snapped off my leather gloves and gently pulled hers off, too. I gripped her hand. "What?" I whispered. "Tell me what you want me to do." I listened tautly for planes, approaching trucks – anybody.

Her throat moved as she swallowed. "Tell my family… it doesn't hurt. Please tell them that."

"I will," I said feverishly. "I promise."

She let out a deep sigh. Her fingers grew limp.

"No!" I cried. I squeezed her hand harder. "*Hang on!* Do you hear me? Someone will be here soon to help!"

I could hardly hear her when she spoke next. "Tell them I'm sorry. It wasn't supposed to be like this…"

I'm not sure of the exact moment when she died. I kept crouching there, clutching her hand…and gradually became aware that the only sound of breathing I could hear was my own. The girl's face had gone completely still. Her eyes stared upwards, unseeing.

I felt numb as I let go of her fingers. I slowly reached for her goggles and lifted them upwards. They caught a little in a curl of escaped hair, the brown strands already going stiff with blood. Her eyes were very blue. I could see now how pretty she was.

Heat pulsed through me. "Why didn't you check your mirrors?" I yelled at her. "You're a Tier Two pilot! You're supposed to be better than that!" My voice bounced back at me from the hills. A few rabbits grazing nearby startled and ran, their tails flashing white for danger.

I sank back onto my heels, staring at the girl. Then, remembering my promise, I fumbled to undo her leather jacket. Her body lay still and unresisting. Her ID tags were on top of her shirt – they still felt warm. I lifted them up and peered at them in the faint light.

Concordia Winston, they read.

My throat tightened. "Concordia", for "peace". Just like my own name. From nowhere, I remembered my father saying, *The fight for peace is in your blood.*

I felt empty. I lay the tags back on her chest. "I'll tell them," I said softly. I tugged her jacket closed again as if I thought she'd be cold. "Don't worry."

I stayed beside her until the trucks finally came.

CHAPTER FOURTEEN

THE WAVES ROSE AND FELL. The low noise of them, their sheer power, ached through me and made the music drifting out from the party sound thin and false. If you swam far enough out there, I bet the water was cold, even here in Angeles County.

Dark and cold and endless.

I shivered. A guy standing next to me on the deck – Kyle? Lyle? – took it as an invitation and put his arm around me. "Kinda nice out here, isn't it?" he said. "All the nature and scenery."

"Yeah," I murmured, hardly noticing him. Still staring at the ocean, I rubbed my arms and wondered what time it was.

Vera was in the house somewhere. Coming to the party had been her idea. I wasn't sure why I'd agreed, except that the thought of staying at home alone tonight had filled me with dread, and the poker game had seemed so pointless that I couldn't even fathom it. I'd thought that maybe music and noise and people would drown out the image of Concordia's lifeless blue eyes.

They didn't.

When the trucks had come, I'd been pulled aside from Concordia's body while they tried to resuscitate her. They figured out it was hopeless soon enough. They'd brought a canvas body bag and they slithered her into it, feet first.

One of the team had given me a distressed look. "Miss Vancour, you shouldn't have landed. Pilots aren't supposed to see this."

My voice had been oddly calm. "If I hadn't shot her down, she'd still be alive. Why shouldn't I see it?"

"Hey, you look so serious," whispered Kyle or Lyle. He put his hands on my shoulders and turned me towards him. His lips were on mine before I realized what was happening. I jerked away.

"What are you doing?" I said in amazement.

"Just being friendly." He gave me a smile that was probably charming, if you were in the mood. "Why not? I like you, you like me..."

I felt like a taut wire. "But I don't like you."

His smile slipped. "You don't?"

"No! I don't even *know* you." I pressed a hand against

my head. It was throbbing suddenly. I didn't know anyone here. Not a soul – not even Vera, when it came down to it. And nobody here knew me.

The loneliness felt as if it might crush me.

"I've got to go," I said faintly.

"*Go?* But I thought—"

I left the deck without waiting to hear. Inside the house, I struggled through the crowd as the wild music enveloped me. A cluster of people stood around the piano, laughing, as someone played.

"Amity, what are you doing?" Vera appeared, petite and pretty in a bright yellow dress, just as I found my coat on the sofa.

"I've got to leave," I said.

"But we just got here! I know you must still be upset, but—"

"I'm leaving," I repeated. I felt as if I might fly into pieces. Across the room, a couple had started jitterbugging, the guy swinging the girl around wildly. The piano player stomped the floor with one foot, keeping time to the boogie-woogie as the crowd cheered.

And that's when I realized: there was only one person in the world who I wanted to be with right now.

"Why don't you come, too?" I said urgently to Vera, lifting my voice over the noise. "You could go and see Marcus."

She froze, clutching her glass as if it were a shield. I blundered on: "He usually works Thursdays, right? If you hurry you could make it before closing time! Vera, he really cares about you."

I thought the glass might break in her hand. She stared over at the dancers; I saw her swallow. Finally she looked back at me and gave a small smile that didn't reach her eyes.

"Go, if you're going," she said.

The streetcar ride back to base seemed to take hours. I sat tensely, reading the advertisements over and over. When we finally reached base I leaped up before the car came to a stop. I jogged down the steps and then ran through the main gates, thrusting my pass towards the guard.

I kept running. I staggered on one of my high heels; I skipped for a few steps to yank the shoes off, then pounded across the asphalt towards the airstrip office.

I burst in through the double doors, breathing hard. The board was in the main corridor: a chalkboard with all the pilots' names on it. I'd seen the details of his fight when I'd prepared for my own, though I'd told myself I wasn't looking.

Reed, C. T3, night fight, central fields. The blue circle showing that a pilot was down and safe wasn't beside his name. I rushed to the counter. Myra, one of the pursers, glanced up in surprise.

"Is Collis Reed back yet?" I gripped the counter's edge tightly.

She was addressing envelopes; she shook her head as she licked a flap. "No, he was shot down." She put the envelope aside and picked up another.

My mouth went numb – I snatched the envelope out of her hand. "*What are you telling me?* Is he dead? Is that it?"

Myra looked alarmed. "No! Oh, Miss Vancour, I'm sorry – I just meant that he lost his fight! He had to bail from his plane; they're bringing him back in now."

I was already running again. I bolted out the door to the airstrip – and from a distance, I could see headlights approaching down the road that ran adjacent to it. I jogged to a stop, still clutching my shoes. Tall electric lights blazed overhead. Someone's plane touched down; the fitters ran past me.

The headlights grew closer. A truck came into view. As it veered towards the office I could see that Ruby, the T3 team leader, was driving. Collie sat beside her, slumped in the seat. When he saw me he sat up slowly, frowning.

I'd begun to shiver, though earlier my coat had seemed too warm. I started towards the truck, dimly realizing that my stockings were torn beyond redemption. Ruby pulled up, engine still idling. Collie climbed out and she drove off across the airstrip.

Collie's gaze locked with mine as he came towards me: a tall, lean pilot wearing a leather flight jacket that already looked battered. His goggles hung around his neck; his ruffled hair was dark gold under the artificial lights.

I stopped a few feet away. So did he. Another Dove touched down, its engine roaring in the background.

"Amity," said Collie finally. He had a smudge of oil across one cheek.

I cleared my throat. "I…wanted to see you."

"I was just going to come and find you." His expression was serious, unsmiling. "I heard about your fight. Are you all right?"

"I'm fine. Fine."

His eyes said that he knew better. He closed the distance between us. "Come on," he said quietly.

With one hand lightly on my back he steered me towards the small, bright cafe near the office – it was for pilots, open all hours. Its lights spilled out onto the dark asphalt. When we got inside we were the only ones there. The empty round tables stood slightly askew, like drunks at a party.

Collie settled us at a table and ordered coffee. When it arrived he pushed the sugar container towards me without asking.

"You're supposed to sign in," I said.

"Myra can wait a little longer." He poured cream in his coffee and then handed me that, too. I stirred it in slowly, listening to my spoon hit the sides of the worn white mug, very aware of Collie sitting across from me – the familiar face grown older, the new broadness of his shoulders.

Collie took a gulp of coffee, then leaned forward on his arms. "Tell me," he said simply.

I hadn't known I wanted to talk about it – this wasn't what I'd planned to say to Collie when I'd come running to find him. But once the words started I couldn't stop them, despite the tightness of my throat. I told him everything. It felt as if it was being dredged out of me in harsh, ugly lumps.

"Her name was Concordia," I finished finally. I rapped my spoon against the table, staring down at my inverted reflection – seeing again the girl lying shuddering in the ancient garden. "So I guess…maybe she came from a Peacefighting family like mine. She might have heard the same stories I did, growing up."

Our mugs sat half-empty, the coffee cold and forgotten. "Probably," said Collie softly.

"She said to tell her family she was sorry. What was she sorry for?"

"Dying, I guess."

"Why didn't she check her mirrors? It was like—" The spoon almost bent in my grasp; I tossed it aside. "Like she *wanted* to be shot down."

Collie was silent for a long moment. "You must have been more hidden than you thought," he said finally. "It happens. Don't blame yourself."

"I'm not. I was just doing my job. But I want *her* to have done her job!" I gave a shaky laugh. "I'm angry at someone I've never met! I had to watch her die; I at least want to know that she did everything possible not to get shot down."

Collie's eyes were pained. "Amity, why the hell did you land?" he said in a low voice. "You must have seen it was hopeless."

"I had to."

"When I heard, all I could think about was finding you." His hand found mine across the table; our fingers gripped each other tightly. "For anyone else it would be bad enough, but for you..." He didn't finish his thought.

He didn't have to. Just having someone there who knew was enough.

The crash that killed my father happened in the fields behind our house; he was on his way back from a World for Peace meeting. I was the one who found him. For a long time, I was sure there had to have been a malfunction: someone or something I could blame. But there hadn't been. He'd somehow – a pilot with thousands of hours of experience, on a landing he'd made hundreds of times – brought it in too fast. His plane had somersaulted, its wings crumpling as they went; he'd been thrown clear and his injuries had killed him.

Not immediately, though. It only took minutes, I guess...but each of them weighed on me like lead.

Collie and I sat silently, sharing the same thoughts. His shoulders were slumped as he slowly rubbed his thumb against my palm. "You never cried afterwards," he said at last. "Do you remember? Not once. I wanted to help you. I didn't know what to do."

"You did help," I said. "That day in my room. You came

in and just sat and held my hand. You didn't try to talk to me, or tell me how sorry you were."

"I didn't know what to say. Everything I thought of seemed so trite."

"But at least you understood that. No one else did." I sat back, releasing his hand as the waitress appeared and refilled our coffee mugs. I hardly noticed when she'd gone. I sat studying Collie – this older version of the boy I'd known.

"I'm…glad you're here," I said roughly. "And those words seem pretty trite, too."

Collie looked up. Something went still inside me as our eyes met.

"I was going to find you tonight even before I heard what happened," he said finally. "It's been a month, Amity."

"I know," I whispered.

He scanned me, unsmiling. "I won't say anything else about it if you don't want. I'll wait another month, or two, or three, or—"

"No!" I broke in. I gripped his arm. "Collie, I wanted to find you, too. I had to tell you—"

I broke off. There was too much I wanted to say; the words crowded together in my throat. Neither of us moved. Across the airstrip, another plane came in: a blur of lights speeding in the distance.

"Tell me what?" Collie asked after a long pause. His eyes were a challenge.

My chin jerked up. I was *not* going to cry. "You said that you wanted to pick up where we left off." I sounded almost angry. "And I wanted to tell you…yes."

Collie's gaze stayed locked on mine. "Is this only because of what happened today? Are you going to decide tomorrow that—"

"No! I mean, yes, maybe it was the catalyst, but I've wanted you for weeks now." My jaw was tight. "Do you want me to say it? Fine, I will. You're all I can think about. When I go to sleep at night, all I can see is you. When you're in the locker room with me it's like torture, because all I want is to touch you—"

Collie moved suddenly, shoving his chair back. He grabbed my hand and we left the cafe; he pulled me into the shadows near the office. A soft rain had started. Across the airstrip, headlights from a truck swept across the asphalt. The raindrops glittered in its lights.

He took my face in his hands. His tone was low, intense.

"Please tell me that again," he said.

I heard myself let out a moan as I threw myself at him. Collie caught me up tightly, lifting me off the ground.

"Amity…" His voice was hoarse.

"I missed you," I got out. "I missed you so much."

Our heartbeats thudded together, even through his jacket and my coat. I buried my face against his neck, breathing him in – the smell of machine oil, summertime, a thousand memories.

Finally we drew apart a little. Collie stroked my damp hair back with both hands.

"You have no idea how much I've wanted to do this," he whispered.

He lowered his head. When our lips met it was the second kiss I'd ever really wanted. I closed my eyes this time, but stood very still, drinking it in – the slight roughness of his mouth, the shouts of the fitters in the distance, the warmth of his hands on my cheeks.

His lips left mine slowly, lingeringly. He kept his hands on my face as we studied each other. I swallowed and reached up, clasping them in mine.

"Nice night," drawled a voice. Harlan and another pilot passed by on their way to the office. Harlan's eyebrows were up in his hairline.

Neither of us answered. As they disappeared into the building Collie took a half-step back, his left hand still holding mine. "Let's go find someplace where we can be alone," he said.

I was so happy I was scowling. "That sounds like a good idea," I said. Collie smiled slightly and touched my forehead. And the fact that he knew I was happy despite my furrowed brow made me scowl even harder.

He kept hold of my hand even as he signed back into the pilots' register in the office, keeping my fingers folded firmly in his on the counter as he scribbled his name with his right hand.

"I thought you were left-handed," I said. An actual smile

had started now. I didn't care that Myra was watching. I didn't care that pilots never held hands, never got involved.

Collie put down the pen. "I am. It's not my best signature ever."

Myra was grinning. "So I guess you found him," she said to me.

I nodded, not taking my eyes from Collie's face. "Yeah," I said. "I've found him."

Chapter Fifteen

THE LIGHT OF DAWN CREPT through my curtains, giving the room a gentle glow. Collie's arm around me felt strong and firm; our legs were tangled warmly together under the sheets.

"What's that one?" I whispered, pointing to a swirl of plaster on the ceiling.

Collie considered it. "A turtle. See the neck?"

"Really?" I wrinkled my nose. "It looks like a plane to me."

He laughed softly. "Everything looks like a plane to you."

"No, that one over there doesn't. See? It's a running wolf."

"That's a horse, Amity Louise. Look, there's even a saddle."

I sat up a little and studied him. I couldn't stop smiling; it felt as if someone had handed me the sun. I traced a circle around the tiny freckle beside Collie's eye. "I remember this, you know," I said. "From the first time we kissed."

His eyes were dark blue in the dawn light. He smoothed the hair back from my forehead. "I lived on that kiss for four years."

"Now you've got even more to live on."

Collie grinned. With a rustle of sheets, he rolled over on top of me. "Yes, but I don't plan on being away from you for four years again," he said. "Or four hours, if I can help it."

I stroked his back as we kissed. I loved the bare weight of him on me – the warmth of our skin together. I hadn't smiled this much since before my father died.

When we finally drew apart, I nudged Collie off me. "All right, I've got to check something." I stretched across him to my bedside table and snapped on the lamp.

Collie's hands grasped my waist. "Oh, *this* is nice..." He tried to pull me on top of him and then fell back, laughing, as I took the lamp and shone it into his eyes. "What are you doing, you madwoman?"

"Stay still." I stretched his eyelids open, inspecting his right eye and then his left; he squinted and twisted his head away.

"I think this is defined as torture, you know. It's been illegal for a long time."

"Stop complaining; I'm busy."

"Bossy as ever. Do you remember that time when you decided you were going to run away from home, and you insisted that I had to go with you, and—"

"It's no use," I broke in. I sank back. "I can't tell what colour your eyes really are. They're blue when I hold the lamp one way, and green another."

He crossed his arms behind his head and grinned. "Yours are easy. Light brown, like melted chocolate."

I combed my fingers through his hair, loving that I could just reach out and touch it. "And your hair's blond in places and kind of golden in places *and* it's brown in other places...you're a chameleon, Collis Reed."

"Well, I never claimed to be boring." He started to say something else, then glanced around the room and his forehead creased. He propped himself up on his elbows. "Hey, I just noticed – where are all your things? Didn't you bring them with you?"

"What things?" I said after a pause.

"Your books, your models, that little box you used to keep treasures in, your—"

I put the lamp back on the table and cleared my throat. "They're...in the closet."

Collie gave me a quizzical look, then got out of bed, dragging the sheet with him. He wrapped it around himself as he opened the closet door. When he saw the trunk on the floor he crouched down.

"Can I open it?" he asked, looking back at me. His fingers rested on the lid.

Our clothes from the night before lay on the floor – my dress, and the tan trousers and white shirt Collie had changed into after he'd signed in. I pulled on his shirt and buttoned it as I crossed to him.

"Go ahead, if you want." I hadn't opened the trunk since I arrived. Its contents had reminded me too much of Dad…and Collie, I guess.

I squatted beside him. "It's not locked."

He eased open the lid. Everything inside was wrapped in newspaper; it rustled as he undid the first parcel. A framed sepia photo emerged: me, Collie and Hal. The three of us sat in a row on the wing of my father's Firedove, grinning widely. My father stood in front of us, leaning back against the wing with arms outspread.

The caption at the bottom was in his handwriting: *My three kids.*

Collie touched the glass over the caption. "I'm, um… glad you didn't tear me out of this one," he said finally. Still gazing down, he put his arm around me.

"He meant it, you know. He always thought of you as his son," I told Collie in a low voice. "I know he'd be proud of you now."

Collie didn't speak for a moment. "Yeah…I hope so."

He put the photo aside and then turned and took my shoulders. His thumbs caressed my collarbones. "And I think he'd be happy about this – about us." He grinned suddenly. "Well, maybe not about me wearing a sheet in his daughter's bedroom. He might think it was a little sudden."

I leaned close and kissed him. "Sudden, after twelve years?"

I could feel his smile. "True. Maybe the only question is what took us so long."

The night before had been darkness, tangled sheets, the heat of our bodies and mouths. It was as if I'd never been touched in my life. His hands woke up nerve endings that had never existed before him.

"We can wait if you want," Collie had whispered. "I promise I won't mind."

And I'd whispered back, "No – I don't want to wait." Concordia's unseeing eyes had allowed no other answer, even if I'd wanted to give one. *Thank you,* I thought to her now. I might never have said yes to Collie at all without her.

I stroked his arm, feeling the softness of its golden hairs. "Tell me what it's been like for you, these last four years," I said quietly. We'd talked about me some the night before, but had barely touched on him. "Were things…all right in the Central States?"

Collie grimaced. "You don't want to hear about that."

"Of course I do. I've read pamphlets – stuff about people being sent away, and correction camps. Is it really that bad?"

Collie didn't respond at first. He pulled out another wrapped bundle from my trunk. "It's pretty bad," he said finally. "Whatever you've read is probably true."

I sat back on my haunches as I watched him. "What about your parents?"

Collie sighed and put the parcel aside, as if accepting the inevitable. "We lived in Denver," he said. His tone was flat. "It was the most beautiful place I've ever seen, but everyone was scared all the time. You keep your head down and mind your own business and hope no one reports you."

"Reports you for what?"

"Anything. If you're not liked, all someone has to do is claim you've been bad-mouthing Gunnison – then you'll be found Discordant no matter what your chart says."

He glanced at the small tattoo for Leo on the base of his thumb. His expression hardened. "We went to the CS because Dad thought an old crony of his could hook him up with some deals, but it didn't happen," he said. "Then we couldn't leave. He had to take an industrial job. That was what all his big plans came to, just stacking boxes in a factory. I had to do it too, once I got to be sixteen. It was the most mind-numbing, soul-destroying work ever. And meanwhile Goldie was busy drinking herself to death, and…" He stopped and rubbed his forehead.

"There was this girl on our street who'd been found Discordant," he said finally. "Anna."

I closed my fingers around his. "What happened to her?"

"The first year or so after we got there, she just had to wear a 'D' on her clothes. She had this doll she used to play with. I remember she told me once that her doll had a good birth chart, even if *she* didn't…" Collie trailed off.

"And then one day the Shadowcars came," he finished roughly. "I saw them take her and I turned away like everyone else."

I squeezed his hand. "Do *not* blame yourself. Collie, you couldn't have done anything except get taken away, too."

"I don't blame myself," he said, sounding tired. "That's the part I hate most."

Silence wrapped briefly around us. "Anyway…I had a chance to get out and I took it," he said. "I can't tell you much about that. Then I came here and got into training school." His mouth twisted. "That's it. You're all caught up."

I licked my lips. "Why…why can't you tell me about how you got out?"

"Because Gunnison doesn't like it when his good little citizens escape." Collie's tone was short. "You can get out if you grease the right palms, but they're not people you want to cross. I won't tell you anything that could put you in danger, Amity. Not ever."

I didn't know what to say. I wrapped my arms around him and pressed close. Neither of us spoke for a moment. "I wish I'd known what you were going through," I whispered against his shoulder.

The warm breadth of his back felt tense under my hands as he held me. "I'm glad you didn't."

"I would have…written to you, or tried to come to you, or—"

"Don't be stupid. The last thing anyone wants is to get

in to that place." Collie drew away and touched my face. "Hey. I'm here now. Let's forget about it."

I knew that he couldn't forget about it, not with his parents still there, but I nodded.

"And anyway, it doesn't matter about me," Collie added. He stroked his fingers through my hair. "Everything you told me last night...getting arrested, how unhappy you were..."

"I'm here now, too," I said. "We're together. It all worked out."

Collie grinned suddenly and kissed my nose. "True. Yeah, except that you think a turtle looks like an airplane."

We went back to unwrapping things from the trunk: books, more photos. Finally Collie found the tin box I used to keep treasures in and creaked open its lid. "Look," he said. "Remember this?"

I pressed against him and took the small model Firedove from his hand. Collie had given it to me for my tenth birthday. It was cast metal, beautifully painted. It had sat on my desk for years.

"I always wondered how you were able to afford this," I said, turning it in the light.

He smiled ruefully. "I stole it."

I laughed, startled. "Really?"

"From old lady Beasley's shop. I think she knew, too. Don't you remember, for a few years I hated going in there?" He took the Firedove from me. "I painted it myself, though," he added, fingering a wing. His smile had turned slightly bitter. "I wanted to have something really good to give you."

The words felt awkward. "But…you know I wouldn't have cared if you hadn't."

"I cared."

There was a pause. I squeezed his hand and jumped up. "Come on – I want to have it out on my desk again." I felt excited suddenly. "Bring the box, too."

Half an hour later a dozen crumpled sheets of newspaper lay on the floor and my room looked like a place that someone actually lived in, with all my books and photos out on display. The pieces of my life. They didn't even fill a small trunk; why did it make me feel so whole to have them out again?

"You've got a beautiful smile," said Collie softly. He was still wearing the sheet. The sight of him made me wonder why all men everywhere didn't start donning them.

"You've got a beautiful…everything," I said, and he grinned and scooped me up in his arms, flopping us both onto the bed.

"Everything? Even my left ear? Even my nose?"

"Especially your nose." I touched its slightly crooked shape – the thickened bit across the bridge. "Ma used to say it's a good thing you broke it, or else you'd be too pretty."

"Too *pretty*?" Collie snorted out a laugh. "Oh, thanks, Rose."

"Well, it does make you look kind of rugged. Masculine."

"I'm glad you and your mother approve. Anything else I should break?"

I pretended to consider it. "No, I think you'll do."

Our eyes met then...and the laughter faded. From across the hall I heard Vera start up the shower. It seemed to be happening somewhere very far away.

Collie swallowed and ran his hand down my side. "You know...all those years when I was in the CS and everything seemed so hopeless...I used to dream about this happening with us. Exactly this way: you wearing my shirt, your hair all rumpled..."

My throat was tight. I couldn't say the same thing back to him. I hadn't dreamed about him; I'd torn him out of my life and tried to hate him.

But I never could.

"You told me last night that you've had two boyfriends," Collie said quietly. "Were either of them serious?"

"No. Not emotionally."

"That's what I meant." His gaze was level. "It's been the same for me. A few girls, but no one I really cared about." His thumb caressed my cheekbone. "No one who I couldn't get out of my head for four years," he added in an undertone. "Or who makes me feel like my heart's going to explode when I see her standing across an airstrip."

My own heart felt the same suddenly. "Me too." My voice sounded stilted. "I wanted to get you out of my head but I couldn't."

"No matter how many photos you tore me out of?"

I shook my head. "No."

"I'm glad."

The air grew too heavy to breathe. When Collie spoke again, his voice was husky. "Do you remember the day I left? We were in the barn with your dad's plane, and—"

"I remember it all," I said.

His eyes looked very blue now – no hint of green. "I started to tell you something that day. I wasn't brave enough. But now…" He touched my face. "I love you, Amity." He gave a crooked smile. "I think I've loved you since I was about ten years old."

"I know," I whispered. I couldn't say anything else.

There was a pause. Collie studied me with a slight smile. "Do you, um…feel the same way about me?"

I came back to myself, startled. "*Yes.* Collie, of course! I thought you knew that already."

He nuzzled his face against my neck; I could tell he was grinning. "I'd still like to hear the words. If you don't mind."

"Now?" I said weakly.

"Amity…"

"All right." I pulled back and took his face in my hands, cradling the warmth of his cheeks. My voice came out low, almost angry. "I love you, Collis Reed. I didn't want to, but I do. I think I always have. There. Are you happy?"

His chin jutted out pugnaciously; his eyes were dancing. "Yeah, I am. You wanna make something of it, lady?"

I swallowed and looked down. "I'm happy too," I admitted finally.

"I know." His hand closed over mine; he squeezed it hard. "We're always going to be this happy – wait and see. Your term will be over in two years and I'll be finished the year after...then we'll buy a little house somewhere amazing, maybe up in Puget somewhere. We'll fly transport for a living and have a dozen kids."

I smiled at that. "Not on our salaries."

"Don't be so pedantic," he said. "We're going to have it all, Amity Louise."

Now that I'd started smiling I didn't seem able to stop. "All right, we will."

"And you know how we're going to start?" Collie bounced to his knees and grabbed my hands. "If neither of us have night fights, I'm taking you out tonight."

"You mean like a date?"

"Exactly like a date. Do you like dancing? Let's go dancing!"

I was laughing now: this was the enthusiasm that had once spent a whole day building a bridge out of mud and rocks. Collie's face was alive with happiness; I could feel it reflected deep inside me.

I touched his face again. He turned his head and kissed my hand, his lips vital and real.

"Yes, I like dancing," I said.

Chapter Sixteen

The whirr of the projector filled the room. Kay sat silently with the others as Skinner showed a confidential film about the correction camps.

On the screen a too-thin man was being beaten by guards. The black-and-white footage had no sound. Kay winced as silent blows rained over his body. She was glad the room was dark.

Finally the man lay motionless, his eyes empty. Black blood pooled around him, stark against the snow. One arm was bent wrongly. A guard carrying a large knife approached the body.

The film shifted to a row of severed heads mounted atop a chain-link fence. They looked blackened, bruised.

Frost sparkled on them.

Kay felt faint. She wondered if any had been Twelve Year astrologers. *All that matters is that* your *head doesn't end up there,* she reminded herself fiercely.

If she didn't get to Gunnison soon, it might. Her last ploy had failed. The one she was planning today could not.

The week before, a wary rustle had gone around the room after she'd asked about attacking the Western Seaboard. Though her pulse had been racing, Kay had met Skinner's gaze squarely.

"'Attack'?" Skinner's tone had an edge. "Really, Miss Pierce. I believe you are referring to the *Reclamation* part of the plan."

Kay inclined her head. "My apologies. When will the Reclamation begin?"

The photos in the "Operation Mars" file had awed her: troops, artillery, weapons. It was the first fighting force the world had seen in generations...and its troops were currently gathered only a few miles from the Western Seaboard's border. Gunnison believed it his destiny to retake the WS and "bring Harmony" to it.

The astrologer who helped him do so would be set for life.

"Must we waste time on this?" snapped a man sitting across from Kay named Bernard Chester. He had round cheeks and wavy brown hair.

"Yes, spare us," said a woman named Vivian wearing a large Sagittarius brooch. "We *have* covered this in some detail, you know, dear. It's not our fault you've only been around for five minutes."

"Order," barked Skinner. "Miss Pierce, the Reclamation's schedule hasn't been announced. According to Mr Gunnison, the cards show that an unknown puzzle piece is missing from the equation. He'll know when the time is right."

The cards. That meant the Tarot, an ancient divination tool. Gunnison had a habit of consulting it at important junctures. From Skinner's expression, the Chief Astrologer found this galling but was trying to hide it.

Kay hoped that whoever was watching them behind the mirror had noticed this. "Yes, I'm sure he will," she murmured earnestly. "Mr Gunnison knows everything."

"Indeed," agreed Skinner with a stiff smile. "But it's a moot point. Because it still hasn't been settled precisely *where* on the Western Seaboard's border the Reclamation will begin. And on this question…" He hesitated.

Suddenly nobody was looking at the four empty seats and Kay knew her hunch had been correct. None of the Twelve Year astrologers had managed to produce an answer that pleased the Central States leader. Those who'd failed the most flagrantly were probably dead.

Kay took a deep breath. *Tell Gunnison how capable I seem,* she silently urged the hidden lackey. *Make him want to meet me in person.*

"I can help with the location," she said.

Vivian's smile looked very toothy suddenly. "Oh, *do* say you'll try. Please. We'd all love you to."

"How, Miss Pierce?" said Skinner.

"Dowsing," said Kay.

The stunned silence was gratifying. "But…you can't be…*dowsing*?" sputtered Bernard at last.

"No one's taken dowsing seriously for centuries," said Skinner coldly.

"Oh, but that's a great mistake," said Kay. "I've studied dowsing for years, and—"

Skinner's steel-chilled gaze had cut her off. "Turn to Section 2a, please," he said to the room at large.

That evening Kay had walked slowly down the gleaming corridor towards the stairwell. What if the mirror was only a mirror, and there wasn't even an underling to impress? If she couldn't reach Gunnison in person… She shook herself angrily. No. She would.

She rounded a corner and stopped short. Sandford Cain was just entering his office. Her first instinct was to duck back before he could see her. She squelched it and straightened her shoulders.

"Mr Cain!" she called as she approached him.

He glanced at her, his light blue eyes disconcertingly pale. "Yes?"

"I'm Kay Pierce, one of the Twelve Year astrologers."

"*Yes?*"

He can smell fear, thought Kay wildly. She ignored her clammy hands and smiled. "I wonder if I could have a word?

I have some names you might be interested in."

Cain frowned. After a pause, he said, "Why aren't you telling Skinner?"

"Well, I know that sometimes you take care of important cases yourself." In her mind Kay heard again the dull *thump* Cain's blackjack had made as it cracked across Mrs Lloyd's head. She managed not to swallow. "So I thought…why trouble Mr Skinner when he'll just go straight to you anyway?"

Sandford Cain's near-colourless gaze studied her. Kay's smile didn't waver.

Finally Cain opened his door a touch wider. His signet ring gleamed; it showed the stylized crab's claws that were the glyph for Cancer. The emblem seemed to mock Kay. Cancerians were meant to be sensitive and nurturing.

"After you, Miss Pierce," Cain said with a pointed smile.

Now, a week later, Skinner stopped the film and flipped on the lights. On the screen, the severed heads on the fence were still faintly visible.

"As you all know, some of those destined for correction camps have escaped our country." Skinner's face darkened. "The Western Seaboard's role in sheltering so many Discordants is abhorrent. When the time comes, we *must* ensure that they're recaptured so that they can face justice."

Kay kept her gaze from the heads as she added her agreeing murmur to the others. They'd been briefed on this: an upcoming Tier One Peacefight would soon give the Central States the right to extradite its fugitives from the Western Seaboard.

It was not a fight that was going to be left to chance.

A grey-haired astrologer named Francis spoke. "Are we certain that all the fugitives are Discordant? Perhaps some are just ordinary citizens who had reason to leave."

Skinner's eyes narrowed.

"Why do you ask, Frankie?" Plump Bernard Chester almost purred the words.

"Francis," said the old astrologer tightly.

"Oh, but I agree with our president that nicknames keep things friendly. Feel sorry for the fugitives, do you, Frankie? Or...perhaps you have something in common with them."

Pointedly, Bernard sketched on his notes a symbol they all recognized: the circle with the jagged line through it, the tip-off on family envelopes that someone was Discordant.

The grey-haired astrologer blanched; his gaze skittered to the mirror as if only now realizing what he'd said. "Certainly not!" he sputtered. "I'm as concerned about Harmony as anyone! I...I was only—"

Now, thought Kay, her heart beating hard.

"I don't think we need to worry about the fugitives, Mr Skinner," she broke in clearly. She opened her briefcase and took out charts she'd prepared the night before, angling them so that they were visible to the mirror.

"Look: I've cast the birth chart of Sandford Cain, who's going to be in charge of the new extradition law. Mars in the tenth house; very auspicious."

"We've already—" started Vivian.

"I've also done a chart for the fugitive extradition law itself," Kay continued over her. "And here's one showing the destiny of the Western Seaboard, where so many of the fugitives are escaping to."

She laid down chart after chart. "You see? They're all related. Look at Saturn in retrograde in the Western Seaboard chart. And see the Mars overtones in the other charts? In fact, if you look at *this* chart, where I've merged them all, you'll see that the trine aspects are—"

She spoke on, dazzling them with astrological proof that the fugitives had no chance. Linking the wildly disparate charts had been tricky, but the similarities she'd come up with seemed less tenuous if you spoke with confidence.

And she could. Kay had met with Sandford Cain several times now. She felt very safe in making such a strong prediction.

"We've infiltrated the resistance groups," Cain had told her, brandishing a batch of reports. "We have copies of all their lists. All. No matter what name someone's been hiding under, no matter how safe they might feel, we *will* track them down."

Then he'd smiled and rubbed the stylized claws on his ring. "And we'll enjoy doing it."

The fugitives' days were numbered, all right. Soon their heads would be joining those shown on the screen.

Now the room's silence was of the awed variety. Skinner craned to see Kay's charts. She obligingly slid copies across the table, resisting the urge to glance at the mirrored wall.

As Skinner studied her work, he began to smile. The other astrologers eyed her warily.

After the meeting, Skinner stopped Kay in the hallway. "Most impressive, Miss Pierce." His sallow face was practically beaming. "I'll show your work to Mr Gunnison."

"Thank you, sir." Kay's smile was humble. "And please...tell him that I can help find the best location for the troops, too."

At the next meeting, the grey-haired astrologer's chair was empty. No one ever mentioned him again.

Chapter Seventeen

"I'M SORRY THAT THERE ISN'T MORE," said my mother. She scraped the spoon fretfully around the almost empty bowl and shook another bite of mashed potatoes onto Collie's plate. "It's so hard to get what you want in the stores now – and if I'd only known you were *coming*..."

"Don't worry, there's plenty," Collie told her. "This is delicious, Rose."

We were sitting in Ma's cramped dining area: a corner of the living room with a table that folded out. I gazed at the mashed potatoes. If it was harder to get things in the stores now, it was my fault. The loss of our oil rights had hit the Western Seaboard even harder than I'd feared.

I shoved the thought away. I wouldn't let it ruin tonight.

"We wanted to surprise you," I told Ma.

"Well, you certainly did *that*."

"It was Collie's idea," I added gravely. He gave me a sidelong, amused look: that had been my refrain when we were growing up, to soften Ma's reaction to our escapades.

She probably didn't need softening this time. She hadn't stopped smiling since she'd opened her front door and seen us. She'd hugged Collie for the longest time, beaming through her tears. Collie hadn't looked completely dry-eyed himself.

"Well, I still don't understand," Hal said to Collie now, his voice flat. "Why couldn't you write once you left?"

Collie took another bite. "Like I said, I was angry – confused, I guess," he replied after a pause. "Dad had told me that I couldn't write to anyone back home; he wanted to make a fresh start. So I just...didn't. By the time I realized what a stupid mistake I'd made, so much time had passed that I thought you'd all hate me and I stayed quiet. I'm sorry," he added, talking directly to Ma now. "You all deserved better than that from me."

His eyes and voice were serious. I knew how much he meant the apology, even if the rest was untrue. We'd agreed not to tell them that Collie had been in the Central States. It could be dangerous for him if too many people found out.

Hal scowled down at his plate. "It's Amity you should apologize to," he muttered.

"He has, Hal. It's okay," I said, touched despite myself at my little brother sticking up for me.

Collie leaned his arms on the table. "No, you're right," he said to Hal. "I'm just lucky that your sister's forgiven me." Our eyes met, and my heart tightened a little. His expression turned questioning.

Ma, we've got something to tell you. The words stayed poised on my lips, refusing to come out. I hadn't mentioned about Collie and me in my letters home, though we'd been together for over a month. It just seemed too momentous, though really I guess it was very simple: *we're in love.* In person was no better. I thought of the fuss Ma would make when she knew and part of me turned ten years old again and wanted to slither down in my seat.

Collie's gaze became wryly amused; he knew exactly what I was thinking. I sighed and cleared my throat. "Ma, listen..."

She didn't hear me. "Tell us about being a Peacefighter," she said brightly to Collie. "You're Tier Three, aren't you?"

"No, Tier Two," said Collie after a beat.

"Oh, *Collis!*" exclaimed Ma, pressing a hand to her chest.

"You are?" said Hal at the same time. The sullen look that had been on his face since he'd seen Collie faded a little.

I nodded. "He was promoted just last week." My gaze met Collie's; the knowing look in his eyes was like being in his arms, warm in bed. I smiled. "He's pretty good."

It still amazed me that the Collis I'd grown up with had become this lean, broad-shouldered man whose changeable eyes knew me so well. For the last month, either Collie had stayed over at my place or I'd stayed at his. One night we'd gone skinny-dipping in the ocean; the tide was coming in and our clothes on the beach got drenched – the ones that didn't wash away.

I'd laughed so hard that I'd fallen down onto the sand. Collie had sprawled out next to me with a rueful grin.

"This isn't funny," he said. "I'm missing my trousers."

"Want to borrow my panties?"

"I *have* underwear. But—" He broke off, laughing too as he kissed me; his lips were wet and salty. "You're so beautiful," he whispered. "How did you get this beautiful, Amity Louise?"

"Even with sand in my hair?" I murmured between kisses.

"Even with sand here...and here...and here..."

"What are you smiling at?" asked Hal now.

I looked down and cleared my throat. "Nothing."

Later we all moved into the lounge area with coffee. Collie sat next to me on the sofa, one arm resting above my shoulders. Occasionally his fingers brushed the top of my arm, stroking it lightly and making me shiver.

Ma didn't notice. She sat in the armchair, talking on and on to Collie about people back in our old town.

He sounded genuinely interested, though I knew he couldn't care less. He'd always been so much better with Ma than I was – more patient, more giving. No wonder she adored him.

Hal lay on the floor reading a *Peace Power* comic. Finally he stood up. "Maybe I'll go read in bed."

"Just rest on top of the covers," Ma told him. "You'll be sleeping on the sofa tonight, dear, so that Collie can have your room. I've made up Hal's bed with fresh sheets," she added to Collie.

"Oh, Ma, no!" I burst out without thinking.

"No, what?" Her face was almost comically surprised.

"I mean…" I trailed off, cheeks reddening. "Well, Collie and I…"

"You *are* staying, aren't you? Amity, you can't possibly go back this late! I'm sure you must have missed the last train."

"Yes, of course we're staying."

"Well, then?"

I could see Collie's amusement, and wanted to punch his leg. "Collie will be in my room," I said.

Ma blinked. "*You* want to be on the sofa? Sweetie, don't be ridiculous."

"No!" I was almost laughing now: this could not have turned out more terribly. "Collie and I will be in my room together," I said at last.

Ma stared at us, her mouth a small, perfect "o".

Collie leaned forward; he took my hand and laced his fingers through mine. "Rose, I'll sleep wherever you want me to; this is your house," he said quietly. "But Amity and I…"

"We're in love, Ma," I blurted out. My cheeks were blazing now.

"Oh," murmured Ma. "*Oh!*"

The scene that followed was every bit as bad as I'd thought it would be…but maybe it was kind of nice, too, even if I didn't know whether to scowl or smile. Ma actually *cried*, and hugged us both.

"We're not getting *married*, Ma," I protested. I was holding a glass of sherry that she'd insisted on pouring for us. Even Hal had a glass.

"Not yet," Ma said firmly. "But it will happen. I know it. Oh, wait! I have just the thing—"

I opened my mouth to argue again as she bustled off into the kitchen. Collie put his arm around me. "Hey, she's right, you know," he whispered. His lips against my ear sent tingles up my spine; I could feel him smiling. "If you ever marry anyone, it's going to me."

"Suppose I don't want to get married?"

"Fine: if you ever live in sin with someone, it's going to be me."

I grinned sheepishly down at my drink. "Maybe you've got a point," I conceded.

Ma returned bearing a tin of fruitcake. Hal shook his head in amazement. "I wish you'd come home with news like this every day," he said to me. His cheeks were flushed from the drink. "We haven't had dessert in weeks."

"This isn't dessert," said Ma as she sliced it. "This is a celebration."

I went to bed before Collie, taking the newspaper with me and leaving him sitting up talking with Ma and Hal. The paper was all in a mess; Ma was terrible about folding it any which way. In my bedroom I got it neatened again and flapped the front page into place.

I froze.

The headline screamed:

GUNNISON WINS EXTRADITION DISPUTE
AGAINST WESTERN SEABOARD
CS Escapees Now Criminals

The words hit me in the stomach. I read quickly, gulping the story down. I read it twice and then bit my knuckle, staring out at a neon light blinking through the blinds. Inane thoughts whirled through my head. Which Tier One pilot had been defeated? Russ? What did it even matter?

Finally I heard the low murmur of Collie's goodnight. When he opened my bedroom door I jumped up. He stopped in his tracks, then shut the door behind him.

"What is it?" he asked.

"Look." I shoved the paper at him. My hand was trembling.

With a tense frown, Collie read it. "Oh," he said finally. He rubbed his jaw.

"'*Oh*'?" I repeated. My voice rose. "Collie, he can extradite you back to the Central States! It says—" I fumbled to find the place, then read aloud, "*The new law will target those CS citizens who have illegally fled their country, including but not limited to those known as the 'Discordant'.* You're a CS citizen; you *told* me so!"

"Not so loud," Collie said, glancing at the door. He sat us both on the bed and rubbed my arms. "Please don't worry. I'll be all right."

"How?" Fear made me snap the word. "Even the anonymity policy won't help you! It says no exceptions will be made!"

Collie took the paper from me and set it aside. "Look… I can't promise anything. But I have reason to believe that I'll be safe."

I went very still. "What reason?"

"Remember I told you that some people helped me get out of the CS?"

"You said they were people you wouldn't want to cross."

"And they're not – but the ones I actually dealt with in the Resistance were good guys. And part of what they did was to give me papers showing I've been in the Western Seaboard the whole time."

I stared at him. "Is that really true?"

"Of course it's true." When I didn't respond, Collie squeezed my fingers. "What?"

"I don't know," I said. "I'm just remembering the way you lied to Ma and Hal at dinner, with that exact same honest look in your eyes."

I was sorry the second I said it. Hurt flinched across Collie's face. "*Amity*. We agreed to that; you know why I did it! Why would I lie to you?"

"To make me feel better! To stop me from worrying!"

His jaw tensed. "Listen to me," he said. "Gunnison's regime doesn't know I exist any more. The Collis Reed who was in the CS has totally disappeared. That's the absolute truth, I promise."

I hesitated, longing to believe him. He cupped my cheek with one hand, his eyes intent on mine. "They told me that the Guns won't find out about me, and I trust them," he said quietly. "I'm not going anywhere, Amity. Nothing will ever stop me from being with you."

As I studied him, something inside me relaxed a notch, like a clock spring easing down. I felt shaky suddenly. I let out a breath and sagged down onto the bed. I put my face in my hands.

The bed springs creaked as Collie sat next to me. I felt him stroke my hair. "Amity?" he whispered.

For several seconds I couldn't speak. "You really don't have to keep me on my toes like this," I got out finally. "Letting myself love you in the first place was hard enough." I let my hands fall and wiped my eyes. "I need you...don't you know that?"

Collie's expression melted into understanding. He unbuttoned his shirt; his chest muscles flexed as he shrugged out of it. His trousers followed the shirt onto the floor.

"Come here," he said.

He pulled me into his arms and we held each other, pressed close under the covers of my single bed. Collie's skin was warm, his heartbeat steady against mine. The faint hum of traffic drifted in through the closed window.

"Remember Canary Cargo?" Collie said softly. "That's what we'll call our transport company."

I smiled drowsily. We'd talked about how we'd maybe buy a little island up in Puget someday, and fly transport to the surrounding towns. "Canary Cargo" was what I'd called my fantasy business as a child.

"Will we have a bright yellow plane?" I murmured.

Collie stroked my back slowly, rhythmically. "Of course. And when we have kids, we'll teach them to fly in it." He kissed my hair and whispered, "Everything's going to be perfect for us for ever...I'll make sure of it."

The next morning I woke up early. Collie lay on his side, holding me even in his sleep. I kissed his cheek and slipped out of bed. I pulled on my robe.

The apartment was silent as I went to the kitchen. I made coffee and sat at the tiny table, where I gazed out the window at Madame Josephine's sign and hated its blood-black swirls all over again. Everyone who thought they'd escaped Gunnison must be panicking over this new policy.

I idly sketched the shape of Collie's Leo tattoo on the table with my finger. *They'll go into hiding,* I thought. *Or try to get to a country that doesn't have an extradition law.*

And even apart from that, there was hardship. Travelling to Ma's from the station yesterday, I'd seen how much things had changed in the Western Seaboard already. Half the stores had signs saying *OUT OF STOCK* or *NO JOBS TODAY*. Next door to Ma's, the fruit seller's wooden display crates were empty. In dozens of places people had been standing in line, looking washed out even in the sunshine.

"Why doesn't Lopez do more?" I'd heard someone demand angrily on the streetcar to agreeing murmurs. Our president was an honest, intelligent man, though lacking in charisma. His eyes looked worried now whenever I saw him on the telio. The truth was, there wasn't much he *could* do.

There were no shortages back on base, which somehow made everything worse: Peacefighter pilots were subsidized by the WfP. I thought I'd almost rather go hungry. I'd stared out the streetcar window thinking, *All this, for five years – just because that one time I wasn't good enough.*

"Morning," said a voice, startling me out of my thoughts. Hal shuffled in, wearing striped pyjamas.

"Morning," I said. I sat up a little and took another sip of coffee. My job was to fight, not make the policies, I reminded myself. "You're up early," I added.

"Smelled the coffee," Hal said. "No breakfast yet?"

"Not unless you're cooking it."

He made a face and poured himself a cup. His dark hair was sticking up in back. He sat across from me and carefully added two sugars from the sugar bowl.

"So are you going to marry Collie?" he asked.

I shrugged. "Maybe someday."

"I bet you do."

"What do *you* care?"

Hal took a gulp of coffee. "Then Collie would really be my brother. It'd be pretty keen to have two Peacefighters in the family. Plus it might help *me* get in. When the time comes."

He looked so eager. I thought of Stan, shot down over the water. And of Vera. I heard her crying at night sometimes; she'd never gone to see Marcus like I'd urged her to.

After a pause, I said, "Hal, do you know what I had to do a few weeks ago?"

I told him about Concordia Winston. I didn't leave anything out. Not even the terrible red-black of her wound, or how her eyes had glazed over when she died.

"I wrote to her family like I promised," I finished. "But I didn't really know what to say."

Hal was pale. I knew we were both thinking of Dad. "Did you tell them she said she was sorry?"

"No," I admitted. "Just that she hadn't been in pain. But they wrote back to me – this whole long letter, telling me about her childhood and what she'd been like..." I fell silent, remembering: *We never had much money, but Cordy was always smiling, and tried to help out all she could.*

"They told me everything about her," I murmured. "And I was the one who killed her."

"You didn't! Her parachute—"

"It feels like it," I said shortly. "Hal, listen. Rumbles are fast, exciting – it's so worthwhile to be a Peacefighter like Dad. But you should know how hard it is before you decide."

Hal looked down and played with the sleeve of his pyjamas. "Have many of your friends died?"

"Enough. Too many."

"Are you afraid that Collie will?"

"Every day," I said. "I don't let myself think about it. You can't live that way."

He studied me with a thoughtful frown. "Does being a Peacefighter make you feel close to Dad?" he said finally.

My throat felt tight. "Yeah," I said. "It does."

"You never told me any of this before."

"I know. Maybe I liked having a place where nobody knew the whole truth. Anyway, don't tell Ma."

My brother's brown eyes were level. "I won't."

We heard her then, humming as she came down the hallway. Hal got to his feet and stretched, looking tall and gangly, and then surprised me by leaning down and kissing my cheek.

"Thanks, Sis," he said quietly.

Chapter Eighteen

Gunnison's street cleaners were out in full force. Kay passed a pair scrubbing the sidewalk and stepped daintily around them, her skirt swinging about her knees. The sun gleamed on her new Scorpio brooch: smaller than her old one, but pure gold. Whatever else Gunnison was, he certainly wasn't stingy to his employees.

Skinner appeared beside her on the sidewalk, matching her pace. "I have to talk to you," he said.

Kay gave him a sidelong glance. "You're still having me followed."

"I have everyone followed," he said impatiently. He took her arm and ushered her down the sidewalk.

They went to a cafe and sat in a dim corner under a

poster of Gunnison. Skinner ordered coffee for them both and sat tapping his fingers. Kay took in his tension. His eyes were hard, his mouth a thin line. With a mounting sense of dread, she realized that Malcolm Skinner was absolutely furious.

Kay's spine chilled. She still hadn't managed to reach Gunnison in person. Had she taken a wrong step, somehow? The severed heads on the chain-link fence flashed into her mind.

Their coffee arrived. Skinner grimly added a packet of sugar to his, then exactly half of a second pack. He folded the tiny packet closed: one, two, three folds.

"We should have listened to you," he said.

Kay was almost certain that she didn't show her relief. She took a sip of coffee.

"Oh?" she said.

Skinner opened his briefcase and took out a chart. He slapped it onto the table. "*This.*"

It took Kay a moment to recognize it, and then it all came back. A month ago, Skinner had asked to see her privately; he'd handed her a thick sheath of astrology charts.

"These are all the Tier One and Two Peacefighters," he'd said. "Most are unaware of the thrown fights, but we can't take any chances – we're at a crucial stage in the Twelve Year Plan. Tell me if any of them might be a danger to us."

Watching Skinner's reactions, Kay had sifted through the charts. The Grand Cross chart was there, and she'd felt a bolt of distaste for whoever that pilot was, for getting the burning plane down. Kay still felt sick when she recalled how worried she'd been over the appeal.

But the chart that most seemed to interest Skinner had been the chart of a Leo. Some of the charts were well-thumbed; this one looked crisp and new. A fresh copy of an old chart, perhaps?

Or a Leo who'd only recently made it into these ranks.

Finally Kay had decided. She'd laid down the Leo's chart, along with a few others. "Watch out for these pilots," she said. "They're a danger to the Central States."

Skinner had nodded slowly, and then indicated the pile she hadn't chosen. "We may need to approach some of these. Can they be trusted not to cause trouble?"

Well, you *seem to think so,* Kay had thought tensely. "As far as I can tell," she'd said aloud.

Now, in the cafe, Skinner jabbed at the Leo's chart with a furious finger.

"You were the only astrologer to choose this chart," he said. "He's been on our radar for a while, and I admit I had my suspicions, but since there was nothing else to indicate…well. We didn't do anything. And now, all I can say is that we regret it greatly."

Kay gave a quick prayer of thanks to the unknown Leo for whatever mistake he'd made. Or he could be one of the Discordant. That was certainly a hot-button issue with Skinner.

"What's he done?" she asked.

"Not important," snapped Skinner. "The important thing is: what now? How do we proceed?"

Kay hid her rush of triumph. Maybe she hadn't reached Gunnison yet, but she *must* be one of the top-ranked Twelve Year astrologers now. For unless she was greatly mistaken, Skinner had rushed to find her, and only her, the moment this stupid, wonderful pilot slipped up.

As for what to do with him…Skinner had given her the answer the second he slapped down the fool's chart.

Even so, Kay took out her pocket ephemeris and made a great show of casting a dual chart based on the Leo's time and date of birth and the current planetary positions over the next few days. Skinner watched intensely, his coffee growing cold.

Finally Kay laid down her pencil. "I'm afraid there's only one answer," she murmured. She allowed a fretful furrow to ridge her brow.

Skinner leaned forward. "What?"

Kay glanced around them. She lowered her voice:

"He's a threat to Harmony. Do away with him. Immediately."

Chapter Nineteen

THE LOCKER ROOM WAS CROWDED to the gills: everyone's fights had come up around the same time and now the room felt steamy, alive with bodies and shouts and locker doors clanging.

"Hey, Vancour!" Harlan appeared beside my locker just as I was fastening my brassiere. He leaned next to me, his chest bare. "You're still playing tonight, right?"

I nodded as I rubbed lotion into my skin. "Definitely."

"What about Collie?"

"As far as I know." I'd changed the photo tucked into my mirror to the one of me, Collie and Hal on my dad's plane. My gaze lingered on Collie's smile. He'd had a fight that afternoon and wasn't back yet. I closed a lid firmly on the thought and put my lotion away.

Harlan yanked on a T-shirt. "Good, though I could do without how lucky Collie-boy is. Clem's probably still sobbing into his beer over that last IOU he had to sign."

"He'll get a chance to win it back."

"This *is* Clem we're talking about. He'll lose the shirt off his back next. No, wait, he's already lost that."

"His shoes?" I suggested.

"I can hear you, you louses," shouted Clem from the next row over.

Harlan grinned and banged his fist on the lockers. "Can you hear that, too?" he bellowed. He winked at me and said loudly, "Yeah, I hear that ol' Clem's gotten so desperate, he's even lost the shirt off his *fitter's* back."

"Slander!" called Clem.

I laughed. "Maybe we should ask Edwards and get the truth."

Clem appeared around the row of lockers, tucking his shirt tails in. "Who?"

"*Edwards.* Your fitter."

"You been sneaking shots of Harlan's rotgut?"

I frowned. "You're T3, right? Edwards used to be my fitter, now he's yours. Come on, don't you even know your fitter's name?"

"He lost it when he lost the guy's shirt," said Harlan cheerfully.

"Nah, my fitter's Rivera." Clem nodded at someone

behind me. "And he *has* a shirt, I'll have you know, unlike Mr Lucky over there."

I glanced up quickly as Clem withdrew to his own locker row. The confusion over Edwards faded in my surge of relief that Collie was down and safe. He was heading towards us wearing a white towel around his waist, his hair and chest damp.

"Hey, gorgeous," he murmured as he reached me. He dumped his flight gear on the bench and scooped me into a hug that lifted me off the floor. I laughed at the wet-skinned enthusiasm of him. We didn't usually touch in the locker room.

"You won your fight," I guessed. "So did I."

"I know; I saw on the board. Listen, Amity Louise, find something amazing to wear. I'm taking you out tonight."

Harlan straightened, glowering. "What? You are not. Unless by 'taking you out' you mean 'going to Harlan's to play poker'."

"Nope," said Collie. "It's a special night, and I'm going to take my best girl out."

Harlan wrinkled his nose at me. "That's not a *girl*," he said. "That's a pilot."

"Fine, I'm taking my best pilot out."

I spread my arms. "You heard the man."

Harlan shook his head as Collie started getting dressed. "You two are wreaking havoc on my poker game." He pointed at me. "Tomorrow night." It sounded like a curse.

"We'll be there." Once he'd gone I glanced at Collie. "Why is this a special night?"

"Patience," he said. He gave me a teasing look as he fastened his trousers. "We'll go dancing, how does that sound? I know just the place; you're going to love it. And champagne – oh yeah, this is a champagne night."

Ignoring the busy locker room, I stepped over the bench and grabbed his arm. "All right, *tell* me!" I laughed.

"Do we really need a reason? We both won our fights… spring's coming…and today we've been together for two months."

His words hung in the air, deliberately casual. A smile grew across my face. "We have?"

Collie's mouth twitched. "You know how they say there's always one person in a relationship who's more romantic than the other one…?"

"All right, so I wouldn't have known. I'm a terrible girlfriend."

"The worst," said Collie sadly. He ducked his head and kissed me. "But I guess that's just my lot to bear."

That night everything that had been on my mind – all the troubles in the Western Seaboard – melted away.

The dance floor of The Ivy Room seemed to spin gently as Collie held me close, moving us in time to the music. The place had low, rosy lighting; on each table a candle flickered in a glass bowl, like captured fireflies.

"*Love me in May...oh, please say you'll stay...*" Van Wheeler himself was singing. The famous crooner swayed dreamily, clutching the mic stand. He and his orchestra all wore tuxedos.

None were as handsome as Collie in his rented tux. I didn't look bad either: my knee-length black dress had a full skirt and a sleek, strapless bodice; a pair of rhinestone combs glittered against my dark hair. An orchid from Collie was pinned to my chest – the first flower anyone had ever given me.

"Where did you learn to dance so well?" I murmured against his neck.

His lips brushed my temple. "In the CS," he said. "There was a youth club; it was almost the only thing I was allowed to do. Dad thought it would look good."

"I can't imagine him caring."

"Things are different there," Collie said shortly. "Everyone worries about appearances. You have to."

I studied the set of his jaw. I could count on one hand how often he'd volunteered information about his life in the Central States. That time he'd told me about the Discordant girl on his street had been the most he'd ever said.

A woman danced past wearing a glittering Taurus brooch. At the sight of it, I started to ask Collie another question about the CS. The music changed to a quick, Latin beat.

His face split into a grin. "Hey, do you know this?"

He put his hands on my hips, showing me the exotic rhythm. I laughed when he spun me, glad that fate had intervened to keep me quiet.

Finally Collie got us two more glasses of champagne. We wove through the crowded room towards a table. My orchid was wilting, and one of my combs was coming undone. I didn't care. I felt happy, loose.

"I could dance all night!" I said, leaning towards Collie to be heard.

"That's the idea." He put his arm around my waist. "More champagne first, and then—" He broke off. Following his gaze, I saw three men talking near the dance floor. One stood much shorter than the other two, though what struck me most was his air of confidence.

The short one turned; he grinned when he saw us and started over. Collie looked slightly taken aback, then he smiled, too.

"It's a guy I knew in training school," he said to me. "I haven't seen him in months."

"Collis! Hey, pal – I thought that was you!" laughed the man when he reached us.

"Jones – hey!" said Collie.

They shook hands. Jones was a little older than Collie, with unruly brown hair and intelligent eyes. He looked me up and down and waggled his eyebrows. "Who's the dish?"

Collie's mouth quirked. "Do you mind? The dish is spoken for."

I stuck out my hand. "Amity Vancour."

We shook. "Mac Jones," he said cheerfully. "Nice to make your acquaintance. You meet our oh-so-charming friend here in the Heat?"

I laughed, still buzzing from the dancing and the champagne. "No, Collie and I grew up together."

"'Collie'?" Mac repeated. He grinned. "Nice – I like that."

"Yeah, but only my friends can call me that," said Collie.

Mac play-punched him. "Everyone's your friend, buddy-boy. Hey, remember that time—"

They reminisced about training school for a few minutes, with people jostling around us. It sounded like it was just as tough as when I'd gone through. Collie kept his hand on my back, gently caressing it.

"So how are things with Greta?" he asked.

Mac winced and scratched the back of his neck. "Ah – not so good, actually. In fact, I wouldn't mind grabbing a quick drink and telling you about it..." He trailed off with a glance at me.

"Well..." Collie's forehead creased as he looked at me, too.

I squelched my slight annoyance and waved a hand. "Go on. It's fine."

Collie rolled his eyes. "No, it's not, actually," he said to Mac. "We're on a date, you lummox, if you haven't noticed."

"Really, it's all right," I said.

Collie hesitated and then drew me aside. "Amity, are you sure? He just has girlfriend trouble, that's all. I feel like a heel."

I wrapped my arms around his neck. "Only for one drink. Then we're going to dance the night away as promised."

Collie glanced back at Mac. "All right, deal," he said finally. He kissed me, then touched my cheek as if he couldn't help himself. He trailed his fingers down it slowly. At the look in his eyes, my heart quickened.

He gave a lopsided smile and let his hand fall. "I won't be long," he said.

Chapter Twenty

At first I didn't mind sitting at a table on my own and watching the dancers, all moving to the music as if it were controlling their heartbeats. But after a few songs I started feeling restless. Thoughts I'd been avoiding all night crept in.

In the month since Collie and I had visited Ma, things in the Western Seaboard had gotten steadily worse. I read the papers compulsively, hating what I was finding out.

Breadlines were longer, jobs scarcer. Up north, where it was cold this time of year, lots of people couldn't afford heating. In some places there wasn't enough fuel for it. The government had set up relief programmes for food and shelter – but resources were so limited they didn't do much good.

Each time President Lopez appeared on the telio he looked older and more defeated. "We *will* get through this crisis," he kept saying.

Are you and Ma all right? I'd written to Hal, knowing Ma would pretend everything was fine, even though our old place in Gloversdale hadn't had any tenants for months. She was trying not to sell – to hang onto it for me and Hal.

My brother had replied that they were getting by: "Ma says she has a little put away." It was news to me. I sent as much money as I could, wishing it was more.

You'd think that with times so hard, all that occult guff would be the first thing to go. Instead the WS had gone crazy for astrology. Practitioners were springing up like poisonous mushrooms. I grimaced, recalling that envelope at Ma's with *Vancour Family* on it. Even in the Heat now you could find the astrologers' stark red-and-black symbol.

Maybe it would have been a craze anyway, but it felt like another outcome of my failed fight. Far worse, Gunnison's men had started entering the Western Seaboard to seize escaped CS citizens. The papers hinted that they had long lists of names, locations. I still hadn't gotten over my fear that Collie might be discovered, despite how he'd tried to put my mind at ease that night at Ma's.

I sighed. Both of us had needed this night out. I wanted to be enjoying it, not still sitting on my own.

I finished my drink. When I glanced across the room Collie and Mac were still sitting at another table talking. I made a face and looked down at my empty glass, tapping it on the table.

"If I give you more champagne, will you let me sit here?" said a voice.

I looked up. A tall guy of maybe twenty or so had appeared; he had a riot of crisp black curls and dark eyes. He held up one of the glasses of champagne he was holding and raised an eyebrow.

I shook my head. "Thanks, but I've got a boyfriend."

"And I've got a girlfriend. Who I've been abandoned by –" the guy nodded at a table where a group of girls sat talking – "while you seem to have been abandoned by your boyfriend. And there are no other seats. So." He put a glass of champagne in front of me and sat down, leaving an empty chair between us.

"I didn't say yes," I said.

"Yes, I heard you not say yes." He stretched out his long legs, gazing moodily at the girls' table. "I don't actually need your permission. I was only asking to be nice." Then he glanced at me; after a beat, the corner of his mouth twisted.

"I'm harmless," he said.

I sighed. "Fine." I toasted him with the champagne glass. "Cheers," I said. We clinked glasses and drank without speaking. The music changed to a foxtrot, then a rumba. My new acquaintance seemed lost in his own thoughts, drumming his fingers on the table.

Finally he leaned towards me. "So what's your name?"

"Amity. What's yours?"

"Ingo."

"What?"

"Een-go," he repeated. "You've heard the name Inga? Ingo is the male form. Germanic."

"Oh. I didn't realize you were foreign," I said.

He gave me a look that was just this side of patient. "We're all foreign," he said. "The Heat's neutral territory."

I was already cringing. "Sorry. I meant that I didn't realize you weren't from one of the Americas. You speak very good English."

Ingo leaned back with one arm hooked over the back of his chair; his tie hung undone around an open collar. "My mother's from New Manhattan," he said. "I went to school there for a while."

"But you're from the European Alliance?"

"Yes – Germanic Counties, down near the Med. You?"

"Western Seaboard."

"Ah, one of the lucky ones," he said dryly. "Put your toe across the neutral border and you're home."

I think it struck us both at the same moment. "You're a pilot," I said.

"And I think you are, too," he said, narrowing his eyes. "You have that way about you."

"What way?"

He shrugged. "Oh, you know. Like you may be here in a fancy club in a pretty dress, but you'd be happier in a cockpit at ten thousand feet. Shooting the hell out of some other pilot, preferably."

I had to smile slightly. If I had that way about me, so did Ingo. I'd never seen anyone look so uncomfortable in a tux. Even with his tie undone, he kept tugging at his collar.

"We're opposing pilots. We shouldn't really be talking," I said.

Ingo didn't look concerned. "They can't put us all together in this place and expect that we'll never meet – all that matters is whether we can still do our jobs tomorrow. I can. Can you?"

"Of course," I said.

He smiled then. "Yes, I can believe it. You have lethal eyes."

I raised an eyebrow. "Is that a line?"

"No, I mean it. You look as if any choice you had to make, you'd take it with no hesitation…" He trailed off then, looking intently at me. His expression slackened slightly; he said something in Germanic under his breath.

"What?"

"You're *her.* You're the mad pilot!"

"Mad?"

"Insane. Crazy." He was grinning now. He moved into the empty seat beside me. "You can't have forgotten. Unless you do that sort of thing every day? You're Second Tier, yes? I shot you down, and your plane was on fire, and you *didn't bail.* You *landed* the damn thing!"

I stared at him, remembering the pilot who'd cruised along beside me, shouting at me to bail. Dark, curly hair. The glimpse of brown eyes I'd gotten from behind the goggles.

"You're *him*," I said.

Ingo laughed. "I thought I was about to have a kill – believe me, I was cursing you for it. Why did you do it? No, wait, let me toast you first." He clinked his glass against mine again. "You are an excellent pilot, you know."

"So are you," I admitted. "Whenever I recognize your flying, I know it's going to be a good fight. I mean, *hard*, but good."

"Yes, same for me." Ingo's face was alive now, all signs of moodiness gone. "I never know what you're going to do next. All right, now tell me – why didn't you bail that day?"

"How could I?" I looked bitterly down at my champagne glass. "Have you seen the Western Seaboard's losses recently?"

"Ah," he said. "So you're one of those. The ones who read the papers," he added at my uncomprehending look.

"Don't you?" I don't know why I said that. Yet for some reason I wasn't really surprised when Ingo nodded.

"Yes, of course, when I have the stomach for it. Not every day. But I have to know what my own fights were about. The EA hasn't been doing so well, either, you know," he went on with a frown. "That win against you was the first big one for a long time."

"Why was there a rematch, do you know?" I found myself leaning towards him intently. "What was wrong with the first fight – the one where I *did* beat you?"

Ingo shook his head. "I don't know. The writing is so flowery sometimes in our papers—"

"Ours too; I *hate* it."

"Oh, me too. But the best I could make out was that it was some irregularity to do with the original claim. Not the fight itself."

"A loophole, then," I said.

He lifted a shoulder. "There will always be. Our job is just to fight, and keep the world from destroying itself."

A silence fell between us then, though not an uncomfortable one. We sat drinking our champagne. On the bandstand, Van Wheeler was still crooning. *The stars in your eyes…can tell me no lies….*

"How did you get to be a Peacefighter?" I asked finally.

Ingo gave me a wry look. "The same as you, I'm sure. We don't want to have small talk, do we?"

"It doesn't really feel like small talk this time," I said. "But I know what you mean. I hate it, usually."

"I don't do it very well," said Ingo with a reckless smile. "I am extremely rude. If you haven't noticed."

"I noticed. So are you going to tell me, or not?"

Ingo gazed across at the dance floor; something flickered behind his dark eyes. "All right," he said finally. "I became a Peacefighter because I wanted it more than anything. You?"

"The same," I said after a pause.

He regarded me. His lean face was full of angles; his black curls framed it like a lion's mane. "I think you are telling me the truth...but that there's more to it than that," he said.

"Really? Because that's what I think about you, too," I said.

Ingo shrugged. "Fine, so we're both right. Shall we talk about something more interesting? Which one is your boyfriend? No, I'll guess." He twisted in his seat and scanned the room. "That one," he said, pointing at an old man with pink skin and a bald, gleaming head.

"How did you know?"

"I can tell from here. It's true love."

"No, that one, actually." I motioned to Collie.

Ingo looked across at the table. "Which one?"

"The tall one with the blond-ish hair."

A waiter appeared at their table and put fresh drinks on it. Collie didn't look up from whatever Mac was saying. I sighed inwardly, wishing I hadn't told him this was okay.

Ingo shook his head, gazing over at him. "This is insane," he said. "My girlfriend is talking to other girls, your boyfriend is talking to another man – and here we both sit, alone together. Do you think there's something wrong with us?"

"Which one's your girlfriend? No, *I'll* guess." I examined the table of girls. One, a small, vivacious blonde, tipped her head back as she laughed.

"The blonde?"

Ingo's expression turned complicated as he studied her. "Her name is Miriam," he said at last.

"She's very beautiful."

"Yes." Ingo didn't seem to want to talk about it. Abruptly, he rose and held his hand out to me. "Come on," he said. "Let's dance. I can make her jealous, and you can make your boyfriend jealous."

When I hesitated, he grinned and waggled his fingers. "You must confess it's appealing."

"What's appealing is the thought of dancing," I admitted; the music was tugging at me. "All right – let's."

Ingo wasn't the dancer Collie was. He held me too carefully, and I could tell it was only through force of will that he wasn't studying his feet. But I enjoyed it. Dancing with Collie kept me on edge; the touch of his hand was electric. Dancing with Ingo just felt comfortable, as if I'd known him a long time. I smiled at the contradiction.

"You're laughing at my dancing," Ingo said gloomily. "I don't blame you."

I shook my head, my hand on his shoulder as we moved. Ingo was as tall as Collie, but thinner. When I explained what I'd been thinking he laughed. "*Comfortable?* Fine, so my attempts at seduction are a bust."

"Is that what you're attempting? I don't think you're doing it right."

Ingo gave a bitter shrug; his smile faded. "No. That blonde witch over there has my heart, I'm afraid."

I didn't know what to say. I glanced back at the girls' table. Miriam saw us and gave a cheerful wave. She blew Ingo a kiss before turning back to her friends.

"Very jealous, as you can see," Ingo said dryly.

"Well, I don't think my boyfriend's even noticed, so you're ahead on that score," I said. Collie was still talking, his back to the dance floor. To my irritation, two other men had joined their table now.

The music changed. Ingo stopped in his tracks suddenly; he held me away from him and gave me a considering, up-and-down look. "You know, you're prettier than I expected," he announced.

I burst out laughing. "Your line's improving."

He grinned as we started dancing again. "All right, that was bad even for me. But you keep shooting me down, damn you. Whenever I imagined you, it was always as some...hag of the air."

"Seduction straight ahead, definitely."

"I'm not trying for that. I'm just telling you a fact." After a pause, Ingo added, "I was sorry when you lost your appeal."

My voice turned short. "Don't be ridiculous. Of course you weren't."

"All right, I was glad for the EA, but..." Ingo made a face as we moved to the music. "Well, we both know it was just your bad luck that your plane went down."

"Not bad luck. You got my air bottle."

"I did?" He smiled then. "Ah, so that's why you stopped

firing. Well, that was clever of me. I wasn't sure whether I'd hit you at all up till then."

I grimaced, remembering the bullet holes. "Oh, you hit me, all right."

"Good. I can take more satisfaction in the win now."

"How much more satisfaction do you want? You shot me down."

"You know what I mean." Ingo studied me, his angular face thoughtful. "Don't you? I think we're very much the same when it comes to flying – even if you're crazy. I followed you down, you know. Shouting at you to bail the whole way."

I thought of Concordia and my throat tightened. "Yes," I said. "I know exactly how you felt."

"Ah," Ingo said softly. "I'm sorry to hear that."

We danced in silence for a while. When the music changed to another romantic number, I glanced over at Collie's table, ready to go drag him away if I had to. My steps slowed abruptly.

The table stood empty. Two couples were just sitting down at it, laughing, the guys holding the chairs out for the girls.

"What is it?" asked Ingo.

"I don't believe it – my boyfriend's gone!" I left the dance floor with Ingo behind me; I scanned the crowd as I went. No sign of Collie. "But I don't understand," I said blankly. "He wouldn't just leave."

"Shall I check the men's room for you?" said Ingo. "What's his name?"

"Collis."

"I'll be right back."

While he was gone I did a quick circuit of the club, even stepping out onto the balcony. There was no Collie anywhere. I couldn't see Mac, either. "*What* is going on?" I muttered. *Had* Collie left? Maybe he'd been having a better time with Mac than I'd thought.

But he wouldn't leave without telling me.

As I went back into the main room, I ran into Ingo. "No, he's not in there," he said. "Would he have stepped outside for a cigarette?"

"He doesn't smoke."

Ingo gave a rueful smile. "Maybe we succeeded too much in making him jealous."

Irritation lashed at me. "He wouldn't be jealous," I snapped. "And he wouldn't just leave."

Ingo raised a dark eyebrow and leaned a shoulder against the wall. "Oh? He appears to have done just that."

"Yes, thanks for pointing it out. I'd better go try and find him." I started to leave, then remembered to say, "Thank you for the champagne. And the dancing."

"Wait." Ingo straightened as I started from the room. "Are you just going to wander around the Heat?"

Remembering the stories of Gunnison's men dragging CS citizens away, fear was starting to curl inside me. "I don't know," I said tersely. "I'll look around a few places nearby, I guess."

"I'll come with you," said Ingo.

"Don't bother."

Ingo glanced over at his girlfriend's table. His eyes hardened. "I might as well," he said. "Besides, you wouldn't mind having company, would you? It can be a lonely business, searching."

He said it like he knew.

"Fine," I said finally. "Come on, if you want."

Chapter Twenty-one

I COULDN'T GET MY COAT back from the coat-check girl because Collie, wherever he was, still had the ticket. It didn't matter; my anxiety over Collie was keeping me warm enough on its own. Ingo and I went up and down the different streets, looking into clubs and bars.

In a smoky Parisian speak, a trio of EA pilots greeted Ingo enthusiastically. "It's Friday night!" cried one. "Why aren't you here with us?"

They lapsed into speaking Euro; I heard "*Por que el fraulien, jah?*" as one threw me a teasing glance.

"*Jah*," Ingo said shortly.

"What were they saying?" I asked after we left.

He shrugged. "That Miriam would be upset if she

knew about you. A lot they know."

The glow of the street lights pooled at our feet. We passed a club that had been built over ruins, with a section of ancient wall left in place for effect. The grey rubble looked stark, depressing – though not as depressing as the astrologer's sign nearby. Its red-and-black Harmony symbol blinked on and off against the ruins.

As Ingo and I walked in silence, I rubbed my bare arms. My chest felt very exposed.

He glanced at me, his hands in his pockets. "I wish you'd take my jacket," he said. He'd already offered it twice.

"I don't want it."

"I feel like a louse."

"Well, you told me yourself you're extremely rude."

Ingo gave me a look. "All right, how about some coffee?" he said. There was a French-style bistro in front of us, with tables out on the street. "We can keep an eye out in case he passes."

It seemed a better idea than trying random places – and The Ivy Room was only a few doors down. I'd be able to spot Collie if he went back in. We sat down and ordered cappuccinos. When they arrived, Ingo tipped sugar into his.

"I still can't understand it," I muttered, warming my hands around the mug. I gazed over at The Ivy Room, hoping that my worry was ridiculous. "Tonight was supposed to be a celebration."

Ingo snorted.

I stared at him. "What?"

He shook his head. "Sorry. It's just that Miri and I were celebrating, too. So maybe it's not a good night for it."

"What were you celebrating?"

He looked down, stirring his coffee. Finally his mouth twisted. "All right, I'll tell you. Today was my peak day."

A Peacefighter's peak day was a big deal, as everyone in this complex knew. He'd made it halfway through his three-year term. Pilots threw wild parties for this, caroused all night.

I went silent, thinking of Miriam at the table of chattering girls. "Did you have an argument, or—"

"No." His tone cut off further questions.

"Congratulations," I said after a pause. "Sorry. I should have said that instead of anything else. I can be pretty rude too, sometimes."

"Yes – you're appalling." Ingo studied me with a small smile, the cafe lights glinting off his dark curls. "You know, if you didn't have a missing boyfriend, and I didn't have a neglectful girlfriend…"

I looked over at The Ivy Room as a crowd headed inside. No Collie. "Skip it," I told Ingo absently. "You wouldn't get anywhere with me anyway."

"Probably not. Story of my life."

I couldn't tell if he was kidding. After a pause, I glanced back over at him. "Is Miriam a pilot?"

He gave a bark of laughter, and I raised an eyebrow.

"What's so funny? I wouldn't have pegged you as one of those people who think women shouldn't fly."

"I think *you* shouldn't, the number of times you've shot me down," he said. "Women like you should definitely not be flying. You're a menace."

"What, then?"

"Miriam would never have the patience to learn to be a pilot."

"She sounds charming." The words were out before I could stop them.

"Oh, believe me, she is."

I thought of the slim perfection of Miriam's throat, her sleek hairdo. "What's she doing here in the Heat? I can't imagine her working in one of the restaurants."

"Her father's a WfP official." Ingo gave me a keen look. "Is it my turn now to ask about the esteemed Collis? For instance, why would he leave you alone in that club with wolves like me around?"

Yes, why would he? I shrugged, hiding my growing anxiety. "Are you a wolf? You're not acting very wolflike."

"I'm not trying."

"Anyway, I can take care of myself."

"I'm sure you can. But that doesn't answer the question."

The street was having one of those odd pockets of quiet that come sometimes in the Heat at late hours. We were the last two people at the cafe; inside, the waiters leaned against the bar talking.

I stared over at The Ivy Room and rubbed my bare

arms again. *Collie, where are you?* Unwelcome thoughts had started pounding through me…thoughts about what Collie might have done to escape the CS, and those two other men who had appeared at his and Mac's table. I shivered.

Ingo pulled off his tux jacket. "Here," he said, tossing it onto my lap. "Don't argue."

I sighed and drew it around my shoulders. "Thanks."

"So what were you and Collis celebrating tonight?" When I hesitated, Ingo raised a black eyebrow. "I told you mine," he said.

His jacket smelled of some exotic cologne; there was a slight bulge in one pocket. I investigated and found a soft, folded handkerchief. "It's our two-month anniversary," I said finally. "But I've known him all my life."

Ingo's smile did look wolfish now. "So it *is* true love. How nice."

"Just like you and Miriam," I snapped. "And yes, it is, actually." Ingo inclined his head in a *touché* gesture. I was starting to wonder why I'd liked talking to him in the first place.

Before he could say anything else, gunfire rang out.

One shot.

Two more.

Then silence.

My eyes met Ingo's in a startled clash. I leaped up and bolted towards the sound of the shots, with Ingo right behind me. The street was almost empty. A pair of men came tearing from an alleyway and went running past The Ivy Room. I caught a blurred glimpse of curly hair; a bald head.

I plunged into the alley and stopped short.

Light fell from a window above. In its faint glow I saw my team leader, lying sprawled in a widening pool of blood.

"*Russ!*" I ran to him and dropped to my knees.

He wore the same pinstriped suit he'd worn to my appeal. His fedora rested beside his outstretched hand. His torso was a dark, soggy mess.

No. *No.* I gripped his lapels, frantic, almost shaking him. "*Russ!* Please say something! It's me, Amity!"

Incredibly, Russ's head moved. He blinked as he struggled to focus on me. A drop of red bubbled at his mouth. "I shot it," he muttered thickly. "Amity...I shot it..."

"*What?*" I could hardly hear what he was saying. "Russ!"

With a ragged sigh, his head slumped. His brown eyes grew dull.

He didn't speak again.

Ingo kneeled beside me, looking grim. "You knew him?"

In slow motion I let go of Russ's lapels and sank back. "My...my team leader."

A low, steady drumbeat had started in my head. Russ's blood looked so dark, so glistening. Like my father's. Like Concordia's. Why did all broken bodies look the same?

"This man was a *pilot*?" Ingo said.

"Yes," I replied shortly.

"Well, someone didn't like him much." Ingo took my arm. "Come. We have to find the police—" He broke off. "What the hell are you doing?"

I was going through Russ's pockets. I knew I wasn't acting rationally, that I must be in shock, but I felt taut with clarity. My fingers scrabbled into the pockets one after the other.

Nothing. Then I touched a small, slim square and quickly drew it out. I angled it towards the dim light, but couldn't see details – a packet of some sort. I shoved it into the pocket of Ingo's jacket, still around my shoulders.

Ingo's eyes were as black as the alley's shadows. "You *are* insane," he hissed.

"Someone's just killed him. I want to know why," I said.

"Are you sure you don't want his watch as well?"

"I wasn't trying to rob him!"

"The police will—"

"*Amity!*"

I leaped to my feet as Collie appeared at the mouth of the alley, his blond hair rumpled. He stopped short, gaping at Russ's lifeless form. "What happened?"

Suddenly I was shaking. I rushed to him and we hugged tightly. "Where have you *been*?" I cried.

"Looking for you!" Collie gasped. He swore as he dropped beside Russ and felt for a pulse that wasn't there. Slowly, he let go of Russ's wrist, his face pale. "But who…?"

"I don't know! We saw two men, but I didn't really get a good look. Did you?" I added to Ingo, and he shook his head.

Collie tore his gaze from Russ. "Who's this?"

Now that Collie was here safe in front of me, I knew just how deep my fear had been. "He's no one!" I snapped. "Just some guy I met. We were having coffee and heard the shots—"

The sound of sirens interrupted me. Autos with curved, grilled fronts and long gleaming hoods screeched to a halt in front of the alleyway, their headlights flooding the passage with light. Two pairs of policemen swarmed in – asking questions, searching Russ's body. It turned out the cafe waiters had heard the shots and called them.

A crowd had gathered outside the alley – mostly from The Ivy Room, judging by their clothes. One of the cops wrote down what I told him about the two men. "So you heard the victim say something, miss?"

I swallowed. "I'm not sure what. It sounded like 'I shot it'. Or maybe 'I shot *at*'..." Though I was trying not to look, I could see Russ's hand lying on the ground, palm up, dark fingers curled.

The policeman scribbled. "Sure he didn't say 'I *was* shot'?"

I gripped my arms tightly. "I don't know. Maybe."

"Ingo Manfred," Ingo was saying to another policeman. His lean face looked tense. "A pilot for the European Alliance."

"How do you know Miss Vancour?"

"I don't. We met at The Ivy Room and had a coffee together, then we heard the shots. That's it." His eyes didn't meet mine. I licked my lips. I'd been positive that he'd mention me rifling through Russ's clothes. The fact that I'd done so felt like temporary insanity now.

The small, flat packet was still nestled in my borrowed pocket. Several times I'd opened my mouth to admit what I'd done and hand it over; each time the words wouldn't come.

And each time they didn't, I knew I was digging myself in deeper, until it would be impossible to mention it at all.

My hands felt sticky. I glanced down and saw Russ's blood smeared across my skin. Collie saw my expression and quickly put his arm around me, steadying me.

"You okay?" he whispered.

"Fine," I got out. Russ lay staring up at the stars. I took a shuddering breath. "Who would do this? *Why?*"

Collie looked shaken. "I have no idea. It doesn't make any sense." After a pause he shrugged out of his tuxedo jacket. "Here," he said softly, offering it to me. "You can give that guy his jacket back."

I pulled Ingo's lapels more securely around me. "No, that's all right...I'm really cold."

Collie always knew when I was lying. He frowned, though he didn't call me on it; the ambulance had just arrived. The glittering crowd parted as men with a stretcher appeared and checked Russ's vital signs. His body was limp, unresisting.

How's my favourite wildcat?

I swallowed hard and turned away as they lifted him onto the stretcher, my eyes prickling. When I could look again, someone had pulled a sheet over his head. He was carried from the alleyway.

"Robbery, that's my guess," I heard a policeman mutter to the others. "His wallet was stolen. Big guy like him, he probably tried to resist."

Ingo heard, too. I saw him give me a look. Whatever was in my borrowed pocket felt pointless suddenly. It was true; there had been no wallet. Russ had simply been robbed.

But what was it he'd tried to say to me?

The police let us go soon after that. "We'll be in touch if we have any other questions," the first cop said. "Thanks for your cooperation."

"All right, people, break it up!" called one of his colleagues, clapping his hands. "Nothing more to see – move along."

The crowd reluctantly dispersed. Collie, Ingo and I left the alley and started back towards The Ivy Room. Collie's hand rested protectively on my back. "All right, what's going on that you're not telling me?" he said in a low voice.

I swallowed and stared down at my bloody palms. "I've got to wash my hands," I said. "And get my coat."

A few minutes later I stood in the gleaming restroom of the club, watching pink water swirl down the plughole as I scrubbed my hands again and again. Even when they were clean, I could still feel Russ's blood. Then I went into one of the cubicles and took out what I'd found in his pocket.

It was only a matchbook. I stared down at it, feeling blank with dismay. I opened it, turned it over. Nothing unusual – though its shamrock design looked a little familiar. Slowly, I put it in my coat pocket, wondering why I was bothering to keep it.

All at once I felt exhausted. When I emerged from the restroom, Collie and Ingo stood waiting in the lobby.

"Here," I said as I handed Ingo's jacket back. Upstairs, dance music still played, thrumming around us. "I'm sorry that I got blood on it," I said. "I'll pay for it to be cleaned if you send me the bill."

"Don't be stupid," Ingo said shortly. He checked the jacket's pockets and gave me a wry look. "As I'm sure you know, that's the least of my concerns tonight."

"It...wasn't anything important," I said. "Just a matchbook."

"How comforting."

Collie's gaze was intent. "Amity, *what* is going on?"

I hesitated. "Not here."

Ingo snorted. "Well. I'd say it has been a pleasure, but..."

"Thank you for not saying anything," I said to him.

"For being a fool, you mean? I'm not thanking myself, I assure you." Without another word, Ingo turned and went up the stairs that led to the main dance hall. Miriam might still be there, I remembered. And it was after midnight now – it wasn't Ingo's peak day any more.

It probably hadn't felt like much of a high point.

"I can't believe you took it without even knowing what it was." Collie stood in his bedroom staring at me. I could hear Wayne, his housemate, snoring through the wall.

I sank down onto the bed. It felt as if The Ivy Room, the dancing, had happened in another lifetime.

"I know," I said. "It was stupid."

"The police were *right there*, Amity! If they'd seen you, they might have—"

"Suspected me in Russ's murder," I said softly. "Yes. I realize that."

Collie started to say something else, then stopped. He pinched the bridge of his nose. "All right," he said finally. "Let's forget it." He sat beside me and put his arm around my shoulders. Though I wanted to be comforted I found myself pulling away, unable to relax.

The matchbook with the shamrock cover lay on the bedside table. I picked it up and stared down at it. Shamrocks were supposed to be lucky.

A smudge of red stained one corner.

Collie took the matchbook from me and placed it back on the table. His voice was hoarse. "Look...it's been a terrible night. Let's just go to bed, all right?"

I barely heard him. All I could see was Russ lying in his own blood, shot for whatever money he'd been carrying.

"Amity…"

I looked at him. For a second it was as if I'd never seen him before. "Where were you?" I asked, remembering suddenly. "I was on the dance floor, and when I glanced over, you'd gone."

Collie's eyebrows rose. "You were dancing with that guy?"

I shrugged. "He sat down and we got to talking."

"Oh," said Collie after a pause. "Well, after Mac left, I couldn't see you at any of the tables. I didn't think to look for you on the dance floor. I just figured you must have gotten fed up with waiting and left."

Emotion started to stir as I stared at him. "But I wouldn't do that."

"I know. I'm sorry. I'd had a few too many; I guess I wasn't thinking that clearly."

"Who were those two men, anyway?"

"Friends of Mac's. I left a few minutes after they sat down, and then I couldn't see you anywhere."

Remembering my fears about Central States authorities dragging Collie away, my voice sharpened. "Well, you couldn't have looked very hard. We searched everywhere for you." I hated how peevish I sounded, but couldn't stop. "In all the clubs and bars – you weren't anywhere."

Collie gripped my hand, looking frustrated. "I was doing exactly the same thing! We must have just kept missing each other." He paused, studying me. "We?" he repeated.

"Ingo came too."

Collie's mouth thinned. "You got pretty pally with that guy, didn't you?"

I laughed out loud: a harsh, brittle sound. "Don't tell me you're jealous! I wouldn't have spent two seconds with him if you hadn't gone off with Mac."

"You told me it was all right!"

"It *was*, but not for almost an hour!"

He shoved his hands through his hair. "Amity, he was practically crying into his drink. What the hell was I supposed to do?"

My dress felt pinched and too tight as I massaged my pounding head. I didn't know what Collie should have done. I especially didn't know why I was nagging him about it tonight, of all nights.

"Can we just…not argue, please?" I said at last. My voice came out small.

Collie's muscles sagged; he took me into his arms. This time I pressed close. As I leaned against his firm shoulder, his embrace tightened.

"I'm sorry," he said roughly against my hair. "Amity, I wanted tonight to be so perfect for us…"

"I can't believe Russ is really gone," I whispered. Then a thought came, and I gave a shaky laugh. "We were already in the Heat. We could have given him his send-off."

Collie pulled away and touched my face. His expression was heavy with things left unsaid.

"Come on," he said finally. "Let's go to bed."

He eased my clothes off as if I were a child. My dress sagged as he unzipped it; a moment later it slithered to the floor. My stockings followed. His hands were gentle, warm against my skin.

Suddenly I'd had enough of death. I wanted life – I wanted Collie. When he'd finished undressing me I pushed his jacket off his shoulders and started unbuttoning his shirt, my fingers deft and sure.

I took off his cufflinks and laid them aside. Collie had gone completely still, letting me undress him the way he'd undressed me. His eyes stayed locked on me, pure green, his pupils very dark.

"Do you remember that time we went swimming in the river?" I whispered.

"Which time?" His voice was husky.

I tugged his shirt free from his trousers. "I'd just turned thirteen. I think it was the last time we went. I was wearing that new swimsuit."

"It was blue," said Collie. "It had a red racing stripe. Right here." His finger trailed slowly up my side, stroking the side of my breast on its way. "Yeah," he said. "I remember."

"I was so embarrassed," I said. "It felt like I'd suddenly grown a figure all at once. I think I spent the whole time hiding in water up to my neck."

Collie's lopsided smile came, a little rueful. "You think *you* were embarrassed? All I had on was that old pair of trunks that were too small. I was terrified you'd see what you were doing to me and never speak to me again."

It had never occurred to me that Collie might have been as unsettled as me that day. I stroked his chest, savouring the contrasts: firm muscles, soft golden hairs. Collie leaned forward to kiss me; our hands found each other and our fingers entwined tightly.

"You were so beautiful," he murmured against my lips. "The way the water ran down your skin…I'd been dreaming about you for years…I never thought this could happen between us."

"Why not? I loved you even then."

"Don't ever stop."

I heard myself groan as his other arm slid around my hips and pulled me tight against him; our kisses took on an urgent beat. "You can see what you're doing to me now, too," Collie mumbled.

"I want to see – I want to do more than see—"

The rest of his clothes were kicked and tugged away by us both. He fumbled in his bedside drawer for a proph and I helped him put it on. My fingers stroked it down as I kissed him, our mouths hot and fierce, his hand cupped behind my neck.

"Amity…" he whispered hoarsely.

We fell back against the pillows. The night dissolved into fire, skin against skin – the flexing muscles of his back under my hands – a happiness so wild it was like being set free.

Collie...Collie... I thought.

After the last shudder we were both breathing hard. We lay without moving, our eyes locked on each other. I swallowed. I stroked Collie's hair from his face; he turned his head to kiss my wrist.

He slid off and pulled me tightly into his arms. I hugged close against his warmth. And though I'd thought I'd never be able to sleep that night, a gentle darkness claimed me and I sank into it with relief.

Chapter Twenty-two

When I was eleven, my dad did a lot of work in the main World for Peace building in Heatcalf City, not five miles from where I was now. One time my mother and I travelled down from Gloversdale to meet with him and see the sights. Hal stayed at home with a friend, so it was just Ma and me.

Even back then, I often found Ma irritating. I remember my awkward silences on the train as I tried to tune out her fluttery comments, her insistence on babying me. "Oh, Amity, look! Cows!" she'd cry, pointing out the window.

Did she think I was three? I grunted and stared down at my book, wishing that Hal was along to be a buffer.

I forgot it all the second we got to Heatcalf City.

Visitors were allowed in with special passes. I was so proud of mine. It hung around your neck on a slim cord and I kept fiddling with it, hoping everyone would notice the name *Vancour.* I wanted the whole world to know who my dad was.

He was busy when we got there, so Ma and I left our things in the hotel room and hit the city. To my disgust, Ma's idea of exploring turned out to be going from shop to shop. I slouched grumpily along after her as she tried on dresses that all looked the same. Why couldn't Collie have come along? Then even this would be fun.

Finally it got to be a quarter past five. I heaved a sigh. We weren't due to meet Dad till six and I wasn't sure how I'd survive until then.

"Can I go on to meet Dad?" I asked.

We were in yet another dressing room. Ma turned this way and that, inspecting herself in the mirror. "I'm not sure," she murmured, then seemed to have heard me. "Not on your own. We'll go soon."

"Please? I know where the WfP building is. I just want to look at all the cases." Dad had told me there were glass cases full of Peacefighting memorabilia in the WfP lobby.

Ma's forehead creased. "Oh, honey, I'm not sure. What if you get lost?"

"I won't! Please? Please?"

She let me go in the end, though her eyes were worried, just as if I wasn't her oldest child and could fly a plane almost by myself. If Collie had been there, she wouldn't have blinked. She had this idea that he was competent and trustworthy. He *was*, but she didn't seem to believe it about me too, which infuriated me.

I found the WfP building easily enough: an imposing tower with a laurel-leaf emblem at its top. I felt grown-up as I showed my pass to the guard and explained that my father worked there.

Inside it was white and gleaming. The way Dad had described the display area, I'd expected a museum. Instead there were only three cases. I peered dutifully in at their contents. A model Firedove, goggles worn by one of the very first Peacefighters, a few other knick-knacks. I'd seen everything in less than five minutes, then still had over half an hour to wait.

The air of hush felt daunting. I perched on a white leather bench. After a few minutes of shifting idly, I went up to the receptionist. "May I have a piece of paper and a pencil?" I asked.

Back on the bench I composed a letter.

July 12th, 1934

Dear Collie, I wrote. *Well, here I am in Heatcalf City. You would just love it here. There are Peacefighters everywhere and shops that sell real flying gear, but I think maybe those are for buying presents to send home because the pilots must get their things from the WfP, don't you think? Anyway I haven't gone into one of those shops yet because Ma is going CLOTHES shopping, can you believe it? She could do that anywhere. I really wish you could have come but maybe next time we—*

I heard a familiar voice and glanced up. Dad had just slid open the elevator's metal-diamond door; he and Madeline stepped out. I grinned and was about to jump up and run over to him. The expression on his face stopped me.

He hadn't seen me; he and Madeline were deep in conversation. They came a few paces into the lobby. Dad shoved his hands into his trouser pockets, regarding her with a complicated look I'd never seen him wear before. It was like he was angry, or sad, or wanted something with all his heart…yet none of those things quite described it.

I sat frozen. In that moment my father became a stranger. I'd always had the dim, unarticulated sense that he was holding something back from us; now I saw how right I'd been. I'd never seen his face look so raw – so full of emotion.

Why didn't he ever look that way around his family?

Madeline wore a long, thin skirt and white gloves. She touched his chest and said something. My father snorted slightly, and then smiled – a real smile that should have warmed me but didn't. Madeline tucked her arm through Dad's. As they started through the lobby she talked earnestly, peering up at my father's face. His dark head was down; he nodded.

My skin had gone prickly. It felt like everything had been ruined, but I didn't know why. I wanted to run away; I wanted to run over to him.

Madeline glanced up. Surprise flickered. "Amity!" She dropped her arm from my father's and smiled.

Dad looked up, too. He grinned and came loping over. "Hey, you're here!" He scooped me into a hug: strong arms, the smell of his cologne.

"Where's your mother?" he asked as he put me down.

"Shopping," I said. "I came early. I wanted to see the cases. I mean, you've told me so much about them. So I wanted to see them…see all the Peacefighting stuff."

I was babbling. I fell quiet, scowling.

"Oh…yeah," said my dad. He glanced over at the cases as if he'd never seen them before. Then he smiled and chucked me under the chin. "That's my girl."

His smile didn't reach his eyes. It rarely did. I hadn't known before; I'd never seen the difference.

But now I had.

The four of us had dinner together that night: Ma, Dad, Madeline and me. We went to a fancy place in the Heat – as Dad told me that part of the City was called – where I picked at the duck breast on my plate.

"What have you been up to, Amity?" asked Madeline cheerfully.

The question usually brought a flood of chatter;

Madeline was one of the few adults who seemed interested in me *and* who I could talk to. Tonight I felt reserved, a bit resentful.

"Not much," I said.

"Just hanging out at the swimming hole with Collie, huh?"

"I guess."

Ma had on one of her new dresses: sleek, satiny and low-cut, with ruffles across the chest. She clutched Dad's arm. "Oh, look, they have cocktails! I just saw that man order one. Tru, darling—"

"Say no more," said Dad in a dramatic tone. He summoned the waiter.

"I adore cocktails," said Ma to no one in particular, when in fact she hardly drank. She was never at her best around Madeline – or maybe it was just the contrast. She seemed sillier, giddier. She giggled and flirted with the waiter and Dad and whatever other men were in sight until I wanted to hide under the tablecloth.

Dad didn't seem to mind; he laughed a lot too, that night. He and Ma had their teasing banter down to an art form. I'd always seen their constant hilarity as evidence of how crazy they were about each other.

But now I thought about the raw look on my father's face as he'd gazed down at Madeline...and it occurred to me that maybe someone who was really happy wouldn't have to work so hard at it.

If he wasn't happy, then what was he? I watched

my mother with cool eyes that night, comparing her giddiness to Madeline's relaxed smile. And I thought I knew the answer.

I held a grudge against Ma for a long time after that. I thought it must be her fault, even though I wasn't really sure what "it" was. But surely, if she were on Dad's wavelength, he'd show her the same kind of real emotion he'd shown Madeline. As to why he'd never shown me anything like that, either…I stumbled over the thought.

I wasn't old enough, that's all. Someday he would.

Whenever he was home after that I spent as much time with him as I could. I probably got on his nerves, the way I hung around. I couldn't help it. There was a whole other Truce Vancour who I didn't know, and I longed to.

"Dad, why did you become a Peacefighter?"

"What was it like when you were growing up, Dad?"

"How did you and Ma meet?"

"Oh, you know," he'd say, usually with his face half-hidden as he fixed an engine or mended a fence. "I've told you that story a hundred times."

"Yes, but…" I'd trail off in frustration. Maybe I knew all the words, but there had to be more to it than just words, didn't there? If he'd only talk to me the way he talked to Madeline, I could maybe figure out the secret to him.

I started thinking about masks a lot. Did everyone wear them? I didn't think I did. Or Collie. Although I wished I *did* have one to hide behind sometimes. More than that,

I wished my father would take his off around me, just for a few minutes.

The only time he ever did was the day he died.

Hal and I had been messing around in one of the fields when we heard his plane. We'd whooped happily – he was hours earlier than expected – and raced for the long, flat strip where he always landed.

"Beat you there!" I flung over my shoulder at Hal as we ran.

"No fair!" he shouted. "You've got a head start!"

I laughed and burst out through a stretch of birch trees. I stopped, the smile melting from my face. The Gauntlet was almost down, a yellow, racing blur with sunshine glinting off its wheels. *Fast* – he was coming in so fast.

Too fast.

I knew what I was going to see before I saw it. Ice gripped me. I pounded towards the field.

"No!" I shouted. "Get the nose up!"

The plane hit the ground before it reached the runway and did a somersault. A wing crumpled with a loud crunch, like someone taking a bite from an apple. In a blurred tumble, my father was thrown clear. I saw him hit a barbed-wire fence.

"*Dad!*" I screamed.

I ran faster. The plane skidded and came to a mangled halt. I could hear my heart crashing in my ears, and Hal screaming somewhere in the distance.

My father sprawled motionless with the section of fence

collapsed around him. I reached him and dropped to my knees. My breath was short, panicky.

A piece of barbed wire was tangled around his neck. Blood was pulsing – so much blood – I gasped and pressed my hands over the wound. Barbed wire bit at me. I could feel Dad's artery throbbing, and the blood's warm slickness as it painted my fingers.

"Dad…" whispered Hal from behind me.

I twisted towards him. "*Go!*" I screamed at my brother. "Get Ma – anyone – *hurry!*"

Hal's face was white, streaked with tears. As he stumbled into a run, he began to sob.

His footsteps faded. There was the sound of the grasshoppers chirping and the wind whispering through the grass. My father was making a terrible gasping, rattling noise, his chest heaving. One of his hands clawed at the ground, white-knuckled.

I was crying, too. "No!" I burst out. "Dad, *please!*"

I wanted to hold his hand. I couldn't let go of the wound. I'd keep him alive no matter what, I thought wildly – I'd hold his life force inside his body.

It was already spilling away around my fingers.

Dad's eyes met mine. I saw him try to form my name and fail. He groped to touch me, still struggling for breath.

"Dad…please…" I choked out.

The tears were damp on my face, yet I could see him so clearly. Time seemed to slow as we gazed at each other.

He died without managing to touch me. I stayed

crouching with my hands over his neck, refusing to believe he was gone, even though his eyes had turned blank and his blood was cooling against my skin.

When Ma came running up with a neighbour who'd been visiting, it took both of them to pull me away. "No!" I shouted, struggling. "Let me go! I've got to save him!"

My mother gripped my shoulders and shook me. "Amity! He's gone! You can't do anything. He's gone."

She pulled me into a tight embrace. When she released me I stood trembling. I saw for myself it was true. My father lay with one arm flung out, gazing upwards. His body was still.

"Oh, Truce," Ma cried. She kneeled beside him and started to sob on his chest. I backed away a few steps, staring. The neighbour woman tried to hug me but I pushed away.

I looked down at my bloody hands. I wished so much that my father had been able to touch me.

And then I realized that he had, even if not physically. When our eyes had met, he'd gazed at me with love...and with something like wonder, as if he'd never really known he had a daughter named Amity before that moment.

Most of all, his brown eyes had held regret.

CHAPTER TWENTY-THREE

"NO...NO, PLEASE...*NO!*"

The cries awoke me with a start. For a tangled moment I couldn't think where I was; then I knew. "Collie!" I whispered, shaking his shoulder. "Collie, it's only a dream!"

He moaned but didn't awaken. I smoothed his hair from his face. The blinds were slightly open; in the glow from the street lights I could just make out Collie's full lips, the rugged shape of his nose.

"It's all right," I said. His hair slipped softly against my fingers. The motion of my hand was steady, soothing. "Shh...it's all right..."

Soon his breathing became regular again. I pressed against his solid warmth and he put his arms around me in his sleep. "Amity," he murmured, not as if he was aware I was there, but as if I were part of his dream. A happy part now, from the sound of it.

I let out a breath. Collie had nightmares once or twice a week. Always the same, with his head lashing back and forth on the pillow and him pleading to someone, though he said he could never remember what they were about. I wasn't surprised that he'd had another one tonight.

Russ.

I lay staring at the ceiling. When I'd first arrived on base, people had ignored me just like they had Collie. Russ hadn't. He'd taken me under his wing, shouted at me more than he did anyone else – always pushing me to fly harder, faster. To survive.

How's my favourite wildcat?

My chest felt leaden. The matchbook still lay on the bedside table. I swallowed and picked it up. Its cardboard cover felt smooth against my fingers. The stylized shamrock looked dark grey now.

Slowly, I opened the cover and closed it again. Something about the way the shamrock looked in this faint light... I frowned at a sudden memory of wailing jazz, and of Harlan putting a shot glass in front of me.

The night of Stan's send-off, I'd sat playing with a matchbook just like this one.

My eyebrows drew together as I recalled that night in the speak for the second time: Russ sitting with two men, leaning intensely across the small table as if he were arguing. A man with curly hair who'd laughed and wagged a finger. The other man had been bald.

One bald, one with curly hair. The same men I'd seen running from the alley. How had I not made the connection before?

I sat up straight, my scalp electric. *It hadn't been a random robbery.* Russ had *known* his attackers. I fumbled the matchbook open again. Brand new, only one match gone.

Russ had been at that same speak tonight. Had he met those two men there again? Yet they hadn't seemed like friends the night of Stan's send-off. More like business associates.

Why would a pilot like Russ need business associates?

That night in the speak, Russ had quickly tucked something in his jacket as Harlan and I approached. Something those men had given him.

The next fight, my air bottle had seized up.

Well, that was clever of me. I wasn't sure whether I'd hit you at all. Ingo's comment on the dance floor suddenly seemed ominous. We were both experienced pilots. He hadn't been sure he'd hit me, and I hadn't felt the hit.

A malfunction, I'd thought at the time. And then, with the odd sense that Russ had been celebrating after my lost appeal, I'd fleetingly suspected sabotage.

But I'd been wrong. Hadn't I?

As Collie slept beside me I pressed my fists to my forehead and willed myself to remember every detail.

I'd found my old Dove, its bullet holes scorched by the fire that had forced me down. I'd run my hand over the holes, dug my fingers in them. Then I'd creaked open the panel and shone my flashlight on the damaged air bottle. A bullet hole had been there, too.

It had glinted in the light.

I went stock-still. My plane had caught fire *after* Ingo shot it. My air bottle had been a melted lump. If the bullet hole had really come from my fight, it should have been as blackened as those on the hood.

Yet its edge had glimmered like diamond dust.

Amity...I shot it.

My breath curdled as the meaning of Russ's dying words hit me. Russ had shot that section of my plane after it burned, to make it look as if my air bottle had been hit mid-battle like he'd told me...but then he'd been a bit careless about charring up the fresh bullet hole afterwards.

He had never expected me to land that plane.

"No," I whispered aloud.

Edwards, I thought frantically. He'd know the truth; my fitter had been the one to check out my Firedove after the crash-landing. Except that while I'd been grounded, he'd been reassigned to Tier Threes. Thinking back, my spine chilled: had I seen Edwards on base at all since I got the burning Dove down? If I had, I didn't remember it.

And Clem, who was T3, hadn't known who he was.

My blood hammered at my temples. I slipped out of

bed and crept through the dark house. In the living room I switched on a lamp beside the phone and flipped hastily through the base directory. It was a new one, out only the week before.

There was no entry for "Edwards, Joshua".

I dialled "O", almost too tense to work the dial. A few moments later I slowly hung up the heavy black receiver, the base operator's words echoing through my brain: "No, I'm sorry, Mr Edwards left months ago. No, I don't know where he went."

In a flash I saw again the night I crash-landed: Russ's muscular form striding off towards the hangar.

Had Edwards left of his own accord? Or had something happened to him?

I stood trembling with shock. I had no idea why those two men had killed Russ tonight...but suddenly I was pretty sure I knew what the three of them had been up to.

No.

I rushed back into Collie's bedroom, where I kept a change of clothes. Groping in the dark, I yanked them on. Collie's breathing stayed gentle, rhythmic. I grabbed up his leather jacket and slipped again through the house, pausing only to take the flashlight from the kitchen.

I let myself out and eased shut the front door.

Outside the street lights cast an eerie glow, with dark palm trees arching overhead. I walked briskly down the sidewalk. The direction I took surprised me; I'd planned to return to the scrapyard. But there was no point. I knew what I'd seen.

"You couldn't have done it," I muttered, the words keeping a fierce rhythm with my stride. "Russ, please, this has got to be a bad dream."

Finally I reached his street. He'd lived in one of the single-dwelling houses that Tier Ones get, more spacious than the place I shared with Vera. The screened-in porch made me think of lemonade and Sunday afternoons.

I felt on edge, every nerve singing. I snuck across freshly-mown grass to the backyard. A lot of pilots didn't bother locking their doors…yet I wasn't really surprised when Russ's screen door was latched.

It was my chance to back out. I looked up at the silent house and licked my lips, wavering.

No. If the truth was in there, I had to know.

I went to the side of the house and started trying windows. None opened. The cellar doors lay flat against the ground, padlocked shut. When I tugged at the handle the latch rattled; its screws were loose. I hesitated, then stood on the doors to deaden any sound. I kicked at the latch with my boot until it shivered apart.

I creaked open the cellar door. The smell of earth and concrete wafted out. I started down the steps; once below ground, I pulled the door shut. Blackness encased me.

I snapped on the flashlight.

I was in an ordinary cellar, with a boiler in one corner and a workbench against one wall. Some distant part of me watched in disbelief. *Amity, what are you doing?* I steeled myself and walked quickly up the stairs that led to the main part of the house.

The cellar door opened into the kitchen. Here, too, everything looked innocent – and at the same time, nothing did, not even the mug on the draining board. I hesitated and cupped my hand over the flashlight, dimming its glow. I had no idea what I was looking for.

Instinct took me down the corridor. I opened doors until I found Russ's bedroom. The sight of his bed, looking vulnerable and unmade, almost defeated me. I wanted to leave, forget any of this had happened.

Russ's dog tags lay on his dresser. They stiffened my spine. Hardship was gripping the Western Seaboard because of my lost fight – if Russ had done what I thought, he'd betrayed everything we stood for.

I searched quickly, pulling drawers open, rummaging through them. Socks, underwear, T-shirts. My spirits leaped when I found a slim metal box under the bed, but it held only photos.

I shoved it back. Frustrated, I yanked Russ's bedside table drawer open so hard that it fell onto the floor. Its contents clattered everywhere. A thermometer, a box of prophs. Nothing that told me anything – nothing!

I sank onto the bed. My breathing sounded too loud in the silent room. *Think, Amity!* Where would Russ hide something? What was important to him?

A sudden image came: Russ standing in the sunshine

offering me a cigar, waggling it seductively as he grinned.

I lunged off the bed and rushed for the study, where I'd seen a wooden cigar box on the desk. If that was where he'd kept his beloved stogies, then he'd spent time in there.

I rifled through the desk. A stack of payslips from the World for Peace. Completely standard, just like the ones I received. I shut the drawer and glanced tensely at the packed bookshelves covering one wall. If Russ had hidden something there, it would take hours – days – to look through everything.

I stiffened.

Footsteps.

My nerves tingled as I listened hard. No, I must have imagined it. I started to move, then froze as it came again: a faint, steady tread.

More than one.

I snapped off the flashlight and stood tautly motionless, straining to hear. People passing by outside, maybe? Pilots came and went at all hours. Or had someone seen my light despite the closed blinds and called security?

Russ's study was at the front of his house. I sucked in a quick breath as the footsteps passed near the window. I heard the furtive murmur of voices.

And then a key in the front-door lock.

My heart went wild. There was a small alcove between the bookshelves and the adjoining wall; I sprang for it and pressed into its shadows.

The front door opened and closed. Two sets of footsteps approached down the hallway. Male voices floated in: "Think there'll be anything?"

"If there is, you know what to do. Take the bedroom. I'll take in here."

A bright circle of light entered the study. My pulse battered at my throat. I kept my cheek tight against the bookshelves, trying not to breathe.

The man holding the flashlight jerked open the desk drawer and shone the beam inside. Its reflection gleamed faintly on his bald head as he searched. He slammed the drawer shut and lifted up the blotter. He'd just reached for the cigar box when a shout came:

"Hey! Someone's already been here!"

The man's head snapped up. He swore and hurried from the room.

The cigar box. I didn't stop to think. I stepped out and took it from the desk, then slipped into the hallway, tiptoeing, my brain screaming, *Run, get out!* When I reached the kitchen I started quietly down the cellar stairs.

"Damn it! They're here *now*!"

Forget sneaking. I raced the rest of the way down, then barrelled across the cellar and up the steps to the trapdoor. For a second it stuck and my heart leaped into my throat – then it swung open and I burst out into the star-coated night.

Shouts came from behind. Still clutching the cigar box, I raced for the street, my footsteps thudding with my pulse.

Halfway down the block I heard someone coming after me.

In a frenzied backwards glance I saw a shadowy, running form, not nearly far enough away. With a burst of speed I turned the corner, then ducked away into the shadows.

Panting, I crouched behind a rhododendron bush in someone's yard. The footsteps slowed, stopped. I huddled tight against the branches. The cigar box jabbed into my ribs.

A second pair of footsteps. Low voices came, hissing with anger as the men began to search. In a sickening flash I saw again Russ's body, sodden with blood.

I was trembling. *Move – now,* I ordered myself. I gripped the cigar box and somehow eased away from the bush, keeping close to the house's blanketing shadows. Step by step, I crept through the darkness. Behind me, I heard the men rustling at the bush's branches.

I turned another street corner and ran.

Chapter Twenty-four

"Ramirez, Tier Two fight against the European Alliance…Stanford, Tier Three fight against the Central States…"

I sagged against the metal folding chair. Collie didn't have a fight today. To my relief, Hendrix passed over my name, too.

The base clearly already knew that Russ was dead. A palpable sadness hung in the air; there were more than a few red eyes. I no longer knew what to believe. Who had Russ really been? The gruff team leader who used to scoop me into a bear hug…or the person I'd uncovered once I'd finally gotten home the night before?

I could see the back of Collie's head a few rows away,

and guessed how much he wanted to turn and catch my eye. I'd returned to my own house after running from Russ's; all Collie knew was that when he'd woken up, I'd been gone. I gazed at his sun-streaked hair. I still felt sickened by what I'd found out.

But if I was right, it would change so much more than I'd thought.

With a faint rustle, Hendrix put the roster to one side. He rubbed the bridge of his nose. "I'm deeply saddened to announce the death of one of our own," he said. "Russell Avery was found murdered in Heatcalf City last night, the victim of a violent robbery. Let's have a moment of silence."

Quiet draped over the hangar. I closed my eyes and recalled the man I'd thought I'd known. The one I *wanted* to remember.

Finally Hendrix cleared his throat. "Pilots stand," he said quietly.

"I swear to fight fairly.

I swear to defend my country to the best of my ability.

I swear to honour the sanctity of life."

My vow echoed with the others. I kept my gaze on the two flags at the front. No matter what Russ had done, I would not allow it to taint what Peacefighting meant to me.

When the meeting finished I started to make my way to Collie. Commander Hendrix stopped me, his brown eyes concerned. "Amity, I saw on the report that you were the one who found Russ last night," he said. "Are you all right?"

"I'm fine," I said awkwardly. I could tell he was thinking about Dad. "But, sir, I wonder if—"

I broke off as I noticed the cluster of administrators standing nearby. I had to be careful. Even just asking to meet was better done in private.

"What is it?" asked Commander Hendrix.

"Nothing," I said. I managed a smile. "I mean…thank you, sir."

The base commander studied me, and then nodded. "All right," he said. "Let me know if you need anything."

As he left I headed over to Collie. When we reached each other his brow creased and he touched my arm. "What happened to you last night? I woke up and you were gone."

"I know. I'm sorry." I glanced over my shoulder and then leaned close. "We need to talk."

Once we were in my bedroom with the door shut I dug out the cigar box from the depths of my closet. Collie eyed it warily as I sat beside him on the bed.

"Why have I got a terrible feeling this has something to do with Russ?" he said.

"I broke into his house last night. Don't say it," I added. "Just…don't, all right?"

Collie sat staring. "Tell me this is one of your unfunny

jokes that I'm just not getting," he said at last.

"No joke."

The bed creaked as he gripped my arms. "What were you *thinking*?"

"I had to know what he'd done!"

"Have you lost your fucking mind?"

I jerked away. "All *right.* But it's done now. And I'm glad I did it." I told him everything that had happened, from checking my plane months ago to running away from the two men.

"I had to go, don't you see?" I finished. "Collie, Russ was taking bribes! If I hadn't gone there, those men would have destroyed the evidence."

Collie sat running a fist over his mouth, back and forth. "All right, what exactly is this evidence?" he said finally.

"Look." I opened the box's lid. The scent of tobacco rose up; dozens of cigars in slick cellophane wrappers filled the space. Hidden flush against one side was a slim notebook. I handed it to Collie.

He took it, his reluctance clear. The notebook was slightly grubby, with a cover of grey card. Collie flipped through. "It's a date book. So?"

"Look at the dates!" I shifted next to him on the bed. "Some are marked with a star. Like here." I pointed at February 3rd. "That's when Russ lost the Tier One fight that gave Gunnison extradition rights. And here—" I flipped back through time. "November 29th. When they sabotaged my air bottle before I went up, so that I couldn't fire."

"You don't know—"

"I do know! My air bottle had a bullet hole that wasn't charred – what else could that mean? Russ shot it *after* my plane burned, to make it look like it was damaged in the fight!"

Collie put the notebook aside. "A date book with a few stars doesn't prove anything," he said tightly. "These could be family birthdays for all you know."

"Of course they're not!"

"*You don't know that.*" He took my shoulders. "Amity, *listen* to me. You are playing with fire. Whoever those men were—"

"Yes, what about them? Do you really think they were looking for Russ's innocent little birthday reminders?" I snatched up the notebook and flourished it. "*Why* would they want this, unless –" I hated the words so much that I almost spat them – "unless Russ was taking bribes, throwing fights, betraying all of us? At first I thought it was just my air bottle, but it was worse than that!"

I flipped through the pages. Some were back from when Russ had been a Tier Two. "On *this* date and *this* one and *this* one, he lost fights. Three more losses, three more stars."

Collie's expression held reluctance mixed with dawning dread. "Maybe he marked his losses."

"With a star? Who would do that?"

"Fine! But even if you're right, this won't prove anything; it could just be enough to get you killed! Russ had to have been shot for a reason—"

"He wanted more money," I said. "I think maybe he was threatening to expose everything unless he got it."

Collie's head snapped up; apprehension crossed his face. "How do you know that?"

"Because there's more." I fumbled at the bottom of the cigar box; my fingers found again the tiny catch that I'd discovered last night. A drawer slid open at the box's base.

It held newspaper clippings.

I handed the top one to Collie. Its familiar headline read: GUNNISON WINS EXTRADITION DISPUTE AGAINST WESTERN SEABOARD – CS Escapees Now Criminals. What wasn't familiar was the margin note in Russ's handwriting: *10K Cs = BULLSHIT!*

The clipping creased in Collie's grip. "Ten thousand credits," he murmured hollowly.

The other clippings were similar: stories of Western Seaboard defeats with scribbled sums on each. I'd always felt a comradeship with Russ because he read the papers like me. But that meant he'd known exactly what his thrown fights had brought about.

He'd known.

"The losses are against different countries," I said finally. "He must have been making deals with all kinds of people. Or illegal gambling, maybe."

Betting on the Peacefights was a felony, but people did it;

there'd been a big gambling scandal only a few months before. That was just *betting*, though. For a Peacefighter to throw fights…I couldn't comprehend it.

Collie's jaw was tight as he shoved the clippings back in the drawer. "Why the hell would Russ even save these?"

"I don't know; it doesn't matter." I gripped his hands. "But don't you see? *This* is enough evidence! We can get these results overturned, including the extradition law. Collie…you'll be safe."

For a moment I saw something flicker in his eyes. Then he got up and started pacing. He shoved his hands through his hair.

"No – no, we've got to think this through," he muttered. "We can't go off half-cocked."

I got up too and stopped him, putting my hands on his chest. "Didn't you hear me? Once the extradition law's overturned, you can't be shipped back to the Central States! Gunnison won't be able to touch you."

"Oh, you are so naïve!" Collie gripped my shoulders; I recoiled at his raw anger. "Do you really think it would be that easy? You have no idea what the world is like!"

"What are you talking about?"

"How did those men get past the guards onto the base, for a start? Somebody had to help them!"

"Or they snuck in, or deceived someone, or—"

"Grow up! You are in *danger*, can't you grasp that? Did they get a good look at you?"

I recalled the shadowy, running form. "I…don't know."

"You don't know," repeated Collie.

"I don't think so."

"But you don't *know.* Amity, there aren't that many female pilots! If they saw you, it wouldn't take a genius to track you down."

"They won't! It was dark; I was wearing your jacket. All they saw was someone running, okay?"

Collie blew out a breath. Still holding my arms, he rested his forehead against mine. Neither of us spoke. I could feel the tension in his hands.

I stroked his hair. "You're right to be worried," I whispered. "If they'd caught me I'd be dead now. But the dangerous part's over with. I just have to show this stuff to Commander Hendrix – then the fixed fight results will be overturned, and with any luck we'll win the rematches." My muscles tightened as I thought of all that would mean: our country solvent again, eastern land rights returned, Collie and the other fugitives safe.

And a pilot who'd betrayed everything I cared about wouldn't have gotten away with it.

Collie's body was as tense as steel. At last he said, "No… no, don't go to Hendrix."

"*What?* Why not?"

"Amity, those men murdered Russ to keep him quiet! We don't know what the hell's going on or how deep it goes." He gripped my hands. "*Please* – don't tell anyone yet. Let me check it out first and make sure you'll be safe."

I stared. "Check it out how?"

Collie's mouth hardened. I saw some sort of mental battle going on. Then he sighed.

"I have…contacts," he said.

The house felt very still around us. Faintly, I could hear the hum of the icebox.

"You mean the people who helped you get out of the Central States," I said. Collie nodded.

I stood motionless. He'd said they were dangerous people, but that some of the ones he'd dealt with had been good guys. Then I recalled the look in Collie's eyes last night at the dance club, before he'd gone off with Mac… the way he'd paused and touched my face.

I heard myself say, "Is Mac one?"

Collie hesitated. "Yes," he said finally.

Fear stroked my spine. "What's wrong? Why did he want to talk to you?"

"Don't worry! Everything's fine." Collie sat me down on the bed with him. "He just had to tell me about some precautions for the new extradition law. I didn't expect to see him last night, or for it to take so long. But since we were both there, it saved trying to meet somewhere else."

"So 'How's Greta?' is a code?"

Collie's wince was all the answer I needed. "Please don't ask me anything else," he said softly. "But I trust Mac, okay? He wouldn't betray me. Just give me a while to check this out, all right?"

My throat clenched at his expression. "Collie…I can't. People are being affected. There are lives at stake."

"*Please.*" He touched my cheek; his other hand was a tight fist. "If anything happened to you…"

"Nothing will happen. I think you're wrong." But my voice didn't come out as strongly as I'd intended.

Neither of us moved. Collie's eyes searched mine. And somehow, without even speaking, I knew that I'd just agreed.

He let out a breath and kissed me. "I'll take the stuff and hide it at my place," he said in a low voice. "I don't want it anywhere near you, in case those men suspect who you were."

I swallowed. "No…your house is too risky." Collie and his roommate had a broken latch on one window that they hadn't fixed. The base was usually so secure there was no need.

"Amity—"

"Don't worry! I'll hide it somewhere really safe. I don't want it to be found any more than you do."

Reluctantly, he nodded.

I took his hand and turned it over. I traced the glyph for Leo at the base of his thumb, following its small, blue-black curves. I thought of Collie's nightmares, wondering again what he'd been through.

I closed his fingers over mine. "A few days for you to check it out," I said. "That's all."

Chapter Twenty-five

The army camp stretched for as far as Kay could see: tidy-looking temporary buildings, the gleam of jeeps and tanks in the sun, people moving like ants in all directions. This hot, dusty land was one of the areas "won" from the WS.

Kay had had a vague idea that she might run into Rita, her childhood friend. Gazing at the reality of a hundred thousand troops, the thought was ludicrous. She turned her attention back to what Chalmers, her guide, was saying:

"...could be ready to go at three hours' notice; that's how crack-trained they are. But of course we need to know exactly where the first stage of the Reclamation will take place. That's where you come in, I guess."

Kay smiled, and tried not to give away that she was frantically scanning the small knot of people near the administrative buildings. A few days ago, Skinner had informed her that her offer to dowse for the best location had been approved. She'd insisted that only one date would be suitable, and had made sure it was when Gunnison was due to inspect the troops.

There was no sign of him. And she wasn't sure how much longer she could stall.

Skinner had been checking some paperwork in the office. As his thin, narrow-shouldered figure rejoined them, Chalmers cleared his throat. "So, Miss Pierce, if you'd like to begin, I'm sure we'd all—"

Kay gave him a bright-eyed look. "You know, I'd be fascinated to learn how this operation has remained secret. It's so *big.*"

To her relief, Chalmers swelled with pride. "Well, of course this whole area is restricted," he said. "And we're in a no-fly zone, so it can't be spotted from the air. But yes, there have certainly been challenges. For instance—"

The desert sun was merciless; Kay's spine felt slick beneath her silk blouse. Skinner grimaced and dabbed at his forehead with a handkerchief.

"Shall we get on with it?" he interrupted.

She could put it off no longer. Yet without Gunnison to subtly point her towards whatever location he privately favoured, she was lost. Kay slowly started to unsling the leather case that she carried over one shoulder.

Make up some problem, she thought, trying not to panic. *Some reason why I can't do it today after all—*

The sound of an approaching engine. Kay glanced up and saw a long, dusty black auto arrive. As it halted, a pair of red-and-black Harmony flags on the hood fluttered and went limp.

The sudden smile Kay shone onto the two men was dazzling. She pressed a hand to her heart. "My goodness! Is that who I think it is?"

As they approached Gunnison, Kay had a few moments to take him in. A man of average height, solid with muscle, with thick blond hair going grey at the temples. He looked like an ageing farm boy, but wore his suit easily: he stood relaxed, hands in trouser pockets, nodding at something Charles, one of his aides, was saying.

As they drew near Gunnison saw them; he raised a hand with a smile. "Mal, hello! Be with you in a moment." His voice was as drawling and resonant as on the telio. He turned back to his aide. "Well, we can't be having insurrection in the camps. You know what to do."

Kay kept her expression cheerful. She managed not to think about severed heads mounted on a chain-link fence, their blackened skin sparkling with frost.

Charles's gaze flicked to Kay. "So I have your permission to use…ah, the methods we've discussed, sir?"

"Of course, Chuck." Gunnison glanced over a document

that the aide held out. He grimaced. "Ah, such a shame. But it's their own fault." He scribbled a signature.

"Also, sir, I spoke to Mr Cain about that Western Seaboard matter," added the aide.

Gunnison glanced up. "I'm sure Sandy's already got it under control."

The aide nodded tensely. Recalling Sandford Cain's cold, pale eyes, Kay thought Gunnison was wrong this time: a nickname did not make Cain friendly.

Finally Gunnison capped his pen and turned again towards Malcolm Skinner and the others. "Mal! How are you?" he said heartily.

His smile broadened when Skinner introduced Kay. "So this is our dowsing astrologer! Very pleased to meet you, Miss Pierce." He shook her hand warmly. His grip was broad, strong, like shaking with a friendly bear.

And to Kay's surprise, she couldn't help giving a genuine smile back. The full impact of John Gunnison was like a physical force; his smile was contagious. *I have to keep my wits about me,* she reminded herself sharply. *This man has the power to kill me.*

"The pleasure's all mine, Mr Gunnison," she said. "This is such an honour."

"Aw, stop it," he said with a grin. "And what's this 'Mr Gunnison' crap? The only people who call me that don't like me. Call me Johnny."

Kay's eyes widened. She'd heard that Gunnison often said this to people...but beside her, Skinner looked as if he'd just swallowed a moth. Clearly Gunnison had never offered his first name to him. Divide and conquer?

Or maybe he just liked her.

The thought was dizzying in what it could mean for her; apprehension followed. She could *not* let down her guard.

"All right...Johnny," she said. "And please call me Kay."

"Deal!" Gunnison clapped her arm and then gazed at her leather case with undisguised curiosity. He rubbed his hands together. "Good stuff, I see that I got here in time. Hey, why don't you talk us through this thing?"

And just like that, Kay was in.

She unslung the leather case from her shoulder and opened it. A long, forked stick lay inside.

It had taken for ever to find one the right length, then whittle off the bark and polish it. Kay carefully stroked it up and down; finally she grasped the forked ends of the stick lightly, one branch in each hand. She turned from side to side as if feeling for some kind of force, and kept an eye on Gunnison.

"Dowsing was once used mostly to locate underground wells, but you can use it to find anything," she said casually. "You just follow the tug of the stick. The reasons are complicated – essentially, it has to do with the earth's electromagnetic field and the dowser's own biomagnetism. Not everyone can do it. I feel very lucky."

Skinner's mouth was tight. He didn't comment.

As Kay angled herself to the north, she saw Gunnison's

gaze narrow. She paused, making the stick quiver in her grasp, then turned a touch away. No, she hadn't imagined it: Gunnison let out an almost unnoticeable breath. She moved to the north again.

"This way," she said firmly. "Maybe we should take one of the autos."

Gunnison looked impressed. "Hey, can you really do that in a moving vehicle?"

Kay dimpled at him. "Well, of course." The confused thought struck her that she was flirting with the leader of the Central States – a man at least thirty years her senior. But Gunnison – Johnny – just grinned in return.

The presidential auto had red leather seats and a gleaming black dashboard. Gunnison sat in the back with Kay; Skinner went in front with the driver. A glass screen kept the back of the vehicle private.

Noting how Gunnison settled against his seat as the auto started down the road, Kay surmised that the location he favoured for the attack wasn't close. She snuggled against the seat as well and rested the dowsing rod on her lap.

"I'll be able to feel it if it starts to change direction," she said.

"Well, that's just fine." Gunnison opened a small compartment and took out a decanter of water; he poured Kay a glass. "Sorry it's not champagne," he said, and Kay giggled. The water tasted fresh and cool.

As the auto purred through the dusty landscape,

Gunnison produced a worn deck of Tarot cards from his jacket pocket.

Kay went taut. She recognized the pattern on the back of the deck from a dozen black-and-white newsreels. She hadn't known until now that it was a vivid green.

Gunnison handed her the cards. "Here you go – shuffle."

She hesitated, all exuberance gone. She'd studied the Tarot. The selection of cards was totally random. If Gunnison didn't like what the chosen images said about her…

Yet to refuse would be unthinkable.

Slowly, Kay rested her glass on a small tray. She took the deck. The cards were larger than playing cards; as she shuffled she had to concentrate not to scatter them all over the back seat. She knew you shuffled until you "felt" the time was right – wildly, she wondered if she could just keep on with it until the auto stopped.

Finally she could put it off no longer. She handed back the deck, feeling stiff with dread.

"Here, Johnny," she said.

He tapped the cards against his opposite palm. Kay watched the motion, sickly mesmerized.

"They're shuffled enough?" he asked. "You're sure?"

"I'm sure," she said faintly.

Gunnison fanned out the cards in one of his large hands. "All right, choose three."

She chose. Her fingers were trembling now – she hoped he'd put it down to the auto's motion. Gunnison tucked the rest of the deck back in his pocket. Carefully, he laid the chosen cards face down on his tray.

"Well now, let's see what we have here," he said with a roguish glance. Kay managed a small smile and took a sip of water. With ceremony, Gunnison turned over the cards one by one.

The Hermit. The Five of Wands. The Tower.

"Interesting," said Gunnison. "Very, very interesting." He narrowed his gaze and tapped the Hermit. "This'll be you, Kay. You're kinda a private person, huh?"

Before she could answer – it hadn't really been a question anyway – Gunnison went on: "And the five o' sticks…hmm. Lots of strife going on, though it *can* mean challenges. Bet you're facing a lot of those right about now, aren't you?"

His tone was friendly. The cards were all right. Kay felt her spine melt away against the soft leather seat. "There *are* a lot of challenges in my new position," she confessed giddily. That was putting it mildly.

"Finally, the Tower," Gunnison said. "Well. That speaks for itself, doesn't it?"

"Great change," said Kay. There were at least four other Tarot cards she could think of that meant the same. The Tower was just the most dramatic-looking: an exploding tower with falling human figures.

Gunnison nodded slowly. "Great change," he echoed.

In a sudden motion, he took out the rest of the deck and added the three cards. He shuffled them all quickly, expertly, then cut the deck and glanced down at the chosen card.

A private smile. He tucked the deck back into his pocket. "Well, Miss Kay, I think you and I will work together very well," he drawled.

Kay's heartbeat trebled. What did that mean? Was she the top Twelve Year astrologer now? Then as Gunnison folded his tray away and glanced out the window, she abruptly realized that his demeanour had grown expectant.

She made a show of gripping the dowsing rod. She pretended to let it tug at her grasp. "Johnny, I think maybe…could you ask the driver to slow down?" she said, her tone urgent.

Gunnison pressed a button and gave the order. Kay noted the subtle sense of triumph in his shoulders. She was close, all right.

She waited, resisting the urge to hurry this. The minutes ticked past; the auto kept slowly on through the desert. In the front seat, she could see Skinner's tension in his neck muscles.

It wasn't until a faint frown appeared on Gunnison's brow that Kay whipped about in her seat, pointing the stick at the road behind. "No, stop, we've gone too far!" she gasped. "It's back there."

An hour later, the three of them stood on a small rise. They'd walked two miles from the road where the presidential auto was parked and were now on the very edge of the land which Gunnison had secured through his manipulated Peacefights.

This patch of desert looked exactly like the rest of it… except that in the distance, just across the border of the Western Seaboard, Kay could make out a dusty town. She knew there were other WS towns close to the Central States' border, too, many far larger. What was special about this one?

Clearly, to Gunnison, something was. He had his hands behind his back; though his brow gleamed with sweat, he somehow looked cool and unrumpled as he surveyed the view. Kay had the sense that a smile was just out of reach.

"This is the place, all right," he murmured. He shot her a glance. His eyes were dancing. "You know, I think maybe we've been setting our sights a little low, Miss Kay."

"Have we?" She didn't understand, but it didn't matter. Gunnison's unconscious body language had not let her down.

"Oh, yes." He gazed out at the desert again. "Oh, yes."

Skinner's mouth was tight. "Sir, if I may comment? Other areas would be far more advantageous. There's really very little here. All the charts that I've cast indicate that—"

"There's a lot more here than you might think," said Gunnison. Then he looked at Skinner. "You've cast charts about this place?" His tone was too mild. If Kay had liked

Skinner more, she'd have winced on his behalf.

Skinner hesitated. "It didn't seem worth showing them to you, when—"

"Show them to her." Gunnison jerked his head towards Kay.

Skinner peered at Kay. Though the Chief Astrologer had warmed to her of late, Kay had the feeling he was changing his mind again.

"Sir?" he said.

"You heard me. I want to know what this little lady has to say about those charts of yours. In fact, no – I want her to recast 'em herself." Gunnison grinned at her. "You'll do that for me, won't you, Kay?"

Kay's spirits were cavorting, leaping. "I'd be delighted," she said.

And she knew, without a doubt, that her interpretation would squarely back up Gunnison's own feeling: that this unlikely spot was the ideal place to launch their attack.

Gunnison gazed out at the town again. "I believe that Harmony is more than just an ideal…it's a conscious force." He glanced at her. "Did you know that, Kay?"

She shook her head.

"Well, it's true. Astrology is just one way that Harmony shows itself. I pray to Lady Harmony a lot, you know." He studied the hot, dusty town, his form as solid as a mountain, blue eyes squinting against the sun.

"We're very close now," he said. "As soon as I get the sign from Lady Harmony…the Reclamation can begin."

Kay felt emboldened enough to ask, "Do you know when that will be, Johnny?"

The leader of the Central States shook his head, still watching the desert. "No. But it'll be soon. You bet."

For a moment he seemed lost in his own world. "She's told me to go in with fire and fury," he whispered. "And oh, we will. Fire and fury. They'll pay for sheltering our Discordants. We'll make them harmonious even if it destroys them."

Despite the heat, Kay shivered.

Gunnison turned to her and smiled. "Shall we go?"

Chapter Twenty-six

DURING THE NEXT FEW DAYS I kept on with my job. I had a fight against the Scando-Finns. A fight against the Central States, which I won, to my hard delight. A fight against the EA, where I could tell the pilot wasn't Ingo and didn't know whether I was sorry or glad.

I hid the documents from Russ's house under a piece of insulation in the attic. With each day that passed they somehow felt more exposed.

"We can't keep hanging on like this," I hissed to Collie. We were in the cafe; he had a fight soon and I'd just returned from one. "What exactly is going on?" I went on in an undertone. "When will Mac say it's safe to turn the documents in?"

Collie shook his head tersely. "It's only been three days."

"People's lives are at stake. *Your* life!"

"I've told you I'll be okay!"

"Yes, because *Mac Jones* says so. Who *is* this guy, anyway?"

Collie raked his hands through his hair. "Someone I trust," he said. "Look – I saw him in the Heat the other night and he's checking it out. That's *all I know*. You can't just call these people up for a quick chat. There are…ways. Routes you have to go through."

"Collie—" I slumped my forehead against my fists. Anyone watching probably thought we were having a fight. Maybe we were.

Even here on base where people didn't always follow the news, knowledge of what was happening was rife. Just that morning, I'd read about a Western Seaboard man who'd been beaten for trying to protect his Central States-born wife from arrest. The new law gave the Guns the right to use "reasonable force". The only reason he hadn't been shot was that she'd given herself up.

I had the means to stop all of it. And so far I'd done nothing.

Collie touched my arm. His fingers felt warm and familiar. "Please, you've got to trust me," he whispered.

"I do. It's Mac I'm not sure about."

A group of pilots sat down nearby. Collie glanced at them and lowered his voice even further. "Well, you're wrong. I'd trust Mac with my life." He snorted softly.

"Hell, I *do* trust him with my life."

Through the window I could see the muscular lines of a Firedove touching down, its tan and grey swirls vivid against the sky. The silence between us grew heavy. Collie sighed and tapped a spoon against the table, gazing out at the plane.

"Please tell me again that the documents are somewhere safe," he muttered to me.

"They're safe," I said shortly.

He studied me; I could almost hear him biting back whatever he wanted to say. He glanced at his watch and stood up. "All right. I've got to get ready for my fight."

I rubbed my temples and didn't answer.

"Amity…" His voice held a hint of pleading.

None of this was Collie's fault, I reminded myself. I stood up too and gripped his hand hard. There was too much to say, so all that came out was a whispered, "Good luck."

The hot water couldn't wash away my thoughts, but when I stepped out of the shower later I felt a little better. Collie wasn't a fool. Even when we were kids, it had always been Collie who'd grab my arm and pull me back if he thought something wasn't safe.

If he trusted Mac, I had to do the same.

I stood towel-clad at my locker and briskly dried my hair with another towel. It felt invigorating – soothing.

I was just reaching for my comb when Harlan came up. "I'm not playing poker tonight, so don't ask," I said.

"I wasn't going to, *actually.*" He propped a burly shoulder next to me and cracked his knuckles. To my surprise, he looked ill at ease. Harlan, who was like a steamroller.

"What?" I said.

He had on only a pair of khaki trousers. The tattoo of the scantily-dressed woman on his bicep wriggled as he shrugged. "You and Vera are friends, right?"

"Right," I said blankly.

"So is that Marcus guy out of the picture? Last few times we all went to the Heat, he wasn't around."

I'd started to get my clothes out of my locker; I stopped mid-motion. Harlan met my gaze pugnaciously.

"Why do you want to know?" I said.

"No reason."

"Well, he is out of the picture," I said after a pause. "But it wasn't really what she wanted."

Harlan jammed his fists in his pockets and looked away. "So you don't think..."

"What?"

"Nothing," he muttered. "And I'm just – you know – looking out for her."

"Let me guess," I said slowly. "You think she's a girl, not just a pilot."

Harlan glared. "Do you have to say *every* damn thing that pops into your head, Vancour?"

"Sorry."

He scraped a hand over his blunt jaw, still scowling. "Yeah, well…mention it to her and I'll deal you bad poker hands for the rest of your natural life."

I was about to say something else – crack some joke, maybe, though I was terrible at jokes and Harlan wasn't in the mood anyway – when I straightened, my eyes widening.

Two officials had entered the locker room. They wore grey uniforms with silver buttons that shone. A swirling red-and-black symbol was stitched on their breast pockets. Gunnison's men – here.

My lungs turned to ice. *Collie.*

"What the hell…?" muttered Harlan, his face slackening.

The Guns weren't alone. A base security guard was with them, looking uncomfortable. But our base was Western Seaboard territory. The Guns could enter it as easily as the rest of the country now, if they had reason.

The locker room had gone still, everyone staring. After a quick conference, the trio started towards the lockers. The Guns' polished boots rapped against the floor as they headed for my row. I had a quick, fierce flash of thankfulness that Collie was away on his fight.

They will not take him, I thought. *I'll die first.*

They passed by and went into the next row over. A voice floated across to us: "Pardon me, sir, are you Clement Acland?"

Harlan and I threw each other a startled glance and

darted for the next row. We stopped just inside it. Clem stood with one arm half in a sleeve, staring at the men in grey. He completed the motion with a small shrug. His face was so pale that I thought of fish that lived deep underwater.

When Clem spoke, his voice was devoid of emotion. "Yeah, that's me."

"Then, Mr Acland, we must ask you to come with us," said the first Gun.

I felt dizzy with relief – with horror. "Why? What's he done?" I burst out. I stepped forward and felt Harlan's large hand grasp my arm.

"Careful," he muttered.

I was still wearing only a towel. The Gun looked me up and down sardonically. "I'm sorry, miss, but I don't have the authority to give out that information. Now, Mr Acland, will you come of your own accord? We'd hate to have a struggle and upset your former teammates."

That's when I saw the pistols at their hips. I felt the blood leave my face. Harlan looked sick.

Clem's eyes pleaded with me to keep quiet. "I'm originally from the Central States," he said in a low voice. "We escaped when I was just a kid. I never thought they'd come after me...I mean, I was only seven..."

"There's a bit more to it than that," said the second man. "I think you'll find, Mr Acland, that you have rather unfortunate stars. But our correction camps are very fine places. Now turn around."

"No!" I lunged forward as the handcuffs appeared; Harlan grabbed me and held me back. I struggled against his grip. "That law's not legal!" I cried. "I can prove it! *Stop!"*

"If you don't want to get shot, then for the love of all that's holy, *shut up*," hissed Harlan in my ear. I subsided, panting; my towel slipped and I clutched at it blindly.

Clem stood with his head down as they snapped the cuffs on him. Our security guard watched, doing nothing.

"No," I whispered.

They led Clem away, a Gun on either side of him and the security guard following behind. Clem stared downwards. He didn't look back at us as the locker room door swung shut behind them.

A chilled silence fell. Harlan had his forearm locked around me from behind, his hand grasping my shoulder. He slowly let go and scraped a hand over his face.

"Did you know Clem was from the CS?" he said finally.

I shook my head, still staring at the door. It felt as if the tide was roaring through my brain.

Harlan swore; with frightening suddenness, he slammed his fist against a locker. "*Dammit!* And there's nothing we can do, that's the hell of it! It's a law, fair and square."

My hand holding the towel was clenched so tightly that my muscles screamed. Without answering, I turned and headed for my locker – my clothes. Harlan was partly right; there was nothing he could do.

But there was something I could.

* * *

Commander Hendrix's office was set away from the other administrative buildings: a large bungalow with palm trees swaying overhead and a gleaming Firedove statue in front, endlessly frozen on one wing.

Inside, his secretary Norma sat typing with a quick, clattering sound. She glanced up. "Miss Vancour, what can I do for you?"

"I need to see Commander Hendrix. It's urgent." I kept my hands tight in my pockets. Hidden under my jacket I had an envelope with the information from Russ's house pressed between my arm and my shirt.

Norma hesitated, her fingers still on her typewriter keys. She glanced at Hendrix's closed office door. "Well, he's busy, but...wait a minute; I know he wanted to see you."

She wiped her hands nervously on her skirt before she rapped on the door and stuck her head in. After a low murmur of voices she returned, her relief obvious. "Yes, you can go in."

When I entered I saw to my dismay that Commander Hendrix wasn't alone. Another man sat across the desk from him, showing him something on a sheet of paper. "She's an excellent pilot," he was saying in a low voice. "And Miss Pierce confirmed her weeks ago."

"It makes sense. And in fact, there's another reason why—" Hendrix broke off as he saw me. He rose with a tired smile. "Amity, come on in. Perfect timing; I was just about to send for you. This gentleman will be sitting in, if that's all right."

Could I see you alone, sir? I didn't say it; I gazed uncertainly at the desk. The stranger had turned over the piece of paper. Was it me they'd been discussing?

The stranger rose too, and offered his hand. "A pleasure, Miss Vancour."

He had unremarkable features that looked strangely familiar. Confused, I shook his hand. His eyes were such a washed-out blue they were almost colourless.

"I'm sorry, I don't think I caught your name," I said after a pause.

"Oh, my apologies," said Hendrix. "This is Sam Cartwright, a liaison officer. We've been working on various matters together. Have a seat," he added, motioning. "Would you like some coffee?"

I sank into the remaining chair. "Thanks, but I came because—" I broke off, glancing at the visitor. I *had* seen him somewhere before. Where? I didn't know, but was almost positive that "Sam Cartwright" wasn't his name.

A liaison officer for who?

"Because…?" prompted Hendrix.

"I…it's private," I said slowly. Some instinct made me grab for the first explanation that came to mind: "I may need to ask for leave again soon."

Hendrix nodded. "Of course; I'm sure we can arrange that. You're very valued here, Amity." He sighed and rubbed the bridge of his nose. "I suppose you've heard about Clement," he added.

My muscles tensed. "I was there."

"A terrible business," said Mr Cartwright.

Hendrix nodded, his expression pained. "I hope that what I have to say to you will be on a cheerier note, Amity."

I was hyper-aware of the envelope hidden against my side. I was being ridiculous, I told myself. All I had to do was ask for a moment alone with Hendrix and show him exactly what Russ had been doing.

I hesitated, and then said, "I hope so too, sir. What is it?"

Hendrix looked down, fiddling with a pen. "I served with your father, you know. Tru was a fine man."

"I know," I said blankly. What did my father have to do with anything?

Hendrix turned the pen over in his hands. "I'll get to the point," he said. "Russ's death affects us in more ways than one. We haven't just lost a good team leader; we've lost a Tier One pilot." He glanced at me and smiled slightly. "He called you 'Wildcat', didn't he? Very apt. Amity, I'd like to offer you a Tier One promotion."

I'd dreamed for months of him saying those words. Now that he had, I felt wrong-footed. I could see Mr Cartwright in my peripheral vision, watching me.

Who was Miss Pierce, and how exactly had she "confirmed" me?

"Thank you," I said. My voice sounded stilted. "It's a tremendous honour."

Mr Cartwright reached for a glass on the desk then and took a sip of water. My scalp crawled. His gold signet ring had two stylized swirls, just like on those astrology charts of Ma's that had reminded me so much of Gunnison.

Memory surged. *That was it.* I'd once seen this pale-eyed man in a news photo...and in a grainy black-and-white telio programme, where he'd stood waving beside John Gunnison while thousands cheered.

I felt locked into my chair with shock, with dread. The man I now knew to be Sandford Cain spoke again.

"Yes, it *is* an honour," he said with a small smile. His fingers were long and thin, his gaze intent. "The world will be depending on you to make the right choices, Miss Vancour. You mustn't let it down."

"Choices?" The word was out before I could stop it.

Commander Hendrix tapped the pen against the desk, and then carefully put it to one side. "I hope very much that we're all on the same wavelength, Amity. I think that we are, aren't we?"

My mouth had gone dry. I didn't respond.

Commander Hendrix leaned forward. "We have a proposal for you."

Twenty minutes later I left my base commander's office with the documents still hidden under my jacket. Somehow

I managed to smile at Norma. Somehow I managed to appear relaxed as I grabbed a streetcar and rode into the Heat.

I found a drugstore with a payphone and slid the booth's wood-and-glass door shut behind me. I dropped a coin into the slot and spoke briefly to the operator, gripping the smooth black receiver to my ear and leaning close to talk into the mouthpiece. As I waited, I tapped the shelf that lay under the phone, too tense to stand still.

A cheery voice answered: "World for Peace, may I help you?"

I quickly turned my back to the drugstore. "I need to speak to Madeline Bark, please."

Chapter Twenty-seven

The view outside the train window shifted slowly from palm trees to mountains and oaks. I gazed out, unable to enjoy the gentle greenness of the approaching spring. Collie looked up from the book he was attempting to read; his expression was unsmiling.

"You're sure you can't tell me what's going on yet?" he said in an undertone.

"I'm sure," I said softly.

When the train pulled into our stop, it was just as I remembered: a weathered sign that read *Gloversdale* and a depot that could use a fresh coat of paint.

"Strange being back," said Collie as we stepped onto the platform.

My nerves relaxed a fraction at the scent of pines. "It's good, though."

"Is it?"

I took in the hard line of his jaw. I'd always had a lot more reason to like this town than he did...but once we could see my old place again, it would be all right. That had always been his home as much as mine.

I'd been desperate to get away from the base for a few days. Thankfully Collie had been able to get leave, too. He shot me a glance as we headed down Main Street.

"All right, we're here now," he said. "What's going on? Is this about Russ?"

I clenched my handbag. "Wait until we get to the guest house."

"You don't seriously think anyone's listening?"

"No. But I can't do it here."

As we walked I noticed in dismay how much my home town had changed. Gloversdale had never been large, but between the lumber yards and the paper mill, it had flourished. Now some of the stores had shut down, their windows dark squares. The consequences of my sabotaged fight had reached here, too.

We'll get the result overturned, I vowed to myself. I winced as I noticed an astrologer's sign across from the library. The red-and-black swirl looked brand-new. Apparently it was one of the few places around that was thriving.

Even here, people were being taken in by that garbage.

Collie started to say something else. His head snapped up as the sound of shouts reached us – the harsh crack of knuckles against skin. I broke into a run without thinking, heading for the two men scuffling in front of the hardware store. Collie dropped our suitcase and passed me, long legs pumping.

"Hey, *hey*!" He shoved in between them – was jostled fiercely as he held them apart. "Knock it off!"

"You stay out of this!" one shouted. "He took my job!"

"They fired you, Evans!" the other one bellowed back. "It's not my fault I can take less pay! I still gotta eat, don't I?"

"*Cut it out!*" Collie's voice broke in sharply. "Come on, can't you work this out without whaling on each other?"

A small crowd gathered, gawping at the scene. I stood watching with wide eyes. I shouldn't have been surprised. Collie had always been the peacemaker of playground fights.

Evans's eyes narrowed. Slowly, he said, "Say…you're one of the Reed boys, aren't you?"

I was probably the only one who saw Collie's shoulders tighten. He dropped his hand from the man's arm. "Yeah, I'm a Reed. What of it?"

"Which one? Hank's boy?" Before Collie could answer, Evans snorted and said, "You know, your Uncle Matt screwed me good on a deal for new roofing. Haven't seen hide or hair of him since."

Collie's lips were white. "I haven't spoken to my Uncle Matt in years," he said levelly.

"You Reeds have always got an angle, haven't you? No matter what –" Evans gestured towards the closed stores – "you *Reeds* are all right, like rats licking off the cream for yourselves—"

"Hey!" I was in front of the man before I knew it. I saw his faint alarm; realized fleetingly how wild I must look as I spat out, "You don't know what you're talking about! He's a Peacefighter. He risks his life every day."

Evans's lip curled. "A Reed, a Peacefighter? That'll be the day."

"It's true! Collie, show him your tags."

"I don't have to show him anything." Collie put his arm around me and led me away, pausing only to grab up our suitcase. His fingers were tense on my shoulder. I could hear the crowd murmuring. We hadn't gone ten paces before jogging footsteps caught up with us. Collie whirled, looking ready for a fight.

The other man held up his hands. "Hey, take it easy! Listen, thanks for stepping in. You're okay in my book, even if you are a Reed."

"Thanks," said Collie dryly.

"You're really a Peacefighter?"

"Yeah. I really am."

The man gave a low whistle. "Well, good for you, pal. We appreciate your service."

Collie and I didn't speak again until we were in our

room at the guest house, with its old-fashioned high bed. I'd signed us in as *Mr and Mrs C Reed*, and had longed for the landlady to raise an eyebrow at the name, so I could give her a piece of my mind.

She just smiled and showed us to our room.

I wrapped my arms around him. "I'm sorry," I whispered against his neck. "We should never have come here. I forgot how bad it always was for you."

It was coming back now, though: the dozens of times Collie and I had walked down that very street and I'd been aware of sideways glances. When I was nine, I'd heard a woman say, "Well, if she were *my* daughter, I'd put a stop to it." I hadn't known what she meant until I saw Collie's blazing cheeks. Then I'd wanted to fly at the woman and claw her eyes out.

Collie stroked his hands through my hair and we kissed. "It doesn't matter," he whispered roughly. "I'd live it all over again in a second. I'd never have met you otherwise."

The words I wanted to say wouldn't come. I could only kiss him back as hard as I could. Finally Collie pulled away a little. His expression was still bitter. "But it's not true, you know," he said. "Reeds do not always have an angle."

"Collie, don't you think I know that?"

"I mean, I know my father does, and my uncles, but—"

I popped my hand over his mouth. "Stop it," I snapped. "*I love you*, you big jerk – remember?"

The corner of Collie's mouth lifted. "Who says romance is dead?" he said after a pause.

I curved my palm against his cheek, feeling the slight prickle of his stubble. Collie let out a breath, then took my hand and kissed it.

"All right," he said. "And I love you too, you infuriating woman. Now tell me what's going on."

I'd meant to lead up to the news gradually. Instead I blurted it out like vomit.

"Hendrix offered me a bribe to throw fights," I said.

Collie slowly let go of my hand. His eyes were very blue – wide with shock.

"It's true," I said, though he hadn't argued. "It was when he offered me a Tier One. You were right. This thing goes a lot deeper than just Russ."

Collie dropped onto the bed as if his legs had been kicked from under him. His throat moved; he scraped a hand over his jaw. "Hendrix...Hendrix actually asked you to throw a fight?"

From outside came the sound of children skipping rope, chanting: "*Twelve signs, all divine, yes it's true, here's the one for you! Aries-Taurus-Gemini-Cancer—*"

I banged the window shut. "Not yet," I said into the sudden silence. "But it was made very clear that if I took the promotion, I'd be expected to throw whatever fights they wanted and that extra payments would come my way if I did. And...it was also made very clear what would happen if I told anyone."

The memory stung. At the end of our meeting, Hendrix had cleared his throat. "I hope you'll stay loyal to our agreement, Amity," he said. "Not like your friend Stan. That was a very sad waste."

I'd somehow managed not to react. *Stan*, with his quick smile, whose offbeat compliments had always made me laugh. I'd never have believed he was involved in this… except that the day he'd died, Stan had wanted to celebrate doing something he "should have done months ago".

Had he just told them that he wouldn't play their game any more?

The bedsprings squeaked as Collie quickly rose and came over. He gripped my arms. "What did you tell Hendrix?"

"Don't worry, I played along," I said sourly. "I told him it was just the opportunity I'd been hoping for."

Collie's shoulders sagged with relief. "This happened two days ago and you didn't *tell* me?"

"I've wanted to a hundred times! But Madeline—"

"Who?"

"Madeline Bark. Remember?"

Memory slowly lit Collie's eyes. "Yeah," he said. "I remember. Is she still at the World for Peace?"

"Yes, and she's checking into it. She made me promise not to tell anyone, but…" My mouth tightened as I recalled the cold, golden glint of a signet ring. I had to tell Collie or I'd go crazy.

"There's more," I said finally. I sat on the bed and drew him down beside me. "Someone else was in that meeting too, Collie. I've done some checking since and…" I turned his hand over and touched his tattoo: the swirling glyph for Leo.

"It's bad," I told him.

Collie had gone deathly pale. After a beat, his fingers closed around mine.

"Let me have it."

When I called Madeline and started to explain, she'd interrupted the moment she realized what I was saying. "Come see me," she said. "*Now.* Use the officials' private entrance on Lennox Street. I'll meet you down there."

Once we were safe in her office she went through the paperwork from Russ's house, asking me question after question. She frowned as she studied Russ's scrawled notes on the news clippings, then glanced up. Her voice was hoarse.

"And you say *Commander Hendrix* offered you a bribe?"

I was pacing her office, too restless to sit still. "Yes, but Madeline, it's even worse than that." I described the man I'd been introduced to as "Sam Cartwright".

"It was Sandford Cain," I said. "I'm certain of it."

She froze. "*Cain?* Are you sure?"

"Positive. I've only seen one photo, but his eyes are very distinctive. It was him."

Madeline licked her lips. "I hope you're wrong."

"I wish I was." I dropped into a seat. I felt on edge, almost sick to my stomach. "He said someone named

Miss Pierce had 'confirmed' me. What does *that* mean? And why was a CS representative there at all? It doesn't make any sense!" I motioned to the pile of clippings. "Russ threw fights against all different countries, not just the Central States!"

Madeline's voice was urgent. "You could swear in a court of law that it was Sandford Cain? You're absolutely positive? Amity, most people in the WS barely know his name!"

I nodded. "The things I'd read about him stuck in my head, so when I saw his photo once, I really studied it. Yes, I could swear it in court. The only thing I'm clueless about is why Gunnison's right-hand man was sitting there while my base commander offered me bribes."

My words hung bitterly in the air. Outside, I could hear two Firedoves fighting somewhere over the bay: the faint drone of the engines, a distant burst of gunfire.

Madeline was pale, with a single spot of colour high on each cheek. Finally she said, "Well...at the very least, it seems we're looking at collusion to influence the Peacefights. And from what you say, two people have already been killed." She slid the clippings back in the envelope. Her hand was trembling.

I leaned forward. "What are you going to do?"

She closed her eyes and pressed her index fingers to her mouth. "First I'm going to make some very discreet inquiries," she said finally. "We don't know how deep this thing goes."

I felt physically cold, as if an Arctic breeze had swept in. "You think the *WfP* might be involved?"

"Certainly not all of it. I hope none of it. But before I try to get these fights overturned, I need to know exactly what's going on." Madeline studied me tautly. "Who else knows about this?"

Collie's name came to my lips. I didn't say it. Given his own link to the Central States, I didn't want him implicated, not even to Madeline, in case it somehow put him in danger.

"No one," I said.

"Good. Don't say a single word. Don't arouse *any* suspicion."

"If they ask me to throw a fight, I won't do it."

"Of course not! Just play along as best you can. I don't need to tell you that these are dangerous people, Amity."

Madeline locked the documents from Russ's house away in her safe. As she spun the dial, a tense frown creased her freckles, and I recalled all the summers she'd flown with Dad. That same intent expression as she surveyed the runway up ahead.

She hugged me when I left. Her hazel eyes were deeply troubled.

"Keep safe," she said softly. "I'll be in touch soon."

* * *

The house where I'd grown up was vacant and needed a coat of paint. When Collie and I went there the next day I hated how abandoned it looked, though I'd have resented seeing someone else living in it.

Inside the rooms were empty of furniture but full of ghosts. In the kitchen I gazed at the spot where the table had been. My father had sat in here the night before he died.

I stood silently as it all came back: how I'd heard him and crept down the stairs. The strangeness of his mood. It had scared me a little; at the same time, I'd longed to understand what he was saying. I'd felt that if I could just do that, I'd finally have the key to him.

I swallowed and turned away. Collie stood leaning against the doorjamb, massaging his forehead. He'd been strained and silent since yesterday afternoon, when I told him what I'd found out after I left Madeline's office. Last night we'd made love with a kind of desperate passion that had said more than words.

"Let's go out to the barn," I said.

Collie glanced up. "You don't want to see upstairs?" he asked after a pause.

"No."

We stepped out into the sunlight and walked through the overgrown yard. The fields were growing wild, too. Collie didn't speak. He had his hands in his pockets, gazing down at the ground, his mouth tight. I wished that I could help with what he was feeling, but I couldn't. I felt the same.

In my father's old barn, his Firedove still crouched.

I thought I must be imagining things, but when I got close it was still there. I'd assumed Ma had sold it. I stroked the plane's side gently, hating whoever had left it here without its canvas covering. Cobwebs lay thick on its surface.

Collie propped himself beside me – just like that day four years ago.

"I still can't believe it," he said finally.

I let my hand fall. "It's true," I said. "Everything leads back to Gunnison."

Chapter Twenty-eight

When I'd left Madeline's office that day I could feel something nagging at my brain – some detail I'd forgotten.

It hit me the next afternoon, when I drew a few circulars from my mailbox in the base office and saw a letter in the box next to mine. It had an Alaskan grizzly bear stamp, just like on the letter I'd received from Concordia's parents.

Concordia.

And suddenly I knew with icy clarity: Russ hadn't been the only corrupt pilot. I stood clutching the circulars as her parents' words rushed back. *We never had much money, but Cordy was always smiling and tried to help out all she could.*

The way her plane had cruised along below mine, as tempting as a dangling worm to a fish…Concordia had thrown her fight. It was why she'd wanted me to tell her family she was sorry, because doing so had ended up killing her. Who'd been paying her? Had Sandford Cain been involved in *that*, too?

But why? To what end?

My sabotaged fight against the EA. Concordia's thrown fight against me.

Finding out the rest had only taken a few hours. I'd sat in a corner of the library, scanning books of news clippings. And when the puzzle pieces all clicked into place, every fight that didn't directly benefit Gunnison had been explained. Stunned, I stared down at two headlines.

LAND RIGHTS CEDED TO GUNNISON
BY RUSSIAN STATES

EUROPEAN ALLIANCE JOIN
WITH SCANDO-FINNS IN DEAL WITH
CENTRAL STATES

The barn was silent, save for the soft rustling of pigeons in the eaves. "Every thrown fight that we know about leads back to him," I repeated. "Every one. That fight I lost that ceded our oil rights? The European Alliance turned right around and gave those rights to Gunnison."

Collie winced, but I had to go on.

"The same for the fight I won against Concordia – *it* ended up helping Gunnison, too. The Western Seaboard's agricultural department sold those land rights to the Russian States, who ceded them to the CS the *very next day*. It was all in place. All arranged."

My throat tightened as I recalled Concordia's hand going cold in mine. The prettiness of her face under the blood. And Russ. Stan. What had driven them both to betray the world's trust? Money troubles? I'd had the impression sometimes that Stan's family didn't have much.

Maybe that explained it...but it didn't make what my friends had done any easier to bear.

Collie looked as if he'd never smiled in his life. He gazed through the open barn door to the fields beyond. "If Gunnison's really behind all of this..." He didn't finish.

"I don't understand it," I said tightly. "Why would anyone want that madman in charge? All these fights benefiting Gunnison: *why?* They could add up to him taking everything over someday, if they aren't stopped."

Collie glanced down at his tattoo; his eyes hardened. "His followers are passionate like you can't even imagine," he said. His lip curled as he added, "And don't forget, Gunnison can get rid of the Discordants. Believe me, people like having someone they can blame their troubles on, as long as it isn't them."

There was something about the way he said it. The barn felt vast around us as I stared at him. "Collie...you were found Discordant, weren't you?"

His jaw went taut. "No."

"You *were.* That's why you had to escape – leave your parents—"

His eyes flashed; for a second he looked as if he hated me. "*Drop it,* Amity."

I hesitated, remembering his nightmares: his head lashing back and forth as he pleaded with someone. What had happened to him?

"It's dropped," I said.

I wrapped my arms around him. Collie let out a breath and hugged me hard. Finally he drew back. In the barn's dimness his eyes were dark green, intent on mine.

"Okay, look," he said. "I was up all night trying to decide what we should do."

My forehead creased. "Do? I've already told Madeline about Gunnison being behind it all. What else *can* we do?" I'd met her in an out of the way diner in the Heat. The dread in her eyes had told me clearly just how much worse this new information made things.

"Please! Just listen to me," said Collie.

"I'm listening," I said after a pause.

He took a deep breath. "All right. I think we should leave now and never look back."

"*What?*"

Collie gripped my arms, "Amity, Sandford Cain is infamous in the CS. He's a killer. And he knows who you are. When they realize what Madeline's up to, they'll know *you* were the one who reported them."

I started to speak. Collie rushed: "You'll be killed and it

won't even make any difference! If Gunnison's behind all of this, believe me – he is not going to be stopped."

He kissed my palm, then folded his fingers tightly over mine. "*Please*," he said in a low voice. "Come away with me. Let's go into town, catch the next train and just go."

My heart twisted. I pulled away and gazed at my father's Firedove. It was just like the one he'd flown in so many fights. And in every one, he'd believed in what he was doing.

"We can't." My voice was curter than I'd intended. "Madeline's in danger too; if we run they'd know something's up. Besides, we're Peacefighters. That still means something."

Collie spun me to face him. "I know what you're thinking! Well, I knew your father too, and Tru would *not* have wanted you to get gunned down in some alleyway for the sake of an ideal!"

"You're wrong." The whispered words needed no thought. My father's story of Louise – her family murdered by troops; the way she'd helped turn the world back from its fatal path – had given me the answer long ago.

"This isn't *an* ideal," I said shakily. "It's *the* ideal. It's worth more than anything."

"More than us?"

"Of course!" I slumped against the Firedove, not knowing whether to laugh or cry. "We're just two people, Collie! What does it matter what happens to us?"

"*It matters.*" He clutched my arms, his expression fierce,

pleading. "Amity, we're finally together – we actually have a shot at happiness! *Please listen.* If you go back, you will get killed."

"You don't know that."

"It's obvious!"

"I can't just run away! What kind of a person would that make me?"

"A smart one! An alive one! One with a man who loves her more than anything, who's begging her on his knees to—"

"*Shut up! Just shut up!*" The words echoed around the barn. I stood with my hands pressed to my head, trembling.

Silence settled over us like a heavy blanket. Collie's expression was tormented. He jammed his fists in his pockets and stared out at the fields again. They rippled in the breeze, flashing first green, then silver. In the rafters, one of the pigeons cooed.

When he finally spoke, his voice was as dull as when he'd told me he was leaving that day. "I knew that you'd say this. Every last word."

"You know I'm right," I said softly.

"There's no way that I'm going to convince you, is there?"

I slowly shook my head. "No."

Collie gave a slight shudder, still staring out at the fields. I could see the tightness of his muscles even through his shirt. "I should go away on my own," he murmured finally. "Just leave this. Leave all of it."

I started to answer. I couldn't. He turned then and studied my face as if he'd never seen it before.

"Except that I could never leave you," he said.

Words had never felt as useless. "Collie...I have to go back and play along like Madeline asked. It could ruin our only hope of exposing the corruption if I don't. Nothing will happen. I'll be all right."

"Do you even believe that yourself?"

"I have to believe it. We both have to."

I put my arms around him. He held me tightly. He was almost trembling. "I am never giving you up," he said in a low voice. "*Never.* Do you understand me?"

My throat clenched. "I'm glad to hear it." I drew back and touched his face, trying to soothe its tautness. "Canary Cargo, remember?" I said. "With a bright yellow plane."

CHAPTER TWENTY-NINE

"AND SO, OF COURSE, WITH MARS in the fourth house, I decided that..."

The young astrologer had been talking for some time. Kay made polite noises, hardly listening. They were in the lavish Aquarius dome; the party in Gunnison's state offices was a glittering array of perfect dresses, crisp tuxedoes. She took a sip of champagne and gazed over to where John Gunnison stood talking in a small knot of people.

His blunt features and solid farmhand's body should have looked ridiculous in a tux. Perhaps technically they did, but Kay felt drawn to him anyway, and knew she wasn't the only one. That voice. The way he held himself.

Look at me, Kay willed him. The dress she wore was the

most beautiful thing she'd ever owned: blue sequins and airy net.

Gunnison did not look in her direction.

He hadn't looked in her direction all night.

Kay licked her lips. They'd had several lunch meetings by now, and Gunnison had been unfailingly warm – had made Kay feel that her input to the Twelve Year Plan was essential. She'd often wondered whether Gunnison really believed in "the power of the stars" but by now she was convinced of his sincerity. It shone from his face, his words.

The knowledge should have made him easier to read. Instead Kay had found herself falling more under his spell, strangely intrigued by his belief, even if she didn't share it. When she'd gotten the invitation to this gathering she'd been thrilled – for more reasons than what it meant for her personal survival. But Gunnison hadn't even greeted her when she arrived.

As the astrologer at her side talked on and on, Kay tried to still her icy dread. The image of severed heads on a chain-link fence hovered at the back of her mind, reminding her of what happened to those Gunnison disapproved of.

No. She was being ridiculous.

A guy a little older than Kay appeared. Short – just barely taller than her – with rumpled brown hair. He gave her an earnest look. "Miss Pierce, isn't it? Say, do you mind if I ask your opinion about something?"

The astrologer at her side blinked and stopped talking. Kay regarded the newcomer in surprise.

"No, of course not," she said.

"In private, if that's okay." The man took Kay's arm and led her away. When they reached the other side of the room he let his hand fall. "I don't really want your opinion," he said cheerfully. "I just thought you needed rescuing."

Kay tried to smile. "I suppose so. Thanks."

He stuck out his hand with a grin. A small diamond bull glittered on his lapel.

"Mac Jones," he said.

They shook. "Are you with the World for Peace?" Kay asked politely.

Thanks to Gunnison's skilful manoeuvring, he had many important supporters, both in the World for Peace and in key positions in other countries. A number of these were present tonight.

Mac Jones shook his head. "No, I work mostly with Mr Cain."

Kay remembered his name then. "That's right, you've been helping him find the Discordants in the Western Seaboard, haven't you? Getting the lists from the resistance groups."

Mac waggled his dark eyebrows. "Hey, you know all about me."

Kay resisted the urge to glance at Gunnison again. She shrugged. "Not really. But Mr Cain's been pleased with your work."

Mac turned serious. He looked over at Gunnison himself. "I hope so," he said with a frown. "You wouldn't believe how many Discordants the Resistance has helped to get away."

"How do you do it?" Kay asked, for lack of anything else to say. "Get hold of their lists, I mean."

Mac snagged a glass of champagne from the tray of a passing waiter.

"Oh, the Resistance trusts me. I spend a lot of time working in the Western Seaboard. They think I'm on the up and up, helping out Discordants on the run." He shrugged. "Well, I *do* help them. Got to. It means I get access to what we need. I turn in whoever I can, though, if the other side won't suspect me."

Gunnison's voice lifted over the crowd for a moment. Kay tensed, but couldn't make out his words.

"A double agent, then," she commented. "How interesting."

Mac grinned as if he knew she didn't mean it. "So you're one of the Twelve Year astrologers? Very prestigious."

"Thanks. I do my best."

"Sure, we all do." Mac took a gulp of champagne and looked again at Gunnison. He seemed restless, but turned back to Kay. "Heard about the Conflict Council decision?"

"About our new challenge against the WS?"

Mac nodded. "They finally passed it. Once we win the Peacefight, we'll be able to extradite *all* Western Seaboard Discordants...even if they're WS citizens. We can start cleaning the place up before we even take over." He lowered his voice. "Just between us, I hear we've already sent people in to start laying the groundwork."

Despite Kay's tension, her interest stirred. "So soon?" she asked in a murmur. "But how can we check anyone's chart over there before we have access to birth certificates?" Though key members of the Western Seaboard's press were Gunnison supporters, by and large the government weren't. They wouldn't provide information before they had to.

"Simple – if people have been using astrologers of their own accord." Mac clinked his glass against Kay's. "Hey, did you know some of the astrologers have even been marking family envelopes for us? Enemies of Harmony will no longer be tolerated. Quite a victory."

Kay knew what a landmark ruling the upcoming Tier One fight had been. It nearly hadn't passed; the Conflict Council's secret Gunnison followers weren't in the majority. Kay thought how galling it must be for Gunnison to have to depend on the whims of the Council to approve the fights he needed.

If things went the way he planned, he soon wouldn't have to.

A week had passed since Kay had dowsed for him. The army was still poised near the Western Seaboard, waiting to attack. Kay had no idea what Gunnison's missing "puzzle piece" might be – and didn't think he did, either.

Over their last lunch, he'd confided that the new

extradition law would be his offering to Lady Harmony, who hated all Discordants. Soon he hoped that he'd receive the sign he needed to begin the Reclamation. From what Kay had heard, many in the Western Seaboard were envious of their more prosperous neighbours. They'd probably be relieved when Johnny took charge...once the "fire and fury" was over.

When it happens, I will be there to advise him, Kay promised herself. She fingered the stem of her champagne glass and glanced at Gunnison's group again. She wished she had the nerve to join them.

If Johnny would give her just the merest glance, she'd do it.

One of Gunnison's aides appeared then and touched Mac's arm. "Mr Gunnison would like you to join him," he said in an undertone. "Hester from World for Peace has arrived; they're going to go over the Vancour matter."

This seemed to be what Mac had been waiting for. "Of course," he said quickly. He nodded to Kay, and the two strode off towards the group.

Kay stood alone, rigid with sudden apprehension. Unlike Gunnison, the aide *had* looked at her. His gaze had been flinty.

She stared over at the small cluster of people. Next to Gunnison stood Hester, the World for Peace official – a statuesque black woman. The others were clearly hanging on her every word. Gunnison said something; Hester looked serious as she replied.

What was going on? Unable to help herself, Kay edged closer. The young astrologer she'd been rescued from stood munching a canapé near them. Kay planted herself at his side and gave him a dazzling smile.

"I was so fascinated about what you were saying earlier," she said.

He beamed in surprise and started talking again. Kay glanced surreptitiously at the group, straining to hear their conversation. Skinner was there. So was Bernard Chester, with his plump cheeks and wavy brown hair. Only Sandford Cain was absent; he was currently in the Western Seaboard.

Skinner said, "Well, frankly, I was concerned about Vancour from the start."

Who's Vancour? thought Kay wildly.

The WfP woman looked strained. "Yes, from what I hear she's very determined. And knows enough now to make a great deal of trouble." She turned to Mac. "I understand you've met her?"

Mac grimaced. "Briefly. Not long enough to form a useful impression."

"We already *have* an impression, unfortunately," said Hester. "We're just lucky that Sandford's already out there and can deal with her."

Gunnison had been standing grimly silent. At the mention of Sandford Cain he nodded. "Very lucky." He glanced at an aide. "Has Sandy checked in yet?"

"Not yet," said the aide.

"Well, I want to know the moment he does. And I'm not happy that we weren't aware sooner that Vancour could be a danger. No wonder Hendrix got it so wrong. Show me that chart again, Mal. It wasn't even *flagged*?"

"I'm afraid not," said Skinner tautly. "We perhaps put a bit too much trust in Miss Pierce."

Icy fear swept Kay; she looked quickly over. Skinner held an astrological chart. He and Bernard pointed something out to Gunnison, who nodded. Even from here, Kay could see the square with an "x" through it.

She breathed in sharply. *The Grand Cross chart.* She'd once wavered over it, but then hadn't chosen it as a danger.

Gunnison looked up then. His gaze met Kay's. For a moment they were the only two people in the room. He studied her, briefly, deeply, his look both disappointed and coolly measuring. Kay clutched her glass.

What's happened? she thought in terror. What had this "Vancour" person done? She started to go over and find out, but Gunnison looked away then, obviously dismissing her, and it felt impossible.

She stood frozen, her thoughts tumbling, not even pretending to listen to the young astrologer.

No one else spoke to her for the rest of the night.

Chapter Thirty

The day after we got back to base, Collie was made a Tier One pilot.

Ordinarily I'd have been jubilant: he'd been a Peacefighter for less than six months. Now the news brought a chill.

We were in the canteen heading towards a table when he told me; I stopped short. "You're *what*?"

"Tier One," repeated Collie. He glanced at the busy room and nudged me. "Come on – let's sit down." His face wore the taut lines that it had worn since I'd refused to run away with him.

We found a table in the corner. I leaned close. "Tell me everything."

Collie added sugar to his coffee and then fiddled with

the canister. "Not much to tell. There was a note in my mailbox this morning to see Hendrix. When I went over, he offered me a Tier One promotion."

"That's all?"

"That's all."

"He didn't mention—" I broke off, glad of the canteen's buzz.

"No," said Collie. "And he was alone."

My voice was barely a whisper. "But why would he offer *me* bribes, and not you?"

Collie shook his head tensely. "I guess he's already got his crooked Tier One pilot and doesn't need another one."

Since we weren't team leaders, our jobs still included taking Tier Two fights if needed. The relief that morning when Hendrix hadn't approached me about anything untoward had been immense.

Suddenly it was as if I were seeing the canteen through a red lens that made everyone's faces distorted, avaricious. How many Peacefighters took bribes? For the first time, I was glad my father was dead. This would have devastated him…along with everything else that was happening in the Western Seaboard.

Anger was the mood of the country now. It had been just over three months since my failed appeal and the loss of our oil rights. Long editorial screeds filled the newspapers, complaining about President Lopez, the long breadlines, the scanty resources…and lauding Gunnison for being a "shining example of strong leadership". They stopped just short of saying, *He should be our leader, too.*

Worse, people were still being taken away. There were stories daily about former Central States citizens who'd been found in hiding and dragged off by the Guns.

I felt hollow. It all seemed to be spinning out of control. I held my coffee mug tight between both hands. "We'll make everything right again," I muttered. "We *have* to."

Collie's expression was torn between sympathy and cynicism; our argument in the barn hovered between us. He glanced at his watch and rose from his chair.

"Right, well…I have to meet the administrator and go check out my new quarters."

I looked up. "You accepted one of the Tier One houses?"

"Yeah, why?"

"No reason," I said after a pause. I'd told Hendrix that I liked rooming with Vera and that maybe I'd move later. There was no way I wanted a new house from him under the circumstances.

Collie's face darkened as if I'd said the words out loud. He propped his hands on the table and leaned close.

"You know what?" he said softly. "If it were up to me we'd be long gone by now – someplace safe where Sandford Cain could never find you. So yeah, sweetheart, you better believe I took the bigger house and the higher pay. I'll take whatever I can before the whole damn thing explodes."

* * *

Once Harlan had asked what a Virgo was. No one would ask that now; astrology was in the very ether. The next night Collie had a Tier Two fight and Vera and I went into the Heat. I saw three more astrologer's signs there; the flashing red-and-black swirls seemed to taunt me. When a woman passed us wearing a golden crab brooch, it felt like the last straw.

"That's Cancer the crab," I said to her.

"That's right." She fingered the brooch with a smile. "Pretty, isn't it?"

"But why are you wearing it? You don't have to show your sun sign here, not yet."

She stared at me like I was crazy. "It's only a brooch."

My voice rose. "Do you know what they do to people in the Central States who refuse to show their sun signs? No, you probably don't, because you'd have to read the papers with a magnifying glass to find any mention of it, but—"

The woman took a step back. "It's only a *brooch*," she repeated.

She strode off.

Vera stood gaping. "Amity..."

I pressed my hand over my eyes. "Sorry," I said. "Sorry."

Finally I couldn't stand it any more and called Madeline from a payphone in one of the Heat's diners. "Who's calling, please?" asked the WfP switchboard operator.

"Louise," I said, twisting the phone cord. Would Madeline remember my middle name?

I waited for a long time, listening to the heavy weight of silence through the receiver. The sounds of the diner came muffled through the phone booth's door: the clinking of silverware, people's conversations.

"Hello?" Madeline's voice was cautious.

I jerked upright. "It's me. What's happening?"

"Nothing I can say over the phone."

"Fine, I'll come to your office—"

"*No.*"

"But—"

"Listen to me!" Her voice was quick, urgent. "Do not call me again. Do not come here. I'm doing everything I can, but things are at a very tricky stage. You need to just keep doing your job and not raise any suspicions. Can you do that for me?"

My fingernails dug into my palm. "Yes," I said at last.

"Good girl," Madeline said softly. "I'll be in touch as soon as I can. We *will* beat this thing, I promise."

The line went dead. In slow motion I hung up the receiver…and tried not to think about the undercurrent of fear in her tone.

Hey Sis,

I hope you're doing well and winning lots of fights. Remember those astrology charts I showed you? Well, these two men came today and asked to see them. I don't know how they knew Ma had them but they did. One of them wrote something down and his cufflinks had

Gunnison's symbol on it. When they gave the charts back they wouldn't explain anything, they just said they'd need to do more checking. I asked what they were checking but they told me to be quiet and left.

Ma's nervous even though she's trying to hide it. I'm kind of nervous too. Amity, do you know what's going on?

Your brother,
Hal

"Don't panic," said Collie. "Amity! Calm down."

"How can I?" I snapped. I paced back and forth, almost wearing a trail in the rug. We were at Collie's new house. At least they hadn't given him Russ's old place; it would have been more than I could bear.

"I really don't think they're looking for me," Collie said again. But he'd been pale ever since he read Hal's letter… and I knew we were both thinking about the chart in Ma's house with his name on it.

"Of course they are." I sank onto the sofa, Hal's letter crumpled tensely in my hand. "What else could it be? *My* family aren't CS residents!"

I'd phoned home as soon as I received it – using a payphone in the Heat again, which I hoped was more anonymous than the base switchboard. Hendrix was clearly Gunnison's lackey; the less that got back to him, the better.

Ma had assured me everything was fine. "They haven't

come back," she said, her voice deliberately cheerful. "They were probably just taking some kind of survey."

I'd gripped the receiver hard. "Ma, if they come again, don't let them in, do you understand? They don't have any rights over you!"

"Really?" Ma had sounded doubtful. "Well...they seemed very sure of themselves."

"Ma! *Do not let them in again.* Promise me."

She'd agreed, though I didn't have high hopes. I knew how she wilted when confronted with authority; she assumed anyone in a uniform knew best.

"They must have found out your link to my family," I said to Collie. "They could be talking to Ma's friends this instant; you know she's told them all that you're a Peacefighter. Collie—" I broke off and touched his face, stroking the slight roughness of his stubble.

"No," I said hoarsely. "I won't let them take you."

He gripped my hands. "Listen to me! They are not looking for me. I'd bet money on it. I don't even exist in the Central States any more, remember?"

"How can you be so sure? Because *Mac* says so?"

"Yes! Amity, you've got to tell Rose and Hal to keep safe. Tell them not to let them in again."

"I already have. Well, I told Ma. Hal was at school."

Collie knew Ma as well as I did. His grip tightened. "Tell Hal, too. Call him and warn him to be careful. Tell him not to call the base. Promise me!"

"You don't have to make me promise. Of course I will."

He's my brother, I almost said, but in all the ways that counted he was Collie's brother, too. "He's only fourteen, though," I added quietly. Hal had had a birthday the month before. "I don't know how well he could stand up to the Guns, if it came to that."

Collie winced at the word "Guns". He turned away and didn't speak for a moment. "No…it's not easy to stand up to them," he said huskily. "But he's got to try."

Though he might not want to face it, we both knew Collie was the only reason Gunnison's men might be interested in my family. I sank onto the sofa again. The house was silent. Very distantly, I could hear a Firedove engine overhead.

"I'm scared," I admitted after a pause. "When I talked to Madeline, she sounded worried."

Collie looked quickly at me. "Have you changed your mind?"

"No! We can't just *leave.*" I pressed my hands to my throbbing temples. "It could destroy everything she's trying to do."

Collie sagged. He closed his eyes. "You know, I'd throw you over my shoulder and take you out of here by brute force if I could," he said finally.

"And just abandon the whole world to Gunnison? Let the corruption continue? You can't be serious!"

Collie rubbed his forehead and didn't answer.

I let out a long ragged breath and slumped against the sofa. I stared at the ceiling. "Besides…being a Peacefighter still means something," I whispered into the silence. "It's just got to."

"You'd better go." Collie's voice was dull.

"What? Why?"

He went to the sideboard and poured himself a drink. His shoulders were carved in stone. "Because all I want to do right now is make love to you and never hear the word 'Peacefighter' again for as long as I live, that's why."

I was close to tears and hated it. I stood up and grabbed my jacket. "Fine. Being a Peacefighter is still an honour, Collie, even now. Maybe *you* should leave, if I'm the only reason you're hanging around."

He stiffened. He turned and regarded me coldly. "Don't think I'm not tempted."

"Nichols, Tier Two fight against the European Alliance... Patterson, Tier Three fight against Mexico..."

I sat stiffly on the metal folding chair as Hendrix read the roster. Vera leaned towards me. "Do you want to have lunch together, if your name doesn't—"

I touched her arm, silencing her. Hendrix had just reached the Rs.

"Ramirez, Tier Two fight against Indasia...Reed, Tier One fight against the Central States..."

Tier One? A murmur went through the hangar.

I turned quickly in my seat. Collie sat with some of the other pilots. Our eyes met. I saw his shock – his apprehension.

I faced forward in a daze. What claim had Gunnison made against our country now? But the Tier One had been given to Collie, so they wanted it fought fairly. Had Madeline already made a difference behind the scenes? No, surely she'd have been in touch.

Vera gazed worriedly at me.

"Sorry," I murmured, not looking away from the World for Peace flag. "I can't do lunch today."

My own name wasn't called.

When Hendrix dismissed us, I made my way over to Collie. We hadn't spoken since the night before, but he didn't seem surprised when I joined him to walk over to the Deciding Room, where he'd find out where and when his fight would take place.

Outside it had just finished raining. Everything had a bright, freshly-washed look – even the trucks passing by. We took a shortcut through the administrative housing. The path was slightly overgrown with weeds.

"What do you suppose it means that there's another Tier One fight against the Central States so soon after the last one?" I said in an undertone. This was our second Tier One in just over two months. The papers hadn't even hinted that anything was brewing.

Collie shook his head. "Nothing good."

A few pilots passed; I kept quiet until they were out of earshot. "At least they want you to fight it and not me," I said. "Collie, it feels like something must have happened."

He gave me a sharp look. "With Madeline?"

"What else?"

"I don't know, and that scares the hell out of me," he said curtly. He stopped and rubbed his fist over his mouth. We were in a vacant lot beneath a cluster of palm trees. A soft pattering fell around us: remnants of rain dropping from their jagged leaves.

I hated how much we'd been arguing lately. Our eyes met. I hesitated and put my hand on his chest. I could feel the steadiness of his heartbeat under my fingers.

Collie's expression didn't soften. Almost roughly, he took my head in his hands and we kissed. "Amity, please be careful," he whispered. "If everything explodes, you're the one they'll be gunning for."

I swallowed. "I will be. You, too."

His jaw was taut. "Have you thought that Madeline might already be dead? You could be staying here for nothing. A sitting duck."

Fear sharpened my voice. "I have to take that chance. I don't have a choice."

"Of course you have a choice!"

"Collie, you of all people should understand—"

He gripped my shoulders hard. "Yes, *me of all people!* Because I've *been* in the CS – I know! You think anyone can stop Gunnison if he's determined to take over? Fighting him is *pointless*! All you can do is survive."

I started to answer and stopped.

Collie's voice was low. "I will ask you this one more time. Come away with me before it's too late." He cupped my cheek with his hand; his skin was warm, familiar. "I love you, Amity. I always have. Don't throw it all away. I'm begging you."

His eyes stayed locked on mine. And in that moment I longed to abandon Madeline, leave Peacefighting to its corruption, and grab the next train to anywhere, as long as it was with Collie.

"*No*," I jerked away, almost trembling. "I can't leave. You know that." The Deciding Room was just across the street. I nodded stiffly to it. "You've got a job to do… or have you forgotten every last part of your Peacefighting vow?"

Collie straightened, his face tight. "Yeah, sorry. Stupid of me to care about your life when *you* don't give a damn."

He turned and walked towards the Deciding Room. As he crossed the street I stood frozen under the palms, watching the set of his shoulders, the way he moved. I wanted to call after him and snatch the words back – but then he was gone and it was too late.

Three hours later, Collie was in the sickbay.

Chapter Thirty-one

I'D JUST SAT DOWN FOR a required training film. The door to the lecture room opened; the messenger's gaze flew straight to me. "Miss Vancour is needed immediately for a fight."

I grabbed my things and hurried from the room. "What's going on?" I asked as we headed down the hallway.

"One of the other pilots is sick. You've got to take his Tier One."

"*What?*" I stopped short. "But Collie's fine! I saw him just a few hours ago."

"It's some kind of vertigo; he can't stand up without vomiting. Miss Vancour, the fight's in less than an hour—"

"*Vertigo?*"

The messenger looked startled. "That's what they said."

I stood there, staring. Collie had the steadiest sense of balance in the world. When we were kids he used to show off with it, practically dancing across fallen logs. He'd never suffered from vertigo in his life.

My hands went cold. "I've got to see Collie first," I said, and started towards the doors.

"But I was supposed to bring you straight to Commander Hendrix!"

I was almost running now. "Ten minutes – that's all!" I called back.

I expected an argument to get in to see Collie. Instead the sickbay nurse hastened me down the corridor. "He's been asking for you," she said. "He seems very distressed."

As we reached a door I could hear Collie's voice: "I've got to see her! You don't understand—"

"Mr Reed, *please* calm down—"

The nurse swung open the door. Collie was struggling weakly with a young aide, trying to sit up. When he saw me, relief flooded his pale features; he sagged against the bed.

"Amity," he mumbled. "I've got to talk to you…"

"Collie!" I rushed to sit on the bed beside him and clenched his hand between both of mine. His skin felt clammy. "Are you all right?"

"I'll leave you alone for a few minutes." My nurse motioned the other one out and closed the door.

Collie's face looked waxy – his thick blondish hair was dark with sweat. "I can hardly move without throwing up," he said hoarsely. "Amity, I think…" He trailed off, closing his eyes.

What had they done to him? I gripped his fingers hard. "Somebody gave you something to make you sick, didn't they?" I said in an undertone.

Collie's hand clutched mine convulsively. "I don't know. Hendrix gave me a cup of coffee, so he could have slipped something in. Amity, please – *please* – you can't fly my fight. Promise me."

Somehow I locked away my fear for him. I stroked Collie's hair from his damp forehead, trying to buy time while I thought. If they'd made him sick, it must be that they wanted this fight thrown after all – and they thought I'd do it. The messenger wouldn't have been instructed to take me to Hendrix otherwise.

Which meant…what? Was Madeline still working behind the scenes? Or had she been found out?

I didn't know. And so for now, I had to keep playing the game. The realization filled me with dread.

"*Amity.*" Collie struggled to sit up again; his face abruptly drained of all colour. "Promise," he gasped. "Don't fight. Make up some excuse—"

He broke off with a moan and I grabbed for a basin. Hunching over, he threw up bile into it, his broad shoulders flexing again and again. When he'd finished he slumped back, breathing hard.

I wiped his damp face with a moist cloth. "Don't worry," I told him softly.

"You won't fight?"

"No. I'll think of something to tell them."

He took my hand; his fingers felt fretful in mine. "You promise?"

"I promise." I gently stroked the cloth down his bare arms, too. Suddenly I saw a little boy lying feverish in a dingy room while his mother danced drunkenly – and heard my own voice asking, *Did you bathe Collie's hands with a damp cloth?*

I swallowed and put the cloth aside. "Get some rest, okay? I'll come back and see you again later."

Collie's muscles had relaxed. He closed his eyes. "We'll leave," he whispered. "As soon as I'm better. Promise me that, too."

"We'll be fine," I said, because there was a limit to how much I could lie to the man I loved. Later, I knew Collie would notice that I hadn't really answered. Now he just nodded weakly.

"I was so worried that you'd fight," he murmured. "Amity, I thought I'd go out of my mind…"

"I'll see you soon." I kissed his forehead, letting my lips linger against his warm skin. "Everything will be all right."

As I left his hospital room, I prayed that the fact Collie had been made sick meant that Hendrix didn't suspect him of knowing about the thrown fights. That he'd be safe, once he was over whatever they'd given him.

And I hoped that he'd forgive me.

* * *

The meeting with Hendrix was short and perfunctory. My commanding officer was on the phone when I came in. "Yes, we'll see to it," he said, and hung the gleaming black receiver back onto its cradle. He studied me.

"You've heard about poor Collis, I suppose. Such a shame – and for a Tier One fight, too. Well, plans change. You'll fly it for us instead, of course?"

"Of course," I said levelly.

"Don't let us down," Hendrix said, his voice intent. "Remember what we discussed and things will go very well for you."

Collie's fight was scheduled for half an hour before sunset: 18.10. I had less than fifteen minutes to get geared up. As the messenger drove me to the admin block, I gazed tensely at the buildings reeling past – remembering the *No jobs* signs, Clem being taken away, Collie's pale face against his pillows.

A Tier One fight. I could not lose, at least not on purpose. But they'd undoubtedly be watching. I'd have to look as if I were trying to throw it, yet still win. Was that even possible?

It has to be, I told myself. If I didn't make this good, they'd shoot me like they had Russ.

The messenger pulled up with a squeal of breaks. I hopped out and jogged into the main building. As I started for the changing room, a flash of white in my mail cubbyhole caught my eye. I almost kept going, then stopped and pulled out the letter.

It was from Hal.

A chill swept me. What was happening at home? I hesitated, and then slipped his letter in my pocket. Whatever this was, I couldn't afford to let it distract me just now.

I geared up automatically and pulled on my leather jacket. Before I headed for the airstrip, I gazed at the photo of Collie, Hal and me on my father's plane, taking in Dad's wide smile. *My three kids.*

Then I reached for my dog tags – my father's and mine – and looped them around my neck.

Three minutes to get out to my plane. I ducked into the storeroom adjacent to the airfield. The parachute marked *Vancour* was waiting on a shelf; as I started to take it, I saw the one labelled *Reed.*

"Everything all right, Miss Vancour?" called an attendant.

"Fine," I called back. On impulse, I reached past my own parachute and grabbed the other one instead. Somehow it felt right: my father's tags around my neck, and Collie's chute on my back.

My plane waited on the airstrip, its swirling pattern bright in the slanting light of sunset. "Nice night for it," said Regan as I jogged up.

I paused to shrug into the chute and fasten its straps around my ankles. "Perfect," I said.

And if flying was all that mattered, it was true: the air was mild and warm, with just a tang of the ocean. The palm trees lining the airstrip seemed to arch endlessly against the sky.

Regan gave me a boost up onto the wing. I slid into the cockpit. Within seconds, the engine was roaring in my ears as I flicked switches and read dials. All the while my mind was ticking through options. So much depended on who I was fighting – how they would react.

I could not get this wrong.

Regan leaned into the cockpit to help with my straps. "Fly safe, Miss Vancour," he said, lifting his voice over the engine. "Show the Central States what's what!"

"That's my plan," I muttered.

Regan jumped back down to the ground and shouted to the other fitter, who ran to pull the chocks away from my wheels. I yanked the hood closed, encasing myself in the world of the cockpit, and then pulled my goggles down over my eyes as Regan signalled the all clear.

"Here we go," I said out loud. I started down the runway, my undercarriage bumping; the plane picked up speed until the palm trees were a blur. I eased back on the throttle – a final bounce, and I was airborne.

The fight was being held over the amphitheatre: our name for a particular dip in the eastern hills. It must have really been one at some point, or something similar – it was a flat, oval space surrounded by hundreds of tiered rows, all long-covered in grass. When I caught sight of it in the distance like a giant's footprint, I briefly fingered my tags.

My first Tier One fight, yet I could take no pride in it.

Once closer, I spotted the other plane circling over the amphitheatre's western lip. The world angled sideways as I banked and drew into position on the other side. My clock read 18.09. No cloud cover, and the sun was too low to hide in its glare.

Short and brutal – that was what fights in these conditions were like.

As my engine droned, I quickly scanned the grassy slopes. I'd expected someone posing as a broadcaster; there was nobody. My opponent would file a report, though. And is Hendrix realized I'd tried to win... I steeled myself.

18.10. We were on.

At precisely the same moment, the other plane and I headed for the centre of the airspace. My fingers felt poised on the stick.

"Time for my training to come in handy," I murmured. Once during practice, my opponent and I'd fired fatal shots almost at once. I'd been a hair faster. In a real fight, I'd have taken critical damage while still winning.

A claim of mistiming: that was all I had.

The sun glinted off the other plane. Just before firing range, I pulled up abruptly and went for height. The other Dove's swirls blurred together as it did the same, both of us battling for prime position.

Nine thousand feet. Twelve thousand. I gritted my teeth. "You will *not* win," I muttered to Gunnison's pilot. Façade be damned; too much was riding on this.

My opponent was a hundred feet below, climbing fast – but I had the advantage. I pushed the stick forward. My plane howled into a dive. The other Firedove slid sharply away and I got it in my sights, keeping right on its tail. The amphitheatre spun below, its green oval turning on my wing.

My scalp felt electric. The other Dove's fuselage swung into the crosshairs. *There.* Just as the other plane whipped about to fire on me, my thumb jammed down hard on the trigger.

The world exploded.

Fire – a roar that filled my ears. My straps gouged at my shoulders as I slammed against the port side of my plane. Thick black smoke smothered the cockpit, and then drifted away.

I gaped down at my starboard wing as it fell, on fire, to the ground.

How? No time to wonder. My plane was falling, too, like a real dove shot from the sky, the world spinning faster and faster. With icy hands I fumbled to undo my straps and then shoved back the cockpit hood.

Wind screamed past, tugging at my clothes. *Fall away from the spin:* we'd all learned it in training. I didn't let myself think. I half-stood and let gravity do the rest, tumbling from the cockpit.

My stomach dipped; I was in free fall. My spinning plane howled above – I had to get clear. Concordia's fate flashed into my head. I shoved it aside and clutched my ripcord, feverishly counting *one banana, two banana.* When I reached ten I yanked the cord.

The parachute billowed up, snapping me to a slower fall. With a gasp of relief, I pulled hard on the cords to steer away from the falling wreckage. Then saw in confusion that I was heading *towards* it. *How?*

My heart chilled. No – it was the other Firedove. Its port wing had been blown off, too.

I had not caused that damage. No way in hell. As I steered frantically away, I saw the other cockpit slide open – saw the other pilot bail, tumbling gently out into the sky.

One banana. Two banana.

At ten, I shouted, "Pull it! You're clear!" I don't know if they heard me, but I saw their parachute unfurl above them…and drift away.

I stared stupidly after it: a white circle flapping and turning against the sunset. The other pilot was falling. There was no parachute.

They were falling.

I could hear them screaming now. Him. A male voice. It woke me up. "No!" I yelled. I tugged hard on my straps, trying to steer myself to reach him – but I was going far too slowly. He'd already passed me.

It takes longer than you might think to fall from ten thousand feet. I watched his figure grow smaller, my eyes abruptly full of tears behind my goggles. I ducked my head away as he hit almost in the exact centre of the amphitheatre. Such a small noise…but the crunch of it shuddered through me. The planes crashed seconds later, one after the other.

Silence.

My chest was heaving; I forced myself to calm down. The ground below looked littered with abandoned toys. The other pilot's body was small and still. I clutched my cords. *Who had done this?* Cain?

Staring down, I was suddenly struck with how isolated this place was.

The low drone of an approaching engine. A truck entered the amphitheatre from a dark tunnel to one side. My first thought was that help had come – my second was that I was an idiot.

I'd taken the wrong parachute. I'd been supposed to die, too.

The truck stopped. Two men got out and stood gazing up at me. One reached inside his jacket; I could see the movement even from this height.

I was drifting right towards them. Frantically, I yanked on the cords to steer myself away. *Too slow, too slow!* I tore off my gloves and fumbled in my jacket pocket for my penknife. I flipped open the blade and sawed at one of the cords; it gave way with a fraying of threads. The parachute jounced – I fell faster. As I started hacking through another cord I had no idea if this was a good idea, but I was too perfect a target up here.

A bullet screamed past. I gasped and kept sawing. The men ran towards me, their shadows long and spidery.

One was bald; the other had curly hair. Grass swarmed up at me – I pedalled my legs and stumbled as I hit the ground. I undid my straps, shrugged out of the chute and ran.

Shouts. Bullets thudded past, the noise strangely flat, competing with the roar of my pulse. I pushed myself to go even faster, weaving from side to side, wishing feverishly that it was just a little bit later – a little bit darker.

Another tunnel lay ahead, gaping like a hungry mouth. I sprinted into it. The scent of moist earth enveloped me.

Within seconds I could hardly see. I groped quickly along, one hand on the wall – it was some kind of ancient concrete, weeping with damp. Water pooled on the floor. Soon the route narrowed; there'd been a cave-in at some point. I gasped in dismay. I could be trapped in here.

Going out again wasn't an option. I steeled myself and clambered over the rubble. I'd just squeezed past a stone block as big as I was when I heard voices. I pressed flat against the wall, my heart hammering.

"Should we go back for the truck?"

"No, look – it narrows here; we'd never get it through. *Damn* it. Where does this place come out, anyway?"

"Don't know; it's all woods on that side. We'd better call in."

"Right, buddy, *you* can tell Cain she got away. Bitch can't have gone far. Give me your lighter."

The voices drew closer. Blood roared through my brain. I dropped silently to my hands and knees; fumbling,

I found a small, cave-like space in the rubble and crawled into it. I pulled my knees hard against my chest and buried my head against them.

My uniform's brown, my hair's dark, I thought wildly. *Please, just let me merge into the shadows...*

A dull *thud* as a rock fell. One of the men swore. When his voice came again it was much closer, whispering. "Okay, it opens out again. Hold that light up."

My fingertips gouged into my legs. I didn't move. Didn't breathe.

"Nothing," hissed the voice finally. "Damn it, this was supposed to be an easy job – just put a bullet through her head if she was still twitching."

"Shut up; she'll hear us. Listen, you better go climb the hill – keep an eye on the other side, in case she makes it out."

"Got it."

Footsteps moved back towards the entrance; I heard the man make his way over the rubble. The other continued down the tunnel past me.

My mouth was dust. What now? The one who'd just left would see me if I tried to escape the way I'd come in. And soon this place would be swarming with the clean-up crew. A very special one, no doubt, who wouldn't question two planes with their wings blown off and a parachute with cut straps.

For a few long minutes I stayed silent, listening to the footsteps fading down the tunnel. Finally, when enough time had passed for the other man to have reached the hill's crest, I edged out from my hiding space.

My heart raced like a rabbit's. I felt far too exposed, but forced myself to creep back towards the entrance. I could hear the faint *drip, drip* of water – my own footsteps, startlingly loud.

I reached the rubble pile. Enough light angled in through the tunnel's mouth now for me to see. I moved silently, testing each concrete shard for balance.

At the top a mouse scurried over my boot. I stifled a cry as I stumbled; my left foot shot downwards. Pain jolted my ankle as it wedged between two shards.

No! Pebbles pattered down the rubble as I tugged at my leg. Stuck fast. *Stay calm, Amity.* Breathing hard, I started hefting pieces of concrete away as quietly and quickly as I could.

Too late. The footsteps were heading back. I heard them hesitate...and then break into a run.

Fury trembled over me. No, I was not going to die here like a rat in a trap. I wrenched up. My foot burst free; I staggered and fell backwards down the slope, landing in a sprawl.

A man appeared, looming atop the rubble.

"Well, what have we here?" His mouth curled as he pointed a gun at me; I heard a *click* as he released the safety. At the same moment I grabbed a rock and twisted upwards, heaving it at his face. He stumbled back with a cry. I scrambled to my feet and launched myself at him.

We slammed down the slope in a scrabble of rocks. The gun went flying.

"Oh, you bitch!" the man spat. He struggled to grab my neck – his thumbs dug into my throat, making the world swim. Panting, I twined my fingers in his curly hair and banged his head against a rock. Again. And again. And again.

He stopped moving.

With a shudder, I slowly sat up, clutching my throat. He was still breathing, his head lolling limply to one side. Curly brown hair, ruddy cheeks, a rumpled suit. At his throat was a gold medallion with an archer on it.

I swallowed and glanced over my shoulder at the entrance. No noise. Yet. I shook myself into action and grabbed up the gun. I barely knew enough to put on the safety, but felt better for having a weapon. I shoved it into my belt, then patted through the man's pockets, grimly forcing myself not to remember Russ, and Ingo's voice: *Are you sure you don't want his watch, too?*

A wallet. Cigarettes. I sagged with relief when my fingers closed over the hard metallic shape of auto keys. I took them and the wallet and left him the cigarettes.

When I emerged from the tunnel the sun was still visible, shining down over the amphitheatre in a thin orange slice. Not half an hour had passed since the other pilot and I faced off. The remains of our planes looked dark and twisted, ugly against the faint golden light.

Staying pressed close to the inner curve of the

amphitheatre, I quickly made my way around to the truck. With luck, the gunman up on top wouldn't see me here.

I drew near the truck…and to the fallen pilot. I *knew* he was dead – you don't fall from ten thousand feet and survive – but I still hesitated. Finally, cursing myself, I glanced upwards and then went over, steeling my spine.

I stopped in my tracks when I saw how little was left of his head – and the red spray that surrounded his body like fine mist. I let out a shaky breath. He wouldn't have suffered, at least, apart from the fear as he fell.

"Peace, friend," I said hoarsely, and raced for the truck.

I scanned the amphitheatre's upper rim. No one in sight. The truck's control panel had a talky device; I smashed it to pieces with a rock. I was taking no chances that they could track me with it – because now that the first shock was fading, the puzzle pieces were slotting into place.

Right, buddy, you can tell Cain she got away.

This was supposed to be an easy job – just put a bullet through her head if she's still twitching.

"Her", not "them". This was about me – about luring me to a remote spot and making sure I died. The Central States pilot had been killed just to do away with the witness. If I hadn't taken Collie's parachute, I'd be dead now, too – smeared across the ground just like my opponent.

I slid into the driver's seat; the truck started on the first try. I slammed it into gear and sped across the bumpy ground towards the other tunnel. As the darkness swallowed me I switched on the headlights. They gleamed across the damp surface as thoughts beat at my brain.

They knew now that I was not on their side. They knew I would do anything to expose them.

And that meant that Madeline had been found out.

Fear gripped my throat, along with a knee-weakening relief that I'd said nothing about Collie to her. No matter what they'd done to Madeline, she couldn't have implicated him. No one would have reason to think that he knew anything, apart from how close we were.

Maybe that was enough. Maybe he was in danger, too.

My fingers were tight on the steering wheel. I forced away the mental image of Collie lying weak and helpless in his hospital bed. The tunnel ended with a bump and a shift of surfaces; I emerged into the evening on a quiet road with trees lining each side, their branches lacing together against the sunset.

I'd never driven in these hills before but I'd flown over them a hundred times. I needed to go west. I'd come to a river that led to the sea; there was a bridge there. I'd cross it and keep angling down through the hills.

Because, much as I dreaded it, there was really only one place I could go.

As I downshifted around a hairpin turn, a cracking sound lashed through the truck. The windshield splintered like a spiderweb; shards of glass hit the seat next to me.

My pulse pounded. I screeched around the turn – another hole exploded through the windshield and I ducked my head down, somehow steering while peering up over the dash. *If he gets the tyres, I'm dead,* I thought frantically.

I cried out as the gunman lurched into the road in front of me, still firing – then I set my jaw and floored it, heading right for him. *Okay, pal, if that's how you want to play it.* He dived away in a wild scramble; a second later I heard the whine of metal as another bullet hit the back of the truck – then I turned a curve and was gone.

I let out a shaky breath. How much time did I have before Cain discovered what had happened and sent people out looking for me? The clean-up crew wouldn't be long in arriving; they were probably already on their way.

Be safe, I thought fiercely to Collie. *You have got to stay safe.* They wouldn't do anything to him, would they? Or worse, he wouldn't give himself away somehow, desperate for answers when I didn't return?

Don't. Please. I beg you.

My knuckles were white on the wheel. I couldn't control what might happen and I hated it – I could only hope as hard as I could that Collie would keep his head down and be all right. Meanwhile, if I was lucky, I had maybe a fifteen-minute window to get away clear.

But at least I was going to the one place that I didn't think they'd expect.

Chapter Thirty-two

"And yet you didn't flag Vancour's chart as a potential danger," said Skinner.

They were in a plush boardroom off Gunnison's state offices in the Aquarius building; the marble wall had a motif of golden water-bearers. John Gunnison himself sat a few chairs away. He stroked his chin with a knuckle and frowned. To make Kay's humiliation complete, Bernard was there, too, watching her like a hawk.

"No, I didn't flag it," Kay said.

"Do you realize you were the only astrologer *not* to flag it?" The bald patch on Skinner's eyebrow gleamed. Kay wished that it made him ridiculous, so that she wouldn't feel so frightened.

The Chief Astrologer angled the chart towards him. "*A Grand Cross* – and with those particular planets! Really, Miss Pierce! This may not be a classically Discordant chart, but you're a Twelve Year Astrologer. It should have been obvious that she couldn't be trusted."

Kay glanced at Johnny, willing him to be on her side. He wasn't, of course. Kay had heard by now, in great detail, exactly what Amity Vancour had been up to. As a result of Hester's information at the party, plans had been put into place to take care of the rogue pilot, but Vancour had escaped only hours ago. She could now expose all of Gunnison's plans if they weren't careful.

Skinner tapped the table. His voice was ice. "I had great faith in your...shall we say, unorthodox methods, but I'm afraid it was very much misplaced."

I didn't suspect Vancour because you *didn't suspect her!* Kay wanted to scream. *This is all your fault!*

She lifted her chin. "May I speak?"

Skinner gave a wincing smile. "Please do."

"It's true I didn't flag this chart as a danger." Kay felt a bolt of pure hatred for Amity Vancour. "But I can explain," she went on.

"Well, I for one would love to hear it," said Bernard. "Because it's clear to me that—"

"It's my turn to speak," snapped Kay. She turned to Gunnison. "Sir –" she didn't dare call him "Johnny" just then – "I flagged Russ Avery's chart when no one else did. I was right. He later caused trouble and had to be disposed of. *And* I chose the perfect spot for the first phase of the Reclamation to take place. If you'll just listen to me now, I promise—"

"The Reclamation hasn't even begun yet!" burst out Bernard. "According to *my* calculations, your perfect location's a disaster."

Only if Johnny's wrong, thought Kay. And she didn't believe that for a second. From the faint flicker behind Johnny's eyes, he felt the same.

"Sir, please – may I finish?" she said softly.

"Go on," Gunnison said. It was almost the first time he'd spoken.

Kay pulled Vancour's chart towards her. *Please let me make this good,* she prayed.

In a clear voice, she said, "I didn't flag Vancour's chart because she is not a danger to us. Yes, things seem troubling now...but look at Pluto in retrograde. Her actions are actually going to benefit us."

Skinner blinked. He opened his mouth and slowly shut it again. At his side, Bernard's jaw dropped.

"*What?*" he sputtered.

Gunnison tapped his cheek. "Y'know, I'm not utterly convinced, Miss Pierce."

Call me Kay! she wanted to cry. Her thoughts flew wildly, like startled birds. She kept her voice calm.

"There's more," she said.

Gunnison raised an eyebrow. Kay took a breath, wondering what she was going to say next. What came out shocked even her. "You see...well...I cast your own chart a few months ago."

A vein in Skinner's forehead bulged. "You cast—! That is an *extreme* breach of—"

"It's illegal," corrected Gunnison mildly. He studied Kay, his blue eyes delving. She shivered. Even in this moment of sickening danger, she felt despair that Gunnison had cast her out of his inner circle.

"So I hope you had a good reason for doing it," concluded Gunnison. He hooked one arm over the back of his chair. It could mean a willingness to listen to her... or that he'd already made up his mind.

Under the table, Kay wiped damp palms on her skirt. "Yes, I did. If I can see a copy of your chart now, I'll show you what I found."

Skinner's face reddened; the tiny bald spot stayed deathly pale. "I'm confident I can answer for Mr Gunnison when I say—"

"Nah, no one answers for me," said Gunnison. "Go get a copy of my chart, Mal."

"But—"

"Go on."

Skinner left the room. Bernard sat gazing at Kay with loathing from across the table. It hit her then what his presence here meant: she and Bernard must be the top two Twelve Year astrologers. Or they had been. She had no idea where she'd be after this.

There might soon be another empty chair in the

astrology boardroom.

Skinner returned and handed Kay a chart. His jaw was tight. "I should like very much to know how you got the details to cast this," he said.

"Oh, Miss Pierce is resourceful – that's never been in doubt," said Gunnison. He motioned to her. "Go on."

Kay had never seen this chart before. Skinner was right; the details of Gunnison's birth were classified. She scanned it quickly. Sun in Sagittarius, rising sign Scorpio. How could she use this to support the idea that Vancour wasn't a danger? She had to find a similarity between the two charts – some link she could use—

To buy time, she said, "Well, you know my specialty is merging charts and finding trends. Look at this."

She drew a blank chart from her briefcase and juxtaposed Vancour's and Gunnison's charts. Skinner and Bernard craned towards her, watching. As she worked she studied both charts in more detail, looking frantically for something she could put a spin on.

And then she saw it. Was it enough, though? It would have to be.

"There," she said when she finished. She looked Gunnison in the eyes. "See the trine elements? And how Saturn conjuncts Mercury, in *both* charts? Sir, Miss Vancour's chart shows a clear karmic bond with your own. She may not realize it, but everything she does is helping the Central States."

Skinner started to speak and stopped.

"Preposterous," muttered Bernard, but his eyes were worried. He studied the chart, his gaze flicking over the various elements.

Gunnison sat motionless, looking at Kay rather than the merged chart. "A karmic bond, huh?"

Did he even believe in karma? Kay managed a small shrug. "Call it what you will. The result is the same. Miss Vancour can't harm us."

What are you saying? her mind shrieked. Vancour was on the run this very second. Kay had no idea what the maniac might do. She, Kay, was buying herself a few hours at best.

Gunnison examined the charts. His expression was inscrutable.

"Yes, but what about the Central States' chart?" Bernard said clearly. He drew a copy from his briefcase and slapped it down.

Gunnison's gaze flicked to Kay. "Well?"

Kay fought her panic. "I was just about to mention the CS chart, actually. Watch." She quickly merged it with the other two. To her relief, there was something she could grab hold of.

"You see? A perfect conjunct of Mars and Mercury. Most unusual and most *powerful.*" Before anyone could comment, Kay blundered on: "In fact...in fact, I suspect that Miss Vancour's actions might be the missing puzzle piece we've all been waiting for."

She had the dizzying sense of having jumped off a cliff. Gunnison's eyes widened.

"You mean for the Reclamation?" he said.

It was obviously what he wanted to hear. Kay nodded. Skinner and Bernard sat too stunned to speak.

Gunnison leaned forward on his elbows. "So what is your advice, exactly?"

Kay's mouth felt like cotton. What *was* her advice? "Well...I'd keep an eye on Vancour, of course," she said slowly. "We need to be ready to act at a moment's notice."

"If we could *find* her, that would be a start," muttered Bernard.

"Oh, we have some idea where she might go," said Gunnison, still watching Kay.

"Then monitor her. Make decisions at every turn," said Kay. "We must keep completely on top of this. But I promise you, she's fulfilling the role she's meant to. Her actions will turn out for the best."

She fervently hoped the words were vague enough that she could take credit for anything that wasn't a disaster, yet still be let off the hook for not flagging Vancour in the first place. Oh, why had she brought the Reclamation into it?

Gunnison drummed his fingers. His hair was slightly rumpled; the effect was oddly boyish, despite his greying blond temples.

"The missing puzzle piece," he muttered.

"Sir..." Skinner's voice was a plea.

Gunnison's sudden frown could mean anything. Abruptly, he picked up the charts and rose. "I'll let you know what I decide," he said. "Go home and stay there, Miss Pierce."

As he left the room, Kay couldn't help gazing after him. Even apart from survival, she yearned to get back in his good graces.

The door closed.

The other two gazed wordlessly at her. Bernard smiled a closed-lipped smile, eyes glittering. Skinner poured a glass of water from a pitcher and took a long sip. He didn't offer Kay a glass.

"If you're lucky, you'll just be shot, and not sent to a correction camp," he said at last.

Kay coolly gathered her things and stood up. "For your information, I'll be a lot luckier than that."

It wasn't until she left the room and went into the Ladies that she allowed herself to sag. She leaned against a sink and pressed a hand to her mouth, trembling as she recalled how the severed heads in the film had sparkled with frost.

Bile and terror lurched in her throat. She wheeled into one of the cubicles and dropped to her knees; clutching the sides of the toilet, she threw up until there was nothing left.

Afterwards Kay slumped against the side of the cubicle, breathing hard. The wall felt smooth and impersonal against her cheek.

She didn't believe in luck. She never had.

Chapter Thirty-three

As I approached the Speak, the music pulsed around me like a second heartbeat. I wore an unfamiliar parka. I'd found a woollen cap in one of its pockets and now it was nestled on my head, down low over my eyebrows. At least it was dark now, and the parka so bulky you could hardly tell I was a woman.

I hadn't encountered anyone else as I drove in the hills. It had terrified me to have the headlights on; I knew how easily I'd be spotted from the sky. As soon as I'd been able – about a mile from the sprawling expanse of Peacefighting bases – I'd ditched the truck and walked.

Entering by one of the main gates was out of the question. Word would be out by now; my pass would get me arrested in seconds. The outer fences only had periodic patrols, though. And in one place I'd hoped there wouldn't even be those.

I'd cut across sea-bitten fields and scaled the scrapyard fence in the moonlight, using my leather jacket to edge over the rusty barbed wire. As I dropped to the ground I saw no one. The front gate lay past the Western Seaboard's section, its planes ghostly in the silvery light. I was desperate to reach my destination, but when I came to where my plane had been, I glanced upwards.

Gone.

The hairs on the back of my neck stiffened. I stared at the empty space atop two sprawled-together Doves. They had actually gone to the trouble of *moving* a wrecked plane. When?

I broke into a run, terrified it might already be too late. In the small office I found a blue parka, the same as that worn by hundreds of Heat workers. I grabbed it and hid my flight jacket deep in the yard. By the time it was found, I'd either be dead or safe. I hoped that "safe" was still an option.

I'd never been so thankful of the Heat's enormity. Striding through its streets an hour later, no one had given me a second glance. Now I stood in front of the noisy speak with my hands jammed in stolen pockets. A group of pilots entered, laughing – you could always tell the pilots, somehow – and for a second I straightened.

He wasn't among them. I let out a nervous breath and

glanced at my watch. After nine p.m. Had I missed him?

I had no choice. I'd have to go inside.

I pushed open the door. The music leaped upwards as cigarette smoke enveloped me. Onstage a woman sang about *le vagabond*, throwing her arms out to her sides. People sat clustered around candlelit tables; the buzz of conversation battled the music.

At first glance I couldn't see him. I struggled to the bar and ordered a glass of red wine, lifting my voice to be heard. As the bartender poured it I tugged off my cap – I'd stand out a lot more with it on. Part of me expected gunmen to surge in at any moment.

They shot Russ in an alleyway – not a crowded speak, I reminded myself tensely.

I stood at the bar and sipped my drink, trying to keep my expression as bland as during a game of poker. As I pretended to watch the singer, I scanned the tables over the shifting crowd. I couldn't see a head of wild, crisp black curls anywhere.

It's Friday night, his friends had said. *Why aren't you here with us?*

I clutched the wine glass. It was Friday night now. But he hadn't been here *that* Friday night...and so maybe he wasn't here tonight, either.

As one song ended and another began, I saw a flurry of movement in the far corner. A tall figure pushed back a chair and stood up. He wore grey trousers, a tweedy sports jacket flecked with green. As I got a look at his face I shoved my almost full wine glass onto the bar and plunged into the crowd.

He was heading for the door; in another second he'd be gone. "Ingo," I called, pushing past people "*Ingo!*"

He paused and looked back. When he saw me, his dark eyes widened.

"What are you doing here?" he asked as I reached him. The expression on his lean face wasn't particularly friendly.

"I have to talk to you."

"Well, I'm leaving now. I'm supposed to be somewhere."

"Please – it's important."

"I'm already late."

I gripped his arm. "You *must* talk to me," I hissed. "Five minutes. It's vital. I wouldn't have come looking for you otherwise."

Ingo's face darkened. Without a word, he took my elbow and led me to a small table in the corner; a couple were just getting up from it. "What are you drinking?" he asked. The tabletop was already littered with empty glasses.

I sat down and pulled off my parka. "I thought I only had five minutes."

"I'm not talking to you without a drink. What'll it be?"

"I don't care. Wine. Whatever."

He paused, studying me. "Yes, this is more like how I always pictured you," he said dryly.

He meant my rumpled flight gear and limp hair. Before I could snap an impatient reply he disappeared; he returned a few minutes later with two glasses of red wine.

He sat down and pushed one across the sticky tabletop towards me, then took a sip from his own glass and leaned back, his gaze intense.

"All right – what do you want?" he said.

I leaned forward on my elbows. "I have to break into the World for Peace offices. I need you to help me."

Ingo's jaw slackened. "You *what?*"

"I'm sure you heard me."

"Why would I help you do such a thing?"

"Because you care about the fights as much as I do. You care about what they stand for."

Ingo took another slow sip of wine, watching me narrowly. "Explain," he said at last.

"Do you remember the last time we met? You said that you didn't think you'd hit my plane before I stopped firing."

His black eyebrows drew together. "Yes, and you assured me that I *had* hit you. Your air bottle, you said."

"Well, I was wrong. My plane was sabotaged. My air bottle had a bullet hole, all right, but someone put it there afterwards."

"Put it there afterwards," repeated Ingo.

"Listen – you think I'm crazy, but I'm not. This whole thing—" I paused and shoved my hands through my hair. All of a sudden I felt exhausted, unreal. In a too-vivid flash, I saw the downed CS pilot again, surrounded by that fine red mist. When they removed the mangled mess of his body, the grass would still bear its outline.

It was several moments before I could keep on. "Fights are being thrown to favour Gunnison," I said finally, my voice a taut wire. "My base commander knows; he offered me a bribe. Russ was shot because he wanted more money. I think at least some members of the World for Peace are in on it, too."

Ingo stared at me. The speak buzzed around us, the music reaching a crescendo. Over his shoulder I could see a faded poster of the ruins of Sacré Coeur cathedral, its ancient half-dome gleaming against the lights of Paris.

"Do you know what you're saying?" Ingo said. "I mean, do you have any idea of the ramifications?"

"Obviously." I took a swig of wine to try to steady my shaking nerves. "Insult me however you like, but don't insult my intelligence."

He snorted, his gaze raking over me. "Yes, very intelligent – you're claiming that your loss against me was because of sabotage, to benefit *Gunnison*? I'm a European, sweetheart. I don't fight for the madman across the border."

"I thought you did read the papers, though – *sweetheart.*"

"What are you talking about?"

"I don't have the newspaper clipping with me. It was on December 16th – there was a story about how the EA ceded oil rights to the Central States. Didn't you read it? Didn't you wonder how your country had any oil rights to spare? Or don't you even remember what our fight was about?"

Ingo's almost-black eyes seemed even darker suddenly,

and I realized he'd gone pale. "That proves nothing," he said.

"Don't be a fool! You said yourself you didn't think you'd hit me! So what do you think happened? Malfunction? Those planes are checked and double—"

"All right!" He took a gulp of wine and scowled over at the singer. She wore a glittering brooch with a pair of fish on it. *Pisces,* I thought, and hated the fact that I knew that.

Finally Ingo turned back to me. He tapped his fingers on the table. "Tell me everything," he said.

I did, leaving out what had happened today. When I'd finished Ingo was quiet for a long moment. "Let's say, for the sake of argument, that I believe there might be something to this insanity," he said finally. "What am I supposed to do about it?"

"I told you. I have to break into the World for Peace. The only concrete evidence I have is in there –" my hand tightened on the stem of my wine glass – "and I strongly suspect the person I gave it to has been found out."

Ingo gave a humourless laugh. "I might have known you'd have some mad plan. What has breaking into the World for Peace got to do with me, lady? Do you think I work there on the sly?"

"No, I think you have a girlfriend whose father's an official there."

Ingo stiffened. "No," he said. "You are *not* dragging Miriam into this." He knocked the rest of his wine back. "I've heard enough."

I clutched his wrist across the table before he could move. "So what now? You're going to just leave and pretend you never heard this? You can't – you're not capable of it."

He jerked away. "You don't know the first thing about me."

"Yes, I do. You're a pilot who reads the papers. You like to know the truth. Well, here it is, Ingo! Or are you too cowardly to face it?"

"Is that supposed to make me leap to my feet to save my honour? Why should I give a damn if you think I'm a coward?"

"You shouldn't! You should give a damn that the system you believed in is corrupting itself to put Gunnison in power!"

Ingo grimaced and scraped a hand over his chin. "My first instinct about you was right," he muttered. "You really *are* a hag of the air."

"Fine, insult me. Will you help?"

I'd hardly touched my wine; Ingo picked up my glass and swirled it, gazing into its depths. "How can I?" he said finally. "It's Miriam's father who works there, not Miri."

"But you go to her house sometimes, don't you? There's that private officials' entrance at the WfP – he must have keys for it!"

Ingo glared at me. "Oh, so now I'm to be a thief? Her family has been good to me – and I'm supposed to betray them?"

"Have you got a better idea?"

"Yes! To forget all about this!"

But we'd already established that he couldn't.

When Ingo spoke again his voice was reluctant. "Yes, there are keys. And I should be at Miriam's right now; it's where I was going when you stopped me. I said I'd give her this." He pulled a battered paperback from his jacket pocket. *Poems of the Old World*, read the title.

Ingo's mouth twisted as he rifled through its pages. "Do you know what's in here?" he asked.

"Poetry" didn't seem the right answer. I didn't reply.

There was a pencilled note in the margin of a poem. Ingo's black curls fell over his forehead as he studied it. "The best that humankind has to offer – apart from Peacefighting," he said. "And now you're telling me that even our best is corrupt. It's preposterous."

My throat was tight. "But you believe it anyway," I said. "Ingo, please. There's no time to lose. There are things I haven't told you, but...I'm in danger. If I don't get that evidence back, there won't be proof of any of this. We won't be able to stop what's happening."

Ingo gave me a dark look as he tucked the book away into his jacket pocket. "'*We*'," he echoed wryly. "What a terrible word that can be."

"You'll help, won't you?"

He shoved his chair back. "I'm leaving now."

I leaped up, too. "Wait! Will you help?"

Ingo spun towards me. "I don't know!" His sudden

vehemence took me aback. "I have to think. And I'm late to see Miri."

"We haven't got time for you to mull this over!" I snapped.

"You'll damn well give me time, or you won't get what you want. I don't even know if I *can* get it."

"One o'clock," I said desperately. I glanced at my watch. "That's over three hours from now. I'll meet you at that same cafe where we had coffee. All right? Will you be there?"

"I'm not promising anything."

"Ingo—"

His eyes flashed. "*Drop it*," he said. "Or I swear you will never see me again."

"Wait!" I grabbed his arm. "I…I need to ask you to do something else."

He stared at me in disbelief. I steeled myself and went on. "Call the Western Seaboard base. Ask to speak to Collis Reed. See if he's okay. Don't mention that you saw me – say that you're with Canary Cargo." I licked my lips. "Please. Please do this for me."

Ingo jerked away. "I'm not your message boy, lady. Make your own mysterious phone calls."

He left, his tall, narrow form weaving through the crowd. I sank slowly back into my chair, wondering whether he'd show at one o'clock…or whether my last request had tipped him over into deciding not to help me at all.

I gripped my forehead. I had to get the documents

back. But I'd had to ask about Collie, too. Not knowing whether he was all right was killing me.

Finally, my head throbbing, I sat up, grateful that I was out of sight here in the corner. I could feel the letter from Hal in my back pocket, still unread. I wanted to pull it out but now wasn't the time – not here. Onstage the singer was warbling about *mon légionnaire*; some of the audience sang along.

I gazed at her glittering brooch. I could see other astrology signs in the audience, too: Aries the ram, Libra the scales.

Once you started noticing, they were everywhere.

When someone touched my shoulder I started, sure that I'd been discovered. It was only a couple holding drinks. "Do you mind if we share your table?" said the woman. "There aren't any other spaces."

I managed a thin smile. "No," I said. "I don't mind."

Chapter Thirty-four

I stood hidden in the shadows near the cafe, gazing down the street. I felt cold, despite the bulky parka and mild night. Had I been right to trust Ingo? I hardly knew him. All I'd had to go on was the gut sense that he cared about Peacefighting as much as I did.

I glanced at my watch again. 1.37 a.m. He wasn't going to come.

When I finally saw Ingo's lean figure in the street lights, my heart soared with relief. He walked slowly, his reluctance clear with every step.

"I'm here," I called in a soft voice as he drew close. He started and turned to stare at me.

I emerged from the gloom. "You came."

Ingo's expression was hard. "Yes," he said. "And just to top off my idiocy, I stopped at a drugstore on my way and made your phone call for you."

My pulse leaped. "And?"

"And the switchboard operator said that Collis Reed was unavailable."

My hands tightened coldly in my pockets. "Did...did you ask why?"

"*No*, I said thank you very much and hung up."

I took a deep breath and forced thoughts of Collie away. "All right," I said finally. "Thanks."

"And before that, if you're wondering, I stole from my girlfriend's father and then I refused to stay the night with her and we argued. Thank you for a delightful evening."

I let out a short, gasping breath. "You got the keys?"

"How like you to stay focused on the important things."

"All right, so you argued with your precious Miri!" I said impatiently. "Just give me the keys and you can get back to her."

Ingo had his hands in his trouser pockets; he barked out a laugh. "These keys are going nowhere without me. If you want to break into the WfP, it will be with me along."

"*What?*"

"How the hell do I know what you really plan on doing? You could be setting off a bomb for all I know."

My voice rose. "Don't be ridiculous!"

"Am I being? The last time I saw you, you were rifling

through a dead man's pockets. Why exactly should I trust you?"

"Because you know I'm honest! You know the way I fight!"

"That doesn't mean you're not a madwoman." Ingo took a set of keys from his pocket and dangled them in front of me. "Choose," he said. "Keys with me attached – or no keys at all."

I clenched my fists. "I told you that I'm in danger," I said finally. "I meant it. If you come, you'll be in danger too."

He gave me a piercing look. "So I take it that people are after you."

"Yes," I admitted.

"Who?"

"People who are very high-up. And my base commander is in on it. I'm sure he's not the only one – yours could be too," I added. "You could be fighting alongside traitors and not even know it."

Ingo put the keys back in his pocket. "Do you realize how insane you sound?"

Fear made my voice sharp. "So now I'm making it all up? My, how an evening with the lovely Miri puts a different spin on things."

"It does," Ingo said. "And maybe you *are* making it all up – how should I know?"

"I guess you shouldn't."

Ingo frowned over at the cafe. When he spoke again his

voice was quiet. "I need to know if you're crazy...or if there's anything to this. Maybe that's why I have to come and see for myself."

"Apart from not trusting me," I said.

He snorted. "Yes, apart from not trusting you. Don't tell me that's hurt your feelings! Would you trust me?"

"I *am* trusting you – with a hell of a lot, actually," I snapped. Ingo didn't respond. After a moment I sighed.

"All right," I said. "I'll take the keys with you attached."

I'd warned him. That was the best I could do. If I told him that they'd tried to kill me just hours ago, and hadn't thought twice about murdering my opposing pilot to cover their tracks, Ingo still wouldn't hand over the keys... but he might leave and take the keys with him.

This makes me no better than them, I thought as we started down the street.

Maybe not. But I didn't see that I had a choice.

The World for Peace offices were about a mile away. We walked in silence through the early morning streets. When we occasionally passed someone I kept my head averted, the cap pulled down low. I couldn't shake the thought of Collie's hospital bed. There'd been a phone on the table beside it.

What did "unavailable" mean?

No. I swallowed hard and grabbed at something to distract me. "Was it difficult to get the keys?" I asked Ingo.

He gave a curt shrug. "Not really. Miri's parents were out. She was on the phone for a while, and I snuck into her father's study. There's a pegboard where he keeps his keys."

"When will he notice they're gone?"

"He won't; it's the weekend. I'll put them back before he realizes."

He'd realize a lot sooner if we were caught. "What did Miriam say about you leaving her at the club that time?" I asked after a pause.

Ingo glanced over, his eyebrows drawn together. His long, angled face looked almost ominous in the dim light. "Which time?"

"How many times do I know about? Your peak day celebration."

"Oh. That." He grimaced. "Is discussing my love life really necessary?"

"I'm just making conversation."

"Make conversation about something else."

"All right. Sorry."

Neither of us spoke for a few minutes. Ingo walked with his hands in his trouser pockets, frowning down at his shoes. They were highly polished, gleaming like dark liquid. Even in the faint glow of the street lights I could see that the toes were slightly pointed – exotic-looking.

"It's a boring little game we play," he said finally, sounding tired. "She ignores me; I get hurt and storm off. Then she's angry that I left, but she can't admit it – that's part of the game too, you see. She has to pretend she never even noticed. Oh, it's good fun. You should try it sometime."

"It sounds awful."

"Invigorating, I'm sure Miri would say. The make-up sex is good." He gave me a wolfish leer. "Oh, sorry. Am I being too crude?"

"No. I'm glad there's something good about it. Because she sounds like a grade-A bitch."

Ingo studied me, his dark eyes both amused and irritated. "Do you always say exactly what's on your mind?"

"Mostly," I said.

"Well, I suppose it's refreshing, at least. Yes, she can be a bitch," he said shortly. "She's also the most exciting, intoxicating woman I've ever met. Shall we talk about your friend Collis now – the intended recipient of mysterious phone messages?"

I thought of Collie begging me not to fly and cleared my throat. "I'd rather not."

"Trouble in paradise?"

"No. The opposite, if it's any of your business."

Ingo gave me a keen look and fell silent. We turned onto another street. We were nearing the administrative offices of Heatcalf City now; there were no other people on the sidewalk. In the distance I could see the dark bulk of the World for Peace building, with its laurel-leaf emblem silhouetted against the stars.

"There's still time for you to just give me the keys," I said.

Ingo was gazing at the WfP building too. "I think you know I'm not going to do that. So can we avoid having this tedious conversation again, please?" He glanced at me and added dryly, "Dare I ask if you have a plan for once we get inside?"

I didn't take my eyes from the laurel leaf.

"In theory," I said.

The private entrance for officials was too brightly lit for my liking, but was at least tucked away on a quiet side street. Ingo and I stood in the glaring circle of light as he tried key after key.

I peered over my shoulder, straining to see if there was any movement in the shadows. "Can't you hurry?" I hissed.

Ingo didn't look up. "I've only been here once. I suppose *you'd* have memorized which key was used, but normal people don't think like criminals. *Ah.* There."

With a faint click, the door swung open.

Ingo motioned me through. "Ladies first," he said, his voice heavy with irony.

Inside the lights were on, but I couldn't hear anything. There was a small reception area, vacant this time of night. As Ingo entered and closed the door, I ducked behind the desk and started rummaging, pulling out drawers.

"What are you doing?" Ingo's voice was sharp. "You said—"

I exhaled and held up a slim silver letter opener. "We can go now."

A carpeted hallway led to the elevators; I ignored it and glanced at the door to the stairs. Madeline's office was on the fourteenth floor.

"Come on," I said. "We've got a long climb ahead."

The stairwell was dark, lit only by squares of light from the windows of each landing's door. When we finally got to the fourteenth floor I reached for the doorknob. Ingo grabbed my wrist.

"Wait," he hissed. "Do you hear something?"

I started to say no, then heard it too: a low humming noise, rising and falling in pitch. Trepidation filled me. "A vacuum cleaner," I muttered. "*Damn.*"

Ingo's face hardened. I expected him to insist that we leave; instead he cracked open the door and peered out. The lights were on – the noise sounded very close.

"I don't see anyone. The cleaner must be in one of the offices," he said.

Madeline's office was down at the other end; if it hadn't already been cleaned it would be one of the last. "Hurry," I whispered urgently. "We can sneak past without being heard."

Ingo looked like he wanted to argue, but didn't. We slipped out of the stairwell and eased the door shut, then hastened down the corridor. When we reached Madeline's office the door was predictably locked. I crouched down and angled the letter opener into the keyhole.

Ingo glanced back towards where the vacuum cleaner still droned. "Do you actually know what you're doing with that thing?"

"Yes, since you ask," I said shortly. My heart was hammering. I tried to ignore it and moved the letter opener's blade carefully, feeling for the tumblers. The blade was a nice narrow one. Good – that made it easier.

This type of lock hadn't moved on much in the four years since I'd tried this. Just as Ingo hissed, "If you don't figure that out *quickly*—" the tumblers fell into place.

I turned the doorknob; we rushed inside and shut the door. The wall opposite had a plate-glass window. Ambient light from the city cast soft shadows. I went and twisted the blinds closed, and Madeline's office fell into darkness.

"Get the lights," I whispered.

There was a *click*. I blinked in the sudden brightness and let out a breath. The letter opener glinted as I tucked it in my pocket.

Ingo eyed me. "Should I even ask?" he said after a pause.

"A misspent youth," I said.

"You?"

"I was arrested once. Does it even matter?" I scanned the office, not bothering to explain that it had been Rob, not me, who'd picked locks. But he'd taught me how and I'd liked knowing. It had made me feel strong, in control.

Nothing like I felt now.

Ingo was still watching me. "Yes, maybe it does matter. Why the hell did you need me, if you can do that?"

I spun towards him. "Because I couldn't have picked the outside lock – it's about a million times more complicated! I was hardly a master criminal. Can we drop this?"

Ingo's curls looked blue-black in the harsh light. He gave a sardonic nod, though his eyes stayed wary. "All right," he said. "What are we looking for?"

I felt even more apprehensive than I'd expected now that we were actually here. Madeline's office was businesslike, yet feminine – just like her. A vase of yellow roses sat on the desk, the blooms slightly wilted.

This was not the time to tell Ingo that I had no idea what had happened to Madeline. And that what I needed might already be gone.

I went and took down the painting of two Firedoves that covered Madeline's safe. The door looked small, impenetrable. I stared at its dial and tried frantically to think.

"Don't tell me you're a safe-cracker, too," said Ingo.

"Can't you be quiet?" I snapped.

People didn't choose combinations at random. *Madeline's birthday,* I thought. It was March 10th – I'd have to guess at the year. She was my father's age, wasn't she? No, younger: he'd told me once that she was in the year below him at school.

I wiped my hand on my trousers. Slowly, I turned the dial. It made a soft clicking noise. Left…right…left again.

I tugged. The safe stayed locked. I tried again with a different year. Then another one.

I spun the dial in frustration. Ingo appeared at my elbow, hands in pockets. His shoulders looked tense under his sports jacket. "Do you know this woman well?" he asked.

"Yes. I know her well."

"All right, then *think*. What are you trying – her birthday? Try a different one. Who's important to her?"

How well *did* I know Madeline? She'd always been part of my life, yet was too much older for us to have really been friends. I'd told her things, not the other way around. I knew she'd never been married, but had no idea who her friends were, if she had a lover, if she had a child, even – though I didn't think so.

A lover.

The words hesitated at the edge of my mind. I went very still, remembering Madeline resting her hand on my father's chest in the main lobby downstairs – the look in his eyes as he gazed down at her.

A sudden suspicion punched me in the stomach.

I started as Ingo snapped his fingers in front of my face. "I would really rather not be found still standing here tomorrow morning, if you don't mind," he said testily.

I set my jaw and reached for the dial again. Somehow my hand stayed steady. I entered my father's birthday, spinning the dial with neat precision.

6 left. 11 right. 3 left.

With a faint *click*, the safe opened.

Ingo rocked backwards with a wordless bark of surprise. "What did you try?" he burst out.

In a way I think I'd always known, so why did this hurt so much? "Someone else's birthday," I said shortly.

There were some manila folders inside the safe; I snatched them up and started rifling through them. When I found the bundle of information that I'd given Madeline, I gasped out a breath.

"It's still here," I said.

"Let me see." Ingo pressed close and took the folder from me. He didn't speak as he studied the newspaper clippings with Russ's scribbled comments, the diary with dates starred, my careful notes about the fights. I saw his fingers go white as he gripped the file.

"I told you," I said softly. "It's all true."

"Yes. You told me." Ingo shoved the file back at me. His eyes looked fierce, but his voice shook. "The thing that I've given my life to – left my home for—" He broke off. "You're sure it wasn't just this one man? You're sure of that?"

"Yes. I'm sorry."

Ingo turned away, his jaw working. I was surprised at his emotion – ever since I'd met him, he'd seemed so cool and controlled. He swiped a hand over his face. "Fine. So what do we do about it?" he said roughly. His gaze fell on the rest of the files from the safe. "What are those?"

I flipped through them. WfP documents, carbon copies

of memos. It looked as if Madeline had been gathering more evidence. "We'd better just take this stuff and—"

I broke off as I saw my own name. The words on the memo jumped out at me. I frowned and tugged it free from the file. I read the whole thing.

It made no sense.

I read the memo again, gulping down the words. "But…I don't understand," I said in a daze.

Ingo snatched the memo from me. Out loud, he read, "*Hester, in addition, Hendrix was misled by her background and made incorrect assumptions. Amity is very determined and not motivated by money. She won't stop until she's exposed this. I'm extremely saddened but agree that the proposed solution is the only way. Would you take care of it? M.*"

Ingo's eyes flew to meet mine. "You know her well, huh?" He shoved the memo back into my hand.

"Madeline betrayed me," I said hoarsely. "*Madeline.*" I read the words again. "She knew," I whispered. "She helped plan it."

Ingo looked up sharply. "Plan what?"

Fury and fear galvanized me. I leaped for the safe and slammed it closed, then shoved the painting back on the wall. "They tried to kill me a few hours ago," I said. "They sabotaged my plane. The other pilot was killed, too. They murdered him so there'd be no witnesses."

Dawning horror spread across Ingo's face. He grabbed my arm. "You told me you were in danger – that's all!" he spat. "You didn't say—"

I whirled towards him. "Would you have still come? Would you? Or would you have taken your keys and gone back to Miri?"

Ingo's face darkened; he started to reply – instead we both froze at the sound of a nearby door opening.

The vacuum started up in the next office.

I reached to grab the files, and then stopped. There was a notepad on Madeline's desk; I snatched up a pen. *I trusted you*, I scrawled. I ripped off the piece of paper and slapped it in the middle of Madeline's desk.

"Come on," I said.

Ingo stood staring. "You *are* insane," he said.

"Yes, maybe I am!" I snapped. "It feels like it right now, anyway."

Ingo started to say something else; his mouth tightened. Silently, he helped me take the files and we slipped away from Madeline's sanctuary with its fading flowers. The sound of the vacuum amplified as we opened the door.

We crept past and then ran for the darkness of the stairs. When we reached them, we travelled down, down into the gloom.

Chapter Thirty-five

Dear Amity,

I'm writing again because I need to tell you that those men came back. I tried not to let them in like you said, but they pushed past me and I couldn't stop them. Ma kept saying not to antagonize them, to let them do what they want. They checked our charts again but this time they went straight to mine, they didn't seem to care about the others. When they left they took my chart away with them. They told me not to go anywhere or I'd be in trouble.

I'm scared, Amity. Why would I be in trouble? They can't really do anything to me, can they? They're Gunnison's men, not ours. I've been reading the papers to try and find out what's going on but I can't see anything. Ma said not to bother you and that it's probably nothing but I knew you'd want to know.

I hope you're all right. Say hello to Collie for me. I sure wish you two could come home again soon.

Your brother,

Hal

I folded Hal's letter and tucked it back in my pocket just as Milt appeared with two cups of coffee. Around us, the roadside diner was full of truckers. In their large hands, the silverware looked tiny.

I'd read Hal's letter a dozen times now. I wasn't sure what was going on, but urgency filled me. It seemed that Collie had been right – it wasn't him those men were after. I couldn't call home; switchboard operators might have been told to listen in on Ma's line. If I hadn't had to meet with Milt, I'd have been on my way to Sacrament already.

Hang on, Hal, I thought. Deep down I added Collie to that plea. My fear for his safety was like a gnawing rat.

I added cream and sugar to my coffee and took a gulp; I'd hardly eaten today. "Thanks for meeting me here," I said to Milt.

He shrugged. "Kind of out of the way, isn't it? Guess that's the idea."

Milt's shabby sports jacket was the same reddish-brown as his hair. His ruddy cheeks gave him an outdoorsy look – just like when he'd first approached me in Heatcalf City after my appeal. I'd pitched his business card in the trash, but to my relief had remembered his name.

As Milt stirred his coffee he gave me a keen glance. "Heard the news?"

I'd just started to pull the files from the brown paper shopping bag I'd been carrying them in. I looked up in apprehension. "What news?"

"You, of course. At least, I assume it's you. Yeah, you're pretty big news, Miss Vancour. Here you go – courtesy of the evening papers." He took a newspaper from a battered briefcase and slid it across the laminated tabletop.

WESTERN SEABOARD PILOT CHARGED WITH MURDER – "WILDCAT" ON THE RUN

My hands went cold. "*What?*" I grabbed up the paper.

During a Tier One fight yesterday a Western Seaboard pilot – who cannot be named under the anonymity policy – opened fire on her Central States opponent as the defeated pilot parachuted to the ground, brutally murdering him. The WS pilot, nicknamed "Wildcat" by her team leader, eluded arrest upon landing and is now on the run.

It is thought that "Wildcat" killed her opponent to stop his disclosure that she had approached him about the possibility of making money for thrown fights. Both the World for Peace and the Western Seaboard have

> denounced Wildcat, and every effort is being made to find her and bring her to justice.
>
> "I'm sickened," said Base Commander Hendrix of the Western Seaboard. "She was a Tier One pilot, trusted with the utmost responsibility the world can give. Clearly our trust was tragically misplaced."

Milt took a gulp of coffee, his gaze not leaving my face. "So is it you, Wildcat?"

I shoved the paper away. "This is just...just a complete pack of lies from start to finish!"

"Is it? Sure seems like it'd be a good reason to kill someone."

Heat surged through me. I leaned forward. "*These – are – lies.* If you don't believe me, I might as well leave right now."

Milt chuckled. "Hey, relax. I'm a journalist. I ask questions. But if you want to get your version of the story out there, I'm your man."

He took in the denims and shirt I'd bought that morning. There hadn't been enough money in the stolen wallet to get rid of my boots, too. "So where are your flight clothes?" he asked. "It says you eluded arrest upon landing."

"I didn't land – my plane was sabotaged," I said tightly. "My parachute was too, only I took the wrong one. The other pilot wasn't so lucky. He tried to bail and fell to his death from ten thousand feet."

Milt gave a low whistle. He pulled a notepad and pencil from his inside pocket and started to write, the stubby lead flying across the page. "Keep talking," he said urgently.

"*I'm* the one they want to silence, because I found out about the bribes. Hendrix is as corrupt as the rest of them. I've got all the evidence. Everything. Right here."

Milt's head snapped up; he looked at the shopping bag. "What kind of evidence?"

"Notes from one of the corrupt pilots, WfP memos and documents—"

"Let's get out of here." Milt flipped his notebook shut. "I've got my auto – we'll find someplace more private." He glanced at the bag again. "If you've really got what you say you've got...well, sister, this thing is going to explode like nobody's business."

Milt drove us to a wooded road high in the hills. The tang of pine scented the air. I knew I'd never smell it again without seeing myself back in this moment: sitting in a battered coupé, parked off an empty dirt road and gripped by tension.

I told Milt everything as he went through the documents, snapping photos of them with a silver and black camera as large as his head. I hated the undercurrent of excitement in his voice. This was only a story to him, the biggest of his career. But he asked good questions and listened to my answers.

He blew out a stream of smoke through the open auto window. It was the third cigarette he'd lit. "*Hendrix was misled by her background,*" he read aloud from Madeline's memo. "So what 'background' is she talking about?"

"No idea," I said.

His eyes flicked to mine. "Really?"

"Really." Though it was true I had a vague sense of guilt, as if I *did* know what Madeline had meant. From somewhere deep down a thought tried to surface. I pushed it away and shook my head.

"I don't know," I said. "Maybe it's that I was arrested for shoplifting once – I told the WfP about it during my Peacefighting interview. I was only fifteen then, though."

"*Background,*" mused Milt again, drawing the word out. "Yeah…maybe."

In a strange way, the files' contents had been a relief. They'd made it clear that most Peacefighters upheld their vows – that many in the World for Peace had no idea about the corruption. But the depth of Madeline's involvement sickened me.

I'd thought I'd known this woman. My father had been a Peacefighter with her; she'd romped with us through my childhood summers. Yet in another memo, I'd read:

> *Yes, of course I warned Hendrix not to approach her; I can only assume the communication went astray. However, I stressed the need to take great care in recruiting* any *pilot, since few would deliberately lose*

fights for their country regardless of recompense. In general he acted competently. Apparently Russ Avery had gambling debts and Stanley Chaplin's family was in financial crisis – this, along with their birth charts, made Hendrix initially think them good prospects.

As I read, anger and sadness clenched my throat. Concordia's family had been poor, too. Is that what they did – preyed on pilots with the "right" birth charts who needed money? But then why ask me? Ma might be struggling a little; we weren't destitute.

Outside the auto, the pine trees stirred in the breeze. Milt had put the other memo aside and was scribbling something in his notepad. "All right, does anyone else know what's going on?"

"No," I said flatly.

Milt's pencil stopped in its tracks. He looked at me, eyebrows raised.

"I can't tell you that," I said, relenting a little. "Surely you can understand. People's lives are in danger." Not only Collie's, but Ingo's – he'd been furious, and scared, when we'd left the World for Peace building.

"What the hell am I supposed to do?" he'd hissed at me as we hurried through the dark streets. "How can I go back and fight now, knowing this is going on?"

But we'd both known that he had to. Though I was as filled with dread as Ingo, what I was trying to do now was our only hope of stopping this.

Milt shrugged. "Yeah, I got you. Okay, I'll skim over that part in the piece." He glanced again at documents from the Conflicts Council, showing approved fights. My suspicion was that they were also fights that had been thrown.

"I haven't been able to check how many of those wins benefited Gunnison yet," I said.

Milt's brow was furrowed. "Don't worry, I'll do it... Hey, kind of strange that you were able to get this stuff, isn't it?"

"Well, it wasn't exactly given to me."

He replaced the papers in the file. "No, I'm sure it wasn't. But listen, you say this Madeline dame's known you from when you were a kid, right? So when the plot to kill you didn't work, what's the first thing she should have guessed you'd try?"

My skin prickled as I stared at him. "You mean – she let me get these documents on purpose? That's impossible! She couldn't have known I'd be able to get into the World for Peace building."

I'd glossed over how I'd managed it, and Milt didn't pursue it. "Must have known you'd give it a shot, though," he said. "Sounds like she knows you pretty well. And middle of the night, things are dead in Heatcalf City. If they were watching for you, they'd have seen you. But they didn't capture you. Why?"

"I didn't see anyone," I said. I'd almost said "we".

"Lots of shadows there at night."

"No – it doesn't make sense." My voice rose. "Why would they let me get this information on purpose? It incriminates them at the highest levels."

"I don't know. Maybe some of it's a plant. I'll tell you straight, though: it's making my journalistic alarms go off like crazy."

"You believe me, don't you?"

Milt lit another cigarette and tossed the lighter onto the dashboard. He was silent for a moment. "You know, I think I do," he said. "Not that it matters. I'll write a hell of a story either way."

My laugh tasted sour. "So that's all you care about?"

He grinned. "Pretty much. But yeah, since you ask, I think you've uncovered something big here, and the powers that be are scrambling to cover it up." He blew out a stream of smoke as he studied me. "What I haven't worked out yet is if you're as true-blue as you seem...or if you were in it up to your neck, too, and now you're turning on them to save your own skin."

I couldn't be angry at his cynicism. If I'd been a little more cynical myself, the other pilot wouldn't have died yesterday. I'd have done what Collie asked and refused to fly.

Collie was a cynic. He'd known all along this could blow up at any second.

My chest tightened at the thought of him. I cleared my throat. "Well, while you're figuring it out, maybe you could give me a lift to the station."

"Sure thing – I think I've got everything I need." Milt handed me the files back. "I won't ask to keep these," he said. "The photos should be enough to convince my editor, once I develop them."

"Good, because I can't give you any of this." I ran my pinched fingers down a file's spine. "Will you be able to get the story published? The papers lately have been full of such fluff."

Milt nodded and stubbed out his cigarette in the overflowing ashtray. "My editor's old-school and he hates Gunnison – this is just the kind of story he's been itching for. Once it hits the stands, they won't be able to put the cat back in the bag. We'll get an inquisition out of it and those fights reversed, wait and see."

I nodded tensely. I hoped he was right.

Milt started up the auto. He hesitated before putting it in gear; for the first time, a shadow fell over his face. "The World for Peace, though," he murmured. "Ah, hell… who would have thought it?"

We drove in silence. When we finally pulled up to the nearest train station, Milt glanced at me curiously. "You got someplace to go?"

"I'm not telling you that, and I'm sure you don't really want to know."

He shrugged. "No, you're right. Not a good idea."

I hesitated. I was desperate to ask Milt to check on Collie for me, but then he'd guess that Collie was implicated in all this. I didn't entirely trust Milt not to do something with that knowledge, if it would make for a better story.

I looked away and picked up my parka from the seat. "When will the piece run?"

"Next couple of days, with luck. You better lay low until then." Milt held out his hand. "Take care of yourself, Amity. Those bastards mean business."

"You, too," I said as we shook. "Be careful."

Milt grinned. "Ah, I'm just a nobody journalist. Listen, you know how to reach me if you need to. And here, have a present – something to read for your trip." He opened his briefcase and handed me the newspaper.

For the first time, I saw the headline below my own.

TIER ONE FIGHT REFOUGHT – GUNNISON WINS RIGHT TO EXTRADITE ALL WESTERN SEABOARD DISCORDANTS.

Chapter Thirty-six

THE TRAIN ROCKED THROUGH THE NIGHT. I sat in the open boxcar with my knees drawn tightly against my chest, watching the moonlit landscape pass. A chilly breeze buffeted the inside of the car, empty apart from a few crates.

I yearned to go faster. Hal's letter felt like it was burning a hole of fear in my pocket.

The news story's photo had shown Gunnison with his easy grin. *I'm relieved that we can help our Western Seaboard neighbours by dealing with their Discordant elements*, he was quoted as saying. *We in the Central States have been sorrowed by your recent hardships. Without the Discordants, you'll soon see an upswing in your fortunes.*

It was clear now what Gunnison's men had been doing at Ma's. People in the WS who'd already had their birth charts done had saved the Guns time: they could check them for anything that madman might deem a threat. Though we weren't even his *citizens,* Gunnison could extradite whoever he wanted now and throw them in a correction camp.

Including, unbelievably, my little brother.

The Guns had known that Tier One fight was coming up. They'd known what its outcome would be.

The fight. I rubbed my temple with a cold hand. Had there even been a fight? There didn't really seem a need to go through the charade any more; they could claim whatever they wanted. Or had Collie been set up the same way I had? I imagined his plane exploding in the sky – saw his lifeless body sprawled against red grass.

No. No. I sat huddled, trembling. *Please be safe, Collie. Please.*

I couldn't help him. I could only pray that he was still alive. But maybe, with luck, I could help Hal.

I took a breath and forced myself to straighten my shoulders. I stared out at the silvery fields, with the bright, flat line of the ocean in the distance.

Madeline's treachery.

My father and Madeline together.

One thought felt more impossible than the other, and I hated which one it was. And somehow, as the train slowly ate the miles, I was cast back to the night before Dad died.

Collie had stayed over that night. He did that, sometimes, even with us as old as we both were by then. He had his own bedroom at our place. It was the spare room, really, but Ma always called it "Collie's room", and he kept some books and things there. I knew he liked it far better than his real bedroom, though he got prickly whenever I suggested that he could just stay with us for good.

He didn't sleep over very often. It was as if he were rationing himself, not wanting to get too used to it. But when he did, everyone seemed happier – lighter. Collie always had that effect on us. We'd sit up and pop corn and play games and just...be a family.

I remembered that particular night so clearly. Dad had been home too, so it was like a double holiday. He'd been in such a good mood – joking around with Ma; starting a contest to see who could catch the most popped corn in their mouth. We'd all played Make-a-Word, and arguments had broken out every few minutes, despite Hal running to get the dictionary. At one point a rumba came on the telio and Dad jumped up and said, "I must have this dance, Rose." He pulled her close and they moved around the living room to our laughing groans.

The moon went behind a cloud and I stared out at the blurred darkness. My childhood had generally been happy, hadn't it? I'd loved our house, and running wild through the fields. Yet whenever Collie had stayed over, it was as if a mood had lifted for all of us. Maybe I remembered that night so well because it had been so unusual. For once, the gulf between my father's banter and the real him hadn't seemed so wide.

But now, looking back...I wondered if there hadn't been something a bit too feverish about Dad's high spirits.

After we went to bed that night, I'd woken up suddenly at the sound of shattering glass. Someone was breaking in! I'd leaped from my bed and snatched up a baseball bat; still in my nightgown, I crept down the stairs. My blood pumped in my ears. I'd catch the burglars in the act – make my father proud of me – maybe even get my picture in the paper.

Halfway down, I heard something strange. I stopped, listening hard.

Singing. No, a kind of low, mumbling noise. Then singing again.

I eased the rest of the way downstairs, clutching the bat with cold fingers. My father sat at the kitchen table with a bottle in front of him. As I stopped in the doorway I had a sinking feeling that Collie's mother would know exactly what that amber liquid was.

Dad was reaching for the bottle when I appeared. He looked up.

"Amity, what are you doing awake?"

To my relief he sounded normal. I started into the room and he jumped up. "No, don't – there's glass on the floor. I dropped a tumbler. Don't tell Mommy, all right?"

He whistled as he got a dustpan and brush and cleared

away the mess. I stood watching the glass glint. He never referred to my mother as *Mommy.* He knew she was "Ma" to me and Hal, and anyway, he always called her Rose.

"Onwards, soldier – advance," he said at last.

I entered and sat cautiously on one of the chairs. "Is that Scotch?" I said, eyeing the bottle. *Hall's Best Blended,* read white letters on a black label.

"Yes," said my father. "I'll have to get another tumbler out now and be civilized, hey? Not drink from the bottle like a ruffian. Want some warm milk?"

I shook my head. I hadn't had warm milk since I was nine. Ma wouldn't have made that mistake, but I didn't blame my father. He was too busy with the World for Peace to know these things.

Dad got another tumbler and poured himself two inches of Scotch. He took a swig and then noticed the baseball bat propped against the table. "What's that for?"

My cheeks went red. "I...heard the glass breaking. I thought it was a burglar." There was no way I could mention the singing and the mumbling.

"So you came downstairs on your own to stop him?" Dad gave a low whistle. "That's my girl. Braver than her old man, for sure."

I was too on edge to enjoy the admiring look in his eyes. "No, I'm not," I protested. "You were a Peacefighter."

"Not that kind of bravery."

I shifted on my seat. What kind of bravery were we talking about, then?

"Fighting when your adrenalin's up – that's nothing." Dad took another gulp of Scotch. "You'll see someday, if you're a Peacefighter too. Will you be?" He leaned back and studied me. Somehow the question didn't feel addressed to me and so I didn't answer, thinking guiltily of Canary Cargo.

"I think you might be," Dad decided. "You're the right type, aren't you, Louise?"

He called me that sometimes – the name of our ancestor who'd done so much, fought so hard. "I don't know," I muttered. "I'd like to be." The lie tinted my cheeks.

"Well, you're a legacy, so you'd get in easily enough." My father sounded grim now. His dark hair fell over his forehead as he tapped the tumbler against the table. "I was a legacy, too, of course. Your grandmother. Oh, she had no idea."

"No idea of what?"

My father seemed to come back to himself. He stared at me as if he'd forgotten who he was talking to.

"Nothing," he said finally. "Times change, don't they? Mom knew what it was like for her, but not for me. And if you become a Peacefighter, all you'll know is what it's like for you. No one can judge your actions unless they've been there. Got that? Nobody."

I licked dry lips. "What actions?"

My father gave a sad, reckless smile. "My darling, if I could tell you that, I'd be king of the world." He gazed into the glass, swirling it so that the amber liquid caught the light.

I watched the glinting waves rise and fall. "Dad, you can tell me anything."

"Maybe someday," he said without looking up. "When you're a Peacefighter, too. It's the only thing worth being, Amity…I always knew that."

I sat poised, tense. I felt as if I were on the verge of some great discovery. Here was the mystery of my father, so close I could almost reach out and touch it…only I still had no idea what it was.

Finally Dad looked up. "You should get to bed now," he said, and I was so relieved to have him sound like a parent again that I jumped up without arguing.

"What time will you fly out tomorrow?" I asked.

He had a meeting at the World for Peace the next day. Something crucial, though I knew he wouldn't tell me what. A lot of what he did was classified. I loved telling the kids at school that; the word felt important as it rolled off my tongue.

"Early," said Dad shortly. He took another gulp and then stood up and flung the rest of the Scotch into the sink. "So I'd better lay off this stuff, huh?"

Why had I asked about his departure time? It felt as if a moment had been irretrievably lost. Yet my next question was just as banal: "Will you take the Gauntlet? Or the Dove?"

My father rubbed a hand over his eyes. "The Gaunt, I think."

"Then maybe I could come, too," I said, feeling

desperate. I went on quickly: "I could sit in the lobby and do homework while you have your meeting—"

"Not this time," said my father.

He smiled then. I smiled hesitantly back. "Go to bed, Amity," he said in a soft voice. "I'll clean up in here."

"I'll help."

"No. Go on," he said.

And so I went.

I'd sat in the boxcar's open doorway for so long that my muscles were chilled, but I still didn't move as the shadows juddered past. I could see my father's face so clearly.

For years he'd been blurred around the edges, no matter how hard I'd tried to picture him. Now, like falling back through time, I could see his tanned face; the faint lines around his light-brown eyes; his thin, clever fingers that could fix anything.

No one can judge your actions unless they've been there.

Once I became a Peacefighter I'd thought I understood. Even with the best of intentions, you sometimes killed. Pilots had died, some of them in agony, because I'd shot them down. I'd have to live with that my whole life, just as my father had.

Now I stared out at dark fields and thought about the word *background.* Such a nice, solid word. It rolled off the tongue in the same important way *classified* once had.

My darling, if I could tell you that, I'd be king of the world.

The train rattled on. I blew out a brisk, angry breath. No. What I was thinking was crazy. I was just numb from everything that had happened these past few weeks.

Almost the worst thing of all was Madeline's betrayal. *I'm extremely saddened but agree that the proposed solution is the only way.* The words still kicked me in the gut. I'd admired Madeline – wanted to be like her.

What had happened? How had she taken this path?

All I knew was that she couldn't have been caught up in it when Dad was alive, or else he'd never have been involved with her. I hugged my knees, staring out at the rocking darkness, and wondered bitterly how long it had gone on between them. Had Ma known?

Finally, with relief, I saw the glow of Sacrament coming up. I scrambled, stiff-legged, to my feet. As the train slowed around a bend I gripped the side of the car, watching the dark, rushing grass. I steeled myself and jumped, rolling into the fall.

The impact slammed through me; the world spun in a blur. I staggered up, breathing hard as the train disappeared in the distance.

Forget all of this. As I started to jog I knew I could think only of Hal now – nothing else.

Chapter Thirty-seven

THE SHADOWCAR SAT WAITING AT the kerb.

I pressed against the side of a building and peered out. I was barely inside the Sacrament city limits. The news that Gunnison could now extradite whoever he wanted had clearly already broken – the streets felt quiet, even for this time of morning. I stared at the smoke-grey van. It was like seeing one of the Central States resistance pamphlets come to life.

"No! Please!" Sudden shouts pierced the air. Two of Gunnison's men appeared, dragging a struggling woman between them. "There's no one to watch my children!" she cried.

"Better that than being watched by a Discordant," said a Gun.

"Please take care of my children!" yelled the woman to the silent neighbourhood. She twisted in the men's grasp. "*Is anybody listening?* Take—"

I flinched as a Gun struck her; she cried out and clutched her face. Blood twined over her fingers. They shoved her inside the Shadowcar and slammed the back door.

The van drove away, leaving quiet houses behind.

My blood beat at my skull. *How* could this be happening in the Western Seaboard? With my cap pulled low, I walked as fast as I dared through the streets.

Milt, hurry the hell up with that story, I thought. At least I didn't have the documents on me. I'd left them in a train station locker and hidden the key.

In the two hours it took me to reach Ma's neighbourhood, I saw dozens of Shadowcars cruising like bloated grey sharks. They seemed to be doing a systematic sweep, following the same route as me. By the time I neared the apartment I was ahead of them and hadn't seen one for half an hour.

But they were coming.

"...for extradition to the Central States," said President Lopez's voice, floating out to the street from a telio somewhere. "This Peacefighting result deeply saddens me, but I urge all citizens to abide by the law..."

I could have happily smashed the telio to pieces. I stepped into a doorway to think, my mind racing. The city had woken up. Autos and streetcars pulsed past, and the sidewalks were busy with people on their way to work as if it was just an ordinary day.

I bumped my fist against my mouth. I had to get to Hal but couldn't go to Ma's house. Cain's thugs might be watching it, looking for me. I shouldn't even be here in Sacrament.

A group of schoolkids passed, giggling and shoving each other.

"You're a Discordant!"

"No, I'm a Libra, Libras are great!"

I wanted to shout after them that this wasn't a game. They'd given me an idea, though. I left the doorway and headed for a nearby vacant lot: a rubble-filled shortcut to the high school. Hal probably took it every morning the same as I had. I could only pray that he'd go to school today like always.

A deserted building sat on the lot. We kids had been forbidden to go inside it, and had of course gone anyway. Its walls were coated with graffiti, its floor littered with cigarette butts and beer bottles. It was the kind of place I'd loved back in the days of Rob.

I stepped inside. The door hung half off its hinges. I pressed against it and gazed tensely out at the lot. A path snaked through the rubble from years of teenagers crossing through.

What had seemed a good idea just minutes ago seemed pointless now. Ma must have seen the papers. She was silly sometimes but not stupid; she'd know what Hal's chart being taken away must mean. I had a sudden, vivid image of her frozen with fear, keeping him at home today – playing right into the Guns' hands.

I went still at the sound of voices, then realized it was only two girls carrying leather book satchels.

"Well, I think it's scary," said the first one as they approached. She and her friend wore neat skirts and blouses, their hair carefully curled. "Why should someone be Discordant just because of their zodiac sign?"

The other girl wore a silver brooch shaped like a ram's curling horns. "There's more to it than that, Francie," she said earnestly. "You can tell a lot about a person from their natal chart. If they're no good then why should the rest of us put up with them?"

"Before they've even done anything, though?"

"How do you know? If they're the reason why things have been so hard for everyone recently, then…"

The girls passed by; their voices faded. I stared after them. Was it really *that* easy for Gunnison to take over people's hearts and minds?

Collie had lived through this. He'd known. In a relentless rush, that moment under the palm trees came back, with the rain dripping gently around us and Collie's fingers warm on my cheek. *I love you, Amity. I always have. Don't throw it all away. I'm begging you.*

My heart clenched. I closed my eyes tightly. If anything had happened to him, it would be my fault. He'd only stayed because of me.

Another set of footsteps was approaching. I shuddered

and swiped a hand over my face, somehow burying my fear for Collie.

A lanky, dark-haired boy wearing grey trousers and a short-sleeved shirt came down the path. He had his schoolbooks tucked under one arm and was trying hard to be casual, though his stiff shoulders gave him away.

Relief flooded me…and then I heard shouts nearby. "No! You can't take him! *Please!*"

Hal stopped in his tracks, eyes wide.

"Hal!" I hissed.

He jumped and took a step backwards. "Who's there?" he called shakily.

A tall, rounded Shadowcar glided into view at the far end of the lot. I didn't stop to think. I lurched from the deserted house and grabbed Hal, putting my hand over his mouth as I pulled him back inside with me. He struggled; his books crashed to the floor.

"*Stop it!*" I ordered. "Stay still…" The Shadowcar passed and I let out a ragged breath. "It's me," I said in an undertone. "Hal, it's just me." I let go.

"Amity?" he gasped. He threw himself into my arms and we hugged tightly. From his trembling, I guessed he was struggling not to cry.

"You really came," he choked out.

"Of course I did," I whispered into his hair. I pulled away and clutched his narrow shoulders. "Tell me what's happening at home. Hurry, we haven't got much time."

I could see my little brother attempting to control

himself – to be contained and mature. "The…um… the Guns haven't come back yet," he said. "I think Ma has some kind of plan, but she won't tell me."

"Ma has a plan?" I repeated, incredulous.

"I think so. She said that I had to be seen going to school like always, but to duck away at the last minute. She said to keep moving no matter what, and she'd meet me at the park at ten o'clock."

None of this sounded like my mother. Or did it? I licked my lips, remembering how she'd swooped in to help Collie that time he'd been sick – marching into Goldie's house with soup and comics, ready to call a doctor no matter what Goldie thought.

"So she knows," I murmured.

Hal was pale. "I'm a Discordant, aren't I?"

"Only to someone who's a lunatic," I said shortly. I gathered Hal's books off the floor; a beer bottle rolled away as my hand brushed against it.

"But it's the law now," Hal said. "They can take me to the Central States and put me in a correction camp. Amity, people die in those places! I've seen a pamphlet that said—"

"I've seen them too," I broke in. I straightened and shoved his books at him. "No one is taking you away. I won't let them. Neither will Ma."

Hal's throat moved. He didn't answer. He was old enough to know that there are some promises you can't keep.

A cluster of teenagers passed and we fell silent.

I stared at the cowed group from the shadows, hardly seeing them.

What was my mother's plan? My own plan had been to grab Hal and leave town. I could still do it, but how safe would he be with me? I'd die to protect him; that wouldn't keep him from getting captured if it came to that.

I could feel Hal watching me as I tapped my fist against the grimy wall, thinking about how Ma crumpled before authority...and also remembering her determined mouth when she'd said, *And if I could, I'd take Collie away from that mother of his and raise him right here.*

The lot was empty again. I slowly exhaled, then steeled myself. I put my arm around Hal's shoulders.

"Come on, we'd better keep moving," I told him. "We've got over an hour before we can meet Ma."

The park bench was over to one side of the path beneath some trees; it was as secluded as we'd get here. It still felt much too exposed. I glanced at my watch again. Five past ten. Five more minutes, that was all I could give Ma. Then I was leaving and taking Hal with me.

Hal sat with his dark head down, hands clasped between his knees. We'd thrown his schoolbooks away in a garbage can. I'd seen Hal start to protest – and then go silent as he realized that he wouldn't be returning to school anytime soon.

"We're supposed to elect student council leaders today," he said softly now. It was the first thing he'd said in a while. "Everyone will think it's weird that I'm not there. Do you think they all know?"

I resisted the urge to look at my watch again. "They'll probably guess, with all these Shadowcars everywhere."

Hal winced and kept his gaze on his hands. I glanced at him, wondering what was going on in his head – whether he was actually attaching some shame to this. I bit back a sharp comment. He was only fourteen.

Collie was so much better at these things than I was. "Hal, it might be okay," I said finally. "I can't say too much, but there's information that, if it gets out…well, it could make all of this go away."

He looked up quickly. "What information?"

"I can't tell you. But I hope it's going to come out soon." Eight minutes past ten. *Ma, come on, come on.*

Hal's gaze stayed on me. He frowned, as if really seeing me for the first time since I'd arrived.

"Are you okay?" he asked.

"Oh, I'm just dandy. I'm sitting on a park bench evading Guns with my brother – what could be more fun?"

An unwilling smile tugged at his mouth. "You know what I mean. How are things with you and Collie?"

I looked down, tapping my fingers together, and shoved away the image of Collie in the sickbay bed, begging me not to fight. "Fine," I said curtly. I didn't add that I hoped he was still alive.

"I guess you're pretty upset about Wildcat," ventured Hal.

"What?"

"You know – in the papers. You must have known her, right? Did she really take bribes?"

"Don't believe everything you read," I snapped. "I thought you were smarter than that."

Hal's expression went stiff. "Well, excuse me for breathing," he muttered to the trees.

He's fourteen, I reminded myself. Eleven minutes past ten. I pushed my shirtsleeve down over my watch and cleared my throat. "Okay, look...I think we'd better—"

"Hal!" My mother appeared down the path in a perfumed flurry. Relief swamped me. Hal and I leaped up as she reached us; she hugged him tightly.

"I thought you weren't here at first. *Amity!*" She hugged me, too. "Oh, darling, you shouldn't have come," she said in a fierce whisper. "It's all much too dangerous right now."

She had no idea. "I know," I said. I glanced at Hal. "Ma, what are you planning?"

"No time – those terrible vans are everywhere." She glanced over her shoulder and then tucked her arm through Hal's. "Come on, I've got everything we need."

She led us to the park restrooms and had me go into the Ladies' first to make sure it was empty. Then she took Hal in. "Here, get changed," she said in a rush, handing him a paper bag. "No arguments," she added.

I stood by the door keeping watch, but the park was

empty. A pall had fallen over the city. In the distance I could hear a siren.

Hal opened the bag and stared down at its contents. "Ma...this is a dress."

"Yes, I've got a wig and shoes for you, too. Hurry!"

Hal's eyes flew to mine. He looked panicked. Not by the dress so much; it was as if the gravity of this had hit him all at once. I wanted to hug him. There was no time.

"Do it, Hal," I said.

Ma led us through the streets. She wore a hat with a veil, partly obscuring her face; Hal walked with his head down, unrecognizable in the blue dress and long, dark wig.

I touched his arm, as tense as he was but trying to hide it. "Hey, you're a really pretty girl," I said. "A lot prettier than me."

My brother didn't smile. "Wouldn't take much," he said finally.

We neared our neighbourhood. I licked my lips. I knew I should get away from my family before Cain's men appeared, but I had to make sure Hal would be all right. I thought of the pistol still hidden under my waistband. I wondered if I could use it if I had to.

"I can't go much closer to our house," I said in an undertone to Ma. "I...I left without leave; I shouldn't be here."

Ma wasn't paying attention. She glanced up and down the block. "This way is safest, I think," she murmured, and to my relief she turned off several streets before our own, her high heels tapping against the sidewalk.

Hal's gaze stayed on me, troubled. The wig made his black eyelashes seem longer. "You left without leave?" he repeated. "Why? For me?"

"Forget it, Hal."

"But—" He bit off whatever he'd been going to say. "Do you think they'll court-martial you?" he asked at last.

"I said *forget it*, all right?" At his expression I softened and tried awkwardly to joke: "Listen, that place was getting boring anyway. I'll just have a little vacation and then go back. It'll be fine."

Hal fell silent. After a moment he frowned and glanced at me. I could almost see the gears of his brain working.

Ma entered Hyde's department store; we cut through ladies' wear and the perfume department. We came out on the next road over, adjacent to our own. She hastened us down a side street.

"This is it," she said, stopping in front of a run-down brownstone.

In the window an astrologer's red-and-black sign flashed. *Madame Josephine's.*

"*Here?*" I took Ma's arm and pulled her to one side. "Ma, *no*," I whispered urgently. "She's the one who must have told the Guns that you had charts done!"

"I know. We can trust her," said Ma.

"But—"

"Listen to me!" hissed Ma. "*We can trust her.* Come on."

As we went inside, I was ready to grab Hal and run if need be. Madame Josephine looked like any other woman on the street: middle-aged, with frosted blonde hair. The room had dark, heavy furniture, but seemed ordinary enough…apart from a large astrology chart on the wall. I stiffened at the sight of it.

"You're late," Madame Josephine said hurriedly to Ma. "Hello, you must be Hal."

Hal bit his lip and nodded. He tugged off the wig; his short dark hair appeared. No one laughed at the contrast this made with the dress.

"There's a bathroom there. Go and get changed, sweetie," said Ma, handing him the bag with his clothes. As he turned away, Ma stopped him and kissed his cheek. Her eyes were bright.

Once the bathroom door had shut, I said tightly, "Ma, what are we doing here?"

"Your mother comes here often." Madame Josephine seemed to be preparing for a client: placing a red velvet cloth on the table, arranging candles. She glanced up. "No one will think anything of it if she keeps coming now that your brother's run away from home."

I stood motionless. "You mean Hal will be here?"

"Show her," Madame Josephine said tersely to Ma.

Ma took me to a small bedroom with faded, flowery wallpaper. She opened the closet, then dragged out a battered trunk resting on the floor. She folded back a square of fitted carpet.

There was a trapdoor with a circular metal handle set into the floor. When Ma tugged on it, the door swung open like a mouth; a wooden ladder led down. Peering in, I saw a small, neat room, just large enough for its single bed and table.

"No one will know," said Ma softly. "No one will even suspect. Until all of this passes over, Hal will have just disappeared."

My fingernails bit into my palms. "You're sure we can trust her?"

Ma nodded. "Yes. I have no doubt. The Central States think she's sympathetic to them, but she's on our side – she tipped me off about Hal weeks ago. Besides, she's my friend."

I stared down into the tiny room. All I could think of was how much Hal loved playing stickball with his friends. *He'll go crazy all alone down there,* I thought. But the alternative was unthinkable.

"Ma?" said Hal.

I turned. My brother stood behind us wearing his own clothes again; Madame Josephine hovered in the bedroom doorway. Hal stared at the open trapdoor. I saw his throat move.

Ma grasped his shoulders. "Don't worry, darling," she said, her voice falsely cheery. "I'm sure it's just for a little while."

"Do I really have to?" whispered Hal.

Madame Josephine touched his arm. "I'll spend as much time with you as I can," she said. "So will your mother. It'll be fine, you'll—"

A loud knocking echoed through the house.

Ma's eyes flew to Madame Josephine's. The astrologer went pale; she shook her head. "I'm not expecting anyone just yet. Quick, get him in."

Ma seemed frozen. As Madame Josephine rushed from the room I clutched Hal's arm. "Come on – I'll go down with you."

I could see his relief. We clambered down the wooden ladder. The room felt claustrophobic; I could have touched both opposite walls at once. I found a lantern and lit it just as Ma closed the trapdoor above.

A flapping noise as the carpet covered us – the muffled scrape of the trunk. Ma's footsteps left the bedroom. I felt icy as I stared upwards, my pulse hammering. Strain as I might, I couldn't hear anything. Had Madame Josephine betrayed us? Were Guns at the door right now?

Or had Cain's men found me?

Hal stared at the ceiling too, his fists tight. I put my arms around him; he pressed against me. "Amity, I don't want to be here," he murmured.

"I know. Shush, though." I stroked his hair. Over his shoulder I could see a small shelf on the wall. Some of Hal's books were on it, and a few of his model planes. How long had Ma been planning this?

We started as footsteps entered the bedroom above like thunder. Only one pair – no, two. My heart rate trebled. I tightened my hold on my brother and thought again of my pistol. *You will not take him,* I vowed.

The trunk was pulled away. "It's only us," hissed Ma's voice.

My muscles drooped. I let go of Hal just as light angled into the room from above; Ma's face appeared in the sudden rectangle. "Hurry, Amity, you have to leave now. That was just the mailman, but Josephine has a client coming soon."

I hesitated. I could stay down here with Hal – hide out with him for however long it took. But Ma would suspect trouble; she might even guess that I was Wildcat. I couldn't put her in more danger than she was already in.

I gripped Hal's shoulders. "Listen to me," I whispered fiercely. "Collie was in the Central States; that's why he could never write to us. He managed to escape – and if he were here right now, he'd tell you that this is worth it. *Anything's* worth it to stay out of one of those camps. You've got to do everything that Ma and Josephine tell you. Okay?"

"Collie was really in the Central States?" Hal said hoarsely.

I nodded, unsure whether I was doing the right thing by telling him – knowing only that I had to give him something.

Hal licked his lips and looked around him. Almost

imperceptibly, his shoulders straightened. "Okay," he said. "Tell Collie that...that I'm really glad he escaped. And that I won't let myself get taken there."

Oh, how I hoped that he'd have any say in it. I hugged him hard. "I love you," I said. "I've got to go."

"I love you, too. Amity!" Hal gripped my arm as I started for the ladder. His eyes searched mine. "Do you maybe want to take that wig Ma got for me?" he said in an undertone.

And I knew that he'd guessed I was in danger.

I tried to smile. "No, you might need it," I whispered back. "But thanks."

Closing the trapdoor over my brother was one of the hardest things I'd ever done. I helped Ma flop the rug into place and drag the trunk over it. It felt as if we were burying Hal alive.

Madame Josephine showed Ma and me a back door. "Take care," she said, clasping my fingers. "I'll see you soon, Rose," she added.

"Tomorrow?" asked Ma.

The astrologer shook her head. "Better not, in case anyone saw you come in. Make it the next day." She squeezed Ma's hand, her gaze intense. "I'll take good care of him."

Once we were out on the street, Ma sagged. "Oh, dear...oh, I hope this was the right thing," she murmured.

I hoped so too, but I didn't say it. I took her arm and we started down the sidewalk, away from our own neighbourhood. All I could see were my brother's eyes as I'd shut the trapdoor over him. It was too late now *not* to trust Madame Josephine.

"Ma, what about you – will you be all right?" I said in a low voice. "The Guns might—"

"They've already been to the house this morning. I told them Hal was at school. They'll have gone there by now and found out he never showed up."

My veins chilled. "So they'll come back and search."

"They won't find anything," she said tersely. "I'll cry and act helpless and say he's been threatening to run away for months."

I glanced at her in surprise and she gave a tight-lipped smile. "You'd be surprised how often men fall for that," she said. "Even Guns, I bet."

As we kept walking I suddenly had the feeling that I hardly knew my mother. Would her ruse work? Or would they drag her in for questioning – or worse?

I hated how powerless I felt. "Ma…" I started.

She stopped at the streetcar stand. Without looking at me, she said, "Amity, you have a job to do, and so do I now. Don't worry. I will not let them take my son." Her voice quavered a fraction – yet I didn't doubt her.

My mother. My pretty, fluttery mother.

My throat was tight. *Dad was a fool to prefer Madeline to you, even for a second,* I wanted to tell her. I swallowed hard and looked away. The streetcar was rattling towards us. I couldn't take it; someone we knew might be on it.

"I have to go," I said. I hugged my mother blindly. "Ma…"

"I know, darling," she murmured, stroking my hair. "I know."

Chapter Thirty-eight

I LEFT SACRAMENT AND HOPPED a train to Angeles, just thirty miles north of the Peacefighting complex. Though I felt leery about being so close to the base, Angeles was the largest city in the Western Seaboard: a seething, spiky mass of millions. With luck I could melt away into it.

A day passed. Two. I hardly had any money left. I slept rough in doorways and abandoned buildings and scanned the papers feverishly. The headlines screamed daily about Wildcat – denouncing her for murder, keeping the public at fever pitch. The stories kept quoting "sources close to the base": "*She always seemed so trustworthy. I'd never have guessed what she was really like.*"

Those are not real quotes, I reminded myself harshly.

There was no sign of Milt's story.

Every time I passed a payphone, I longed to call the base. But if Collie was still alive, he already knew he had to keep low. Anyone I called there would be at risk if the base guessed it was me.

Collie, please be okay, I thought over and over. *Please. Canary Cargo, remember?*

On the third morning I stood half-hidden in a doorway with my hands jammed in my coat pockets, staring out at the gloomy city street. The glow from the street lamps daubed at the shadows. In the downpour, the light itself looked streaked with damp.

Distantly, I was aware of the emptiness in my stomach – a hollowed-out feeling as if someone had gouged away my insides. It was two days since I'd eaten, not that it mattered. If I could just get what I needed, I'd be fine.

A light went on in the diner opposite. Five a.m. I could see a bleached-blonde waitress tying on her apron, and silver stools with red leatherette seats. My hands tightened in my pockets. It all seemed so ordinary.

I was desperate to get in there and see a newspaper, but forced myself to wait until other people had drifted in: a postman, a woman who wore sensible shoes like a nurse, a few more. Then, my heart beating hard, I flipped up my coat collar and left the safety of the doorway. My boots splashed in the puddles as I jogged across the street, shattering reflected light with each footfall.

My boots. They were regulation boots, nothing like the

pretty shoes that most women wore. I prayed no one would notice and stepped into the diner.

The sudden warmth and dryness was an embrace. Conscious of how bedraggled I looked, I slipped onto the seat at the end of the counter – the one nearest the door, in case I needed to run.

The waitress came over. Her upswept hair was in stylized curls. "Help you?" she said cheerfully, swiping at the counter with a damp rag. *Betty*, read her name tag, with a symbol beside the letters that looked like a lashing tail. I tore my gaze from it.

"Just coffee, please," I said.

Gunshots rang out as I burst through the bathroom window. I landed on a scattered mess of wood, glass, trash from the alleyway. Pain – my hand was bleeding – I lunged to my feet and ran, pausing only to push over a trio of garbage cans and send them rolling in my wake. Panting, I veered out onto the sidewalk, my boots thudding against the concrete.

By the time I heard distant sirens, I was over ten blocks away. I kept walking until I couldn't hear them any more, until the only noises were the mundane ones of the city. The elevated train was up ahead. No one paid attention when I paused under its bridge. People passed by as the trains rumbled above, shaking the ground at our feet.

A shard of glass glinted from the fleshy part of my

thumb. I gritted my teeth and pulled it free, then found a handkerchief in my pocket and wrapped it tightly around the wound.

The whole time, my thoughts were tumbling, screaming.

I knew that I had not misread the story on page nine. But I pulled out the paper and read it again anyway:

> JOURNALIST KILLED IN AUTO CRASH
>
> Milton Fraser, 28, was found dead yesterday evening after he apparently lost control of his auto and broke through a safety rail, crashing over fifty feet into a canyon...

I swallowed hard as another train rattled overhead and the trash whispered against my ankles in the breeze. They'd killed Milt, an ordinary journalist who they shouldn't even have *known* about. How deep, how broad, did this whole thing go?

Collie.

My sore hand clenched its bandage. He had to still be alive; he *had* to be. And I had to get back to him, somehow – we both had to escape if we could—

With the rain still drizzling down, I started to run.

Finally, blocks later, I forced myself to slow to an unsteady walk. My hand pulsed with pain as I made my way down the city streets, listening for sirens. I felt dizzy. I'd existed on adrenalin for days. Now it had left me, and my knees had turned to cotton.

Occasionally I glanced at the newspaper I still carried. The headline never changed: JOURNALIST KILLED IN AUTO CRASH. Milt had been so certain that his editor would be on our side.

It looked as if he'd been wrong.

The vision of Collie's body sprawled on red grass flashed into my mind again. The paper crumpled in my grip. No. It couldn't be true. Collie wouldn't have flown after what happened to me. He'd have pretended to still be sick even if he wasn't.

The vision wouldn't go away. I could see the drying blood in Collie's sun-streaked hair. His eyes, open, as blue as the sky at which he stared.

Russ was dead. Stan and Milt were dead.

Collie was dead, too. I knew it.

I heard a low moan – realized it had come from me. The sidewalk seemed to lurch. I stumbled as I wove through the steady stream of pedestrians.

I'm just tired and hungry, I thought dazedly. Collie was *not* dead. I'd get back onto the base somehow. We'd leave together; we'd find a way to get the truth out to the world. It was the only thing now that could save Collie and Hal both.

I kept trudging down the sidewalk. I'd held myself together for days, but now it was so hard to think. The base was over thirty miles away. The city's bus stations would be crawling with police; motorists would have been told to watch out for me. I'd have to leave Angeles on foot, then hop a train. The city limits were ten miles from here, but I had to reach them.

"Have to," I mumbled. I looked at the paper again and froze.

The headline read: COLLIE KILLED.

Then the letters rearranged themselves. JOURNALIST KILLED.

Journalist. Collie. Killed.

"Miss, are you all right?"

A man stood in front of me. "I'm fine," I got out. "I just..." I couldn't finish. I groped to steady myself against a wall. There was no wall. I staggered and the man grabbed my elbow.

"Easy, sister! What's the matter – haven't had enough to eat? Pretty common these days..."

He trailed off, frowning at my face. Then he looked down at my boots.

My regulation boots.

"Hey, wait a minute..." he breathed.

Fear pierced through my daze. I jerked away and started to run.

I heard thudding footsteps behind me, felt his fingers graze my parka. "Stop her! That's Wildcat! Stop her!" he bellowed.

In a blur, I saw passers-by turn my way, each face a moon of surprise. Shouts rang out. I put on a burst of speed, but bodies closed ranks in front of me. I tried to shove through – hands grabbed each of my arms.

"That's her! That's her!"

"No!" I gasped. "Let me go – you've got it wrong!"

"Like hell!" shouted the first man, thrusting a newspaper at me. My face stared out from the front page. "Amity Vancour – that's you!"

"It's not what you think – please – the WfP is corrupt; I was trying to expose it—"

"How dare you!" yelled a woman. Her mouth looked wide, contorted; spittle flecked my cheeks. "You've got a nerve, blaming them!"

Shouts filled my ears – pounded through my brain.

"Murderer!"

"*Traitor!*"

"Call the police!"

I was jostled back and forth as the crowd struggled to get at me. "The world trusted you!" screamed the woman. She lunged forward and clawed at my cheek.

I cried out as her nails raked down my face; someone else yanked my hair. The jostling turned to shoving. I stumbled and fell to the sidewalk and they were on me – kicking me, hitting me.

"Bitch!"

"We trusted you!"

"Traitorous bitch!"

Somebody kicked me in the ribs. The sidewalk felt cold and grainy against my bleeding cheek. With a whimper, I curled into a ball as their blows rained against my body.

The wail of sirens.

"All right, break it up, *break it up*!" The order sounded distant. Gradually, the blows became fewer. Someone got in a final kick and was jerked away.

"Get up," ordered a voice.

My chest was heaving; one hand clutched at the sidewalk. I didn't move.

"*Get up.*" Someone grabbed me by the elbow and hauled me to my feet. I staggered as pain burst from every inch. The crowd stood staring, their faces hard with hatred and satisfaction. A policeman held my arm. Another stood just in front of me, his gaze oddly sympathetic.

"Yeah, that's her – even with those nice new decorations on her face," he said. "Let's take her in."

Chapter Thirty-nine

THEY LEFT ME ALONE IN A CELL for what seemed like hours. I lay on a hard cement slab and stared at the wall. They'd taken my pistol from me. There was no mattress, no pillow. My bruises throbbed, but to my amazement, I must have slept. The next thing I knew, I was drowsily raising my head from my arms and there was someone standing at the door of my cell.

It was the black policeman who'd said to take me in. His face was ageless; his eyes looked as if they'd seen centuries pass. With a jingle of keys, he unlocked my cell and swung open the door.

"Come with me," he said.

Sleep had sharpened my senses again. Warily, I got up

and followed him to a small room with grimy walls and a wooden table. Two chairs faced each other across its scarred surface.

"Sit," he said.

I sat.

He took the chair opposite and studied me for a moment. "Messed you up pretty good, didn't they, Miss Vancour?"

"I'll heal," I said.

"If you have time. Know what the punishment is for treason?"

"If I'm found guilty, they'll shoot me." My voice stayed level.

A clock ticked on the wall, measuring out the seconds. The policeman nodded slowly. "I'm Officer Page," he said. "I've got some questions for you."

"No."

"You're refusing?"

"I haven't eaten in two days. If I don't get food, then yes, I'm refusing."

Officer Page raised a dark eyebrow. For a few beats I had no idea what he would do. Then he reached for a squat black phone on the table; he dialled and spoke briefly into it. "Sally, bring sandwiches and coffee for our guest." He gave the last word an ironic twist.

He hung up and leaned back in his chair, his expression unreadable. The clock ticked some more.

"They look like warpaint," he said finally.

I looked at him.

"Those scratches on your face," he added.

It seemed the non sequitur of the century. "I wouldn't know," I said. "My amenities didn't come with a mirror."

He snorted. "Feisty, huh? Well, I sure do hate it when women fight. That crowd was out of control. Can't really blame them, but—"

"I wasn't fighting."

"Oh, no, you were just on the run after evading arrest, weren't you?"

The door opened. A woman entered with a plate of sandwiches and a pot of hot coffee. Suddenly my hands were shaking. I fell onto the food greedily, wolfing it down. The sandwiches were egg salad, which I hated. Nothing had ever tasted so good.

Officer Page waited until I finished the last bite and had poured myself some coffee. "Comfy now?" he asked.

The coffee was strong and bitter. It cleared my head. "Am I allowed to make a phone call?" I said.

"No, you are not. The rules are different for Peacefighters, as I think you know. You're not under our jurisdiction. We're just holding you for your own security force to come deal with. They can decide if you get a phone call or not."

Collie. I squelched the thought harshly. If he were still alive, I couldn't have called him anyway.

"So that means I don't have to answer your questions," I said after a pause.

Officer Page shrugged. "Well, thing is, a crime's still

been committed on my beat. Two, in fact: you evaded arrest and were beaten up by a mob. And I don't like it when things get messy on my patch."

"I'm so sorry."

The policewoman had brought an extra mug; Officer Page poured himself some coffee. "Plus something about this whole scenario is making me itchy," he said. "You see, I spoke to the waitress at the diner. She told me you ordered a cup of joe and asked to see a paper."

I didn't respond. He went on: "Now, I ask myself: why would a woman on the run – who I'm assuming to be reasonably intelligent – put herself at that kind of risk for the sake of reading a newspaper?"

"Because she didn't know the anonymity policy had been lifted," I said.

"Or else she was hoping to find something."

I thought of playing poker with Harlan and kept my face on the mild side of expressionless. "Find what?" I asked.

Officer Page opened a drawer and brought out the crumpled newspaper I'd been carrying when I was arrested. It was folded into quarters, just as I'd left it, showing the headline JOURNALIST KILLED IN AUTO CRASH.

"Milt Fraser," Officer Page said musingly. "I did a little checking, you know. One of his co-workers at the paper said he'd been up all night writing something – the story of his career, Milt called it. Now he's dead. That's kind of interesting, don't you think?"

I didn't answer.

"That crowd that attacked you – a few of them claim you said the WfP is corrupt, that you were trying to expose them." Officer Page waited, his brown eyes watching me.

I was already being charged with treason; there didn't seem much I could gain by denying it. "Yes, I said that," I said finally.

"Pretty wild claim."

"I suppose."

He tapped the newspaper. "You know, this co-worker of Milt's said he was a young guy – ambitious. But very careful about his sources. He wouldn't write something unless he could back it up."

The documents in the train station locker flashed into my mind. Apprehension chilled me. If I trusted this man and he turned out to be another WfP lackey, my only evidence would be destroyed.

I wrapped my hands around the mug. "Well, you know more about Milt Fraser than I do. I've never met him."

A flicker of something showed in Officer Page's gaze. Disappointment?

"Look, I'll be straight with you," he said. "My mother was a Peacefighter, and that means something to me. If there's any truth in your claim, then I want to know about it."

"I'm not a liar," I said softly.

"And I bet you're not delusional, either. So what's going on, Miss Vancour? Gunnison's winning every fight that counts. I don't believe in this 'power of the stars' malarkey—"

I started as the door flew open. A pair of World for Peace security officers entered: a man and woman in matching tan uniforms with the laurel-leaf emblem over their breasts.

"So this is her," said the woman. Her hair was pulled back into a bun; her eyes were a frosty blue. She turned to the man. "Yes, she's the one in the photo. Go call and tell them we're on our way."

As the man left, Officer Page scraped his chair back and rose to his feet. "I was just doing some preliminary questioning."

"No need."

"Well, yes, there is a need – there was a crime committed in our precinct."

The woman gave him a cool look. "The crimes Miss Vancour has already committed will have to take precedence, Officer. Murder is a serious matter."

A surge of heat overwhelmed my fear. "I haven't even had a trial yet."

"There were witnesses."

"*Witnesses?* To an un-broadcast Peacefight? Since when?"

The woman stepped briskly forward. I cried out as she struck me hard across my bruised face.

"Now, wait a minute—" began Officer Page.

"It's time for you to leave, Officer," said the woman, without taking her eyes from me. "I have jurisdiction now. Any hindrance from you is illegal."

Officer Page's mouth pursed. After a moment, he turned and left. The door closed behind him.

"You will speak only when I tell you to," the woman said into the silence. "Like now, for instance." She took out a photo and slapped it on the table. "Tell me about your accomplice."

I went still. The photo was of a pilot with curly black hair and a lean, angular face.

"I don't know what you're talking about," I said.

Her hand flashed as she struck me again; this time I managed not to make a sound. "Let me make it easy for you," she said. "Ingo Manfred, a pilot for the European Alliance. Do you recall him now?"

My cheekbone throbbed – I could taste blood. Already, my mouth felt swollen and clumsy. "I hardly know him," I said. "We danced together at a club once and then had coffee. That was the night Russ Avery was murdered. I never saw him again after that."

"Really? And yet the two of you were seen breaking into the World for Peace building together."

My note to Madeline flashed into my head. "That's not true. I went there, but I went alone."

"How did you get in?"

"I picked the lock."

She took a piece of gleaming brass from her pocket and slipped it over her fingers. "I'll ask again," she said. She tapped the knuckle rings against her opposite palm. "How did you get in?"

I licked my lips, staring at the glinting brass. "I picked the lock."

She punched me in the stomach. The pain was immediate, crushing; a wave of nausea passed through me. I gasped, doubling over.

The woman gave a small smile. "The ways of Harmony aren't always easy, are they, Miss Vancour?" She propped her hands on the table and leaned close into my face. "You're lying," she said. "It's noble of you to protect Mr Manfred, but he's certainly not protecting you."

"What…what do you mean?"

"He turned state's evidence. He's told us everything. About his girlfriend's father, the keys, your wild plans – everything."

She watched me for a reaction. I hoped I didn't give her one, though it felt as if she'd just knocked the breath from me a second time. Had Ingo really talked?

In a way, I couldn't blame him if he had.

The door opened and the male official came back in. "They're expecting us."

The woman nodded and straightened. "We'll enjoy getting the complete truth out of you soon, Miss Vancour. Now get up. We've got a long drive."

I rose slowly, holding my stomach. She grabbed my arm and hurried me from the room. Officer Page was waiting for us in the corridor. His frown deepened as he saw me.

"Can…can I use the bathroom?" I mumbled. "I think I'm going to throw up."

The woman grimaced. "Take her," she snapped to Officer Page.

The bathroom was empty except for a toilet and basin. No window – nothing I could use. I splashed water over my face and then studied my bruises for a long moment in the mirror, gripping the cool porcelain sink.

The scratches did look like warpaint.

I left the bathroom. Officer Page stood leaning against the wall, still frowning. As he straightened, he looked like he was about to say something and then sighed.

"I have to put these on you," he said. He drew my arms behind my back and snapped on a pair of handcuffs. The metal weighed coldly against my wrists. We started down the corridor.

Without looking at him, I said, "The Rosevale train station. Locker twenty-eight. The key's under a loose tile in the Ladies' restroom."

Chapter Forty

They took me in a security van. I'd never seen the inside of a Shadowcar, but I imagined this wasn't far off.

I rode in the back while the two officers took the cab up front. The van's interior was just two benches facing each other; there were no windows. I sat slumped over, too aching and dispirited to try and figure out where we might be going.

Had I done the right thing, telling Officer Page where the documents were? Milt had been killed; what made me think Page would have better luck?

I thought bleakly of the morning meeting back at base. Every day, hundreds of Peacefighters swore to fight fairly – to defend their country to the best of their ability –

to honour the sanctity of life. Most of us meant every word of that vow. The whole *world* believed in Peacefighting. The crowd that had attacked me proved that. If I could just get the truth out to people… I swallowed.

The truth was that I'd soon be shot for a traitor.

And that Collie was dead.

I felt cold, hollow inside. I'd been kidding myself to even hope otherwise. Everyone knew we were a couple. He'd been in danger from the second I stole those documents from Russ's house. Either they'd sabotaged his plane, or they'd made certain that he never left his hospital bed.

I closed my eyes at a sudden memory: the two of us in bed together a few weeks ago. We'd just made love and were lying in each other's arms. The sun had hit Collie's face, making his eyes very green. He'd grinned as he kissed my fingers one by one.

"Canary Cargo," he said. "And at least ten kids."

I'd laughed. "Can't we settle for five?"

"No, you're not thinking this through, Amity Louise," he'd said gravely. "If we have ten, we can have our own basketball team."

I shuddered and pressed my face hard against my shoulder. My mouth contorted. I would not cry. Whatever happened, that woman would not see me with damp cheeks when she opened those doors again.

Finally the van slowed and came to a halt. Silence descended as the engine was killed. I sat up, staring at the double doors. Footsteps headed my way. The doors were flung open and I blinked in the sudden sunshine.

"Get out," said the woman.

My muscles felt stiff. I crouched my way through the van. With my wrists still cuffed behind me, I stumbled as I jumped to the ground.

And then I stared. Our surroundings were as familiar to me as my own hand. "What are we doing here?" I blurted.

She gripped my arm and marched me towards the gate. "Pilots charged with treason are held on their own bases until trial." She gave me a pursed-mouth smile. "Home sweet home. Though your fellow pilots probably don't feel too welcoming towards you right now."

Instead of driving me straight to the brig, they'd stopped outside the main gates. With base security accompanying them, they frogmarched me through the streets. My cheeks burned as people turned to gape at "Wildcat" with her bruised, scratched face.

As we passed the canteen, Vera was just coming out. She pressed her hand to her mouth, her eyes wide. *None of it's true,* I wanted to tell her.

There was no sign of Collie.

The sun burned down as we reached the brig: a squat grey building I'd barely noticed before. Inside it smelled of disinfectant. Base security signed me in. Beside each name was a notation: *drunkenness; disturbing the peace.* Mine read, *suspected treason.*

The woman gave me a smile that actually looked sincere.

"I hope we meet again, Miss Vancour. Either I or my colleagues will look forward to many long discussions before your trial."

Another cell, another hard slab. This one had a thin mattress; it didn't make much difference. I sat against the wall and stared up at the tiny barred window opposite. The tinny sound of dance music drifted in from the office. It hadn't stopped since I arrived. I heard one of the guards humming along:

Love me in May,

Oh, please say you'll stay...

That night at The Ivy Room, dancing in Collie's arms. I hugged myself and tried not to think.

Shadows moved slowly across the cement floor. There was a toilet in the corner of my cell, visible to whoever happened by. I pushed aside my squeamishness and used it. Late afternoon came. A guard slid a tray of food through a slot at the bottom of my door. I ate listlessly, knowing that I needed the energy.

I'd just finished when I heard the outside door open. The guard's voice came to me faintly: "Evening, sir."

I looked up sharply as another voice drifted in: "You can take a quick break. I want a word with our prisoner."

My blood went cold. I scrambled to my feet just as Commander Hendrix appeared.

He stood outside my cell gazing in, his eyes lingering on my bruises. Neither of us spoke. The telio was still on in the background, burbling another tune.

"You made a serious mistake, Vancour," said Hendrix finally.

"No. I did not," I whispered.

My commander looked sad. Angry. "You're nothing like your father, are you?"

I gripped the bars. "I am *everything* like him."

"Hardly. But if I'm honest, I almost admire it. You've got the courage of your convictions, at least." Hendrix shrugged. "Well, it'll cost you your life. It's not what Tru would have wanted."

"You're wrong," I spat out. "It's *exactly* what he'd have wanted, if the only other choice was to be a traitor like you."

Hendrix's forehead creased...and then, incredibly, he gave a small smile. "So you don't know."

His words hung in the air as the dance music played on. With a lurch of dread, I somehow knew that this was the secret I'd longed to know about my father my whole life.

All I wanted was to run away from it as fast as I could.

"Don't know what?" I said finally. My mouth was dry.

"Haven't you ever wondered why I assumed you might be open to our offer? You, one of our finest pilots?"

No. Oh, please, no.

Hendrix stepped close to the bars. “Twelve years ago your father took a bribe for a Tier One fight,” he said softly. “It was what put Gunnison in power.”

Chapter Forty-one

In the silence that followed, images flew at me like wasps. Ma, buying antiques for our house when I was growing up. My father's two planes. Collie's voice from our childhood: *Amity, you have so many nice things.*

Peacefighters did not make much money.

"You're lying," I said hoarsely. "My father believed in what he did."

"Not as much as he believed in looking out for himself – up until the day he died." Hendrix frowned. "I've wondered about that," he added, more to himself than me. "A clear day…a pilot with so much experience…"

"What the hell are you saying?"

"I'm not sure. But you see, another important fight had

come up. Tru was supposed to throw that one, too. Instead…" Hendrix shrugged.

"Instead *what*?" A hot tear darted down my cheek. I hated Hendrix for making me cry almost more than anything else. "He wasn't even a Peacefighter by then! How could he have thrown a fight?"

"But he trained them; he was still in practice. And since he'd thrown the fight that put Gunnison in power, naturally they approached him to—"

"*This is not true!*" I took a shaky step backwards.

"It is," Hendrix said flatly. "And it's part of why we thought you might show some common sense."

My darling, if I could tell you that, I'd be king of the world.

I took a gasping breath and clutched at my face. I stood motionless, breathing hard. When I let my hands fall, Hendrix was still there.

"Get out," I said.

He gave a small, strange smile. "Don't you want to ask about your friend Collie?"

Though I kept my face expressionless, the words rocked me. How much had Hendrix guessed? Was Collie still alive to protect? *Please*, I thought. *Please.*

I lifted my chin and met Hendrix's gaze. "He's no friend of mine," I said.

It had been one of those gilt-edged summer days, with the sun so bright and fierce that it drenched you in heat the second you stepped outside. Collie and I were down by the river that skirted my family's property – we practically lived there in the summertime. We'd already been for a swim. Now we lay side by side on the pebbly bank with dragonflies flitting around us, staring up at the sky with our bare feet still in the warm, murmuring water.

"What would it be like to swim through the clouds?" I mused.

Collie had one tanned leg bent at the knee, the other sprawled straight out. The bent leg swayed lazily back and forth. His hair was bleached flaxen with summer.

"Cold and wet, probably," he said.

I rolled my head against the pebbles to give him a disgusted look. "The sun's *hot*, stupid," I informed him. "So when you go up high, it gets hot, not cold."

Collie crossed his arms behind his head. "*You're* stupid. It gets colder the higher up you go."

His note of authority made me hesitate. "It does?"

"Yep. Miss Owen told us."

Miss Owen was his third-grade teacher. I was only in second, with old Mrs Belvedere, who was deaf as a tree stump. My forehead creased as I studied a billowing cumulus. I'd always imagined clouds to be soft and warm, like cotton candy.

"I don't understand why that should be," I said finally. "I'll have to ask Dad."

* * *

Dad...I don't understand.

I lay unmoving on the hard slab they called a bed. How many times in my childhood had I said those words? And he'd always had an answer for me.

No one could explain what I was feeling now. I squeezed my eyes shut, recalling Hendrix's odd smile when he'd mentioned Collie. It couldn't have meant anything good; I knew it. Yet my flash of hope that Collie might still be alive persisted. It was a torment that writhed in my chest.

Thinking about my father was almost as bad. What Hendrix had told me explained everything, filled in so many gaps. If I could, I'd have taken a knife and sliced the knowledge from my brain.

Distantly, I heard the guard approach, humming. He stopped in front of my cell. "Finished with that tray? Want to slide it back out to me?"

I didn't answer.

"Hey, sister, you hear me? I'm not coming in there after it."

"Go away," I whispered.

The guard huffed out a breath. "Fine, have it your way. No tray, no breakfast tomorrow."

He turned and left. He wasn't humming any more. I pulled the blanket more tightly around myself. The opposite wall of my cell had a spiderweb of cracks on it; a few scraps of graffiti.

I memorized every one.

* * *

After a long time the music from the telio stopped and a news story came on. The words were inaudible to me, but the announcer's urgent tone pierced through my turmoil. Wincing from my bruises, I sat up.

"Holy moly, would you *believe* it…?" the guard muttered from the office. The telio grew louder as he turned the volume up.

"*…as reported previously, shocking new evidence has come to light. It's been conclusively proven that bribes were being accepted by the World for Peace, affecting Peacefighting conflicts up to and including Tier One fights…*"

My scalp went electric; I leaped to my feet. Officer Page had done it! He'd found the documents – made the right people in the media listen. But as the announcer continued, dread touched me.

I gripped the bars, listening frantically. The announcer wasn't mentioning Gunnison! The story made it sound as if the World for Peace had acted on its own, for financial gain only.

"*…such as pilot Amity Vancour of the Western Seaboard, one of the worst offenders, now taken into custody for treason. In the hour since this news has broken, the world's reaction has been swift. Countries who have lost vital conflicts are demanding restitution. Riots have—*"

The announcer's voice broke off. The sound of shouts came through the telio. Another voice started talking – fast, desperate.

"*We're not supposed to tell you this. The Central States have just attacked our eastern border. Repeat! Gunnison has just attacked our eastern border, near Claremont. He's got an army – tanks – soldiers are shooting anyone who resists—*"

War.

I stood frozen, numb. The story continued: "*It's brutal here – no one's ever seen anything like it – the soldiers are showing no mercy—*" On and on, each word more terrible than the last.

From outside, shouts started filling the air. "Gunnison's attacking! Get to the planes!" Someone ran past my cell, their footsteps crunching against the gravel. It woke me from my stupor.

"*Let me out!*" I yelled. I rattled my cell door. "Let me out, do you hear me?" When no answer came, I shouted harder. I grabbed up my tray and banged it against the bars.

"Knock it off!" yelled the guard.

"You've got to release me!" I threw the tray through the bars. It clattered against the opposite wall.

The guard appeared in front of my cell, his eyes wide. "Hey, what are you—?"

"I've got to help fight!"

"Are you *crazy*?"

"Listen to what's going on!" I was almost crying with frustration. "I have to help! *Please!*"

Suddenly the telio was drowned out by a whine from the base loudspeaker. Hendrix's voice boomed:

"The Central States have attacked the Western Seaboard

– repeat, the Central States have attacked the Western Seaboard! I've just received the order from President Lopez that we will fight. All flying personnel, report to the airfield immediately…"

"*All flying personnel!*" I shouted at the guard.

"Yes, but…but I can't just—"

A rhythmic pounding came from the telio. "*I've got the door barricaded; they're trying to get in,*" said the announcer in a rush. "*They're shooting people, forcing them from their homes—*"

Our own door banged open. Light footsteps ran towards us. I stared as Vera appeared, breathing hard. She didn't look at me.

"You have to let her go," she told the guard tautly.

"Miss, I can't!"

"*…tanks in the streets,*" the announcer was saying. "Tanks. *He must have been planning this for—*"

Vera's hands were clenched. "It doesn't matter what she's done! She's still one of our best pilots!"

The guard hesitated.

I gripped his arm through the bars. "*Listen to what's happening!* I have got to help fight!"

Gunshots echoed from the speakers. A long moment later, dance music came on. The bubbly melody played against the sound of shouts from outside, and of Hendrix's voice still echoing. The guard went white.

"Let her out!" yelled Vera. "*Now!*"

His hands trembled as he fumbled with his keys. He

unlocked my door and swung it open. "All right, but.... but if anyone asks..."

I didn't care what would happen if anyone asked. I pushed past him and Vera and I ran for the door.

It was just after dawn. Sirens wailed through the air. As we raced through the palm-lined streets others joined us – pilots, fitters, mechanics, some pulling on clothes as they went. Vera's face was set as she ran beside me.

"Thanks," I huffed out to her.

We rounded the drive to the airstrip. "I don't know if what they're saying about you is true, Amity," she said finally. "It's hard to believe it. But...sometimes you don't really know a person."

I thought about my father and emotions battled in my throat. "What they're saying isn't true," I said. I shot her a glance. "Is Collie all right?" I asked urgently.

She shook her head. "I don't know. I haven't seen him since before he lost the Tier One fight."

"He flew it?" My voice rose in dismay. That was days ago.

We shoved through the outside door to the changing room. Vera nodded, breathless. "I saw him getting ready. He looked like he should have still been in sickbay; he was really pale. I haven't seen him since. I don't think anyone has."

She glanced at me in sudden dread. "Amity, you don't think...?"

I didn't answer as we raced down the corridor. Collie had been forced into flying, though he must have suspected a trap. This was what Hendrix's strange smile had meant. Picturing again the red mist on the grass – the other pilot's shattered body – I wanted to curl into a ball and keen.

You've got the rest of your life to grieve for Collie, I told myself savagely. *Right now, all that matters is stopping Gunnison.*

When we got inside the changing room it was chaos. My old locker had been given to someone else. I rushed to the box where stray items were kept and started snatching things out. Gloves, goggles. I yanked on a flight suit that was two sizes too big.

"Vancour!" called a voice.

I turned, and Harlan tossed me a leather jacket. Our eyes met and he smiled slightly.

Outside, the planes waited. Fitters scrambled over them like ants, getting them ready. As I ran for the Doves, Vera and Levi were ahead of me, Harlan and Steve just behind.

Hendrix's voice still boomed: "Repeat, we've been given the order to fight – all flying personnel, report immediately – pilots, you'll take off in T minus ten minutes—"

I wondered acridly what Hendrix thought of the order to fight Gunnison. I reached one of the planes. "Get the chocks!" I yelled to a fitter. My bruised muscles sang as I swung myself up onto the wing. I ignored them and shoved open the hood.

"Amity!" called a voice.

I glanced back. Vera was just getting into the plane behind me on the runway. She hesitated, studying me in the dim morning light.

"Be careful," she said.

"You too," I told her.

Chapter Forty-two

"*We interrupt this programme for an important announcement. The Reclamation of the Western Seaboard has begun!*"

Kay had been listlessly making herself a sandwich; she stopped mid-motion and stared at the telio. As the broadcast continued, she lunged for the dial and turned up the sound. She huddled on her sofa, staring wide-eyed at the black-and-white Harmony symbol that filled the small screen.

Half an hour later, she hadn't moved. The announcer enthused on and on.

"*…as every citizen knows, President Gunnison's Twelve Year plan has seen us safely through the first dozen years of* *his reign. Now, with the Reclamation under way, we're at last embracing our glorious destiny! Rejoice, fellow citizens! The stars are truly smiling on the Central States today. Soon the entire Western Seaboard will be ours, the two countries again united under our beloved President Gunnison's rule...*"

Finally the national anthem started playing. Kay swallowed, her thoughts wild. Had Gunnison used her advised location for the attack? What "unknown puzzle piece" had swayed him?

And what did this mean for her?

After Gunnison had sent her home five days ago, she hadn't dared budge from her apartment. Once, and only once, a messenger from Gunnison's office had appeared and handed her an envelope.

Inside was a note:

Vancour met with reporter Milton Fraser, date of birth 08 10 13, time/place of birth 04.53 WST Seattle. She gave him all info from Bark's office. Should story be allowed to break?

Kay had regarded the note with horror. *Damn* this Vancour person – would she never stop? Then her skin prickled with hope: Gunnison must still value her opinion.

"Come back in half an hour," she'd told the messenger, and she'd feverishly begun to work.

How to reply had been simple. No, of course the story shouldn't break. She'd promised Gunnison that Vancour's actions would benefit them – the world would be outraged to learn that fights had been fixed. She'd cast a chart showing the journalist was a threat, and sent it back to Gunnison at once.

She'd heard nothing in response.

Soon after, going crazy with anxiety at the thought of Vancour out there doing who knew what, she'd made a decision. Though she'd claimed the pilot couldn't endanger them, enough was enough; Kay's own life was at stake.

She'd prepared a chart showing it was time to capture Vancour. *Release her photo publicly if you can,* she'd written. *Mercury in retrograde demands it.* Again she'd received no word from Gunnison's office, not even an acknowledgement. And now this.

Kay blinked as she became aware of cheers.

Dazedly, she went to her window and tugged it open. An impromptu parade snaked down the street – trash-can-lid cymbals banged out a jubilant rhythm. A song bawled by hundreds of voices floated up; she recognized "Happy Days are Here Again".

Wes-tern lands are ours again,
Give us the sun and moon and Mars again,
Johnny Gun is here to stay, amen!
Wes-tern lands will soon be ours!

A smile gradually grew over Kay's face.

The tune was contagious – she propped her elbows on the sill and hummed along. Below, a little boy waved a Harmony flag; he shrieked with laughter as his father scooped him up onto his shoulders. A couple danced past, the man twirling the woman dramatically.

"The Central States!" he shouted.

People on the street caught each other's eyes and grinned at the antics. Many raced to join in. Kay had no idea how many were actually celebrating and how many just wanted to be seen as patriotic. It didn't matter. The mood was exultant.

A long, shiny black auto edged through the parade, honking. A pair of red-and-black Harmony flags fluttered on its hood. Kay straightened, her eyes widening as the auto pulled up at the kerb outside her building. The flags fell still.

A man with tousled brown hair a little older than Kay got out. A second later Kay heard footsteps jogging up the stairwell. She whirled, her heart beating fast, as a knock came at her door.

When she opened it, the man had a hand propped on her doorjamb. He glanced up at her with a grin. "Hi," he said. "Remember me?"

"Mac Jones," said Kay.

"The very one." He shook her hand. "Hey, nice to see you again. Can you come downstairs for a minute?"

At street level the music was still playing; laughing shouts filled the air. As Kay reached the long black auto, its back door swung open.

"Get in," said John Gunnison. He was smiling.

In a dream, Kay slid onto the red leather seat. Gunnison

leaned across her. "One of the other cars will take you home," he said to Mac Jones. "Thanks for all your help, bud."

Mac gave a little salute. "Pleasure, Johnny. As always. I'll let you know when Sandy checks in."

Inwardly, Kay's eyebrows rose. She hadn't thought Mac was high-up enough to call Cain "Sandy". Then the auto pulled away and she forgot about it. Gunnison handed her a glass filled with sparkling liquid.

"This time it *is* champagne," he said. "I don't know much about it – more of a beer man, myself – but they tell me this is fine stuff."

"Thank you," murmured Kay. She took the glass and clinked it against Gunnison's.

"To the Central States," he said. "And to us, Kay."

Kay. The warmth of his presence – his smile – was like being near a small sun. Kay melted in its glow. She wished she were wearing a prettier dress. She wished...no, she didn't really wish for anything at all. Just to be sitting here with John Gunnison was enough.

"To us," she echoed.

Gunnison settled back against the leather seats, studying her intently. "Lady Harmony told me this would happen," he said. "Did you know that, Kay?"

He said it so simply, without guile. Kay shook her head.

"Oh, yes. I think I've mentioned that I pray to her a lot. Well, she whispered to me to take your advice when you said Milt Fraser was a danger, and about releasing that pilot's photo. Later on, we found out Vancour passed information to a WS cop. Know what Lady Harmony told me that time?"

"What?" asked Kay faintly.

Gunnison drew a piece of paper from his briefcase and handed it to her.

An inter-office memo. Kay read a few lines and gasped; her gaze flew to Gunnison's.

"Yep," he said. "I released the information to the press myself, through certain channels. Or at least...I told 'em all they needed to know." He gave her a conspirator's smile.

The memo described how the world was reacting, even as Gunnison's auto purred down the streets. *International relations are in chaos. Countries that have lost vital conflicts are questioning the veracity of the Peacefights and demanding restitution. Riots have broken out worldwide and makeshift armies are attacking each other across borders.*

Kay stared numbly at the words. She called herself an expert on human nature...yet she'd never seen this coming. It hadn't even occurred to her, not after a century of peace.

The world was at war.

She dragged her attention back to Gunnison as he held up his champagne glass and studied the bubbles. "You know, at first I couldn't hear Harmony's whisper," he said. "So I drew a Tarot card to help me focus. Guess which one it was."

A chill crept along Kay's spine. It wasn't possible... was it?

"The Tower," she said.

And inevitably, John Gunnison drew that card from his inside pocket. The artwork showed the tiny people tumbling, screaming.

"The fire and fury that was promised," he mused. "The card from *your* spread, Kay. You were right: Vancour was the puzzle piece we've been waiting for."

Kay swallowed. If something still went wrong… "Is… is it over yet?" she asked.

"No, but they can't beat us. The question was how the world would react, and now I think we've got our answer. *This* is why the stars wanted me to wait."

Slowly, Kay nodded. The world was in turmoil; their attack on the Western Seaboard would just be seen as more of the same. Gunnison would silence whoever in the WS needed to be silenced. Once the dust had settled and the borders had changed, would anyone even dare to comment?

She hesitated. "When I dowsed for you that day, you said you'd set your sights a little low."

"Yeah, that's a fact." Gunnison grinned. "You haven't guessed what's so important about that dusty little town? Kay, the whole region is full of uranium."

At her blank look his smile turned roguish.

"The Cataclysm," he said. "I've had scientists working for years to figure out exactly how it happened. Now we know the ancients' secret."

Kay's face went slack; she quickly regained her composure. Suddenly the auto's engine sounded like the hum of incoming bombs. A dizzying image came from her childhood history books: mushroom clouds that billowed towards the sky.

Gunnison took a slow sip of champagne.

"I wasn't certain until you dowsed for me," he said. "It's not only my destiny to bring Harmony to the Western Seaboard, Kay. I'll bring Harmony to the entire world – with fire and fury if necessary."

Kay gave an inward shiver, thankful that she was on the winning team. "That's wonderful," she said weakly.

"But hey, enough of that! We're celebrating something else today too, you know."

The Central States leader covered her hand with his. "Mr Skinner's recent performance has been… disappointing. I need someone with more vision." He squeezed her fingers. "How would you like to be my new Chief Astrologer?"

All other thoughts vanished in a wave of triumph and relief. She'd done it! She would survive and with a vengeance. Kay smiled into his eyes. "I'm honoured to accept, Johnny," she said softly. "I'll serve you the best I can."

Gunnison beamed. "Well, now, that's just fine!"

He poured more champagne. As the golden bubbles frothed from the bottle, he said, "Of course, I don't think there should be any more secrets between us, do you?"

Apprehension fluttered. Kay lifted her glass and took a cautious sip. "Secrets?"

"You know what I mean."

"No, I...I don't think I..."

"Really?"

To her alarm, Gunnison's expression had become measured. Unsmiling.

"I don't like liars, you know," he said.

Kay's blood froze. "I'm not one."

"No?" His gaze flicked over her. "Well, now, this is just a hypothetical. But for instance, if my new Chief Astrologer secretly thought astrology was a sham...then that would be a pretty big lie. Do you agree?"

For a second Kay thought she might throw up. "Why, yes, I suppose it would be," she said after a pause. "But I—"

"Be real careful, Kay," broke in Gunnison quietly. "Skinner's been found Discordant for his incompetence in the Vancour matter. And as far as I'm concerned, liars are even more Discordant. Now, what was it you were about to tell me?"

They'd left the city behind. Low green hills stretched before them, with the sky broad above. In a sickening mental flash, all Kay could see were severed heads atop a chain-link fence.

You could be made a Discordant for not believing, too.

"Well?" said Gunnison.

Her throat was almost too tight for speech. "I...don't know what you want me to say," she whispered.

"The truth. Now."

It felt as if nails were spiking into Kay's skull. Did he really already know? Or was it a trick?

Somehow the champagne glass didn't shatter in her grasp. When she spoke her voice was barely audible: "I've never believed. I went into astrology for the money."

To her amazement, Gunnison threw back his head and laughed. "Now *that* is what I wanted to hear!" When she stared at him, he winked. "Remember when I read your cards, right here in this very auto? I chose one for myself, too. What did I tell you then?"

"You said we'd work together very well," Kay recalled in confusion.

"The card was the Scholar."

The view of the hills slid past outside. She realized she had no words. According to the New Harmony Tarot, the Scholar was a person of great learning, but no faith.

"I've known all along," Gunnison said. "Didn't matter. I needed someone who could look at all of this unemotionally – see patterns others might miss." His small smile held triumph. "And it was all true, you know," he added. "Every last bit, Kay. The harmonic power of the stars works through you whether you believe in it or not."

Kay opened her mouth and slowly closed it again. Somehow Vancour's actions *had* really turned out to be the missing puzzle piece. What had been the odds of that?

Was it the same with the other charts Kay had cast? She felt dazed as she realized that she'd never made anything up. She'd just seen things that others hadn't. Even dowsing…she'd been so certain that she was the one in control, but what if she hadn't been?

Astrology, the Tarot, dowsing: these things *couldn't* be true.

Could they?

"Well?" Gunnison grinned and nudged her. "Is my Chief Astrologer going to sit there staring at me all day, or are you going to say something?"

Kay felt swept by emotions she didn't understand. She swallowed, ridiculously close to tears. "You...you really don't mind that I don't believe?"

"You will," Gunnison said softly. He gripped her hand and released it; he settled back against his seat. "Yep, between you and Ford, I've got quite a team now."

"Ford?"

"*You* know – Sandford. Who did you think I meant?"

"I don't know," said Kay in confusion. "I thought you called Mr Cain 'Sandy'."

The leader of the Central States guffawed. "I can't picture Sandford Cain being a 'Sandy'! Nah, Sandy's one of my inside guys. Pretty smart, all the things he comes up with. You'll meet him soon. He's very loyal."

Gunnison touched Kay's face. His warm hand lingered on her cheek.

"Just like you," he said.

Chapter Forty-Three

We took off one after another – every pilot present on the Western Seaboard's base, over a hundred of us. The desert town of Claremont was an hour away, across the Jacinto Mountains. I flew tensely, keeping with the pack, locking away my grief for Collie.

Once we crested the mountains the land turned harsh, rocky. We saw the town long before we got to it: a thick black column of smoke was streaming up into the sky. A score of smaller fires burned as well, stark against the beige landscape.

High overhead, three large, bloated planes approached, looking too heavy to fly. The red-and-black Harmony symbol gleamed from their tails. As I realized what they were, my hands went clammy.

"Oh, you bastard," I whispered to Gunnison. Bombers were supposed to be ancient history. A flock of new-looking Firedoves accompanied them, like kestrels protecting condors.

The world tilted as I screamed up to meet a bomber. A pair of Doves came at me, filling my vision. My thumb thrust down on the firing button; I rolled away as bullets pelted a Dove's hood. It went down, flames snapping at the air.

Overhead, the bombers kept flying.

As I wheeled back in position the smoke from the burning town swallowed my plane in black gulps. I caught glimpses of other planes through it: a chaos of wings and tails in all directions, attacking each other. Below, tanks rolled through the streets.

I whipped in and out of the smoke, trying to shoot at the bombers – swooped low to get tanks before they got me. The smoke was dark, blinding. Half the time I'd spot a plane only to realize it was one of ours. My hands tightened in frustration. I banked and fired on an opposing Dove; it vanished into the gloom. I couldn't tell what was happening, couldn't tell if I'd brought anything else down.

Meanwhile the bombers were finding their targets.

An explosion thundered; I pulled up sharply as the courthouse erupted below. Shards of roof twisted in the air. The smoke whipped past, blanketing everything. I gritted my teeth and kept easing back on the stick to get above it. I was at less than a thousand feet.

I don't know which hit me, a Firedove or a tank. Suddenly a jolt slammed through the plane. In a flash of orange, a fireball appeared on my tail. No, my tail was gone – the crackling fireball was all that was left.

My plane plummeted, screaming. I swore and shoved back the hood. Wind and smoke rushed past. My eyes streaming even behind my goggles, I bailed, half-falling from the cockpit.

One banana...two banana... With a quick prayer, I tugged the ripcord.

The chute opened.

I gripped the cords as I floated down through the smoke. Doves still screamed above; I couldn't see any more bombers. All was confusion – shouts – the roar of engines. A house went up, almost right under me; the blast blew me sideways. Pieces of plaster and wall whined past. Something big slammed against my chute, tangling in the white cloth.

Shit! I grabbed for my reserve but it was too late; I fell the height of a house. I hit a pile of rubble and cried out at my bruised ribs.

Alive, though. Nothing broken. Panting, I snatched a brick and scrambled up, expecting soldiers to be on me at any second. Nothing happened. I stood motionless, breathing hard. Finally I let the brick fall. I shrugged free of my chute and pushed the goggles from my face.

The street was full of smoke. I could see soldiers in the distance; it looked as if they were forcing people out of town. I swallowed and looked around me. An auto sat leaning to one side, one of its tyres blown out. The house across the street had its front door open.

Everything had the hyperreality of a dream. I walked slowly to the house. The front yard was well-tended. Grass clippings littered the sidewalk, as if someone had just mown that morning. I reached the door and hesitated… then gripped the doorjamb and peered inside.

From my father's stories I knew what I would see, even if it wasn't really there: Louise's mother, dead on the floor. And her brother, sitting headless against the wall.

The house was empty. But I was right.

I stared for several moments at the phantoms in my mind. The brother's head was lying on its side. His eyes were bulging, as if he'd been screaming. The mother's stomach looked torn – mangled – ugly.

My eyes were dry. I felt hard inside, as if I might never cry again. Collie was dead and Gunnison had won.

Another explosion rumbled. I turned and stared back at the street. My ankle was starting to hurt now – I'd jarred it when I fell. It didn't matter. I went back out and started walking.

I kept to the side of the road, close to the houses, and headed away from the soldiers. I didn't know where I was going. I just had to leave this place. Above, planes still whined – far fewer now. Had the others been shot down? Returned to base? The smoke made it impossible to fight in the air, and none of us were equipped to fight on the ground.

Later, I knew how much I would care. Right now, it just felt as inevitable as nightfall: this had been over with before it even began.

The town felt eerily empty. Limping, I turned a street corner and kept walking. Here, too, doors stood open. A burned-out auto was still on fire. An elementary school took up half the block. The Western Seaboard's sunburst flag hung limply from its flagpole, smoke drifting past.

My neck prickled as I became aware of a Firedove's throaty drone. Suddenly a Western Seaboard plane burst from the smoke the next street over.

It flew low for a few blocks, as if searching, then turned and headed up my street. I stared, wondering if one of my former teammates didn't want "Wildcat" to get away.

The plane roared past just above roof level. I couldn't tell who the pilot peering out was.

The Dove abruptly went high, vanishing into smoke. When it reappeared it was coming in for a landing on the school's front lawn. I took a wary step back, ready to run.

The Dove touched down. The hood slid open and a tall blond pilot scrambled out, yanking off his goggles. He started sprinting towards me and the whole world seemed to stop.

"Collie," I breathed.

I pressed my hand hard against my eyes, struggling for control. "Please let this be true," I murmured. "*Please*..."

"Amity!" Collie shouted. It broke the spell. The next

moment I was pounding towards him, not caring about my ankle.

We reached each other and Collie swept me into his arms. He was warm, strong; he smelled of sweat and leather. For an endless moment our heartbeats crashed together. I clung to him, breathing him in – savouring his solid reality. I could feel the slick warmth of my tears against his skin. Maybe they were his tears, too.

He pulled away a little, kissing my hair, my cheeks. "Amity…Amity…I found you…"

"You're really alive," I gasped. I leaned back to look at him.

He winced at my battered face. "Oh, Amity…what did they do to you?"

"I'm fine!" I wiped my eyes. I didn't know whether to laugh or cry, so I was doing both. "Collie, I…I thought you were dead."

He grasped my upper arms. "No – no! I was in the sickbay; I took off just after the rest of you."

"Sickbay?"

"I got concussion during my last fight. I acted like it was worse than it was, so that I could lay low." Collie's tone was grim. He gazed around him at the deserted street – the burning auto. He slowly shook his head as the flames crackled. "I can't believe this has happened."

"I know," I whispered.

He swallowed. "During the battle I saw you bail, but then I lost sight of you. I've been searching every street…

I was so scared that you'd been captured…"

I ran my palm slowly up and down his arm; I thought I might never be able to stop touching him. "I was sure they'd killed you," I said, my throat tight. "I thought they'd guess that you knew as much as I did."

"I pretended to play the game. After you escaped, Hendrix called me in and told me that the Tier One fight was being refought, and—" Collie broke off and rubbed his forehead. "I pretended to play the game," he repeated, his voice husky.

We both looked up sharply at the sound of a loudspeaker. It sounded as if a truck with a megaphone was moving through the streets.

"*Congratulations! This land has been reclaimed by the Central States. All new Central States citizens, report to a Harmony ambassador immediately for further instructions… You cannot stay here; this town contains vital mining interests and is being razed to help promote Harmony…*"

The loudspeaker grew closer. Collie pulled me to the side of a house. Two blocks away, the truck drove down the cross street, blaring its message. The loudspeaker faded.

"Mining interests," I echoed, staring out at the burning auto. The first war in almost a century. For *mining interests*. Finally I blew out a breath and glanced back at Collie. "What happened when you had to fight the Tier One?"

He gave a tired shrug. "I told them I'd do what they wanted, and then I tried my damnedest to win. I lost that fight fair and square, but...if I'm honest, I can't be completely sorry." Very gently, Collie touched my bruised face; his thumb caressed the side of my mouth. "Because I knew you were still alive." He tried to smile. "So I'm kind of glad they didn't shoot me for going against them."

I stood motionless. I couldn't be totally sorry that he'd lost, either...but in my mind I saw the trapdoor as it closed, slicing my brother's face from view.

"Amity? What's wrong?"

"Do you know what the fight was about? What Gunnison won?"

Collie shook his head. I told him in short, terse words.

He went white. "Hal could really be extradited and sent to a correction camp?"

"If he's caught."

Collie stood staring at me. "It's my fault."

I touched his arm. "Collie, no. It's *Gunnison's* fault."

He twisted abruptly away and slammed his fist against the side of the house. It felt as if he'd punched me in the stomach. I wrapped my arms around him from behind and he clutched my hand.

"Amity, I swear to you. I tried to win."

"I know," I said against his back.

He turned and we held each other. He pressed his face into my neck. "Rose and Hal are my family," he murmured. He drew back, scanning me anxiously. "You're sure he's all right? He's well-hidden?"

"I hope so. Ma's done her best."

Collie exhaled; our foreheads touched. I stroked his head, knowing exactly how he felt. In the distance, the megaphone was still bleating. I knew that we should leave but for a long moment I just stood there with Collie's body pressed close against mine.

It felt like the only home I'd ever need.

"There's something else," I said at last. "Hendrix told me that – that Dad took bribes. He was the one who put Gunnison in power."

Collie drew back; he gaped at me.

"I think it's true," I said. I briefly described the encounter with my father in the kitchen that night. *My darling, if I could tell you that, I'd be king of the world.*

"And there were so many other things." My voice came out small, like a little girl's. "So many things when I was growing up that never quite made sense..."

Collie ran a slow knuckle across his lip. "I think you're right," he admitted heavily. "Amity, I spoke to Tru that night too. I'd gone to get some water, and he was in the kitchen. He seemed so...despairing. And he said, 'Are you planning to be a Peacefighter, Collie? Don't do it, son. It'll suck out your soul.'"

I couldn't hear the megaphone now. The silence was almost worse.

"I never knew what he meant," said Collie finally, sounding defeated.

"And then we both became Peacefighters anyway," I said.

He grimaced. "Yeah. We both became Peacefighters anyway."

I swiped my eyes and took his hand. I squeezed his fingers. "We'd better go."

"Where?"

"Anywhere, for now." I slid my other hand behind his warm neck and kissed him; our lips lingered together. "You were right all along," I whispered fiercely against his mouth. "We should have escaped weeks ago."

I felt him give a small smile. "You're admitting you were wrong? This must be a first."

"Come on. You can lecture me later."

We walked to where his plane waited in front of the school. Collie glanced at it, then back at me. "Think we'll both fit?"

"We'll have to, I guess." I took in the plane's jaunty swirls, remembering my father's hand on mine on the throttle, teaching me how to fly.

Teaching me how to live.

A doll lay on the ground with a boot-clad footprint on her dress. I hesitated, then bent down and picked it up. I turned it over in my hands. "Collie...you'd be a lot safer without me, you know."

Anger creased his features; he crouched beside me. "Do you think I give a damn about that? I'd die before I left you." He rested his hand on my hair. His eyes were the pure green of leaves after rain.

"I'd die," he repeated softly.

The truck with the megaphone was audible again. "*...the town is being reclaimed for mining purposes and you will* not *be spared...*"

Collie kissed me and then straightened and swung himself up onto the wing. "Come on," he urged, holding his hand out to me. "If you sit between my legs I think we can just about do it."

I nodded. I started to toss the doll aside...and then placed her tenderly on the ground. I smoothed her dress and stood up. We'd find a way to keep fighting Gunnison – we'd find a way to make the World for Peace worth believing in again.

Louise was my namesake. I would not let her down.

I took Collie's hand and he pulled me up onto the wing. The sunlight caressed him from behind, turning his hair pure gold. My throat tightened. I was so glad he was still alive that I knew I'd never be able to express it in words.

I stroked back a lock of his bright hair, feeling the silkiness of its golden strands.

"Ready, Sandy?" I said.

Collie had been about to climb into the cockpit; he stopped and stared at me. "W-what?"

"Remember? When you were a freshman, everyone at school called you—"

"Yeah," he broke in flatly. "Yeah, I remember." After a pause he gave me a crooked smile. "Sorry. I was just... thinking of someone else who calls me that."

I started to ask who, but then our heads jerked up; the

truck was in the next street now. We clambered into the cockpit. It was tight, but with Collie's arms around me and me working the stick, I knew we'd manage.

The engine was already warmed up. I flicked the starter switch and the Dove erupted into life. We turned the plane in a slow circle.

I felt Collie's lips tickle warmly against my ear. "You know I love you, don't you?" he shouted over the roar of the engine.

"I know!" I called back.

His arm around my waist tightened. His voice sounded rough. "No, I mean…I really do love you, Amity. No matter what, okay?"

I almost wanted to laugh. "Collie, I *know*! I love you too! Can we get going?"

Without answering, he shoved down on the accelerator. We started taxiing, faster and faster. The houses blurred past. I pulled back on the throttle. A few harsh bumps of the undercarriage and we were airborne.

I eased back the throttle and the Dove climbed.

Welcome to HARMONY 5,
where the DISCORDANT are BROKEN.

The rules are simple here: OBEDIENCE or DEATH.

Anyone caught trying to escape is EXECUTED.
But in a world this DARK, what has Amity got to LOSE?

A chilling and compelling journey
of REVENGE, SURVIVAL and LOVE.

ISBN: 9781409572039

Acknowledgements

Broken Sky was a challenging book to write. Not only was the world so ambitious, there was that twist you're probably still cursing me for. Reader feedback was essential, and I'd have been completely at sea without my wonderful editors at Usborne. So, first, my heartfelt thanks and lots of hugs and puppies to Stephanie King (you're amazing and I love working with you), Anne Finnis, Rebecca Hill and Sarah Stewart. The combined efforts of all of you – your insightful comments, probing questions, and flagging of inconsistencies – made *Broken Sky* a far better book than I ever dreamed. Thank you, thank you, thank you. Tremendous thanks also to Katharine Millichope for the gorgeous front cover, and to Amy Dobson in Publicity for all her efforts in putting it out there in front of people.

Once you read *Broken Sky* you can never read it the same way again, and so to get fresh opinions I inflicted early drafts on more beta readers than usual. Lots of love and virtual cake to the following writer-pals who gave their time and comments: Linda Chapman, Keren David, Fiona Dunbar, Caroline Green, Nick Green, Melissa Hyder, Inbali Iserles, Liz Kessler, Katherine Langrish, Gillian Philip, Benjamin Scott, Julie Sykes, and Sheena Wilkinson. (So many of you are also close friends who help keep me sane – an uphill task, I know! Thanks, my lovelies.) Sincere thanks and more cake to Victoria Wilton, who took time out from her A levels to read and comment.

The fictional Firedoves are Spitfires in disguise, and I'd have been lost without expert assistance. Huge thanks to Keith Perkins, the man behind AeroLegends, who answered so many of my questions. Any errors are of course my own. Thanks also to David "Rats" Ratcliffe (flying in the Harvard with you to experience combat manoeuvres was unforgettable – I particularly liked the "rat-a-tat-tat" noises you made as we dove after another plane!), Air Marshall Clifford Rodney Spink, and Andrea Featherby. Thanks once again to Neil Chowney, who's been my advisor on all-things-engines since the *Angel* days. (And by the way, can I just say that flying in a Spitfire is hands-down the coolest piece of research I have ever done, EVER!)

Massive thanks to all the readers and bloggers who've

been cheering me on for the past two years, waiting for this book. Hope it meets expectations. Sincere thanks are also due to Caroline Sheldon for all her support over the years, and to Jenny Savill with anticipation for the future. Thanks and tackle-hugs to any friends I haven't mentioned, both online and off – you know who you are! – and to my family, especially my sister Susan Benson Lawrence.

And to my husband Pete, who brings me flowers for no reason, understands the importance of chocolate, and spends hours talking about my imaginary people with me: thank you for always being there, even when I do mad things like embark on another big, epic trilogy. I love you.

About the Author

L. A. WEATHERLY was born in Little Rock, Arkansas, USA. She now lives with her husband and their cat, Bernard, in Hampshire, England, where she spends her days – and nights! – writing.

L. A. Weatherly is the author of over fifty books, including the bestselling *Angel* trilogy. Her work has been published in over ten different languages.

Catch up with L. A. Weatherly on facebook

@LA_Weatherly

laweatherly.tumblr.com

Can't wait for Darkness Follows?
catch up with L. A. Weatherly's

"Heart-stopping romance." *Mizz*

"Wonderful, original." *The Sun*

"Packed with suspense and drama." *The Daily Mail*

"Sparkling." *Books for Keeps*

"Awesome." *Once Upon a Bookcase*

"Will leave you breathless." *Daisy Chain Book Reviews*

"Stunning." *Book Angel Booktopia* for *Chicklish*

"Made me laugh, smile and cry." *Open Book Society*

"Fresh, imaginative...highly addictive." *Empire of Books*

"Will suck you in and take you on a thrill ride."
Feeling Fictional

"Pure perfection." *Dark-Readers*

"Unmissable." *Jess Hearts Books*

"Mind-blowing, spine-tingling, absolutely brilliant."
Book Passion for Life

Willow knows she's different from other girls. She can look into people's futures just by touching them. She has no idea where she gets this power from...

But Alex does. Gorgeous, mysterious Alex knows Willow's secret and is on a mission to stop her. But in spite of himself, Alex finds he is falling in love with his sworn enemy.

ISBN 9781409522010

Only Willow has the power to defeat the malevolent Church of Angels, and they will stop at nothing to destroy her. But when Willow and Alex join forces with a group of Angel Killers, Willow is still treated with mistrust and suspicion. She's never felt more alone...until she meets Seb.

He's been searching for Willow his whole life – because Seb is a half-angel too.

ISBN 9781409522393

Training a new team of AKs, Alex and Willow's love grows stronger than ever. But with the world in ruins, the angels are enslaving humanity, moving survivors into camps where they devour their energy, causing slow but certain death. When Alex is forced to embark on a deadly solo mission, Willow is left to defeat the angels with Seb – and she has no idea if Alex is ever coming back...

www.angelfever.com

For my husband.

First published in the UK in 2016 by Usborne Publishing Ltd., Usborne House,
83-85 Saffron Hill, London EC1N 8RT, England. www.usborne.com

A CIP catalogue record for this book is available from the British Library.

ISBN 9781409572022 03206/6

JFM MJJASOND/16 Printed in the UK.